UNDER
A
SKY
ON
FIRE

BOOKS BY SUZANNE KELMAN

A View Across the Rooftops
When We Were Brave

UNDER
A
SKY
ON
FIRE

SUZANNE KELMAN

Bookouture

Published by Bookouture in 2020

An imprint of Storyfire Ltd.
Carmelite House
50 Victoria Embankment
London EC4Y 0DZ

www.bookouture.com

ISBN: 978-1-83888-796-4
eBook ISBN: 978-1-83888-795-7

To all the brave women of Britain during World War Two who not only fought and worked but also kept homes, families and the indominable British spirit alive. And to my own grandmother, Joyce Diana Shelley, who when the rest of the world went underground to shelter from the bombing, raced out into the night to face our enemy.

'… A woman of strength knows that it is in the journey that she shall become strong.'
Unknown

'Without courage all other virtues lose their meaning.'
Winston Churchill

Prologue

15 August 1940 – The First Bomb

Hauptmann Rubensdörffer swiped the sweat from his brow and blinked twice, struggling to clear his vision one more time and steady his breathing. In his ears his heart pounded like a drum as he attempted to recover from the attack that had come out of the blue. With twenty-one planes behind him counting on his leadership, he sought desperately to grapple with the fear and anger that boiled inside him. Hot sweat gathered under his collar, prickled the backs of his hands and trickled between his fingers inside his leather gloves as he gripped the control stick harder with the sheer frustration of it. With great fury he recalled the assurance from the intelligence reports he had studied before take-off that the British squadrons had all been destroyed on this route. But now his own airmen were, hundreds of miles from their air base, deep in enemy territory, and they had barely made it through the last attack, losing their fighter support in the process. His greatest fear was upon him: under his leadership the entire bomber squadron were flying towards London alone and unprotected.

Dramatically unbuckling and yanking back the strap of his leather flying cap, stretched so tightly across his throat it felt as though it would strangle him, he struggled frantically to recall the route he had so meticulously committed to memory, but he felt so rattled that everything just swam in front of his eyes. Trying to shake off his terror and orientate himself, he peered across the stretch of the silver wingtip of his Messerschmitt BF 110 as it bobbed and weaved through the hazy cloud, the glint of the setting sun's orange glow blinding him as it flashed along the wing like a lighthouse beacon.

Another terrifying thought suddenly gripped him. What if more fighters were waiting for them on the direct route into Kenley? Surely, they would never survive another attack.

'I'm going to take a different route,' he barked into his radio to the gunner sitting behind him.

'You think that is wise?' came back the hesitant response. 'Why don't we just drop the bombs and get the hell out of here?'

Rubensdörffer could hear the fear in his gunner's voice but reasoned if they passed the target and approached from the north they could drop the bombs and clear the target faster.

Undeterred by his counterpart's concerns, Rubensdörffer leaned heavily on the throttle controls, racing past the target, then banked hard right as the engines shook and whined with the strain. Behind him, the rest of his squadron blindly followed. Diving to a lower altitude, the rush of the accelerated airspeed screeched to a deafening pitch as below them terrified ground crew and personnel ran in a hundred different directions to avoid the attack.

Suddenly, a stream of bullets peppered the side of Rubensdörffer's Messerschmitt, and behind him his rear gunner swore as he swung his guns to engage the new squadron of British fighters. He banked hard away to avoid the onslaught as a fresh trail of bullets blazed over his cockpit window. A Hurricane tore past, diving down then up and away to engage him again. From the other side, another rally of bullets cracked the window behind him and as he swivelled his head back he gasped in shock: he had lost his rear gunner. The man he had flown with, his friend for five years, was slumped over his gun, very obviously dead.

Filled with bottled-up anger and overwhelming grief at his friend's death, he wanted more than anything to get away; he had to get away fast. Rubensdörffer knew his bomber squadron couldn't sustain another attack, especially as he now could see that Spitfires filled the sky and he was completely defenceless. So, making a desperate decision, knowing it was controversial, as there were factories and housing close to the airfield, but not caring, he slammed his hand down on the bomb release. The plane shuddered as the five-hundred-pound explosives were freed from the bomb bay.

All around, his group followed suit, bombs scattering everywhere, missing the intended target of Kenley.

Banking hard away at full throttle, his engines roared. With perspiration now dripping down his face and blurring his eyes completely, he sped towards the Channel, trying to put out of his mind the fact that instead of bombing the Kenley airfield as he had been intending to do he may have just killed innocent civilians. He would explain to his commanders the impossible position he had been in, and of course they would understand, he reasoned.

Suddenly, a deafening explosion slammed into the side of his plane, rocking and rolling it onto its side and he swore as it shook every bone in his body, jarring him practically out of his seat as he cracked his head on the far side window. Fighting to remain conscious, dazed and in shock, he clung on to his control stick more like a life raft than to steer. As his vision cleared he looked down at his control panel to get his bearings as smoke filled his cockpit, choking him, and out of the corner of his eye he could see a ball of fire was engulfing his wing. This was very bad. He thrust the plane into a steep dive, attempting to put out the fire with the updraught. Rubensdörffer felt frantic – he was still deep over British soil and wasn't sure if he would make it back to the Channel where he could be picked up by a German rescue boat. As he tore towards the ground, his engine screaming its protest, the fire smouldered to a grey ugly cloud and Rubensdörffer heaved back on his control as the plane shook violently. It took all his strength to lift the nose as he skimmed high trees and desperately tried to keep it airborne. Beside him his only good engine whined and spluttered, the imbalance of the hole in his wing bouncing him around wildly as his controls jerked aggressively beneath his grip. As he tried to cling onto his life he prayed furiously, prayed he would make it, make it home to see his family again.

Chapter One

Twelve Weeks Earlier

Lizzie Mackenzie inhaled deeply and filled her lungs with the smell of the fresh damp grass and the icy scent of the mountain streams that rippled across the granite rocks. As she closed her eyes and exhaled, she realised this was what she would miss the most, just being out here in the Highlands in her very own world. As a sharp breeze blew across the loch, it swept up the hillside to find her, bringing with it the salty scent of the water; toying with her, it tugged at the mass of red curls piled up beneath her green knitted hat, which finally gave in and broke free to swirl around her face. Pulling wisps of copper strands from her lips and wrapping her arms around herself, Lizzie listened to the familiar sounds of the place she'd come to call home.

Out on the loch, geese were honking one to another, and below her, in the fields, she could hear horses whinnying as they stretched out their golden necks and shook out their shaggy manes. As the wind whistled through the trees and splayed the waving bracken, she relished in the complete peace and spaciousness it afforded her, a timeless tranquillity that she had known all of her life.

Lizzie couldn't imagine what it was going to be like to live in a big city. She had never been to London. In fact, since arriving from the Isle of Barra five years before, she'd barely left her aunt and uncle's farm, but when her papers had arrived, they had informed her that she would be at a training site just outside the capital. Her two younger cousins had protested, wanting to go with her, but as her aunt Marion had reminded them, she needed someone left at home and besides, thirteen and fourteen were far too young to join the Women's Auxiliary Air Force, as Lizzie was doing.

Opening her eyes and looking out across the grey, rippling water, in the sky she spotted an osprey, its cream and brown striped wings extended as it wheeled in long, slow descending spirals searching the loch for prey. Lizzie watched the quiet and graceful way it moved through the sky and thought about her life over the last few years, in the heart of Scotland. She had been fortunate to be staying somewhere with a loving family in a place where she got plenty of fresh air, mountain water, and, of course, there was always food in the home of a farmer. It was a far cry from what she'd expected when her parents had sent her from the island to live with her relatives. But all the better for it.

Alerted by the raised sounds of bleating sheep drifting up from their flock below, her attention was drawn down the hillside. Her uncle had started to round them up for the evening. Lizzie watched the sight she'd viewed what felt like a thousand times, Uncle Hamish surrounded by scores of white, shaggy, long-horned sheep marked with their painted red crosses that identified them as their own, bounding down the hillside for home. Ambling down in his languorous stride, his knotted staff steadying his way, her uncle was wearing his usual flat cap and green plaid jacket that had long started to fray around his neckline and cuffs. But this was his favourite, and even though her aunt had bought him numerous new coats through the years, he still seemed to gravitate to this familiar and comfortable tweed. As he went, he whistled through his teeth and called out to Bob and Chip, the sheepdogs always by his side, communicating in ways that only the three of them understood.

Trudging down the steep hill in her green rubber boots and long wool skirt, her thick coat wrapped around her shoulders, Lizzie made her way towards him. She would be changing into a blue uniform tomorrow night, she thought. Leaving first thing on a 6.00 a.m. train. She would change trains in Glasgow, which would take her across the border and down through England, past big cities she'd only ever heard about, like Manchester and Birmingham, all the way to London.

Lizzie galloped to the bottom field to catch up with her uncle, who had reached the far gate, calling out to him, still far off. The wind whipped up at her back and carried her voice ahead of her to find him. He swivelled around and acknowledged her with a brief wave of his hand, clad in one of the thick black woollen gloves she had knitted for him two winters before.

As she finally joined him at his side, out of breath, he was heaving open the top gate of the lower field, set in the drystone wall he had built with his father many years before. Resting one of his mud-crusted boots on the bottom rung of the gate, he hunched over it as he waited for the dogs, who diligently continued to circle the sheep, steering them towards the entrance as they bleated their displeasure at being herded. As the last of the sheep moved into the lower field, Uncle Hamish pulled the gate shut and took a moment to look down at his niece, a broad smile crinkling his piercing green eyes and spreading across his shiny weather-reddened cheeks.

'Oh, there's my girl,' he said in his usual sing-song Scottish manner. 'Are you all ready?'

'I am,' she said, fighting with the wind that continued to tug loose strands from under her woollen cap, creating a candy floss of hair that whipped around her face.

'All ready for your adventure in the big city?' he continued, widening his eyes with anticipation. 'Though I won't imagine it will be for long, because if Jerry manages to make it over here, he will be sure to turn around and leave once he sees a Mackenzie waiting for him.'

He put his arm around her shoulder and pulled her close for a vigorous side hug as he chuckled to himself. They'd been close since she arrived, the eldest daughter of his twin brother. They'd discovered a shared love of the fields, of the Highlands, and the farming. 'I'll miss you, Lizzie. You have been a great help to me and your aunt. But we've all got to do our bit. I'm very proud of you. I'm proud of what you're doing.'

Now side by side, his arm still resting on her shoulders, they strode through the muddy lower field, that sucked at their boots and was already well marked and grooved with the numerous slotted hooves of the sheep and soft pads of their collies. With his heavy silence, Lizzie could tell her uncle was contemplating something. Maybe he was worried about her leaving.

'It won't be long till I'm back, Uncle Hamish. You wait and see. We'll get this war sorted out, and I'll be back to help here on the farm. I won't be going back to Barra.'

He shook his head, as if that wasn't where his thoughts had been, then taking a moment to answer, he swallowed down emotion before he spoke again, his voice a low rumble. 'I was thinking that this will be a nice fresh start for you, Lizzie. A new time in your life.'

She swallowed too, realizing what he was referring to. The last five years had not been easy for her, and sometimes she forgot just how much it affected her aunt and uncle and their family too. She followed him through the bottom gate and into the farm courtyard, where the sheep were already gathered around the entrance to their pen, bleating their desire for their dinner. Lizzie helped him usher them in and lift the large grain sacks to feed the sheep, taking a moment to remember.

Thinking back to the time five years before, which had been so difficult. Her cousin, Fiona, was that age now. Just fourteen Lizzie had been when she'd fallen in love with Fergus McGregor. The boy from the next farm on Barra. The whole thing seemed so foolish now as she thought back, but she had been convinced she was in love, and they had been barely children, experimenting, caught up in emerging feelings. But what had started out so innocently for her had changed rapidly for him. Lizzie thought back to how it had all turned so ugly so quickly that night and pushed the unbearable memories away. She had confessed it to her best friend, who instead of supporting her had turned against her and turned many of her other friends against her too. The pain of the rejection had been heartbreaking, and she'd vowed she would never trust a friend in the same way again. Lizzie had never told her parents what had really happened between her and Fergus that night and she never would have, if not for the fact that she'd found out she was pregnant. With both families being devout Catholics, they had got together to discuss it in the cold, unwelcoming, visitors' parlour as the two of them had sat there staring at their hands, shame-faced. She was unable to look at him without feeling sick and angry.

There had been much toing and froing between both the families, but eventually it had been decided that she would go away to her aunt and uncle's across the water in the Highlands, have the baby, and give it up for adoption. Everyone had been clear: fourteen was no age to start a family, especially with a baby conceived out of wedlock. Fergus had wanted to finish his schooling and Lizzie had family obligations. It just wasn't right to saddle her with a young one when she was still a child herself, her father had insisted, his hand resting heavily on her shoulder as tears had streamed down her face.

Lizzie remembered the stony-faced disappointment on her parents' faces as they had seen her off onto the boat, and how she had cried with the loneliness on the train journey afterwards. Before she found a kinder home with her aunt and uncle, she had been desperate, leaving the only home she had known on the isle in the Outer Hebrides, wondering what was to become of her. And then again, when she gave up the baby. Which was the hardest thing she'd ever done. Harder even than seeing her own parents turn against her when she'd found herself pregnant in the first place. Quickly, she pushed the painful thoughts away from her mind as she felt the reassuring hand of her uncle on her shoulder again.

'Come on, girl, sheep are fed. Let's get ourselves in for something to eat. We need to get you to bed early tonight if you're going to make that train in the morning.'

She nodded as she walked by his side, across the slate grey cobblestones of the farmyard, and towards the tiny farmhouse that was their home. She sat on a step to pull off her boots and looked out across the Highlands one last time. It had been a grey day, but all at once, the sun broke through the dark clouds as it started to set on the west side of the loch, its rays stretching out across the heathered banks, turning the loch into a sea of molten silver and illuminating the geese still foraging for their food before laying up for the night.

Yes, she would definitely miss this, but she had to admit her uncle was right. This would be a fresh start for her in a place where nobody knew about her past, for even though she'd been whisked away from the isle before she had started to show, there had been stories back home, and even here, as much as she had tried to hide it, people had known. And she'd felt not just the guilt of her decision, but somehow, she'd never been able to let go of the torment of what she had done. And not unlike the sheep in front of her, with their own indelible crosses on their backs, she had also felt marked forever with the pain and the shame.

As she entered the house, the smell of burning peat and the heat from the kitchen range stretched out its fingers to warm her frigid cheeks. Wandering into the kitchen to help her aunt with the stew, she settled her heart to enjoy the last evening that she would spend with her family.

As usual, the house was a hive of activity. Fiona and Margaret were squabbling over a game they were playing.

'She's cheating again,' Fiona was yelling to her mother in the kitchen, one hand firmly on her hip, her face flushed red, as behind her Margaret's guilty smile only confirmed the situation.

Hamish walked to the cooker and kissed his wife on the back of the neck. 'Smells good, girl, smells good.'

Her aunt Marion pushed hair from her damp forehead as she pulled fresh bread from the oven and shouted back at the girls. 'You two are going to have to grow up now,' she remarked sternly. 'With Lizzie leaving us you're are going to have to do more work around here, so you had best try to learn to get on!'

Both Fiona and Margaret tried to plead their case to their father, who just shook his head, smiling, and dropped into his favourite chair by the fire to start reading his paper.

When the whole family finally came together to eat, Lizzie's gaze lingered around the table. All the people she loved most in the world were right here. It was such a far cry from the home she had come from. She couldn't imagine ever going back there. As she pulled off chunks of her aunt's home-made bread and dipped it into the warm, salty stew, she studied them all, trying to capture the scene as a picture within her mind of each one of them. Just like this, gathered talking and eating, sharing and laughing, even of her cousins as they continued to bicker with one another. A picture in her mind she could return to whenever she needed to come home in her heart. Lizzie would remember them just like this. She would miss life on her uncle and aunt's farm, but new things, bigger things, were waiting for her in the capital. And she couldn't wait to see what they were.

Chapter Two

The next morning Lizzie awoke, as she had so many times before, to the sound of nature outside her window. A loud chevron of geese was making its way across the loch, announcing its presence in a lengthy bellow.

The familiar sound comforted her as she stretched awake, her eyes drawn to the shafts of dusky sunlight that were creeping their fingers beneath her daisy curtains.

Lizzie studied them for a moment; she'd barely paid attention to them for years, but wanted to take in every detail of what was familiar on this final morning before she left Scotland for who knew how long.

The curtains billowed a little as a draught found its way through the cracks in the stones – part and parcel of living in a cottage that had been settling for a hundred years. As the daisies rippled, Lizzie smiled at the thought of her favourite childhood flower. She remembered as if it was yesterday her aunt bent over her ancient sewing machine, pins gripped between her teeth as she'd hemmed them to match a coverlet on Lizzie's bed. Hoping to make her niece more comfortable in her new home. First to recover and then as an enticement to stay on and finish her last two years of schooling with them. When Lizzie had written to her parents asking to stay longer, her mother and father had not protested. Even though it had been her desire, it had still deeply wounded her how they had rejected her, and she knew in her heart of hearts they were terribly ashamed of her and her secret. In the time she had lived here, her aunt and uncle had never said a bad word about her parents, but there were knowing looks and quiet whispers when she had been out of earshot that had affirmed to her that they knew the difficulties she had left behind her on Barra.

As the smell of bacon cooking wafted up her tiny staircase, her view drifted towards the ceiling. Lizzie studied the sloping roof, painted in delicate lavender-blue, that when the sun bounced off it bathed the whole room in its cool, comforting glow. Her aunt's mother's dressing table and tiny wardrobe were across the room, her walls decorated with a couple of childhood paintings she had brought with her and some clumsy cross-stitch pictures she had tackled after arriving. In the far corner, her bookshelf was still filled with some of her favourite Enid Blyton books and on the floor was a rag rug she had made the last year in school. Everything familiar and reassuring. When she had arrived, her uncle had offered her the bigger room. But there was something about the attic room, with the creaking stairway to reach it, and the little door her uncle had to bow his head to get through; all of this made her feel cosy and secure. It may not have been the most significant bedroom, but it was the one that she felt the most comfortable in.

From outside, Bob's and Chip's happy barks alerted her to the fact her uncle was on his way to the sheep pen. Swinging her legs out of bed, she moved towards the window, and drawing back the curtains, looked outside. Uncle Hamish was staring out at the loch, as silver shafts of early morning sun rippled across it, bringing it to life. On the banks, fishermen were already making their way down to the edge to prepare for their morning catch.

Slipping on her dressing gown and slippers, she sauntered across her brown linoleum floor, making her way down the creaking stairway into the kitchen. Aunt Marion had already laid the table and had just started cracking eggs into the frying pan when she arrived. Lizzie slipped her arms around her aunt's ample waist and gave her a hug from behind. The older woman responded by tapping her arm and turning around to smile at her niece.

'Well, this is it, Lizzie. Are you all ready? Is your bag packed?'

Lizzie nodded and made her way to the kitchen table. From there, she could look out of the window and see her uncle, who was starting to open up the sheep pen. He called out to somebody to greet them. The farmer next door. People in Scotland had their farms side by side for generations; this farm had been in Marion's family since the 1700s. When her uncle Hamish had met and fallen in love with her, he had left Barra to work her farm. First alongside Marion's father and now alone. And once again, with a shudder, Lizzie remembered that this was one of the reasons she could never go home. As much as she felt a connection with the beauty of the island itself, she couldn't spend her life so suffocated, knowing that Fergus was just next door. He had tried over the years to put things right between them, writing her long letters after the baby was born. But Lizzie had never been able to move on from the pain and the hurt of that one night and that one experience, and could never imagine going home to face her parents or Fergus.

Her aunt and uncle had never spoken about it outwardly, but she knew deep down they thought about it too. Knowing how hard it would be with both families on Barra living side by side for hundreds of years; neither able to just uproot and move somewhere else. So, with no way of going back, Lizzie would have to do that for herself. She loved her aunt and uncle but now it was time to find her own way.

Going to London to join the Women's Auxiliary Air Force had been a noble reason for leaving Scotland. No questions needed to be asked, even if her own reasons for leaving were very different. She wanted, of course, to help the war effort. She could have chosen to join the volunteer effort in Scotland. But she had secretly hoped to be posted to London, and she had been. England's capital city was far enough away for her to get some distance between her and her past, but there was also another incentive, the huge secret she hadn't even shared with her family.

Her thoughts were suddenly interrupted by her aunt Marion, who placed a breakfast plate down in front of her. Hot crispy bacon, fresh eggs, and her aunt's home-made bread made her mouth water. As if alerted by the smell, both of her cousins tumbled down the stairs, falling over each other like puppies to enjoy their last breakfast together. As they all ate, the three girls chatted about Lizzie's new adventure and what it would be like, and one hour later, they found themselves waiting at the tiny train station that would take Lizzie to the central station in Glasgow and then on to London.

As they huddled together on the platform, Lizzie looked at her family, her two red-haired cousins, her crinkled-faced uncle in his town tweed, to see her off, and her kindly aunt, smiling, round and rosy-cheeked. Lizzie was sad to say goodbye. But she also knew she had to do this. This was her chance to get away.

There was also the newspaper clipping folded in her diary, the one she had read and reread so many times, and that had made her hope she would finally have the chance to find her daughter.

Her aunt handed her a wrapped bundle.

'I've made you some sandwiches and some eggs in case you get hungry.'

'I've just finished breakfast!'

'But you have that long journey down to London. You'll be hungry between now and tonight when they feed you. And who knows what they're going to feed you in England?'

Lizzie smiled and took the packed lunch.

'Well, this is it,' said Hamish. 'Our favourite niece going off to win the war for us. We're very proud of you, Lizzie.'

As the train pulled in to the station, he gathered her into his arms, hugging her so tightly she tried not to cry. She would miss her uncle, so different from her father; his quiet presence, their long conversations on the banks of the loch, the sound of him calling to his sheep, and the smell of the fresh outdoors on his farm tweed. She pulled back and hugged her aunt as well. She could hear the tears in her voice.

'Please take care of yourself, Lizzie. We'll write to you all the time. Keep your head down and make sure you eat properly.'

Lizzie nodded, fighting the tears as she grabbed both Fiona and Margaret in her arms and gave them one big squeeze.

Lizzie made her way on board, clutching her grandmother's carpet bag, the only bag that had been big enough to carry her belongings from Barra and now down to London. She pulled down the window and waved as they all waved back furiously. And as the train whistle blared out its final departing sound, Lizzie felt the tension in her stomach and hoped she was doing the right thing. She took in the family faces one last time, each of them looking at her with so much hope and pride.

'Goodbye,' she shouted. 'I'll write as soon as I can.'

'Good luck, take care,' they shouted back.

Before she knew it, she was gone, leaving Scotland behind; the only place she had known in her whole life.

Chapter Three

Diana Downes clutched her new brown leather suitcase by her side and looked up and down the platform of Birmingham New Street station. She'd arrived early, so as not to miss her train, but now she was worried that she might be on the wrong platform, as she was the only one waiting there, except for her mother.

Jessie stood stoically by her daughter's side, her quiet, gentle presence always reassuring and loving. Clutching her large leather handbag under her arm, her mother was wearing a flowery yellow and olive dress and her favourite brown hat. And, of course, the matching brown raincoat she wore year-round, summer or winter.

Diana smiled nervously at her mother and thought about her dad, wishing he could have been there with them, but understanding why he hadn't been able to see her off. As she paced the station platform to work out her nerves, Diana thought back to the conversation they'd had at lunchtime.

She and Jessie had been busy in the kitchen, clearing away the dishes after lunch, when her attention had been drawn to the front room where her dad was still stood gazing out of the window, his corned beef sandwich untouched on a table by the side of his chair. Was the fact that she was going away to fight this war making it harder for him? she'd wondered with a new sense of guilt. What was he thinking about as he stared across his garden?

Were his thoughts back in the trenches? Still locked in the war that had changed him irrevocably? She recalled the stories her mother had told her about her father when he had come back, not only injured from the mustard gas that had created chronic breathing problems for him, but also broken on an emotional level that was both a lot less measurable than his constant wheeze, and less able to be remedied with medication. Shell shock, as it was called, was their daily reminder of a war, fought and won nearly twenty years before, that had left its mark forever, still ever-present to many; whole families, not just hers, who'd had to readjust to living with an enemy that continued to assault its victims long after the ceasefire had been celebrated.

She'd closed the kitchen door and looked across at her mother. 'Is he okay, do you think?' she asked in a whisper.

'Yes, love.' Jessie nodded, drying a teacup in her hand, a gentle smile drifting across her face. 'He will be. Of course, it's hard for him with so many of our friends and family already off to war, and now you're going to join up. But don't worry, his garden will keep him busy.'

Diana hadn't been convinced, and walking into the sitting room, she had observed her dad in a familiar routine, taking out his pipe, tamping tobacco down into it, lighting a match, and inhaling deeply as he continued to stare mindlessly out at the garden.

'Are you all right, Dad?' she asked in a forced, chirpy manner as swirls of blue smoke scented the air with its earthy aroma. When he didn't answer her, she nervously started rearranging the cushions on the sofa, pretending that was the main reason for her being in the room as he made his way back to his favourite chair. 'I don't want you to worry.'

Horace nodded slowly, staring at the floor as if he was considering the zigzag pattern of their brown and cream carpet for answers. Sitting down next to him in the saggy brown armchair with the lacy cotton armrests her mother had embroidered herself, Diana reached forward and laid her hand gently upon his, noting once again with sadness how he still had the tremor he'd been left with. Diana could see he was fighting with emotion.

Finally pulling his pipe from his mouth, he looked up at her with reticent eyes. 'Are you sure you want to do this, Diana? There are plenty of things you could do right here in Birmingham for the war. Why don't you settle down and marry a nice local boy here? You could still do something for Britain. But you could also be close to your family.'

Diana swallowed down the guilt that was now gripping her throat, acknowledging his pain at her leaving. Bringing her hands back together, she began to wring them in her lap. 'I just feel I want to do something more, Dad. Something meaningful. I know I could roll bandages or knit socks here, and there is nothing wrong with that. But with so many of our boys overseas and so many of my friends already signed up…' Her voice drifted away, allowing the silence to fill the end of her thought, and he nodded his head in resignation.

Eyeing her shiny new suitcase in the hall with obvious sadness, he sat back in his chair and took another long draw of his pipe, and Diana's heart went out to him. She had immense love and fondness for her kind-hearted dad, his fragility creating an opportunity for him and Diana to connect on a much deeper level. While other fathers were away all day working, her father had often been at home, helping take care of her throughout her childhood. With his health issues, he had not been able to hold down a job since he'd returned from the war. And though he'd managed to do part-time work here and there, it had been her mother, Jessie, who had become the family breadwinner.

As soon as she was old enough, Diana had supplemented their family's income, working in Birmingham's city centre as a hairdresser. But now bigger things were calling to her and she couldn't help feeling pulled to do something on a much grander scale for the good of her country.

Propelled by the heavy silence, she stood up and strode to the window, folding her arms across her chest. 'Your victory garden's looking good, Dad.'

He pointed his pipe towards the garden. 'The lettuces will be ready soon, and you'll miss the cabbages.'

She turned and smiled, and his warm eyes studied her. Diana thought how strange this was for him, how their roles had reversed. He had been the person to take her and meet her from school, taking his job of protecting her very seriously. Now, in a way, by fighting for their freedom, she was providing that same security for him. Some of her favourite memories were of her father meeting her on a rainy day. He would stand defying the rain at the school gates as she skipped through puddles to reach him. Then he would engulf her in his large grey tweed overcoat with the silky silver-coloured lining, escorting her under his arm all the way home so she wouldn't get wet. Diana remembered how safe she'd felt, walking alongside him, her eyes cast down to carefully navigate her way, following his feet in the leather shoes that always shone. Enveloped by his overcoat, a fortress from the weather. Tucked under his arm, she'd loved the familiarity of being surrounded by the musky scent of his pipe tobacco, mingled with that of his favourite peppermints, which always lingered on the inner fabric.

A station announcement about her train abruptly shook Diana from her reverie. And she noticed with relief that more people had now ascended onto the platform to await its arrival. Pulling down her tight straight skirt and adjusting the belt, Diana wondered if wearing her new shoes – with the two-inch heels – had been a wise choice. She'd wanted to give a good impression and had her thick, brown, curly hair cut by one of the other hairdressers the day before as a goodbye gift, but now she wondered if she would look overdressed. She glanced up and down the platform for guidance, to see if she could spot anybody else who might be going to join up as she was. But most people seemed to be either older men or mothers with young children.

Jessie slipped her hand into her pocket and handed over a packet of peppermints to her daughter, followed by a newspaper she unfolded from her large handbag.

'For you to read on the train,' she stated. 'Such a long way, all the way to London.' The way Jessie drew out the words made it sound as though Diana were on her way to Africa. And though she was a little apprehensive, as this would be her first time in the capital, Diana was excited about what she was going to do. Her only reluctance was about leaving her home and her dad. She hoped he wouldn't fret too much.

Diana skimmed the headlines. As usual, there was no good news. Mostly about Germany's recent invasion of Denmark, Norway, Belgium, the Netherlands and France, also the preparations for the anticipated invasion of England. Nazis had already started bombing the air bases all over the country, and the Battle of Britain, as it was being called, was being waged in the sky over the English Channel.

All at once the train appeared, chugging up to the platform, its steaming, smoking presence dominating the station. It was two minutes early, and Diana's heart leapt to her throat. This was it. She was going. Turning to her mother, she hugged her tightly. 'Take care of yourself and Dad for me.'

Jessie rubbed comforting circles on her daughter's back as she whispered into Diana's hair, 'And you take care of yourself.'

Pulling away, Diana fought her brimming emotions. Noting a hint of her mother's flowery perfume had rubbed off onto her own cheek, she turned towards one of the doors. She hadn't realized how this would feel. All she'd been centred on was getting to the barracks in London. But now she felt such a wave of sadness. If the Germans did attack Birmingham or London, would she see her family again? What would life be like in Britain if the Germans occupied it? She quickly pushed the thoughts from her mind. She couldn't think like that. Mr Churchill had been clear, they all had to be strong and make Britain proud.

Turning to kiss her mother quickly on the cheek, she stepped up onto the train and started to stride down the carriage, waving to Jessie through the windows as she went. Her mother stood resolutely and watched her daughter and slowly lifted her hand in a reluctant wave. And Diana thought she saw a tear leave her mother's eye. This was so hard, so much harder than she had expected. As she continued to walk the length of the train, many of the carriages were already full, but finally, she eyed a vacant seat in one and made her way towards it.

Sliding open the door just as the train started to gain momentum, Diana was thrust inside and didn't see the bag on the floor before she tripped over it. Falling forwards, she was saved by a pair of arms, clad in green paisley knitwear, that grabbed hold of her before she toppled to the floor. The young woman who had caught her deposited her into the worn brown leather seat opposite as Diana tried to right herself, taking in the worried face of the fellow passenger who had saved her.

'Oh God, I'm so sorry. I just pulled it down for a second to fish out my knitting and forgot all about it,' said the woman, who had lively eyes, a shock of red curly hair, and a strong Scottish accent.

Diana caught her breath and straightened her hat, a smile breaking out across her face. 'Well, it wouldn't do for me to break my leg before I even get down to start my war work, now, would it?' she joked.

The other young woman's face softened with relief at Diana's forgiving tone. 'Let me help you,' she implored as she went out into the corridor to retrieve the brown suitcase that was still in the doorway where Diana had dropped it. Then, with little effort, the young woman hoisted it up into the netted luggage rack overhead.

Picking up a ball of blue wool and knitting needles that had fallen from her lap to the floor when she had leapt up to save Diana, she added, red-faced, 'I always knit when I'm nervous, and I have to be honest with you, I'm very nervous. Thought I would get started on a scarf to go with my new uniform. And look at me' – she secured her own large carpet bag back in the overhead rack – 'I can't even take care of people on our side, never mind take on the Nazis.

'My name's Lizzie Mackenzie, by the way,' she continued as she sat down again. 'And as you've probably gathered by my accent, I'm from Scotland. It's not too strong, is it?' she asked, concern furrowing her brows. 'You can understand what I'm saying, right?'

Diana shook her head. 'Sorry? You'll have to say that again. I can't understand a word you're saying.' Then she raised her eyebrows to acknowledge she was joking.

Both girls descended into a fit of laughter and Diana was grateful for a light moment. She had not enjoyed saying goodbye to her mother at the station and was concerned she would fret about her parents all the way to London, but now she was gladdened by this new carriage friend to chat to. It would make the journey go quicker and help stem the homesickness she had already been feeling.

'Ach, get away with ye, you're pulling my leg,' Lizzie joked back.

Diana said, 'And it's no good asking me about strong accents. I'm a Brummie. They probably won't understand either of us down there.'

'You don't have an accent at all to me,' responded the wiry Scottish girl, with surprise. 'I think you sound just like one of those BBC wireless announcers.'

'That's because I'm practising my posh accent,' Diana continued, another smile creeping across her face. 'Just in case I get invited over to Buckingham Palace for a cup of tea with the queen while I am down in London.'

'I'm off to London myself to join the Women's Auxiliary Air Force,' continued Lizzie with a great sense of pride.

'So am I!' responded Diana as she slipped off her hat and coat. 'I'm joining up as well.'

'Fancy that! That's wonderful,' said Lizzie. 'At least I've made one friend. I think…' she said warily, raising an eyebrow with hopeful expectancy and pushing back a silky red curl from her eyes.

'Well, we'll just have to see about that,' responded Diana. 'It depends if you try to kill me in basic training.'

Lizzie shook her head and corkscrew spirals of copper curls bounced around her face. 'I wouldn't put it past me. On the farm, we had so much more room. I'm worried about the big city. All those people. I've never even left Scotland. At least you're from Birmingham, where you're used to people.'

Diana nodded. 'I was not looking forward to leaving my family behind, my mum and dad and all my customers at the hairdressers.'

'Is that what you were before?' asked Lizzie, her eyes widening.

Diana nodded with a smile.

'I could do with a cut myself,' Lizzie said, running her hands through her thick mane of hair. 'You didn't happen to bring your scissors with you, did you?'

Diana nodded. 'I always bring my scissors with me.'

'I want something short. Like they wear it in the city?' Lizzie said, pointing at Diana's fashionable curls. 'A bit like Betty Grable, you know?'

Diana nodded. 'I did four Betty Grables last week,' she chuckled. 'I'm sure we could sort you out. Let's hope they bunk us close together.'

Diana suddenly felt calmer. Everything had been far from fun while she'd been getting ready, and now here she was on the train talking about things that were familiar to her: hair and American film stars. Suddenly she was struck by the adventure of it all. She had wanted to serve her country. She also wanted to have new experiences, and was now having her first. She took in the young woman in front of her who continued to chat about the problems she had with long curly flyaway hair. She was a good six inches shorter than Diana, maybe five foot one or five foot two, with the most beautiful green eyes Diana had ever seen, a pixie chin, and a smile that lit up her whole face. And there was a warmth about her as she talked. But also, there was a sadness behind her eyes,

Diana could see. Her new friend was wearing a green tartan skirt and a thick green cardigan, emphasizing the emerald in her eyes and bringing out the pinkness in her cheeks.

'You would look incredible with those eyes and that shaped face with a shorter cut,' she said to her.

All at once Diana's stomach grumbled and both girls laughed again.

'I'm sorry,' said Diana, putting her hand on her waist. 'I did eat a little lunch, but I was so nervous, you know?'

'Don't you worry yourself,' said Lizzie as, pulling down her red tartan carpet bag again, she plunged into it and pulled out sandwiches wrapped in paper and two boiled eggs. 'I think my Aunt Marion was packing enough food for the whole air force.' She handed half of them over to Diana with one of the eggs, and Diana looked down at them in surprise.

'Eggs?' she said with shock.

'And ham,' said Lizzie, proudly.

'We haven't seen ham and eggs in Birmingham in forever, not in a sandwich like this.'

'Well, that's the perks of living on a farm,' said Lizzie, smoothing out a napkin on her lap. 'Go on, tuck in. Who knows what they're going to feed us down there.'

Diana took a bite of the sandwich, it was delicious.

'Is that where you were living then, on a farm?' she asked, wiping the crumbs from the corner of her mouth that were clinging to her crimson red lipstick.

Lizzie nodded. 'Up in the Highlands in the middle of three large hills and overlooking a beautiful loch. I would tell you the Gaelic name for it, but you'll no' be able to say it. I've been staying with my aunt and uncle and their two girls. Uncle Hamish mainly farms sheep, but they have a whole plethora of animals. It's absolutely beautiful up there,' she mused, staring wistfully out of the window and taking a bite out of her own egg. 'I am going to miss it a lot, but our new prime minister Mr Churchill put the call out and we've all got to do our bit.'

Diana nodded.

'"Arm yourselves and be ye men of valour, and be in readiness for the conflict; for it is better for us to perish in battle than to look upon the outrage of our nation and our altar,"' said Lizzie, quoting parts of the parliamentary speech from a week before as she thrust a fist into the air, doing an impression of their new prime minister, albeit a Scottish version.

Diana chuckled and knew she was going to love this person. She was so grateful to have met her already.

'I didn't think much about it when I signed up, did you?' continued Lizzie. 'But it's nerve-wracking, isn't it? Now I'm actually on the train. I was fretting before you got on, wondering about whether I'd make any new friends in a big city. All the friends I have, I grew up with, and I was worried to death I would be lonely and I'm hoping to God I make it back. And now look at me here, tripping up perfectly innocent people just to make a friend.'

They finished their lunch and continued to talk about their lives before the war, as Lizzie started to knit methodically and Diana stared out at the country that rushed by the window. Everywhere looked so different now. Every train station they stopped at was nameless, because the signs had all been taken down to confuse the Jerries if they ever made it on to British soil. At every station there were dozens of people, many in military uniforms, up and down every platform, and as they went through cities, they passed large municipal buildings, each of them now masked with taped windows and surrounded with barbed wire fences and sandbags around entrances piled high in case the Germans ever attacked the towns.

As they chatted away their time together, they were in London before they knew it, and the train conductor informed them they were at their destination. They grabbed their bags and cases as the train came to a screeching full-stop, brakes creaking and hissing steam under the strain. Peering out of the window, Lizzie pointed to a tall, thin man wearing an air force uniform and carrying a clipboard.

'I bet he's for us,' she said, seizing hold of Diana's arm with nervousness. Then, 'I wonder if he's single,' she whispered into Diana's ear and they both started to laugh again. 'Not a lot of choice in Scotland for me – not that that's the reason I'm here, of course,' she said with a glint in her eye, and Diana nodded.

'You'll do,' she joked back.

'Do you have a boyfriend?' asked Lizzie as they waited their turn to file off the train.

Diana shook her head. 'Not much time for it,' she said. 'And as a hairdresser all my customers are women.'

'I don't think we'll have much chance here, either,' responded Lizzie with reluctance, 'with all the men away, and I'm sure the air force will have plenty for us to do.'

As they clambered down onto the station platform, they made their way towards the gentleman with the clipboard and then noticed there were three other girls behind them who must have been further down the train. He nodded to all the young women and called out names. Lizzie and Diana were two of them. Lizzie approached him.

'Excuse me, Flight Lieutenant Stone,' she said, as he'd introduced himself. 'Do you think it would be possible for Diana and me to bunk together at the barracks?'

The officer looked up from his clipboard. 'I don't really assign barracks, I just get you there,' he said with a curt smile.

Lizzie did not seem deterred and persisted. 'Please, could you put a word in for us? We made friends on the train. I'd love to be close to her.'

He looked from one to the other, and Diana was aware that Lizzie was gripping her arm so tightly she was losing feeling. They must have looked as desperate as a pair of refugees.

He nodded. 'I'll see what I can do,' he said. 'Friends are important right now for all of us.'

There was a sad tone to his statement and Diana wondered what had happened in his life for him to comment in that way, and all at once she was aware of the seriousness of being a member of the fighting forces.

He led them all outside, and Diana noticed the city was alive with life. Parked outside the station was a canvas-covered troop truck, which the officer ushered them towards. Diana looked down at her tight skirt and high heels and wondered how she would get herself up into the back of a truck. This hadn't been the best choice. She hadn't even thought about it.

'Up you go, girls,' he said in a jovial manner as he saw Diana look down at her clothes and shoes. 'I'm afraid Queen Mary was using her carriage today, so we've had to make do with this,' he joked as he made his way to the front of it. All the girls helped hoist Diana into the truck, and they laughed at her predicament. Once they were settled, Flight Lieutenant Stone's driver started the engine and they rattled away.

As they went through the streets of London, Diana looked out the back of the truck as the tent-like flap waved up and down in the breeze, their backs bouncing against the canvas walls with the smell of petrol leaking up through the floor. Lizzie sat opposite her and smiled and said exactly what Diana was thinking.

'Well, whatever happens, it's going to be an adventure.'

Diana nodded and looked around at the other girls in the truck. This was going to be something different. She could feel it, and she was so grateful to have met Lizzie, who was already making her adjustment a pleasant experience.

When eventually they arrived at the RAF station on which their training barracks were situated, on the far western outskirts of London, Flight Lieutenant Stone must have had a word with the woman who was taking care of them because she joked about them.

'I guess you two are the Siamese twins who want to be together,' she announced, noting Lizzie latched onto Diana's arm again. They both nodded. 'Come on then,' she said. 'I'll get you settled in.' They followed behind the older woman, who walked towards the barrack block that was to be their temporary home, and as her stomach tightened, Diana felt a growing anticipation.

Chapter Four

The next day, on a different London platform, the high-pitched screech of the steam train whistle pierced the hot, stagnant air of the crowded station, forcing soldiers up and down the platform into a frenzy of activity as they dragged themselves from the arms of their loved ones to begin boarding the awaiting troop train.

Catching her breath and drawing him close for one last lingering hug, Julia Sullivan clung to her husband and tried desperately not to cry. Burying her face into the coarse weave of his khaki-brown army uniform, she inhaled the scent of the family soap on his neck, a familiar luxury which by some miracle she'd managed to buy, but which was now only a cruel reminder that it was John who was going to war this time, not a neighbour or some distant stranger. Her own precious husband.

Even though Julia attempted to gulp down her tears as she drew away to study him, she was aware he noticed her resolve was crumbling and reproached herself for letting her anguish slip, especially as she had been so good at hiding it from him for weeks. Somehow, she had put on a brave face, from the bitter blow of John receiving his call-up papers all the way through to helping him pack his kitbag.

Even as he'd held his two children for the last time on their doorstep, scarcely an hour before, with Maggie sobbing uncontrollably in his arms and Tom's pale face and trembling bottom lip conveying all of his dread, even then, Julia had managed to keep it together, wanting to be strong for them all. But now her well-constructed wall was disintegrating right in front of him.

'Come on, gal, chin up. I'll be back before you know it,' he whispered into her ear, the lilt of his London accent reassuring her above the clatter of train doors being wrenched open and kitbags being thrown inside. Sliding his hand beneath her blonde curls, he cupped the back of her neck gently to tilt her head up to meet his gaze as he brushed her lips with a gentle kiss. His tone was light-hearted, but as he drew away and his green eyes searched her own, gone was his usual twinkle of mischief and in its place a real look of concern. Julia knew what every facial expression signified from this person she had known all of her life and had watched grow from a boy to a man, knew that even behind his easy tone and staunch patriotic determination, he still needed her strength to get onto the train.

'I'll be fine,' she insisted, drumming up all the false bravado she could muster, fighting the quiver in her voice and her trembling knees. 'I'm sure the War Office will have plenty for me to do while you're gone.'

John nodded and swept his thumb across her face, gently wiping away a tear that had betrayed her show of strength and had trickled down her cheek without her realizing.

All at once, a torrid wind ripped down the platform, swirling the stale air into hot spirals that tousled hair, rustled newspapers, and turned up the corners of a poster that hung on the red brick wall with a beaming woman holding a cauliflower encouraging them to 'Dig For Victory'. As it whipped around the back of her bare knees, Julia stepped back from John's arms to cling on to her new cornflower-blue cloche hat she had purchased especially to see him off.

'It matches your eyes perfectly,' the shop assistant had insisted the morning before, folding her arms over her ample bosom when she and Julia had considered it in the mirror together. It had been a frivolous expense during wartime and had taken most of her pin money for the month, but she'd decided it would compensate for the lack of silk stockings available. Julia wished his last memory of her to be a meaningful one, one he could carry in his thoughts for as long as was needed.

Watching her with amusement, he quirked an eyebrow and his usual mischievousness returned. 'You don't want to lose your new hat, gal. That would never do,' he stated, beaming.

Clinging to her brim, Julia returned his smile. Just then the train whistled a second time, its urgency palpable. Sucking in a full breath of the muggy air, Julia panicked and looked around, hoping for someone to give them permission for just a little more time, but all around her were scores of serious, ashen faces looking as desperate as her own. Mothers, brothers, sisters, children, all staring wistfully at young, uniformed men, and she reflected with sadness how this was taking place in stations all over England.

Activated by the urgency of the train whistle and stomping out cigarettes under the toes of shiny new black boots, a swarm of brown uniforms merged with the train, as soldiers clambered up, pushing and joking with one another. Further down the platform, a lively group started singing a jovial rendition of 'It's a Long Way to Tipperary', and it lifted into the air, cutting through the heat of the day, attempting to lighten the sombre mood and stifle the sobs of loved ones left behind.

Running her hand slowly down John's arm, Julia considered the unfamiliar, coarse cloth of the uniform, drew his hand to her lips, and kissed the tip of his knuckles before interlacing her fingers with his and strolling by his side towards the train.

As he shifted his bag onto his shoulder, he leaned in. 'Promise me you'll take care of Mum,' he urged her above the din of lively banter as soldiers all jostled to find a seat. 'I don't want her to worry herself to death.'

Julia nodded, thinking about how stone-faced and fearful Agnes had looked that morning as she'd watched him leave from their doorstep. 'Of course. She's just next door. I can pop in and see her all the time,' she assured him. 'Promise me you'll keep your head down.'

In response, he saluted her comedically and stepped up into the carriage and away from her just as the vast cylinders on the train exhaled, letting out a hiss of white, hot steam that encircled her bare legs again, its acrid smell and fumes causing her to shut her eyes and hold her breath momentarily.

John pulled the door shut and slid the window down to look over at his wife one last time.

'I love you, Julia,' he whispered in an unusually intense manner. 'Kiss the kids every night and tell them their father is winning this war for them so they will have the hope of a future, and I'll be home before you know it.'

Unable to resist, she rushed up onto the train's step to kiss him one last time. In her exuberance to run her hands through his thick dark hair, she knocked his army cap askew.

'Steady on there, gal,' he laughed. 'I can't meet Mr Hitler half-dressed now, can I? I don't want to let the side down.'

She tenderly straightened it and stepped down to look at him, framed in the window, and even though there were dozens of people milling about on the platform, she could only see him in that moment and her heart was desperately sad. But more than anything, she was proud, proud of this amazing man with the carefree and loving nature who made every one of her days better for being in them.

'I'll write,' she called out above the final train whistle that blasted out its urgency again in three long lingering shrieks. 'Every day,' she assured him over the clamour of what sounded like a thousand goodbyes all up and down the platform.

He nodded. 'I'll write when I can too,' he shouted back as the train began to chug, vast metal wheels starting their slow arc, grey smoke billowing from its chimney and cylinders, hissing and spluttering.

Julia followed the train along the platform as long as she could, waving vigorously, until finally it became nothing but a spot on the horizon, John's hand waving out of the window in a sea of other brown arms and nothing but the faint echoes of, 'It's a long way to go…' that reached all the way back to the platform then dissipated into the air. As soon as all trace of the train was out of sight, she let the tears flow freely down her cheeks as she attempted to gather herself to adjust to life without the man she loved, and suddenly she felt incredibly lonely.

Chapter Five

Julia brushed away the tears that blurred her vision as she crossed Westminster Bridge on her way to work. As she strode at a clip, she gave herself a stern talking-to. Lots of people were putting their husbands on trains. She had to pull herself together, be strong for her children, for Maggie and Tom, show a brave face. Besides, she had important war work to do.

Turning off Whitehall Road onto Whitehall Place, she crossed the street and entered the building on the corner. With its impressive Edwardian Baroque exterior and splendid restored rooms and stairways inside, it was a well-known and much-beloved London landmark. That, as well as being a palace at some time, with a history that extended back to the reign of Henry VIII. Even Cardinal Wolsey, the Lord Chancellor, and the Archbishop of York had used the London residence, which had formerly been called York Place. Now the outside of the old palace was a pitiful sight, with each entrance marked with the evidence of war: piles of cream-coloured sandbags stacked eighteen feet into the air.

Breezing swiftly through the entrance, she presented her pass to the soldier there on duty. As he nodded to her, she raced past him, her feet echoing across the floor. Inside, the white marble hallway was a magnificent spectacle, with its grand cream Grecian-style pillars and stone staircases ascending up through the building, but Julia had no time to admire the decor today; instead she sprinted up the stairs to her office on the first floor.

Since the beginning of the war she had been working in one of the typing pools.

It was her department's job to document all of the artillery needed for the ground forces and her days were repetitive and predictable, which in many ways was a comfort to her. But not today, because as she dashed into the enormous room, with the dozens of rows of typists, she was taken aback to see quite clearly that her supervisor, Mrs Hathaway, was waiting by her desk.

Julia tried to muffle the echo of her high-heeled shoes on the wooden floor as she hurriedly tiptoed to reach her, speculating as to why she could be waiting there. She knew she'd informed her boss she'd be late today because she would be seeing John off, so the only other possible explanation would be that there was something wrong with her work.

As the woman who had been pacing in front of her desk turned to see Julia coming towards her, she let out a gasp of relief. 'Oh, Julia, I wonder if you could step into my office for a moment. There's something I need to talk to you about.'

Attempting to catch her breath, Julia followed behind her supervisor, snaking through the long line of desks. Feeling uncomfortably warm, and sensing a trickle of perspiration forming under the brim of her new hat, she averted her gaze from the many curious expressions she sensed all around her. It was as though the whole typing pool paused to watch this unusual occurrence, the two of them parading back to the office at the very end of the room. Julia tried to wrack her brain about all the work she'd finished the day before. Never had her supervisor called her into her office. Mrs Hathaway usually handed out packages of work to them at their desks. As she turned to shut the door, Julia's eyes swept across the room, noting the many raised eyebrows and open-mouthed stares that had followed her inside.

'Take a seat, please, Julia,' Mrs Hathaway encouraged, her pleasant, professional tone not giving away anything.

Still, Julia rushed into a long flowing excuse for why she was late. 'I am so sorry I wasn't here on time, I had to see John off today, you see.'

For a moment the woman looked puzzled and then shook her head. 'Yes, yes. I remember you telling me yesterday. It's not about that.'

Julia sat down with a sense of dread. This must be about her work. Her mind had been so full of John leaving and her children being left fatherless she had been preoccupied. Had she made mistakes?

'I hope everything is okay with my work,' she continued, anticipating anything her supervisor had to say. 'I have been a little distracted lately with everything going on in my family.'

The woman smiled and raised a hand to stop her. 'We've all been distracted, Julia. There's a war going on. No, this has nothing to do with that.'

Julia noticed Mrs Hathaway seemed nervous. She rose and walked to the window, playing with a silver cross on a chain around her neck as she stared out, apparently trying to find the right way to put what she needed to say. Julia hoped to God she wasn't being sacked. But the next words out of her supervisor's mouth took her by complete surprise.

'Julia, we have something we want you to do. The higher-ups have been on to me, and they need another girl. They asked me to send the best I've got.' She swivelled on her heels and peered directly at her. 'And that, of course, would be you. You're the fastest in the pool by far and the most accurate. I know I can always count on you. This afternoon you need to go and meet with a Mr...' She strode to her desk to review a note she'd placed there. 'A Mr Woodbridge. They're going to ask you a series of questions and have you take a typing test, and if it all works out, you'll be doing some work for them.'

Julia began to panic. She loved the office she worked in and had a number of kind work colleagues. Though she wouldn't call them close, they were familiar to her. She'd already felt so much emotion today, the last thing she wanted was her nice, secure, easy job to change into anything more uncertain. 'Another office?' she enquired meekly. 'Will I still be in London?' The panic was evident in her tone.

Her supervisor shook her head. 'I can't tell you any more than that. You need to go up and see him this afternoon at one o'clock. If it all works out, I can tell you more about the situation later. Go back to work now and try to put it out of your mind till then.'

Julia nodded, taking the piece of paper that was handed to her with the unfamiliar name scrawled on it, and felt apprehensive. Returning to her desk, and even with her supervisor's urgings, she was unable to put anything out of her mind. She typed away absently, considering a thousand different scenarios this could mean, and none of them felt good.

At break time the girls were eager to know what was going on but Julia was none the wiser than they were. When she asked if any of them knew a Mr Woodbridge, they all shook their heads. 'She was waiting for you for about twenty minutes, pacing up and down in front of your desk. Whatever it is, it must be important,' surmised one of them.

At a quarter to one, she left the typing pool and climbed the stairs to the number of the room she'd been given, on a floor where many of the prime minister's own staff worked. Finding the correct door, Julia's heart was pounding as she knocked on it, and from beyond it a polite upper-class voice reached out to her. 'Come in.'

Inside was a neat-looking man with a balding head sitting behind an enormous mahogany desk. He peered up at her over the top of his half-rimmed glasses. 'Ah, Mrs Sullivan,' he announced, as though he already knew her, but they had never met. 'Come on in and sit down.' She did as he asked and sat down in front of the desk, hovering on the edge of the seat, one of her fluttering hands nervously smoothing down her skirt. 'Did Mrs Hathaway tell you anything about the position?'

Julia shook her head. 'She just said she would tell me more once I've been through a test.'

The man nodded his approval. 'All right, then we'll get started, shall we?'

Julia nodded.

'First of all, I have to ask you a series of questions, and I need you to answer them as honestly as possible. Then I need you to do a typing test, a shorthand test and a transcription test. All of those skills will be needed for this particular job.' He must have sensed her apprehension because glancing over at her his businesslike expression softened and his tone mellowed. 'Mrs Hathaway tells me you're the best they have down there. I'm sure you'll do fine,' he added, encouragingly.

Taking a document from a file, he started to ask her a number of questions. Many she'd been through in her first security check a year before. Questions such as: did she have any family that had ties to the IRA or was she affiliated with any pro-German societies, or did she have German relatives? As she answered them all, a little bemused, he looked at her attentively for each response as though checking carefully that she was telling him the truth.

Finishing the questions, he made a mark on the form and then asked her to sit at a typewriter at a small desk in the corner where he instructed her to type a letter copied from another written document. He started a stopwatch and Julia began typing. It was a straightforward letter of request, something similar to those she had to type every day. As she finished it, she rolled it out and handed it to him.

After that he tested her shorthand skills, which she was the most nervous about, because it wasn't her greatest strength, then Mr Woodbridge asked her to add another sheet of paper to the typewriter. She did as she was told and noted that her hand was still shaking as she rolled the barrel and wedged the paper down inside. Julia wished she knew what this was about. He then dictated a letter at quite a rapid speed, but Julia kept up with ease. Transcription was one of her strengths, and her mind was able to process well ahead of her fingers, so she never really had to stop and ask him to repeat anything. He spoke for about three minutes and then stopped. As he reached his hand towards her, she rolled out the paper, and he reviewed everything for a few minutes that felt like an eternity.

She sat there, apprehensively chewing on her cheek. Nothing to keep her attention but the movement of the black Gothic hands and the thrum of the large mahogany wall clock as it ticked methodically, the faint smell of polish from the wood of the desk, and the constant buzz of the traffic outside. He finished reading, took off his glasses and beamed. 'I think you'll do fine,' he said. 'You're definitely very fast. Mrs Hathaway was right.' He took out a stamp and stamped the three pieces of paper and added them to a file. 'If you could go back to Mrs Hathaway, she'll furnish you with the details of your new assignment. Tell her you passed the test with flying colours.'

Julia acknowledged his words with a little frustration that she still didn't know what this was all about. As she stood to leave, she was aware her whole body was trembling. At the door he called out to her.

'Julia.'

She turned.

'Thank you for all your hard work, I'm glad you're on our side.'

She allowed herself a small smile.

When she got back down to her own floor, she went straight to Mrs Hathaway's office. Most of the girls were still having their lunch and her supervisor was halfway through a sandwich when Julia knocked and entered the room. Mrs Hathaway swivelled around in her chair and beckoned to Julia when she saw who it was. 'Come on in, Julia. How did it go?'

'He said to tell you I passed with flying colours.'

Mrs Hathaway looked relieved. 'I knew you wouldn't let me down. Sit down.' Her boss placed her sandwich down on her desk and, wiping crumbs from the corner of her lips with a tissue, she became quite animated, almost excited. 'Julia, we've had a request from the top. For someone with impeccable character and with high skills to move downstairs into Mr Churchill's war rooms. He is losing one of his main secretaries down there.'

Julia swallowed, beginning to understand what she was suggesting. Was Mrs Hathaway telling her she was going to be working with Mr Churchill himself in the war rooms? 'It's an honour,' continued her supervisor, 'and you'll be greatly needed during the war. You should be very proud that you've been chosen to do this work. There's one thing we need to consider though, Julia. This work will not be easy. You'll work very long hours, sometimes into the evening and maybe even through the night. How is your situation at home? You have children, don't you?' Julia nodded. 'Well, I think that you need to think very seriously about them before you take the job. Have you considered sending them away?'

Julia fixed her gaze on a spot on the carpet in front of her and felt a familiar twinge of guilt. So many parents were sending their children to the country to live where it would be safer if the cities were attacked. She hadn't had the heart to send her own children away before John left. She knew she was doing nothing but putting it off. What if the Germans never attacked in this phoney war, as it was being labelled, and she sent her children away for no good reason?

The memory of Maggie's tear-stained face and Tom's pale, quivering lip from that morning swam into her thoughts. Could she deal them another blow? Putting them on a train to God knows where without her?

Mrs Hathaway seemed to sense her predicament. She leaned forward and did something very uncharacteristic for this woman who always seemed to be so aloof; she placed her hand over Julia's. 'I know it's hard, my dear. I had to send my three off last week, but it really is for the best. Not just for them, but for the country. Do you have relatives somewhere that would take them in?'

Julia looked up. 'I do have an aunt that lives in the Cotswolds. She wrote to me last week saying she had plenty of room and if I wanted to send the children, they would be well looked after there, but I hadn't got the heart to send them. Particularly as their father was going to war today.'

Mrs Hathaway sat back and drew in a thoughtful breath. 'That is understandable, but it may only be a matter of time before it becomes mandatory, my dear. Particularly if Herr Hitler starts getting closer to the city with his bombs. And God forbid if he makes it onto British soil. Would you rather your children be in London with the Nazis or maybe out in the country where they might have more of a chance? It would be less adjustment for them if you sent them now. Let them get established somewhere, in case things do turn badly.'

Julia wrung her hands. This all made total sense, but she'd been dreading it even though the children had started to complain that their classrooms had pretty much emptied around them overnight.

'Why don't you take some time to think about it?' continued her supervisor. 'Mr Churchill doesn't need you till next week. That will give you a few days to decide and get the children organized. I must encourage you to think now though, dear. This kind of opportunity doesn't come along every day. And there would be a substantial pay rise. It would be a fine feather in your cap, and you may end up sending the children away anyway.'

Julia acknowledged that and then rose and strode to the door. 'Thank you, Mrs Hathaway, I appreciate this opportunity,' she affirmed, gratefully. As she wandered back down to the typing pool, she wished more than anything that John was here to talk to about this, or that she had a sister, or a close friend. She had lost both her mother and father years before, and she was an only child. There was really just her husband, who had been a next-door neighbour of hers, and they'd grown up together. He was like a brother as well as a partner. She did have her mother-in-law, Agnes, but she was such a worrier and she'd become incredibly upset about this war, about her son going away. Agnes wasn't someone that Julia could talk to. Now she wished she and John hadn't kept themselves to themselves so much. Now she was all alone to make this very difficult decision.

She ambled back to her desk, where she sat trying to decide what to do until the other typists joined her after lunch. When she shared the news with them, they were all excited for her. 'Of course you've got to take it,' said one of them. 'This is an incredible opportunity.' Julia was conflicted, still feeling the turmoil of letting her children go.

She spent the rest of the day distracted, thinking of all the pros and cons, but really there was no decision to make. She had to take it. All of this made sense. But her stomach twisted into knots when she thought about her children. They were all the family she had here now. If she sent them away, she really would be alone, and Julia didn't know whether she could stand that.

Chapter Six

All the way home, Julia contemplated the position they had offered her, knowing everything that had been said to her was the truth. Her children weren't safe here in London. But would she be capable of putting them on a train as well? She stepped down off her bus and took her time making her way home. There was no rush because each day, Agnes, who lived next door, picked the children up from school while Julia was working and would watch them at home until she got back.

Julia meandered through streets that were experiencing a light drizzle, which was refreshing and seemed to clear away the dust of what had been an unusually warm day for the time of year. All at once she had an idea of who to ask for advice. She couldn't think why she hadn't thought of it before. But she wouldn't make any rash decisions until she had spoken to her favourite aunt on the telephone.

As they didn't have their own telephone at home, she picked up her pace and made her way to the corner of her street and pulled open the red metal door of the telephone box. Dialling the number, she deposited the right change and heard the strong, self-confident voice of her auntie on the other end. When she told her the dilemma, Aunt Rosalyn was just the comforting voice she needed.

'Darling, you must put them on the train. It's the most sensible thing to do. And who knows? Maybe this rotten war won't last forever, and it would be like a summer holiday for them down here in the Cotswolds. I have this big empty house with just me knocking around in it on my own, and we have the dearest country village school with lots of children Maggie and Tom's age. And you can come down and see them any time you want. The earlier they come down, the sooner they can settle and be ready to start the school year right here. Things are only going to get harder for you there in London, even if you don't take this job. And besides, it sounds like a wonderful opportunity, Julia darling. Let me know what you decide, but I will look forward to seeing them towards the end of the week. On Sunday we have the village fete. If the children make it before, then I can take them there. There'll be pony rides and fun and games. They'll have a wonderful time.'

Julia smiled at the picture and the charming world that her aunt was a part of and even though it was so different from her own she wouldn't change a thing, she loved the buzz of London. But maybe right now for the children it was the best place.

Julia hung up the phone and wondered why she'd been so worried about it all. Her mother's sister made it all sound so sensible and obvious and by the time she pushed open the telephone box door, it had stopped raining and a sweetness greeted her. The smell of spring flowers in full bloom drenched by the rain, scenting the air.

Striding down the street, she opened up her front gate and made her way down the path. As she put her keys in the door, she could hear the children in the front room already arguing about something. In a way, it made her happy. They'd been so forlorn just that morning, that to hear them in their usual evening discourse reminded her how resilient children were and how they knew how to live in the moment.

Agnes was putting the kettle on, sour-faced in the kitchen. 'I can't believe he's gone,' she said as she shook her head vigorously. She hadn't moved on from John's departure. 'This wretched war is taking all the best people and I can't help but be angry about it all.'

Julia stifled a deep sigh. She was glad she hadn't asked Agnes to help her make the decision. She knew she was John's mother, but she was always very negative and quite a difficult person to be around.

After they'd had a cup of tea, and Agnes had left, she decided to broach the subject with the children over supper. 'My aunt Rosalyn has invited you down into the Cotswolds for a bit of a holiday.'

They both continued eating, obviously not realizing the significance of this.

'She tells me there'll be a fete there on Sunday, so I was thinking of sending you down there for a break.'

Tom looked up, fear crossing his face. 'But you'll be coming with us, too, Mummy, won't you?' he asked, the panic evident in his tone.

Julia swallowed. 'Mummy has a lot of work to do here in London, and so many of your friends have already left to go and stay with their friends and relatives. And with Daddy now gone, I thought it might be a nice break for you to go and have some time with Aunt Rosalyn. She's a lot of fun. I loved going to her house when I was a child.'

'Isn't that the lady who has a pony next door?' asked Maggie thoughtfully as she spooned baked beans into her mouth.

'Yes, that's right,' said Julia, not sure if the woman's horse was still alive next door but amazed that Maggie, who had just turned nine, had remembered that. She'd been quite young, about five, the last time they'd been there.

'I've always wanted to learn,' said Maggie. 'Learn to ride a horse.' She stabbed at a potato with a fork. 'No room for a horse here, is there? Maybe Aunty Rosalyn could introduce me to that lady next door so I could learn to ride her horse.'

Julia smiled. 'I'm sure there'll be something that you can do like that. There's lots to do in the country. And Mummy can come down and visit you at any time. It's just things could get very difficult here in London. We want you both to be safe.'

'Will you be safe, Mummy?' asked Tom in a timid voice.

She could have kicked herself for saying that with her tender-hearted son present. 'Of course I'll be safe, Tom. Mummy works for the government, and the government must take care of us. They have special places for us to stay if anything happens. You can't worry about me.'

'I don't want to go,' he said, screwing up his little face.

'I do,' said Maggie. 'I want to ride the ponies.'

'But I don't,' snapped Tom, his voice rising to a yell. 'I want to stay here with Mummy.' He slammed down his fork and rushed upstairs.

After she'd cleared away the tea things, she went up to sit on his bed and talk to him. 'I need you to be grown up, Tom, and so much more grown up than you are. All of us are having to grow up in some way or another, even Mummy. Without having Daddy here, I have to be Mummy and Daddy, and it would help me a lot if you would go to the country with Maggie, and then I won't have to worry about you because Aunt Rosalyn will take really good care of you.'

'But I love you, Mummy, and I don't want to be away from you.'

'I know, me neither,' she said, brushing a curl from his damp forehead where it had fixed itself with the exertion of crying, 'but the government may ask you to go away anyway. And at least this way you get to go somewhere where you're with my auntie. I need you to be very brave, Tom, and do this for me.'

'Is that because I'm now the man of the house?' he said with a small sniffle.

Julia swallowed down a laugh. She had no idea where he'd heard that before. 'Well, that's right. You are the man of the house now that Daddy's not here. I need you to support Maggie and be good to her and be good for Aunt Rosalyn. I promise I'll come down as soon as I can. And I'll write to you all the time.'

'What about my comics?' Tom sounded mulish.

'I'll send your comics through the post, don't worry. And they have comics in the village where Aunt Rosalyn lives as well. Everything's going to be just the same. You're going to make lots of new friends, and before you know it, this rotten war will be over, and you'll both be able to come home.'

There was a long pause while he appeared to be considering her words as he toyed with the buttons on her cardigan, then his green eyes flicked up to meet hers. 'Are there tractors down there?' he asked, brightening a little.

'Lots of tractors,' said Julia, sensing an opening. 'And animals and fields and streams you can play in.'

Tom's eyes started to widen. 'I've always wanted to climb trees in a wood, are there woods and trees in the country?'

'Lots of trees,' continued Julia. She could see the tide was turning. She brushed his damp forehead with a kiss. 'Get off to sleep now, love, and we will talk more about it in the morning. You will be able to take your bear,' she added, tucking him in and smoothing down the fur of the bear that was snuggled next to him, noticing as her heart melted a little the threadbare corner of its ear where Tom rubbed it in order to fall asleep. 'And all your favourite toys,' she continued, fighting the quiver in her own voice.

Tom nodded.

She rose and tiptoed to the door and turned off his light, his tiny voice finding her through the darkness.

'You'll be okay, won't you, Mummy, without us?'

He sounded so much older than seven and she fought the truth. 'Of course I'll be okay, Tom. I'll miss you terribly. But I have important war work to do for our prime minister here.'

Even in the darkened room, she could see his eyes widen with the gravity of what she was saying.

'Then you must do it, Mummy, and I promise to be good. I'm getting good at writing now and I'll draw pictures of the tractors and send them to you.'

'Sounds lovely,' Julia said, now fighting the croak in her voice as the tears started to rise in her chest again. After she closed the door that night, and after Maggie had gone to sleep, she sat at the kitchen table and cried. She cried for a whole hour. For the man that she'd put on the train that morning and for the children she'd be putting on a train at the end of the week. Everybody was leaving her. And she wondered if there would ever be a day when they would be a normal family again.

Chapter Seven

Lizzie woke with a start and sat up in bed, her heart pounding. She had been dreaming about Fergus; she struggled to steady her breathing and quieten herself. As she peered out into the gloomy room, she tried to work out where she was. Where was the sloping ceiling, the daisy-patterned curtains being sucked in and out by the night air? This room was square and had a vaguely antiseptic smell. It was then that she recognized where she was, as she focused on the blackout curtains at the window. It had taken her a moment to acclimatize her vision, but now she could see more clearly. Just a few feet to her right was Diana, her back turned to her as she slept in the large room they shared with the other recruits. She was in West Drayton, just outside London, in the WAAF training barracks.

Clutching at her nightdress she realized sweat was dripping down her chest, and her hair was matted around her face and neck. She needed to get out of bed and go somewhere where there was some cooler air.

Lizzie slid her legs out of bed and into her slippers and, grabbing her dressing gown, stepped into the hallway. Attempting to inhale gulps of the thin, dry air, she ran her hand through her damp hair and tiptoed to the tiny kitchen, which they shared among the four rooms that were her small group. Her hands were still shaking and her palms sweating as she placed the kettle on the stove and, tentatively peeling aside the blackout curtains, she cracked open the window in hope of some fresh air. Outside, the first pink blush of morning was smeared across the blue velvet sky. All was unusually still around the barracks and Lizzie closed her eyes to enjoy it. Somewhere, far off, birds began to welcome the day and just the familiarity of the rise and fall of gentle birdsong took her home to Scotland and calmed her instantly. She took a long slow moment to inhale deep, ragged breaths of the cool morning air until her breath was even, her heart rate returned to normal and the clock in the kitchen, ticking merrily, informed her it was five o'clock. Feeling her equilibrium return she shuffled to the stove and dropped a teaspoon of tea into the pot, and only then did Lizzie consider the dream again.

She had been back in the barn just as it had happened five years before. When the two of them had started kissing, and their heavy petting had shifted into something else, something more sinister. Lizzie remembered with a shiver the sound of his breath roaring in and out of her ears as he panted, his hair matted with sweat, his hands groping her body, his clammy cheek next to hers, as he'd clumsily kissed her neck. Lizzie had stared up at him, confused about the intense emotion that was causing his face to contort in a way that made her fearful. They had kissed many times before but nothing had felt like this time. Lizzie shuddered, remembering her naivety as she continued to recall the way he had pressed down upon her with the whole weight of his body, stealing the air from her lungs. In the kitchen Lizzie drew in a deep breath, needing to feel that freedom now as she remembered. Back then she hadn't enjoyed the experience, and had tried to push him off. 'Come on, Fergus, I need to get home. You know Father is strict about my curfew.'

But instead of his usual jovial response, he had tightened his grip on her arms, narrowed his eyes and appeared not to hear her as he attempted to quiet her with an intense kiss on the lips.

Eventually, she had thrust him back harder, and red-faced, he had looked desperate.

'You can't do that, Lizzy. You can't just lead a boy on like this,' he had spat out at her. 'There is a name for girls like you, and it isn't nice.'

Lizzie had been shaken. He had never spoken to her in that way before, and her cheeks had reddened, too. She suddenly felt guilty, responsible for his angry mood. She hadn't meant to lead him on. This wasn't the first time they'd ever kissed. Why was this so different?

'Oh, get away with you,' she'd responded, trying to sound cheerful and keep the tremble from her voice. 'You know that isn't the case.' Once again, she'd attempted to raise herself, pushing up from her elbows. Eventually, frustrated, he'd let go of her arms, thrusting them away from him and had rolled over and lay next to her on the straw. He was furious.

'It's not right, Lizzie. We can't go on like this,' he said, unable to keep the frustration from his tone.

Now angry herself with the pressure she was feeling from him, Lizzie had jumped to her feet, and attempted to leave when he'd grabbed her arm again.

His voice dropped to a whisper as he started to plead with her. 'Lizzie, I'm sorry. Please don't leave like this, please!' he'd whined, pulling her back down onto the hay next to him. 'Please just stay a little while longer. I love you, I don't want us to part like this.'

She'd sat back down but a million thoughts had whirred through her mind, as she'd measured what he'd said. Had she been leading him on? She hadn't intended to, she knew how babies were made and just didn't want to get pregnant. She had to admit she'd been more than curious about what all that meant, but something about this evening just didn't feel right to her. Fergus had become intense and brooding.

'It's just I love you so much,' he whispered into her neck, trying to reassure her. 'People who really love each other want to take it further. And everyone knows, you can't get pregnant the first time, any rate. And I've tried to be so patient because I love you, Lizzie, but if you really loved me too, you'd want to do this. Don't you feel anything? Don't you love me?'

'You know I do,' she insisted, confused by her conflicting feelings. She did love Fergus, didn't she? Why didn't she want to take it further if she loved him?

Lizzie had started to doubt her own conviction. Was Fergus right? Was there something wrong with her? As she'd contemplated all this he'd carried on coaxing and reminding her they were in love and one day would be married and besides he would stand by her whatever happened. Interspersed with his cajoling he'd continued kissing her neck, her face, stroking her hair and telling her how beautiful she was.

And finally, concerned about the time and not wanting them to fall out, he'd worn her down with his persistence, assuring her he promised to stop if she wasn't enjoying it. It had still felt wrong and she hadn't enjoyed it at all. In fact, it had been really uncomfortable, though she had just wanted to get it over with at that point.

After he'd finished, she'd laid back on the straw, tears pricking her eyes, feeling completely confused and a deep sadness as Fergus had lain catching his breath, smiling contentedly by her side. Surely that wasn't what love was supposed to feel like, was it? The love she had read about in books and seen on the films once a month in the church hall.

After they'd parted that night, things had been different. She found she couldn't trust him any more; they had gone into the barn that afternoon as lifelong friends and left as strangers.

Lizzie had felt thoroughly ashamed of herself. The whole incident would have been terrible enough. It would have been the unfortunate end of a friendship. But when she had found out she was pregnant, the whole thing had taken on a whole new seriousness.

The kettle whistled and jarred her from her memory. Pouring the water over the tea, she noticed that her hand was shaking again. Now she was older, Lizzie saw it for what it was: Fergus had manipulated her, making her feel guilty as though, somehow, she'd caused how he was feeling; but with age and hindsight she felt nothing but anger at him and self-loathing for not standing up for her own convictions: that would never happen again.

As the tea steeped, she slipped back into her room, where Diana sighed and turned over in her sleep. Lizzie pulled the newspaper clipping from her handbag and went back into the kitchen to read it one more time. She opened it and smoothed it out on the table. Three smiling faces looked up at her from the photograph. It was an article that had been in the local Scottish paper about the work that was being done for orphans all over the country. This story was about London orphans and how the orphanages were dealing with the influx of children that was happening because of the displacements during the war. When she'd first read it in her uncle's newspaper, her heart had pounded in her ears because she'd recognized somebody in it. In the photograph was the woman who ran the orphanage, but next to her was an older woman in a nurse's uniform who she'd recognized instantly as the nurse who had snatched her baby from her five years before. The woman who had been so cruel to her, and to the other young nurse who'd allowed her to hold her baby for a moment.

This had been the first clue she'd had about the whereabouts of Annie, the name she had given her daughter, since that day when she'd been taken from her arms, and here was a picture of that woman. The nurse she would never forget, who had stood in the doorway and looked at her with such cold contempt. Underneath the picture there was the name of the orphanage – St Barnabas. She reread it. It was down here in London, and she was determined to find it. As soon as she had leave, she was going to find Annie and make sure that she was all right. Tears sprang to her eyes again as she thought about her daughter, and as the world started to come to life outside Lizzie sipped her tea and came up with a plan. 'I'm going to find you, Annie,' she whispered into the empty kitchen.

Chapter Eight

After that first night when Julia had told them, the children seemed to come round relatively quickly to the idea of being sent to their great-aunt's in the Cotswolds. It had helped that at school that week, a friend of Maggie's had sent a letter to the teacher, who had read it out to the class, about all the marvellous things she was doing at the seaside since she'd been evacuated. Maggie had told Tom at supper and that had doubtless aided the situation and abated some of her children's fears, and Julia had been grateful for the teacher's clever idea.

Also, Julia had been spurred on by the ongoing discouraging news about the war in Europe. All week the papers had been full of the evacuation of Dunkirk in France, where hundreds of thousands of British soldiers had been rescued from the shores of Europe by the navy and a flotilla of small craft owned by everyday people. The fact that Europe was now defenceless added weight to current concerns that Britain could soon be invaded.

But too soon the day Julia had been dreading arrived. Early on Saturday, she rose before dawn to collect herself and finish any last-minute packing for her children. Sitting at her kitchen table, she wrote the labels that were to be hung around the children's necks with their names and addresses on them. With a hand wrapped around a steaming cup of tea, she stared out of the kitchen window, watching the royal-blue night turn into a gorgeous cerise dawn, and contemplated how odd it was, to be labelling her children like luggage.

When Maggie appeared, following Julia down early that morning, her nervousness revealed itself in the way she began to babble to her mother in one long jumbled thought. This was her daughter's usual way of dealing with things that worried her.

'What happens if they put me on the wrong train, Mummy? Or what happens if they put me on the right train, but they don't tell me when to get off at the right stop, Mummy? Or what happens if Aunt Rosalyn doesn't remember us, or when we get to the station, she's not there, and nobody tells you, and we can't phone you because we don't have a telephone here? And what will happen to us then?'

As Maggie burbled on, Julia tried to clear her thoughts. She turned to her daughter and gently upturning her distraught face, she smoothed down her frizzy hair and kissed the top of her head, saying, 'Now, Maggie. You must stop worrying about everything all at once. There are lots of kind people that are going to help us along the way. Women in uniform, they are called the WVS, and they are going to take you all the way to the Cotswolds. You'll be assigned to a person who you'll know both on and off the train. That's why I made these tags, you see.' Julia showed her the labels she had just finished addressing.

'Your London address is on here and on the back is Aunt Rosalyn's. I've also put the phone number down where I work at the War Office, so if anything goes wrong, you can just give this label to somebody, and they'll be able to call me. Lots of people have gone down to be with their families, and all of them have got where they're meant to have been. I need you to be strong for Tom, Maggie. You know how much he relies on you.'

As if on cue, she heard the light tripping on the stairs of her son, also up early for a change. Most mornings, to get them off to school, Julia had to literally heave them out of bed. This morning both of them were up half an hour before they usually got up. As he moved down the stairs in his green striped pyjamas, his bear tucked under his arm, she could see the anxiety etched on his white face.

Julia swallowed down her guilt and concern. Tom had barely spoken for the last two days, just nodding or shaking his head when she'd asked him questions. With an uncommon silence both children sat down at the table and peered up at her. Julia fought the lump in her throat. They looked so young. She tried to continue in a cheerful manner. 'Now, what can I get you both for breakfast? I managed to get some eggs, and would you like some toast?'

Maggie slumped back in her chair and nodded her head reluctantly as Julia moved around the kitchen. As the water boiled, she opened the cupboard and pulled out a couple of small wrapped parcels.

'I've bought you both a little gift to take with you. Just a present for being so brave.'

Their attention at the table stirred as all eyes were upon the presents. She handed out the parcels and instantly, both the children started to unwrap them. A colouring book and pens for Tom. His eyes widened. He loved to colour. 'So, you can draw those tractors for me, Tom,' she said with a smile.

Maggie opened her gift, a doll with golden ringlets and a little green striped dress. She looked up in delight. 'She's lovely, Mummy! This is the one that I wanted. The one I told you about in the window. You said it was too expensive.'

Julia nodded. 'Well, I thought you would need a playmate to go with you, and I had a little bit of extra money saved.'

Both the children's moods lightened as she placed the boiled eggs in the egg cups and toast on the plate, then scraped the butter on and off again as she'd read about in a women's magazine in order to make it last longer.

After breakfast, Julia sent the children upstairs to get dressed as their two little suitcases waited for them in the hall. Then, brushing their hair for the last time, she hung the tags around their necks, they slung their gas masks over their shoulders and the three of them all trundled out of the door. As they walked up the road and towards the train station, Julia tried to jolly them along, glad she had asked Agnes to say goodbye to them the night before. She didn't think she could have stood her sorrowful and judgemental expression this early in the morning.

'I've already started writing a newsy letter to you—lots of fun cartoons in it for Tom. As soon as you're on the train, I'm going to post it. It will be with Aunt Rosalyn in the next few days, and you can look for it there. It'll have your very own names on it.'

Sullen, the children just nodded.

When they got to the train station, it was bustling, and Maggie's mood started to sour as her fear started to bubble up again, the new doll already forgotten. People were leaving from all over London now and there were lines and lines of children. As they waited, Julia straightened Tom's hat on his head. He just looked at her through sad liquid eyes and then back down to the ground.

'Oh, come on, Tom,' she encouraged, gently stroking his icy cheek. 'Put on a brave face, son. It's what Daddy would have wanted. Look at all these children; they're all leaving their mummies and daddies, too. And there are even younger children than you, that may need you to be brave for them, and Aunt Rosalyn will take excellent care of you.'

Maggie grabbed her sibling's hand, defensively. 'I will take care of my brother,' she snapped, 'now you no longer want to care for us.'

Even though Julia knew where this was coming from, her daughter's words still stung her. 'Maggie, you know that's not true.'

'And you'll be able to do all the fun things, won't you? All the fun things here without us now,' Maggie added.

Julia didn't continue the argument. She knew Maggie was just hurt and scared. Tugging Tom away from their mother's side, Maggie stomped towards the line of children waiting on the platform, trying ever so hard not to look back at her mother. Julia quickly raced up and hugged them both tightly, kissing the top of their tiny heads, getting a light waft of flowers from Maggie's newly washed hair. 'Take care of each other,' she whispered, her voice hoarse with her own emotion. 'Promise me you'll write and draw lots of pictures.'

Maggie set her chin, though her bottom lip was quivering. She was trying so hard to be brave; it was all coming out as anger though, and Tom just looked so incredibly young. As the children stumbled towards the train, a woman in uniform tapped Julia on the arm. 'Best if you leave them here, dear,' she whispered to Julia in a kindly tone. 'Don't want any big emotional scenes right next to the train. They'll be fine with us. Don't worry. We've done this lots of times.'

Julia began to panic and almost pushed past her, but understood the sense in what the woman in the grey and red WVS uniform was saying. But she so desperately wanted one more minute with her children as she watched them disappear into a sea of tiny brown caps and plaited hair.

All at once, the hiss of the air brakes alerted her to the fact this was really happening. Why did she seem to spend all of her time at train stations saying goodbye to the people she loved? Balling up her fists until her nails cut into her palms, she reminded herself this was for the best. Her children needed to be safe. The train whistle sounded, and members of the WVS organized them all into two lines and started to walk them towards the train. Julia bit her lip so hard she nearly drew blood. She couldn't cry. She couldn't show them how upset she was.

'Please look round,' she willed her daughter. 'Maggie, please. Just one more time.' Maggie didn't look round but Tom turned and waved pathetically, and even from the distance she could see there were tears in his eyes.

Briskly, she followed them as they walked along the corridor. She watched them until they were escorted into a compartment and sat next to one of the windows. They seemed so young and so vulnerable. What kind of life was this war, where you put your children on trains and sent them away? Nothing about this felt natural.

Suddenly, fresh fears gripped her. She hadn't instructed Rosalyn how to comb Maggie's hair just the right way to get the tangles out or told her that Tom's favourite food was custard, and how it was the surest way to get him to eat if he was pining. She'd have to put that in a note to her auntie as soon as she got home. As she watched them waiting for the train to move, Julia felt the grief about all the things that she would miss out on, all the things that Rosalyn wouldn't know.

As she was working through these fears in her mind, the whistle of the train announced its departure and steam hissed up from the wheels, masking the windows where the children were sitting. Reaching out abstractly, she grabbed hold of a woman's arm next to her, who too stood watching her own children. The woman responded in the same way. No words were spoken between the two of them, but they both stood there clutching each other in silent solidarity during the most inhumane thing in the world, giving up their children to someone else. Knowing deep down, this could even be the last time they actually saw them.

Julia pushed the thought from her head and started to wave vigorously as the steam cleared, and she could see Maggie's wan face peering out the window. The platform was packed and Maggie didn't see her mother, but Julia continued to wave vigorously, following the train at a gallop as she had done with John.

Right at the last minute, she caught Maggie's eye, and finally relenting, Maggie nudged Tom, and they both waved. She saw her mouth the words, 'Goodbye, Mummy. Goodbye, Mummy.'

And Julia stood at the end of the platform until the train was completely out of sight and the emptiness she felt was bottomless. Her children had just left her, and she was now completely alone. The shock of that reality numbed her to everything around her. She didn't remember walking home or posting the letters she had in her bag for them. She didn't remember putting the key in the door. When she got home she just stumbled upstairs, and still in her coat and hat she lay on the bed, and started to sob. Tomorrow she would find the strength for what she needed to do, but today, this was all she was capable of.

Chapter Nine

Julia took the weekend to get over the heartache of saying goodbye to all of her family, her pain being greatly eased by a short letter from John on Saturday saying he was well, but because of censorship he couldn't tell her where he was, and a cheerful phone call with the children on Sunday, where they had described the fun they'd had at a local fete.

So, by Monday morning, she was ready to start her new job. Stepping off the bus, she hurried along the street. She would be entering the Whitehall building by a different entrance now, and she'd allowed herself time to find that. But she had to admit she was nervous. As she crossed the road, towards the right gate, she felt as if she needed to pinch herself and was still a little in awe that they had chosen her for this work.

Joining the line to get in, she smoothed down her skirt and straightened her new hat that she'd matched with a navy skirt and pale blue blouse. She'd even managed to talk her local shopkeeper into giving her some stockings on account, explaining how she was starting a new job.

'Can't have you doing that with bare legs,' the shopkeeper had said, shaking his head and glaring at her over his glasses as he slid the stockings across the counter.

As she waited her turn, she nervously fingered the new orange identification card a very serious-looking government official had issued her the week before and looked around the vast Regency crescent that marked this end of Whitehall Palace. It was quite impressive, with its white stucco façade, so popular in the Regency period, smooth cream-coloured pillars, and arches with intricate detailing. The whole building glistened under the morning sunshine, though soot marred many of the corners and crevices, due to all the coal fires burning in the city that earned London the nickname of the Big Smoke. Still, even with these blemishes, the beauty of the building was undoubtedly striking. Taking her turn at the gate, she handed the guard her pass, which clearly stated she'd be working in the war rooms. Finding her name on his list, he checked it off, and nodding to her, he ushered her through. As she walked towards the main door, her heart pounded. She was really going to do this. She would actually work for the prime minister himself.

Julia checked her watch and noted she was early, so without a need to rush, she allowed herself a moment to admire the architecture along the way as she sauntered into a long, broad corridor. To her right, sun streamed in through a line of elegant bowed windows, the leaded glass creating square pools of light that highlighted the tones of a highly polished cherrywood floor. From this vantage point, Julia got an excellent view of London. In one window she noticed a plump pigeon sitting sunning itself on one of the black wrought-iron guard rails, its eyes closed and its green and purple iridescent neck feathers shimmering in the morning sunshine. She smiled to herself as she passed it. Sometimes it was hard to believe a war was going on when nature treated it with such contempt.

The bright sunlight also bathed the wall to her left in a gentle, warming glow, illuminating statues and portraits of noted people of the past that hung there. Their stately figures were highlighted in arched recesses of white-coloured stone. Julia moved past paintings of starched-looking admirals and distant ancestors of the royal family, tripping lightly along the floor, not wanting her echoing shoes to draw attention to her. As she marvelled at the beauty and the heritage all around her, she hoped Mr Churchill would protect this. She would hate one of Hitler's bombs to flatten all this impressive history. Reaching the end of the corridor, she moved through a grand archway into a marble-floored entrance hall, with more cream stone staircases ascending through the building. This morning it was alive with activity as people bustled about their business, the rolling echo of their collective conversations bouncing around the stone walls along with the sound of their hurrying feet. Julia had been instructed to head towards a doorway at the end of the room where another soldier stood on guard. Showing her pass once again, the soldier looked at it, handed it back, and allowed her inside, closing the door behind her.

The other side of that door was a world away from the rest of the building. It was such a contrast to the hallway she had just left that it took Julia a moment to see and get her bearings. Grey brick walls were illuminated by dim lighting and riveted to the walls was a heavy iron staircase with criss-cross metal treads that reached down into the bowels of the earth. It felt more like a fire escape than the way to the war rooms of a prime minister. Everything about it spoke of the industry of war: behind her was the grandeur of the British empire and in front of her was the future work to be done. It felt as though this staircase was a gateway to the inner workings of the machine that was driving the British war effort. She imagined it wasn't much different from being on an elegant steamship and taking a wrong turn and suddenly finding yourself in the heat and dust of the engine room. As she had worn her high heels, she couldn't help but clank down the metal stairs, feeling very self-conscious.

At the bottom of the staircase stood another soldier waiting by another enormous iron door. This one was in full dress uniform and studied her pass in much more detail than the guards before.

'You're new?' he challenged, an edge of distrust in his tone.

She nodded. 'My first day today.'

He peered at her again before slowly turning her pass over and running his thumb across the front of it, scrutinizing all the words, inspecting it for irregularities. Eventually, he handed it back to her.

'You will need to wait here for your supervisor. You need an escort your first time in here.'

He went inside, closing the heavy steel door behind him with a clang of metal.

In the dimly lit hallway, Julia waited and shivered. Outside, it had looked as if it was shaping up to be another lovely day, but down here it was damp and cold. The beauty of the Whitehall building above her seemed a million miles away from this dim, cellar-like room that smelled dank. It reminded her of a trip she'd taken with her parents to Warwick Castle years before. The dungeons had felt cold and damp like this. As she looked around her, she hoped she wouldn't feel claustrophobic down here. Julia shook that thought from her head. As challenging as it was, this was an incredible opportunity that she was getting. The door opened again, and a short, square woman with heavy, dark-rimmed glasses and black hair wound into a prim-looking bun eyed her with interest. The first word that popped into Julia's mind was schoolmistress. The woman thrust out a cold, dry hand, accompanied by a tight smile.

'Hello, Julia,' she said, 'welcome to the bunker. My name is Mrs Scriber.' Her manner was businesslike but the pitch of her tone was such that Julia felt it would grate on her nerves if she had to listen to it for too long. 'Come,' she commanded, striding back inside, her square, matronly shoes whispering on the brown linoleum as Julia attempted to keep up with her guide's fast pace. 'I will be your supervisor down here. If you have any problems or questions, you come directly to me,' she echoed over her shoulder as Julia nodded blankly to the woman's back. 'My job today is to show you around so you can familiarize yourself with the place. It can feel quite like a rabbit warren when you first arrive, but you'll soon get used to it.'

As Mrs Scriber turned corners and snaked down hallways, Julia looked around her in awe. She hadn't known quite what to expect from the war rooms. Maybe a couple of offices or separate rooms downstairs under the building. But she had never imagined anything quite like this. This was a hive of industry that burrowed throughout the depths of Whitehall. Along walls of cream-painted bricks that were dusty and smoke-marked, her guide led her past room after room of people working, with gas masks and signs warning them about what to do in an emergency everywhere, all illuminated by gloomy light bulbs.

Mrs Scriber stopped at the doorway to one room. 'Telephone exchange,' she announced, with a quick sweep of her hand.

Julia looked inside. Seated back to back in two rows of four, eight switchboard operators sat in front of floor-to-ceiling mahogany boxes, moving neat rows of telephone plugs in and out of their pegboards. Already busy routing calls, heads were bent low as they spoke quietly into receivers.

'Morning, girls,' Mrs Scriber greeted them, brightly.

Hands lifted up haphazardly around the room but none of them moved their gaze from their equipment or broke from the intensities of their calls.

Her supervisor didn't stop as she continued to weave Julia through the honeycomb of rooms, sweeping her arm towards another corridor where, lined along the walls, were dozens of bunk beds stacked with grey army blankets and clean sheets.

'If you need to stay overnight, you can sleep here. During emergencies we can work well into the night. Sometimes there's no point going home,' she said with another tight smile.

As she marched on, her guide continued, 'We have our own filtered air down here in case of a gas attack. We can be down here for days at a time if we need to be.' She pulled back a curtained area. 'Everybody is required to use the heat lamps that are supposed to combat the lack of light we all receive down here. You need to use those at least once a week. Strip down to your underwear and sit here for thirty minutes.'

Julia shook her head. She hadn't expected any of this.

'The canteen,' Mrs Scriber said, continuing on her whirlwind tour, her hand pointing out the room to their right. The smell of something like shepherd's pie – the war-rationed version of it, no doubt – drifted through the service hatch amid a mass of steam. In front, a large metal water boiler was steaming, lines of white mugs on a vast metal tray beside it. Through the hatch, the cook wearing a chef's hat and a crisp white apron acknowledged Mrs Scriber with a nod as beside her a young girl in a blue-and-white checked pinafore, her hair wound up in a scarf, was making sandwiches. They passed by another room with a closed door.

'The war rooms, dear,' she said, cracking open the door. There was no one inside. 'You will not be allowed in here unless you're invited. But I wanted to let you know what it was.'

Julia peeked inside; mahogany desks sat in a large square formation, all facing one another, pads of papers and ink pens lying ready for people to take notes. Her supervisor pulled the door shut as Julia caught a glimpse of an enormous map on one wall outlined in red and green.

'Also out of bounds without permission is the map room,' she whispered, nudging open another door as a wave of blue smoke drifted out. Inside, it was teeming with life. Military personnel of all branches of the fighting services were moving around the room, conferring with one another and staring at graphs and maps that covered every inch of the wall space. Numerous desks were piled with papers and a bank of telephones dominated the centre of the room.

As they turned the next corner, Mrs Scriber slowed her pace and whispered to Julia, 'Here are Mr Churchill's own quarters. He has a bedroom and an office here. As one of the typists, we may call upon you to type for the prime minister. Just be aware, sometimes he likes you to type while he's in bed. I realize this is unusual, but you can't be squeamish down here. He's an interesting character, but he's getting the job done.' She broke out into a smile.

Julia acknowledged what she was saying, absorbing all she was seeing.

'I know it can smell musty down here,' Mrs Scriber continued, 'and I wish people wouldn't smoke, but you can't tell people what to do. There is a lot of pressure, so you'll get used to that. We all have.'

Julia nodded, still struggling to get her bearings. The oddest thing about being below ground like this was that there were no windows. Once again it felt as if she was below the deck of a huge ship.

Finally, they arrived at the typing pool, where four girls were already seated at desks, illuminated by long black metal pendulum-style lights. On each desk along with their typewriters were wire in-and-out trays filled with typed papers, a notebook, a stack of carbons, and a tin with sharpened pencils.

Her guide introduced her to the other women. They all stopped typing and looked up.

'This is our new girl, Julia Sullivan. She'll be replacing Emily, who as you know struggled with the pressure of this kind of work. Make her feel at home, won't you?'

They all acknowledged her as Julia contemplated her supervisor's last comment and wondered what she had let herself in for as she moved towards the empty desk and sat awkwardly down in front of the typewriter.

'I'll leave you to get settled in, Julia.' As she marched off, Mrs Scriber's departing words were, 'She's very fast; she'll keep you all on your toes.'

There was a general hum of laughter around the room as Julia's face reddened. After she had gone, one girl with platinum blonde curls and cornflower blue eyes at the desk in front of Julia's leaned over her typewriter and spoke to her.

'Hi, my name is Carol, and don't take too much notice of Scribie. She can come across quite stern, but it's all an act. Her bark is much worse than her bite.'

'She's actually quite friendly, brings us chocolate sometimes,' added another willowy girl with short brown hair and a swan neck who was whisking through her notebook, a pencil clenched between her teeth. She removed it and smiled, 'I'm Stephanie, by the way, and we are a friendly bunch down here. I organize all our social activities.' All the girls laughed. 'Which, of course, to most of us are non-existent,' she continued, 'so it's my way of saying I do nothing. If you want someone to check your work for spelling mistakes, ask Linda, she's a whizz, and smart as a whip.' She pointed her pencil towards a girl with catlike eyes and heavy lids, her hair pinned up in a victory roll.

'The product of a very boring youth, I'm afraid,' purred the girl in question, her voice slow and thick, reminding Julia of Greta Garbo.

'Linda also keeps us all up to date on what the movie stars are wearing and doing,' added Stephanie.

Linda leaned back on her seat and lit a cigarette, blowing out a long slow curl of blue smoke into the air before announcing in a droll tone, 'Welcome to the dungeon. Is it ten in the morning or at night?'

Julia looked shocked as Carol shook her head. 'It's a standing joke down here. Because we never see the daylight, we are like bats. Laughing about it is how we keep ourselves sane.'

'And lastly,' continued Stephanie, 'if you need a good laugh talk to Sally. She is the life and soul of the party. Mind you, she has been very quiet today,' she added, pointing to a girl with ruddy cheeks and fair hair at the back of the room who was staring blankly at her shorthand pad.

'Worse for wear, girls,' Sally growled back, giving the girls a hangdog look. 'Should never have gone out last night with that Welsh sergeant. He had me dancing and drinking till two and my head is still spinning.' She squinted back at her pad. 'I think this word is supposed to be bombs, but it looks like we might be considering dropping babes on Hitler, if I'm to believe my shorthand notes,' she announced with a chuckle, moving her pad further away from her eyes to try and focus better.

Her laugh was infectious and there was a snigger throughout the pool.

'Maybe it's a new propaganda technique to keep those German soldiers busy elsewhere,' added Stephanie drily.

Julia started to relax. She could sense the spirit of camaraderie in the room. Probably developed through hours of being down here alone together.

Carol showed Julia where to hang her coat and hat and told her where the cloakroom was. As Julia uncovered her typewriter, she also instructed her how to deal with the in-tray.

'Are you married?' Carol asked as she helped her stack her files.

'My husband's away.'

'Mine too,' smiled Carol. 'Is yours in Africa as well?'

'I'm not sure yet,' Julia admitted. 'I'm waiting to hear where he will be posted. He just left last week, and I only got a short note from him so far.'

'It can take a while,' Carol admitted, dragging her hand through her blonde curls. 'Mind you, I think Dave used it as an excuse not to write for the first month. He hates writing and it was that long before I actually got four lines on a piece of paper, telling me he was alive. At least in the other three he told me how much he loved me and missed me.'

'Have any of you met the prime minster yet?' asked Julia in a hushed tone.

All the girls nodded. 'Mr Churchill's rather nice when you get used to him. A little unconventional,' Stephanie informed her. 'And he mumbles. You have to be able to type and be able to listen really well. And he hates the clatter of the keys on the typewriter so you have to type softly. He can come across a little bombastic, but he seems like a nice man. He's always pretty nice to us, though he is short on patience. But don't take anything personally. You'll probably be working on his speeches, just like Emily was. You have to type as he speaks. He hates people taking shorthand notes and does a lot of corrections last minute. He's always changing his mind. That's probably why they picked you to replace Emily, because you're fast, and you will need to be.'

'He won't be around today,' added Linda, stamping out her cigarette, bobbing her rolled hair and scrolling up her barrel to check her work. 'He's got meetings upstairs today. Unless Germany attacks, you'll probably have the whole day to get yourself settled in, get used to the warren. It takes a little getting used to, but I'm sure you will fit in fine.'

Julia smiled and thought again, *I'm actually going to meet the prime minister*. For the first time since before John had left, she felt excited. Even though a war was not the best reason for being here, it felt like she could really make a difference. And she hadn't realized she'd be working on Mr Churchill's speeches. As Julia started to read through Emily's notes to her in the in-tray, the exhilaration of that made her cheeks redden. She would have the honour of seeing those speeches presented to the Houses of Parliament or hear them on the radio. Who would have thought it? A girl from Brixton sitting here working, hobnobbing with the prime minister. Pulling out two sheets of paper, she added carbon and rolled it into her typewriter.

Chapter Ten

Diana collapsed onto her bunk. She couldn't recall a time when she'd experienced so much pain. Every muscle in her body ached. She had thought being a hairdresser and on her feet all day would have prepared her for the exertion, but as she peered down at her muddy shoes still tied on her feet, she realized she didn't even have the energy to take them off, though they would need to be cleaned before inspection tomorrow. All she could think about was sleep, even though the mattresses were wafer thin, and it was only six o'clock, she knew she could probably drop off quickly.

As she lay drowsing, she reflected back over the two weeks of activity. She and Lizzie had cemented their friendship. Lizzie had an enormous heart and a wonderful sense of adventure but Diana had continued to sense something else in her new friend. A deep sadness that she glimpsed now and again when Lizzie's guard was down, in moments when she was unaware that she was being observed. Diana wondered about it, and whether their friendship would become close enough for Lizzie to open up, and feel safe enough to let her share in whatever it was that hid just behind her smile. But apart from that small observation Diana had been grateful to her new friend, who would always jolly her along when things were getting tough.

Since they'd arrived, it had been a whirlwind of ceaseless activity. Their commander had had them marching up and down the compound all hours of the day and night, and they'd hardly had any food to eat. Last night had just been a small pie and gravy. At the end of every day, Diana wavered between feeling hungry and exhausted. To get them used to the pressure they could feel once bombs started dropping, they were often roused in the middle of the night, lights flicked on, and had to race to their stations. They had to get dressed quickly. Sometimes to save time Diana slept in her stockings so she didn't have to put them on when she was bleary-eyed and disorientated. There was also further discussion about the final units they could be assigned to. And though she was exhausted, she felt excited about the prospects of what she would be doing in the WAAF.

Diana was nearly asleep when, all at once, the door to the room opened and in came Lizzie. She yipped, gushing, 'Diana, a whole night off!'

'Aha,' Diana mumbled, not even opening her eyes. 'I'm going to stay right here and not move a muscle until tomorrow morning. I'm not even sure I have the energy to get undressed.'

All at once, she could sense Lizzie leaning over her. 'Can't waste a night sleeping, Diana. We need to get out. We haven't even seen London yet.'

Diana forced her gritty eyes open. Lizzie's face was inches from her own.

'Come on, let's go dancing or see a movie or something. One of the girls has to do a delivery in town, and she's offered to give us a lift in.'

'I can't even feel my feet,' groaned Diana, 'never mind go dancing.'

Lizzie sat on the edge of the bed. 'Look, I know it's been a hard couple of weeks, but we're so close to London. We don't even know what we're missing. I've never been to a big city. I'm so excited to see it. Before we know it, it'll be tomorrow, and they'll have us marching up and down again for another week. This is the only chance we'll get. I promise we won't be out late – Scout's honour. We'll just look around, see the town, maybe watch a film, then we'll get straight back on the bus. You can be asleep by ten o'clock. You know they like us to go out in pairs if we can.'

Diana forced herself into a sitting position. Her whole body felt the ache again. 'All right,' she said as she stretched her back. 'Give me a minute, and I'll try to remember what it feels like to be a human being again.'

Placing her feet on the ground and heaving herself up, Diana shuffled across the floor as she stretched her back once more and rubbed her neck. And she had to admit, even though she was tired, it would be fun to see London for a couple of hours before she went to bed. It would make a change from just the barracks, the parade ground, and the canteen. Making her way into the communal bathroom, she started to wash her face and get ready.

As she put on her own clothes again, she was amazed to see how it made her feel so different. The regimented uniform she'd been wearing for over a fortnight had been stiff and uncomfortable. The shoes were practically matronly. Suddenly she started to feel like herself again as she sprayed on perfume and started to put make-up on, running a comb through her curly hair. Painting on her ruby red lipstick, she smacked her lips together in the mirror. *That will have to do*, she thought, even though she still looked a bit tired around the eyes.

Half an hour later, the two of them were bumping along in an air-force truck on the way into central London. They were a jovial pair, laughing and joking about their first weeks and anticipating the first evening out in the West End. The driver dropped them off in Trafalgar Square, and the intrepid pair looked at everything around them in awe, particularly Lizzie. It was still light, so they wandered about the streets looking in all the shop windows, then stopped to have tea and cakes and ate until they were full. After tea they then decided to go to the pictures. A comedy was playing in one of the cinemas, and both of them liked the idea of relaxing and watching something funny for the evening.

'I've never even really been to a proper cinema before,' enthused Lizzie, her eyes wide as they walked into the foyer. 'We had a local fella in Scotland who would come once a month and bring us a film, which he played in the church hall, but I've never really been in anything like this before.'

As they stood in the queue to go into the auditorium, Lizzie turned to Diana. 'I'm just going to powder my nose. I won't be a minute.' Diana nodded as she waited in line, and Lizzie darted back into the hallway. Diana had second thoughts and decided maybe she would pop to the ladies too, and check her make-up. She started to follow Lizzie when she noted that instead of heading towards the toilets, Lizzie had stopped at the phone box in the foyer. Diana observed her friend promptly pull out the telephone directory and after searching the pages, write down something on a slip of paper then thrust it into her bag. Diana watched with interest. Why was she being so secretive? Was is something to do with the sadness she saw in her friend? Lizzie took a deep breath, apparently to steady herself, before heading back to join the line. Not wanting to let Lizzie know she'd seen her, Diana slipped quickly back into the queue. Lizzie arrived back just in time for them to walk into the darkened room. The film hadn't started yet so they made their way into the centre of the cinema and took their seats in the middle of the row. Diana waited to see if Lizzie would elaborate about what she had just witnessed but she didn't. Instead, Lizzie just enthused about her anticipation for the film to begin and Diana realized there was still much about this new friend she didn't know yet.

Chapter Eleven

On Friday evening, Julia left work early and made her way home after an exhausting week working in the war rooms, sometimes being there late into the night. She'd only actually seen Mr Churchill once, and that was as he'd rushed by, requesting Carol for the work that he needed. She had worked hard, and the hours went quickly but strangely, and she felt like a mole underground with no windows to inform them all if it was morning or evening. But even though she had barely come up for air all week, she willingly preferred to be at work than at home, which was an echo of a shell of what it had been without her family and with only Agnes waiting for her.

With that thought, Julia's stomach tightened. Since John had left, Agnes had been even needier than before and had become very clingy with her. And without the children to keep her busy, all she did was worry about the war all the time. Julia had tried to help her find other things to do with her time. Still, she didn't seem to care about rolling bandages or volunteering for the WVS; she just screwed up her nose and shook her head when Julia encouraged her to do something with all the nervous energy that she seemed to need to wring out of her hands all the time. Julia had even introduced her to the nice older couple across the street, who were new to the neighbourhood. Mr and Mrs Thompson had only moved in a few months before and had kept themselves to themselves, but had been nothing but pleasant to Julia when she had run into them. But Agnes had only eyed the middle-aged man, who was heavyset and balding, with distrust and had practically spat out a 'no thank you' to his tiny wife, who had a fluttery way about her, when she had asked her to join them for tea.

As soon as Julia got home each night, Agnes would start in about John, fretting about why they hadn't heard any more from him yet. Then once she had worried enough about him, she would methodically move on to everyone else in her life who had left her, going round and round in a manic loop, pulling in her dead husband and her grandchildren just for good measure. As she would prepare her tea while listening to her mother-in-law, Julia felt more and more worn down by the same conversation as the night went on. Then, with a twinge of guilt, she would remind herself that this was her husband's mother; she was alone. And it was hard for everybody right now.

The only evening Julia got respite was on a Thursday, when Agnes disappeared off to bingo. She would scuttle off down the road at six o'clock and not get back till nine, and those three hours were like bliss for Julia. But today was Friday, and with a sinking heart Julia knew she had an entire weekend ahead with just Agnes for company.

Before she went home, Julia decided she would get a cup of tea or something. A chance to gird herself between work and home and facing Agnes, just some breathing space. She'd hardly had time to gather herself since the children had left.

At least she had heard from them again on Tuesday, placing a call in the call box on the corner of her street. Julia had heard their little voices, which felt a million miles away from her, and had fought back her tears as she listened to the eager regaling of their adventures so far. She could tell they were both happy; even Tom had a spark in his tone as he talked about the farm they had visited the day before. Once she had placed the receiver back down, she'd had such mixed feelings, relieved they were happy and safe, but Julia also couldn't help feeling a little resentful. Someone else was seeing her children grow up, combing their hair, feeding them breakfast, reading them bedtime stories, and experiencing all the magic that comes from seeing the world through a child's eyes. Magic that she seemed to need more than ever in the current climate, to fend off the brutal realities of life in wartime.

Julia looked down the road, noting her bus was late, and thought she might walk to the next stop just to get some exercise.

Wandering down the street, she noticed once again how strange it was to see many of the windows were now secured with tape in preparation for a bomb attack. Pausing outside a cinema, she read a cheerful poster advertising the new Arthur Askey film that was playing there, his cheeky face emblazoned on the front, the words 'hysterical' highlighted in solid black letters above his head.

That was what she needed. She needed to laugh. She needed to relax. She looked quickly at her watch. It had only just started. Hurrying to the booth, she paid the money and made her way inside. As she entered the darkened cinema, she put Agnes's face out of her mind. Her mother-in-law would be worried, but Agnes would worry anyway, so she couldn't let that affect her. The cinema was pretty crowded and was playing a newsreel with the stories of the day. As the black and white picture flicked across the screen, it illuminated the auditorium for a second, revealing that it was packed. Through the smoky blue glow, Julia noticed there was a spare seat in the middle next to another young woman.

Apologizing as she went, she manoeuvred herself through the crowd and settled herself down in the seat, just as the announcer in the plummy British accent talked about how well the RAF had been doing in the latest rounds of battles in the skies. Soon the main feature started, and as Arthur Askey performed his comedic slapstick routines, loosely knitted together in a story, Julia roared with laughter, as did her fellow cinema-goers. She was sad when the film came to an end. As the credits were rolling, she looked at her wristwatch and through the dark could just make out the time. She sighed; she needed to get home. But it had been light relief for a couple of hours without the concern of her mother-in-law, the guilt about her children, or the worry about her husband away, who knew where.

As the lights came up, she quickly made her way to the end of the aisle. Hurrying outside, she stood on the street to get her bearings and work out where her closest bus stop was.

Suddenly, there was a hand upon her arm. She twirled around and noticed two women in front of her. One was tall, well-groomed, and dark-haired, the other short with a thatch of red hair. She realized the redhead had been next to her in the row. It was she that spoke, and Julia noticed she had a strong Scottish accent.

'Excuse me,' she said, 'I believe you may have taken my scarf by mistake. Normally I wouldn't mind, but I've spent all week knitting it. And I only finished it this morning. I would hate for you to take it home with you as it's the only one I've got that goes with my uniform.'

Julia looked down at her arm, where she'd gathered up her coat from the chair and noticed, with surprise, the blue woollen scarf wrapped around it.

'I'm so sorry,' she said, untangling it from her coat and handing it to the young woman. 'I don't normally steal people's clothing.'

The three of them laughed politely.

'Not to worry,' said the young woman, beaming. 'It's not so cold down here. Where I come from, I need a scarf even in the summer. And I wanted to wear it out tonight because I just finished it, you know.'

'I take it you're from the Highlands,' said Julia with a smile.

'Oh, what gave me away?' enquired the girl with a cheeky grin.

'You're a long way from home.'

'My name's Lizzie Mackenzie,' she said, 'and this is my friend Diana Downes. We're both down here in London, training at the RAF station in West Drayton to do our bit for our country, if we ever make it to the end of the training. We are going to work for the Women's Auxiliary Air Force. We thought we'd do something brave and mighty for our country. But all we've done so far is march up and down in lines and shine our shoes. So, we're beginning to wonder if we made a big mistake.'

Julia laughed.

'I thought I was coming to London for adventure, and to see the city,' added Diana. 'This is the first time I've been into town since we got here. We've only seen the RAF station so far.'

'Do you know anywhere where we can get a cup of tea or coffee?'

Julia nodded. 'Just down here.' She indicated a cafeteria she sometimes passed on her way to and from work. Its steamed-up windows always seemed to be full of people, even when she came home late in the evening. 'Let me buy you a cup of tea to say sorry for stealing your scarf and to celebrate your first time in London.'

'Only if you will join us,' encouraged Lizzie.

Julia thought about it; she might as well put it off a little longer. Agnes wasn't going anywhere, and it was nice to chat with somebody new. The girls seemed friendly, and she was happy to help them, as they were new to the city.

Making their way further down the road, Julia ushered them into the tea shop that was now packed with locals coming out of the cinema. But still, Diana managed to secure them a table as Lizzie and Julia went to the counter to order a pot of tea.

Once they settled themselves down around the little grey Formica table, they huddled together to be heard over the crowd, many of whom were retelling funny lines and laughing about the film they had all just seen. Diana told them about her family back home. And Lizzie described how beautiful the Highlands were.

'You married? Do you have children?' asked Lizzie as she sipped away at her tea.

Julia looked down at her steaming drink.

'I do,' she said. 'They're away in the countryside right now, with so many of our other children from the city here.'

A sympathetic look crossed Lizzie's face. 'That must be hard for you.'

'My husband's away fighting as well,' added Julia.

'Oh, that must also be difficult,' Diana added, shaking her head.

And once again, Julia realized how alone she was.

'I was afraid I'd feel lonely, too,' said Lizzie. 'But so far, everyone's been so friendly down here.' They finished their tea and made their way out of the tea shop. Lizzie and Diana stood staring up and down the street. 'Someone told me we could get a bus back out to the train station, a number thirty-two. Have you any idea where it might stop?' she asked Julia.

Julia shook her head.

'Look, mine is just coming,' she said, pointing to the bus that was trundling down the road. 'Why don't we ask on there? Maybe he will know.' Racing to intercept the bus as it ground to a halt, Julia asked the conductor who hung off the back.

'Thirty-two?' he exclaimed with disbelief, pushing his cap to the back of his head so he could scratch his bald head underneath it. 'Thirty-two – you just missed it, won't be another one for an hour.'

Both Lizzie and Diana looked ashen. 'But our last train leaves in thirty minutes. Why such a long wait?' Lizzie enquired incredulously. 'Isn't this the big city?'

'It might be, but there's a war on, love. You two haven't got a chance of getting back there tonight, and I just heard from another passenger the tube is down, in that direction. You'll have to hitch a ride.'

Diana looked mortified. 'We've got to be back on the parade ground at nine a.m. tomorrow. And we don't have any money to stay in a hotel. How do you suggest we get back?'

'Don't ask me, darling,' he said. 'I'm not a tour guide. I just take money. So, are you and your friend getting on or what?'

Julia turned to them. 'Look, you may as well come home with me. I only live twenty minutes away. And with my kids and husband gone, I've got two big empty rooms. You could stay the night and travel back with me in the morning.'

'Are you sure?' asked Diana.

Julia nodded.

'What time do the buses start in the morning?' Lizzie asked the conductor.

'Early enough,' he said. 'About seven.'

Lizzie did the calculations in her head. 'That means we could still get back to the station in time,' she said to Diana, who had paled by her side.

He pointed a finger further down the road and continued, 'Just down the road there past that phone box is where you'll pick it up at seven in the morning.'

'As long as we're back in time for duty, maybe no one will say anything and we won't be put on a charge, and end up on jankers,' Lizzie said.

Julia looked puzzled.

'It's a slang word for special duties, that aren't very pleasant,' elaborated Lizzie, screwing up her nose. 'Are you sure you don't mind?'

Julia shook her head. 'It will be fun,' she said. 'Come on, let's go.'

They all paid their fare and clambered up the stairs to the top deck of the bus.

'Always pushing me into trouble,' complained Diana, shaking her head. 'It'll be an adventure, Diana,' she said, in a sarcastic Scottish accent. 'We'll see the big city, she said!' continuing her impression of Lizzie. 'Some adventure, we nearly ended up sleeping homeless on the street.'

Lizzie blushed red. 'I do seem to always be getting you into trouble, don't I, Diana? Maybe you shouldn't stick around with me.'

'I don't have a lot of choice, we live in the same room.' Diana smirked. They all started to laugh.

Julia enjoyed their lively banter. It had been years since she'd hung out with friends like this, before she'd had her children. And when she'd started working for the war department a year ago, the work had been intense, and though she was starting to get to know the girls in the bunker, it was really hard for them to all get time off together, as the pool always needed to be covered. So, there was no one she could really laugh with or have fun with after work since John had left.

The girls regaled her along the way with all the adventures they'd had during their training and how Diana had had to carry Lizzie for a whole mile when she had twisted her ankle on a run.

Getting off the bus, they made their way down the street. But as Julia approached the house, she quietened as she noticed that even through the blackout curtains, with the darkness behind her, she could see Agnes's face looming. Before she'd even got to the front door, her mother-in-law was standing out on her doorstep with her arms folded.

'I thought something had happened to you,' she said in an accusatory tone. 'I've been worried for over an hour. I was just about to call the police, tell them you weren't home.'

Julia swallowed down the hot anger at her lack of decorum, reminding herself Agnes was her husband's mother. 'I decided to go to the pictures,' she responded in an unconvincingly cheery manner. 'These are my new friends, Lizzie and Diana. They missed the last bus, so they're going to be staying with me tonight.'

Agnes eyed them all warily. 'Well, I won't bother you any more then if you've got company,' she said with a sniff, setting her face like stone. And Julia nodded. She wasn't going to buy the guilt. And pushing the door open, the three of them strode inside.

Lizzie whispered to Julia, 'I always thought it'd be really nice to have neighbours, but she's not very friendly, is she? Does she always give you the third degree when you come home late at night?'

Julia shook her head, taking off her coat. 'Well, she is my mother-in-law. She thinks she has more right than anyone else.'

'Oh, God, I'm sorry,' burbled Lizzie, her face blushing crimson. 'I didn't mean to insult your family.'

Julia grinned. 'No, actually, you saved me. I would have had her over here for hours telling me how much she'd worried about me not being home. I think with John leaving, it sent her over the edge. She's always been a little that way, but this war has made her so much worse. She seems to have become paranoid about everything.'

As Julia prepared a cup of tea for them all, Diana and Lizzie went into the front room. Lizzie noticed the photograph of John on the mantelpiece. Picking it up, she called to Julia in the kitchen.

'Is this your husband?'

Julia poked her head in the room. 'He's handsome, isn't he?'

The girls both smiled back, nodding.

'He has a great sense of humour. He makes me laugh every day. He's always so fun to be around. Every day is an adventure with John. Always thinking of things for us to do as a family. I miss him terribly,' she said, making her way to the stove to take off the kettle. She didn't want to cry.

'Have you heard where he will be stationed yet?' enquired Lizzie.

'Not yet, it's been two weeks, but you know, they said it might be a while before they find out. He could be anywhere in the world right now.'

Lizzie touched her arm. 'I'm sure you'll hear soon. If his life's anything like our time at West Drayton, he barely has time to think, trust me. Sleeping and eating, it's all you dream about from the minute you get up to the minute you go to bed.'

'We just run about all day and then collapse in our beds,' Diana added. 'If Lizzie hadn't dragged me out tonight, that's where I'd be right now. I'd have been there from six o'clock. My body aches in places I didn't even know I had muscles.'

Bringing the tea in, once it was made, they all settled down in the front room.

'These are your children?' enquired Lizzie, looking at another photograph next to the one of John. 'They're lovely. Where in the country are they?'

'Up in the Cotswolds.'

'You were right to send them there,' mused Diana, sipping her tea. 'If anything happened, it would be so traumatic for children, don't you think? At least over there they have a chance of being safer if bombs start dropping.'

Lizzie sat back in her chair and surveyed the room. 'God, it's nice to be in a house, isn't it, Diana? It's not so terrible or anything at the barracks. But you don't really get the same facilities, you know, of a home. All they've got to offer us is lukewarm showers we have to run through. Most of the time, we have to make do with a strip-down wash, with a flannel and a sink of water. And the water always seems to be freezing cold. I'm sure they treat prisoners of war better.'

All three of them laughed.

'All I dream about is a nice hot bath when I'm standing there in that lukewarm shower.'

'You can have a bath here tonight if you want,' suggested Julia. 'You'll have to keep it to the regimented five inches of water, I'm afraid. I've already marked the tub up to help me remember. But you're welcome to it.'

'Do you mean it?' squealed Lizzie, her eyes widening.

'I do,' nodded Julia.

'I wouldn't want to put you to any trouble.'

'Look, it's no trouble. Least I can do for two women out there fighting for our nation. It's the smallest way I can pay you back for coming from all over the country to help us fight the war here.'

'I'll take it,' said Lizzie, jumping to her feet. 'Lead me to the bathroom, Macduff.'

'I also have a little shampoo up there,' added Julia.

'God, shampoo,' said Lizzie. 'I feel like I'm at the Ritz. I've been having to use the Lifebuoy soap on my hair and look at it. It's a frizzy mess. Diana has promised to cut it for me. But I, for some reason, had some leisurely idea that we'd have actual time to do that.'

'Are you a hairdresser, Diana?'

'I was.'

'Have you got your scissors with you?' enquired Lizzie, with a gleam in her eye.

'I told you,' reminded Diana, 'I don't go anywhere without my scissors.' She tapped her handbag.

'Would you mind if she cut my hair while she was here, Julia?'

'Of course not.'

Lizzie yipped with delight, running up the stairs. The girls could hear her giggle as she made her way into the bathroom.

Thirty minutes later she was back down, her head wrapped in a towel, her face flushed red with the hot water and with a delighted look on her face, she sank into a chair. Julia brought a kitchen chair into the front room so Diana could cut her friend's hair.

'Where were you a hairdresser?'

'I'm from Birmingham.'

'I didn't detect an accent.'

'She's practising her posh one in case she meets the queen,' added Lizzie, unfurling the towel from her hair.

As Diana cut Lizzie's hair, Julia put on the wireless, and the three of them sang along to the Andrew Sisters' new song.

As she watched the two girls in front of her, Julia thought for a minute that this could be the beginning of something, a friendship. A friendship born out of all their necessity, doing what they were doing for this war. But it'd be nice to have friends, somebody who understood what she was going through, and Julia started to have a glimmer of hope that she might make it after all.

Chapter Twelve

At the beginning of July, Diana and Lizzie sat nervously on their bunks, waiting for the test results after finishing their basic training. In the past two weeks, they'd been tested to see what would be the best placement for them both. Over time, their skills had become more prominent. Diana had become physically stronger, excelling in her athletic abilities, which surprised her most of all. She put it down to having to always carry Lizzie when she got exhausted on their long runs. Lizzie had tested very strong in her verbal reasoning.

Now they both sat waiting nervously for their commanding officer to pin up the results of the tests on the board in the hallway. One of the other recruits poked her head into their room.

'Results are in,' she stated cheerily. Diana grabbed Lizzie's hand and squeezed it tightly as they made their way into the hallway. All the other girls were crowded around the noticeboard looking for their assignments.

Finally reaching the board, Diana ran her finger down the list and, with a sinking heart, saw they were not being placed together. Diana, with her strength and height, had been recommended to work on the barrage balloons, and Lizzie was going to be working as something called a filter plotter in Kenley.

'Well, at least we'll still be in London,' stated Lizzie, trying to be positive as they sidled back to their room to continue packing. Today was Friday, and they had the night off; they would leave on Sunday for their new assignments. Julia had promised them they could come over and celebrate the end of their training together at her house and stay the night. It would be the last time all the girls would be together before they left to start their new work, but it was with a heavy heart that the two girls made their way into London that day.

However, their sadness was short-lived as when they got to Julia's house, she was in a jovial mood, and had somehow managed to get all the ingredients to make a cake and was ready to celebrate the end of their training with them. This did lift the girls' spirits, and they sat there drinking a glass of sherry, reliving all the fun memories over the last six weeks together.

They toasted their freedom and tried to be positive about the situation.

'At least being based in central London, you and I will be able to get together all the time' said Diana, optimistically. 'And Lizzie, it's not that far to Kenley.'

'Especially here to Brixton,' added Julia. 'It's only about thirty minutes.'

They both stayed the night and had fun, but they had to head back the next day.

*

On Sunday, Diana was sad to say goodbye to Lizzie. She held her friend tightly and tried not to cry. It was amazing how close they had become training together. Diana couldn't believe it'd only been six weeks since she'd left Birmingham. It felt like an eternity. And now she felt she had a friend for life. Lizzie didn't hold back the tears. She sobbed uncontrollably on Diana's shoulder.

'I know we're both going to be in London, but somehow it just feels like the end of something,' she said as she wiped her hand across her face. 'We have to try and get the same night off so we can see each other.'

'We'll work it out,' said Diana. 'Don't worry, I'm sure there will be times to be together, go to the cinema or see a play or something.'

Lizzie nodded and ran a hand through her bobbed hair. Her new hairstyle suited her so much, thought Diana as she looked at her. It emphasized her beautiful eyes and pixie grin.

They walked outside to the truck waiting to take Diana to her destination. She climbed up on board and waved goodbye to Lizzie as the truck set off for the barrage balloon training school.

Chapter Thirteen

It wasn't long after Diana left that Lizzie was called as well. Going through her things she folded the newspaper clipping into her bag. Since arriving she had had hardly a minute to herself; now, she would have more time to find her daughter. Grabbing her belongings, she made her way outside to go to her new assignment. As she climbed into the back of the truck, the other girls all around her were caught up in a lively conversation about what they were going to be learning. Radar was a new thing, and they were very excited.

'Apparently, they can actually track the enemy on a screen,' stated one of the girls. 'Kind of like a camera, but moving like a film.'

'Will we be able to do that, do you think?' said another girl, her eyes widening. 'I'd love to.'

'I don't know, but it's all very exciting, isn't it? Amazing what they are letting us do.'

Lizzie looked out the back of the truck as they exited the gates of the RAF station that had been her home for the last six weeks, and as they bumped along the road, she thought about that. Because so many of the men were gone, they were getting opportunities to do things women had never been able to before. The war was frightening, there was no doubt about that, but she was getting to have experiences she had never in her wildest dreams believed was possible for her.

Her thoughts drifted back to the time when she had given up her baby for adoption and the conversation in the family parlour. How they had all wanted Fergus to finish his education instead of being a father. No one had even mentioned Lizzie's school work, and as she thought about the conversation it stung. It had been unsaid that day, but when she looked back with hindsight, it seemed so obvious to her now, no one had cared about her educational development. It was clear that school was just something to keep her busy until she was the right age to marry. Now, as she listened to all the girls talking about the responsibilities and important work they would be trusted with, she wondered, if this war continued, what would it be like afterwards? Was it possible that now women were proving they could all do the same jobs as men, that at some obscure date in the future, they could be afforded the same opportunity as a man if they wanted it? It seemed highly unlikely, but it filled her with hope, that one day a woman would be allowed to choose.

When they arrived in Croydon, all the girls clambered around the back of their truck to get their first look at their new barracks. It was much larger than the one they had come from, and there was a general hum of excitement between them as they took in all the new buildings.

As the truck stopped they jumped down, their new superior officer was waiting to meet them and they automatically lined up at attention to meet her. She was a long, stringy woman, with a high-pitched, plummy accent and a serious overbite, and with a broad smile she stepped forward to greet them with a long lurching stride.

She introduced herself as Sergeant Wheaton and gave them brief instructions about barracks procedures then informing them that though they would be living on base here, they actually would be plotting out of the operations room in Kenley.

There was a ripple of hushed excitement around the group. Once they had settled in, they would begin their new training straight away.

Though she already missed Diana, Lizzie was excited to be working as a filter plotter, or, as it was also known, a clerk of special duties. They weren't given long to unpack before they all shipped over to Kenley to take a tour of the operations room.

The offices, located underground for safety, were attached to the airfield at Kenley. And as they crossed the parade ground, a Spitfire tore over their heads and landed on the runway in front of them to line itself up with more Spitfires that were waiting for duty. Beside her, one of the girls swore in surprise. It was exhilarating to watch the pilots in action, and all the girls cheered as another took off and roared over their heads.

'Go get 'em, lads,' shouted one of the girls, pumping her fist in the air.

Making their way down into the operations room, Sergeant Wheaton informed them that for their first week, they would be observing the work they were training to do and also be in the classroom learning how to plot coordinates correctly.

The girls followed Sergeant Wheaton down a long, cold, dark tunnel, their feet echoing on the damp flagstones as they moved below ground, finally arriving at the plotting room. With hushed revelry, they filtered into the vast room that was alive with activity.

Inside were about thirty or forty people already at work, and the air was hot and alive with conversation and motion. It had the hum and lively energetic movement of a casino Lizzie had seen on a film in the church hall once. Everyone was concentrating on their work, many of them talking to one another via phone headsets all the plotters were wearing.

The room was situated on two levels. On the ground level where they stood, illuminated by long pendant lighting, was a huge map of southern England and the French coast. Gathered around it were the people known as the plotters – men and women, but mainly women, who stood next to the map with a long billiard-cue-sized plotter. Lizzie watched in awe as the woman in front of her received information through her headphones and then pushed aircraft into position on the map with her plotter. This was the job Lizzie herself would be doing in a matter of days.

On the second level, around the room, were officers who helped coordinate the effort. Their job, they were informed by Sergeant Wheaton, was to collect all the information coming in from around the different areas and signal to the plotters what needed to be moved. Sergeant Wheaton continued telling them in a whisper that out along the coastline were the coastal spotters. They were all located in bunkered areas watching for planes through their binoculars, their job to inform this station what kind of planes were on their way, in what numbers, and heading in which direction.

The officer on the second level would confirm this with any radar information that was coming in at the same time. This allowed the commanders to instruct the girls on the floor of what planes needed to be moved where.

All the trainees were allowed to wear headsets to listen in on what the plotters were listening to. The information coming in described the heights, number, and placement of the aircraft on their way in. As the data filtered through, a plotter pushed onto the map a plane marked 'H', which stood for 'hostile', and the direction the plane was flying in from. Lizzie overheard the call come through to the girl she was listening in with, and heard 'six-niner, five-niner.' In response, the plotter slid the planes into a specific position on the map. Another girl responded to the call by adding a plane marked with an 'F' for 'friendly', which gave them all an overview of the British response and which squadron had been scrambled and was going up to meet them.

Lizzie was fascinated. She watched the movement around the map. The phones rang constantly on the upper level. Information was coming back and forward between all of the people in the room. It was intense, but also amazing to watch the war literally unfurling before her eyes. The senior controllers above seemed to work just as intensely as the girls plotting on the floor. And

Lizzie found herself apprehensive as she watched the enemy forces moving into position over England. She bit her lip, hoping that the friendlies, their own boys, would interact with them in time.

Sergeant Wheaton informed the new recruits how important it was to be accurate with the planes and not just put them willy-nilly on the map, because just a little way out could have the aircraft off by miles and have the British squadrons relocated to the wrong area. And minutes could make the difference in loss of life on the ground.

They spent the rest of the morning working to understand the task ahead. When they broke for lunch, their instructor took them to the canteen to eat. The girls all discussed in hushed tones what they'd seen.

'It looked so intense,' said one girl.

'On your feet for the whole time during a raid,' said another.

'At least we're inside,' responded Lizzie, 'and that's warm.'

As they sat eating their lunch, a group of pilots walked into the hall. All the girls turned to watch them.

In basic training, there had been male recruits on the training base, but they hadn't had much interaction with them. The pilots looked so handsome in their uniforms. They laughed and joked with one another and one of them smiled over at the girls.

'Well, at least we've got something nice to look at while we're here,' laughed one of the other girls with a strong Lancashire accent, and they all giggled as they finished their lunch.

In the afternoon, and for the next week, they were observing in the operations room, understanding how the radar worked, how to plot correctly and how to give the right instructions.

After a week in the classroom and observing, they were to start their first shift.

Nervously, Lizzie made her way into the room that morning and took up a place where she'd been instructed. For the first day, she worked alongside another plotter, but still, she felt the intense pressure of what she was doing.

Above her, the phone jangled. Her senior commander, who had introduced himself as Stan, called down into her headset from his direct dial telephone, communicating a coordinate. Nervously, Lizzie pushed the plane she had at the end of her stick with the letter 'H' on it towards the area where he'd commanded her to go. Then came another instruction, and she continued to work steadily, though it was really nerve-wracking.

All around her, people were deep within their work. But as she worked, the girl next to her, who was shadowing her, nodded and smiled.

Fortunately for Lizzie, it wasn't a hectic flying day, but still, the intensity had made her realize how important this job was. And in some ways, it was exciting to feel like she was practically on the front line of the war. Lizzie could see everything that was coming over from the French coast and every time the planes veered towards Brixton, where Julia lived, she would wish she could just call her up and tell her to be careful, they were on their way. But of course, that wasn't possible. Everything they were doing was secret. Besides, there were no public telephones in the room. But she wondered what she would do if something she saw or heard was going to affect someone she really cared about. She couldn't even think about how hard that could be and hoped she would never be in that position.

At the end of the shift she was glad to relax and be off duty, and not feeling hungry, she was eager to see if there had been any letters for her. Unable to get time off yet, she had written twice to the orphanage she thought her daughter might have been taken to but hadn't heard anything yet. When she got back on base she rushed to see if anything was waiting for her. There was only one letter from her aunt and uncle. Lizzie was disappointed as she made her way back to her room to read it. Flopping down on her bed she placed an arm behind her head to read her aunt's words.

Dearest Lizzie,

I hope you are well and not working too hard. We all miss you and talk about you often, especially your Uncle Hamish, who is having to make do with Margaret helping him on the farm and I'm sure you know how that is working out. Fiona is working on a blanket she is knitting for your room as we thought you might be missing some comforts from home, it should be finished tomorrow and I will get it straight in the post. Also, last week Mr McCrae managed to get some chocolate in his little store and I wrangled an extra bar out of Margaret to send to you, I will try and get it in the post tomorrow. All is about the same here, except I wanted to let you know Karen MacAndrews had her baby, a bonnie baby girl they are going to call Ella after her grandmother. She is the loveliest little thing and has brought a lot of joy to us all in the village and helped us stop missing you so much. Looking forward to hearing from you soon about all your adventures in the south.

Much Love, Auntie Marion, Uncle Hamish, Margaret and Fiona

Lizzie reread the words 'a bonnie baby girl' and tried to push down the emotion that fluttered in her chest, as it seemed to reach out grasping fingers that tightened around her throat. She had gone to school for a short time with Karen who had just been married a year ago and she tried not to feel the jealousy that was welling up inside her. Why was Karen allowed to keep her girl and Lizzie was not? She was wrestling with her conflicting emotions when a head appeared around the door of her room.

'Lizzie, did you forget you were on the washing up in the canteen?'

Dragged back to the present, Lizzie forced a smile onto her face. 'Just coming,' she said in a strained cheerful manner, pushing herself off her bed and slipping her feet into her shoes.

Checking her hair in the mirror she noticed the deep sadness etched on her face and swallowed down the pain. As she ran a comb through her hair, she realized things had become so much clearer to her since she had been away from her home. In fact, in the last few weeks she had decided if she found Annie and she was not happy, then she, Lizzie, would find a way to get her back. She wasn't sure how yet, and she still had to find her daughter, but she knew if Annie had suffered as much as Lizzie had from being apart from her, she would find a way to put this all right, no matter what the fallout would be in Scotland.

Chapter Fourteen

On 15 August Diana completed her twelve weeks of barrage balloon training, including the weeks she had spent with Lizzie, and if she'd thought her basic training was physical, it was nothing compared to working with the balloon.

An incredible sight to behold, the barrage balloons were huge, each as big as a grey whale; a silver, bullet-shaped inflatable with a tail, they were launched during an air attack and it took twelve people to operate one.

For the first week they worked solely in the classroom, as they were informed it was really important to understand not just the physical job of keeping the balloon in the air, but they also had to understand the physics of how the balloon floated and how to maintain it while it was flying. That week she learned balloon drill, balloon maintenance, winch driving, winch maintenance, wire splicing, balloon technical, and balloon theory to learn the science of how it flew.

The wire splicing was very hard on all of their hands. Most of them had blisters and cuts from learning how to plait the wire, but as they were told by their commanding officers, their hands would have to harden up and it would be even more difficult if they had to repair a wire while it was flying once they were out in the field under attack.

In the second week, the girls got their first look at the balloon they nicknamed Big Bertha, which would be theirs to fly. They were a merry bunch that day as they travelled out to the field to meet their balloon for the first time, singing, 'She'll Be Coming Round the Mountain' as they went.

It was a beautiful crisp morning, it had rained the night before so the grass was fresh with dew but now they had what was promising to be a lovely warm day. As the truck came to a stop, all the girls crowded around the back to get their first look at Bertha flying in her hangar. As the sun streamed into the enormous building the silver balloon that was chained to the ground inside flashed and glinted as she bobbed and weaved through the shafts of sunlight, stirred by a light breeze.

'Bloody hell, it's huge,' stated a Liverpudlian, who Diana knew was called Kathy.

Jumping down, they marched into the building, their heavy work boots echoing on the concrete floor of the hangar. Diana had long since put away her tight skirt and high heels for the times when she had leave. Now they were all dressed in their new uniforms, especially for this war work. This included heavy blue knitted sweaters, boots and trousers, which Diana loved. These were the first pair of trousers she had ever owned, and though she had seen other women in trousers in Birmingham and Katharine Hepburn was famous for wearing them, she had never bought a pair. But she felt so free whenever she put them on.

The first thing they would be learning that day was how to get the balloon up and down. Diana stared up in awe at the sheer size of it and hoped they would be able to handle it as their commanding officer, Sergeant Sam Daly, briefed them on their duties. He was a short, square, older man with a thinning hairline and a wicked sense of humour. A Cockney born and bred, he was a lot of fun and kept the girls laughing when sometimes all they wanted to do was cry with the physical work they were all doing.

'Right, ladies,' stated Sergeant Daly in his cheerful, sing-song way, 'you have to treat this gal like she's your best china – which is Cockney for mate, china plate, see, for all you poor foreigners sad enough not to be born in London. Not like you would treat your mother-in-law. You have to like her.'

In response, there was a ripple of laughter down the lines.

'And like all good relationships, it takes a lot of factors to make it work properly. First, we have to get her outside. Mavis.' He pointed to a girl with red hair and lively eyes. 'You can drive the truck out and be in charge of winch driving.'

Which meant they would attach the balloon to the truck, then Mavis would move it out into the field. Once they were free of the hangar and in the right spot, Mavis would slowly turn the winch to wind the cables out. Then grabbing the wires attached to the side of the balloon they would all work in four groups of three to steady it.

'Get her out to the site then, Mavis,' stated Sergeant Daly, 'and Kathy, as you seem to be the most talkative, you can be on balloon drill, calling out all the instructions through this megaphone to the crew.' He handed the megaphone to Kathy as another ripple of laughter went around the group.

They marched out behind Mavis and the balloon, which bounced and weaved on freeing itself from the hangar like it was a prize inflatable at the fair. Once in position, they worked in their teams, two on port, the others on starboard, learning how to fly her and bed her down. This was done by releasing the forty-pound sand weights and ballast blocks that anchored the balloon. By releasing the ballast they could then fly her with the use of the cables and guidelines that were secured to rings situated at the base of the balloon. The idea was to get Bertha about five thousand feet up into the air to stop enemy planes dive-bombing. Sometimes planes could even get caught up in the wires, and they would bring the bombers down.

Once in position, Diana stood shivering with the others on her small team, Maisie and Jean, for even though it was warm a sharp wind had picked up, tousling their hair and causing them to button up their coats and pull up their collars. Diana trembled with a sense of excitement and a little apprehension. It was one thing to learn about it; another to deal with the sheer size of the balloon and to control it in the wind. The three of them took hold of the wires attached to the port side as Kathy started to call out instructions. Methodically, Mavis began to crank the winch that unwound the balloon. As she grasped hold, Diana noted again how the wires were brittle and sharp, and with no gloves and the weight of the balloon being buffered in the wind it took all of her strength not to have the cables slip across her palms and cut her hands. As the tallest, Diana stood in front and the two other girls took hold of the wires behind her to anchor her. As they eased away the ballast weighing it down, the balloon started to climb and tugged hard on the wires, wanting to take off, forcing them to dig their heels into the wet grass to keep their balance. As they fought to control it, the wind whistled past their ears and it took all of their concentration to hear Kathy's instructions through the megaphone.

'Hard to port,' she screamed, her Liverpudlian accent more pronounced than ever as a strong gust practically pulled all six of them on that side off their feet and dragged the balloon into the other direction. Diana tugged on the line with all her might, hearing Jean swear behind her and feeling Maisie's breath coming in hard sharp spurts into the back of her neck. They then pulled back so hard the balloon careered in the opposite direction, and the girls on the other side mirrored their performance with many shrieks and gasps of frustration.

It took them the best part of the morning, by which point coats and jumpers were thrown off in untidy piles. But finally, they started to get the hang of it, finding they were able to anticipate the movement of the balloon and compensate before it got out of hand.

Every time Bertha reached her desired height in the air, they would all cheer, but the minute a strong wind shifted around her fins, it took all twelve of them to keep her in position.

'Steady as she goes,' Sergeant Daly would shout as Diana's team of three continued to be lifted off their feet whenever they struggled with a particularly violent gust.

'You'd think they would have given us more to eat, make us a bit heavier,' joked Jean from behind her after being knocked to the floor for the third time.

'I'm definitely putting lead in my knickers tomorrow,' Maisie joked back, as they all laughed and she helped Jean to her feet.

They continued to raise and lower the balloon every day until they could anticipate every movement of the balloon and also of each other.

Daly didn't let up on them, though, having them out in all weathers any time of the day and night. He particularly liked it when it was raining or windy, knowing that would challenge the team and give them a taste of what it could be like to be under attack. He would flick on the lights in their barracks at three in the morning, shouting, 'Wakey, wakey, it's lovely and muddy out there, pouring down and blowing a gale. Perfect night to go on a picnic.' This was his way of telling them Bertha would be flying. It could get quite harrowing in the dark and rain.

One night, Daly called them out to duty in the middle of what was a particularly stormy evening with driving rain. Soaked to the skin before they even reached the balloon, their boots slipped and slid around in the mud as they attempted to get their footing. As Diana raised her head to look up at the balloon the rain poured down her face and neck, and into her ears and eyes, blinding her. The wind whipped around them, building into gusts which caused the sandbags and ballast blocks to fly around their heads. It was harrowing and Diana had to keep ducking and calling out to stop other members of her team from being hit, and it took all their energy, effort and concentration, to fly the balloon and also to keep themselves safe. As Diana trudged back inside filthy, aching and exhausted three hours later, she knew they were ready. If they could survive a night like that, they could survive anything.

They finally finished their training and at the end of it, Diana took her examinations, which she passed with flying colours. They'd now be sent out to a barrage balloon site somewhere in London, where they would be stationed for the rest of the war to fly during air raids.

That morning, after she passed her exams, she marched out onto the field with the rest of the team securing the balloon on its truck to drive it out to its new home. The group she worked with had become close, even though there was no one quite as fun and friendly as Lizzie. She loved working with her crew as they took turns to do different jobs.

The truck finally stopped just near Westminster. They were to fly their balloon on a playing field in that area. There was a light breeze, but nothing of too much concern. It was a beautiful day, positively balmy. Apart from a few rainy days over the last week, they'd been enjoying full sun.

Moving into action they drew a crowd of onlookers as Diana and her team hoisted the enormous silver balloon into the air for the first time over the city. It went up smoothly, glinting in the sun as it bobbed and weaved on its cables, and they all felt a great sense of pride. She thought about her friends and wished they could see her at work. At least now the intense training was done she would have more leave and be able to spend time with Julia and especially Lizzie. They had managed to write to one another over the past few weeks but were both eager to see one another again. As Diana pulled on her cables she hoped it would be soon. Little did she know that within the very next hour, Lizzie's life would be under threat from an attack in the Kenley area, when the first bombs that were the precursor to the Blitz dropped on London, killing dozens of civilians for the first time during the war.

Chapter Fifteen

15 August 1940 – The First Bomb

That same day started out as quite unremarkable for Lizzie, but it escalated into something much more significant as the afternoon wore on. A squadron of German bombers had been tracked by the Observer Corps heading towards the London area, accompanied by Luftwaffe fighters. From Biggin Hill, Hurricanes and Spitfires had been scrambled, but the German fighters had kept the British pilots busy, and the bombers were able to break through the defence and proceed on their route unguarded.

Stan, Lizzie's counterpart, signalled down to her. 'Observer Corps reports twenty-two bombers still heading towards Kenley at three thousand feet. No sign of fighter cover. Squadron 111 has been scrambled.'

Lizzie received the information and advanced the twenty-two German planes into the place on the map with a twinge of concern. Continuing to edge them forward, bringing them closer to the operations room she was in. Kenley, with its abundance of military equipment, was no doubt the bombers' target. It had been targeted before, but she had never been on duty during a raid. Beads of perspiration formed under her fringe and between her fingers as she slid the plotter along the map. All around the room, even though everyone was working, all eyes were watching the twenty-two planes filled with 500 lb bombs that were heading straight towards them. It was always nerve-wracking when she handled planes in the London area. She would push the hostiles closer and closer to the city, and the girl beside her would push the friendlies in to intercept. So far, they had been lucky. Would the fighters make it there this time before the enemy dropped their bombs on them all? As the dogfight continued in the sky above her head, their own planes, Squadron 111, continued to intercept.

She listened intently to the action and willed their fighters into battle. In her mind's eye she could see them, Spitfires and Hurricanes all swirling around their enemy in the sky, swooping in over and over to fire on the German bombers. As everyone in the room waited with bated breath, the clock continued to mark the enemy's ominous advance. All at once there was a call from one of the commanders for them to prepare for an attack and with her heart beating out of her chest she hastily donned her tin hat and sent up a silent prayer.

As she pushed the friendlies closer, Lizzie heard the woman next to her whisper under her breath, 'Come on, lads, see them off.'

All eyes were centred on the map, on those twenty-two planes, and all ears were attuned to the ceiling. She, like everyone else, had been taught in basic training that the bombs made a whistling sound as they got closer to the ground. Lizzie closed her eyes and counted the seconds being ticked off by the room's lumbering clock, trying to focus more intently on any sound above her head. What would it be like to have a bomb drop on top of her? Could the operations room protect them? Or would she be one of the early casualties of the war on British soil?

Her thoughts were interrupted by Stan giving her new coordinates and with a sense of relief she noticed it appeared the bombers had missed Kenley altogether and were flying north. She was surprised – maybe they were heading for Croydon. There were some RAF fighters there on the airfield and it was where her barracks were. But surely with all the tracking equipment here, Kenley was a much more logical target. Over her headphones she listened to the British pilots as they communicated among themselves, trying to make sense of it all.

'Red two, I'm engaging bombers going in.'

'Roger Red Two, coming in behind.'

'Got the lead bomber in my sights – firing.'

'Going around.'

'Coming in from your right – firing. I think I hit the gunner.'

'Damn, what the hell are they doing? The Jerries appear to be panicking, they are dropping their bombs everywhere. The lead pilot is heading for the ground. Staying on him.'

'Direct hit! Direct hit! I got him, his wing's on fire.'

'He's descending to try and put it out. Staying with him. It will be hard to get out of that dive.'

'It looks as if he only just made that but he is hedge-hopping. I'm staying with him, firing again.'

'Direct hit, direct hit! He's losing altitude, heading for the woods, no sign of a chute.'

'He's down! He's down! Crashed in the woods, plane's on fire. I don't think he will be walking away from that.'

Another voice came over their headsets. 'Well done, Red Two. We need you back up here to finish the rest.'

In the plotting room they all breathed a sigh of relief as the lead plane had been destroyed and the squadron continued to pick off as many of the rest of the bombers as they could.

At the end of her shift, she went to have a tea break before she went back to barracks. It was while she was in the canteen that some of their fighter pilots appeared and sat at the table next to her. They were talking in a very animated way, and she could overhear the conversation.

She gathered from what they were saying that even though Kenley had been spared, the Germans had dropped their bombs on RAF Croydon instead, which was four miles north. The Croydon airfield, which had been London's public aerodrome before the RAF had taken it over on the first day of the war, had mainly factories and residential homes all around it. Lizzie felt the air catch in her throat. From what the fighters went on to describe, it appeared there had been a significant loss of life and explosions that had taken place beyond the boundaries of the airfield itself. If this was correct, it would be the first time the Germans had dropped bombs on a civilian area.

Finishing up her tea, Lizzie knew she needed to get over to her barracks to see if everyone was all right. Managing to get a lift from another officer, they started their way across the few miles to the airfield. When they got there, the overwhelming devastation was evident. Lizzie never realized how intense the bombs could be; twisted metal and piles of crumbled stone were everywhere. The acrid smell of smoke and burned wood swirled around them as did the ash that rained down on the truck as if it was snowing. It was hard as they drove for Lizzie to distinguish any landmarks, because the ruined buildings were all just heaped into broken, smouldering masses.

As they inched forwards, making their way as best they could, it was obvious the bombs had hit some of the neighbouring houses as well as the several factories that had surrounded the airfield. It was at the end of the afternoon shift, but the factories would still have been packed with workers. Firefighters were out in force as ambulances tore past them, their bells urgent. Nothing could have prepared Lizzie for this. It was as if the girl next to her read her thoughts.

'God, this is awful. I understand why the Germans would want to take out our airfields. But everyday people? What's the point of that?' she said as they observed a young boy being stretchered from a house that had taken some bomb damage.

Because of the piles of rubble in the road and the many diversions due to dangerous bomb sites, it took them a while to get back to the airfield itself. But as they got closer, Lizzie caught her breath because even from a distance she could see the smoke and fires from the Croydon barracks. At the main gate, the guard informed them that many buildings had taken a direct hit and to be very careful as they made their way inside. The girl driving dropped her at the gate, and as she hurried towards her room, Lizzie passed the mess hall where they ate on the way, which had been levelled to the ground. As she turned the corner to where her barracks had been, she stopped in her tracks because instead of her room she was greeted by a pile of ash and blackened wood, smoke and a fire still blazing, firemen already around it, dousing water onto the flames. It took a minute for it to sink in what had happened.

Even though she'd been trained to expect the worst and to work under pressure, she was grief-stricken; this was the first thing that had affected her personally. As she watched the barracks burning to the ground, she thought about everything inside, all her clothes, her personal things, the blanket she had received that morning from Fiona, her photographs from Scotland. Then, she remembered with a sinking heart, she'd had letters from her aunt and her uncle the day before, and too tired last night to read them, she'd saved them to read later on after dinner tonight. Now she would never know the words in those letters. She also wondered about any other post that may have arrived today, the much-anticipated letter she had been waiting for for so long from the orphanage. What a cruel twist of fate if today had been the day it had arrived.

One of her barrack mates appeared and put her arm around her.

'Horrible, isn't it?' she said. 'Damn Germans. Wheaton wants us all to go over to the primary office for a briefing.'

As many of them huddled together in the office, word having spread fast about the devastation, they were told that while they were being rehoused, they would have to find somewhere else to stay. With nowhere here for them to eat, the air force would try and put as many up in other barracks like Kenley as they could, but if anybody had friends or family in the London area, this would be a good time to go and find a couch to sleep on. Lizzie naturally thought of Julia and wondered if she'd be willing to put her up.

Getting the bus to Julia's, she sat looking numbly out of the window trying to come to terms with it all. Yes, it was only things, not people or friends, but the sudden loss felt acute, as if she had been robbed, and suddenly Lizzie felt very lonely and a long way from home. Would she be able to do this? How would she feel if it was someone she cared about?

Julia was surprised to see her on the doorstep.

'I thought you were on duty for the next three days.'

Lizzie followed her into the kitchen. 'I was, but my barracks got hit today, and everything's gone.' Only then did her lips start to tremble as the shock of what she'd seen sank in.

Julia came and put her arms around her. 'Lizzie, I'm so sorry.'

'At least everybody was okay,' said Lizzie through her sobs. 'We were all accounted for, and most of us were out working when it happened. The few that were off duty were in other places, but still, it's horrible to see.'

'Of course,' said Julia.

'They've asked if I could find somewhere to stay, so I was wondering...'

'I insist you stay here,' responded Julia. 'Don't think any more about it.'

'Hopefully, we'll get rehoused soon, but if you don't mind, that'd be wonderful.'

'Stay as long as you want. It will be lovely to have the company.'

While Lizzie drank a cup of strong hot tea, Julia decided she would put her in Maggie's room and went up to put fresh sheets on the bed.

'Are you sure it's not too much trouble?' asked Lizzie as Julia came back down.

'Of course it's not. In fact, it's exactly where you should be. We all need to stick together right now. Friends are so important to all of us. You and Diana have already been such great friends to me. I was hoping you could think of my home as a place you can stay anytime you want to. It's just me here alone, after all. Besides,' she said optimistically, 'I do have that bathtub.'

Lizzie couldn't help but smile. 'As my aunt says, there is always a silver lining, and I must admit, having some time with a bathtub doesn't sound so terrible.'

After dinner Lizzie made her way up to Maggie's room. It felt so odd going to bed in one of Julia's nighties, without a thing to her name. Not her clothes or belongings, not Fiona's blanket, not even her granny's carpet bag or any of her letters. But out of all her lost possessions what affected her the most was the newspaper clipping. The photos of the woman she had been hoping to show people to identify the nurse that had taken Annie. And not only had that clipping helped her believe she could find her daughter, it was also a tiny touchstone to remind Lizzie that it had really happened to her. Without the visual reminder and clue, she felt desolate; instead of getting closer to finding Annie, it felt as if everything was slipping away from her.

Chapter Sixteen

25 August 1940

As soon as Julia arrived at work that Sunday morning, she perceived something was different. Not only was the building in Whitehall busier than usual for a weekend, but there were also many people in the bunker. There was a buzz, an intense energy about the place. As she moved through the warren of rooms military personnel were heading into the offices and huddled at the cafeteria. Two men stood in deep conversation, one shaking his head, as they both drank a cup of tea. And in the war room's office, places were being set. It had been ten days since the first attack on Croydon, and then last night, for the first time, German bombers had dropped bombs in the heart of London.

Making her way to the typing pool, she pulled off her hat and coat and hung them on a hanger. Carol was already seated at a desk. 'What's going on?' she whispered to her friend.

Carol looked up from her typewriter and ran her hand through her blonde curls. 'They have called an emergency meeting this morning; the war cabinet are on the way down.'

Julia sat down hesitantly, pulling the cover off her own typewriter and started her work from the day before, but the constant activity all around her distracted her.

All at once, her boss strode into the room. 'We will need someone to take notes. Where's Linda?'

Carol shook her head. 'I don't think she's in today. She was feeling sick yesterday.'

Julia knew because of her shorthand skills Linda normally wrote the minutes for the meetings.

Mrs Scriber shook her head. 'Julia, how's your shorthand?'

Julia hesitated. 'Erm, all right, I think,' she said, trying to be honest.

'I've got too much for Carol to do down here. And where are the other two girls?'

'I don't know,' responded Carol. 'I'm sure they'll be in, in a while.'

'Julia, you'll have to do. Come with me.'

Grabbing hold of her pad and pencil, Julia followed Mrs Scriber to the War Room, a place she'd so far only seen when the door was open. A room she'd been told never to go into unless she had been instructed to do so. This was the place where decisions were made, life and death decisions. This was the hub of Churchill's activity, where the overview map was. Where discussions were had that changed the course of history.

Before she went inside, Mrs Scriber turned to her. 'I don't have to remind you, do I, Julia, that everything that happens in here is top secret. You can't share anything of what is said inside with anyone else. Do you understand? Not a brother, or a sister, or a friend, or a husband, or any family member, or even other girls in the typing pool. Is that clear?'

Julia nodded, feeling the weight of her words.

'It is imperative that everything discussed in this room is kept in the bunker. Lives depend on it. People could die if this information gets out.'

Mrs Scriber opened the door and nervously Julia followed her supervisor inside. The catering crew were already in, laying out glasses of water at people's places and making sure pens and paper were at the ready for the war cabinet to take notes. The desks were set up in their usual large square formation so everyone faced one another. This, Churchill said, was to give everyone an equal voice.

There was no head and tail here. Just a group of individuals trying to reach the best decisions they could for the nation.

Mrs Scriber clipped to the back of the room where another small desk was situated.

'You take notes from here,' she stated, pulling out the chair. 'It can get quite heated in here sometimes, so keep your emotions in check. Don't get involved, be detached, but you need to make sure all the information is written down. I cannot emphasize how important this work is. What you write today could be read out in Parliament one day, and will become the official notes about the meeting for history.'

Julia nodded her head as all at once her throat became parched and a light sweat prickled across her forehead. She could do this, she told herself, she could do this. She sat down and noticed that her hand was shaking as she lifted it up to her pad. Sensing her discomfort, one of the catering girls smiled sympathetically and handed her a glass of water which Julia thanked her for, gulping it down.

At ten o'clock, members of the war committee started to arrive, and it was undeniable that weighty situations were being considered. As they came in, in small groups, she didn't have to hear what they were saying to know by the furrowed brows and low whispers that there was a concern. Their worry was palpable.

Julia had observed members of the war committee many times on their way in and out of the bunker, but there was a difference about them today. All thoughtful, contemplative, they moved into their positions and sat waiting for Churchill's arrival. At about 10.15, the prime minister arrived and, bidding hello to everyone, made his way to the end of the table. Removing his hat and his jacket, he took his place, resting his cigar in the ashtray that was provided by his position. Julia tried not to stare, but it was surreal to be this close to the man who was guiding their country through such a dark time. A man she had barely seen here and only heard on the radio or seen in flickering pictures at the cinema.

It didn't take long for them to get to the heart of the situation. Julia's pencil moved at lightning speed across her pad as the meeting started. Each of the heads of the War Council – army, navy and air force – were giving an account of the attack that had happened in Croydon days before, and now another one that had just occurred on civilian London. The navy finished off with the devastation to the docks, but reported that even though they had taken a hard hit, they were still managing to be up and operational.

Whenever Julia had taken shorthand notes in the past, she'd always felt pretty detached from what she was hearing, able to just concentrate on writing things down properly, but as she listened to the numbers of people wounded, the devastation of the buildings and the cost to their life in London, she couldn't help feeling an emotional pull about the situation. These numbers were tough to hear and note down.

The meeting progressed into the stage of trying to figure out what to do, and it became pretty apparent that Churchill had his heart set on retaliation. As the members of the war cabinet discussed this, things became heated, as both sides of the camp – one thinking this was too severe and the other thinking they had no choice – tried to argue their point to the prime minister, everyone trying to weigh the pros and cons of life and death.

Churchill was adamant that Hitler needed to be put in his place. They needed to hit back at him quickly and hard, and he wanted to attack Berlin, sending the message that England was not going to take this lying down.

If Hitler was prepared to attack innocent civilians, then so was Churchill. The opposition in the room let their concerns be known that an attack on Berlin could change everything, and only encourage Hitler to hit back harder. And was it worth shaking the hornet's nest like this? Another member of the war cabinet argued once again that maybe they should have negotiated peace with the Germans, but Mr Churchill was clear: surrender was not an option.

The meeting went on for a long time, with both sides' arguments being weighed heavily. In the end, Churchill could not be swayed from his conviction. British bombers would attack Germany. They would send fifty planes to Berlin, and they would strike targets in the capital that night. Even though some members continued to protest, the decision was made, the majority agreeing with Churchill that something serious had to be done, and the orders were put in place for the raid that night.

As Julia walked back to her desk, she felt a similar feeling as she'd felt the day war had been declared, as though something big had just happened and she'd been a part of it at the inception. Things were about to change. It wasn't that she had feared the progression of the war. They'd been preparing for Hitler's attack for months. But she couldn't help thinking that in retaliating in this way with the Germans, London, her London, and home, would become the trained mark for Hitler's anger. Even so, she actually sided with Churchill. They didn't really have a choice any more. The Germans were going to come no matter what, whether it would be by air or by sea. The only way to defeat a bully was to attack.

She realized as she started to type up her notes that peace was a fantasy, that the war would have to escalate. Carol must have noticed her ashen face as she sat at her typewriter. 'Is everything okay?' she asked in a whisper. 'What's it all about?'

Julia shook her head. 'You know I can't give you details, Carol. But I can tell you this,' she said, 'that I think things are about to change in this war.' She read over the notes, her thoughts across the sea. Things were going to change tonight. Civilians were going to die. And she was a part of it.

The next night she sat down in her armchair and put on her radio to hear the news report about the attack that she had recorded for history, and felt the weight of that bearing down on her.

Chapter Seventeen

7 September 1940

Everything changed on 7 September 1940, the day that history would record as the first day of the Blitz. It was a Saturday, and Diana had been in London doing some clothes shopping and had the afternoon off. It was a gorgeous day. Everybody was out in the city; on her way in on the bus she had been struck by how normal everything had seemed. Friends eating in restaurants or sitting picnicking out on blankets in the park, young children playing, old men reading newspapers or passing the time of day on warm wooden benches, everyone just taking the time to enjoy the weather.

Coming out of a department store with a bag containing a new hat clutched under her arm, Diana noticed that everybody was frozen, staring up at the sky, shielding their eyes from the sun. She looked up to follow their gaze and what she saw made her heart want to skip a beat. Hundreds, too many to count, of German bombers were making their way up the Thames. She'd never seen planes over London like this before, and never in broad daylight. The sound was ominous, like a million insects, their engines buzzing, the sound reverberating around the streets with a deep humming resonance.

Diana clutched her bag to her chest and swallowed down hard. Surely so many bombers weren't just coming to hit their airfields. Surely, they were going to hit targets here in the heart of London. She thought about what the newspapers had said after the Berlin bombs had been dropped and how some people in the government were concerned about retaliation. As she shaded her eyes, peering up at the sky, it felt unreal, unbelievable, something from a film, and deep in the pit of her stomach she had the sinking realization that this was very significant. This felt like the beginning of something and she knew it wasn't going to be good. Why would Hitler send over so many planes if he didn't want to make a statement? And Diana feared London would pay for his wrath. With so many planes she would probably have to get straight to her site. But first, she glanced at her watch – she was supposed to be meeting Lizzie for a cup of tea in town as they had planned to spend the day and evening together. Making her way to the tea shop where they had decided to meet, she sat there nervously staring at her cup of tea, turning it fretfully in the saucer, waiting for Lizzie to appear.

When she did, Lizzie was as shocked and surprised as she was. They discussed what they'd both seen.

'What do you think it means?' asked her friend, the worry etched across her face.

Diana sipped her tea slowly as she tried to think of what the impact might be. 'I believe it is Hitler retaliating for the Berlin bombing. Lizzie, I think we need to prepare ourselves for a rough ride. Sorry to cut short our time together today but I think I'm going to go to my barracks just in case they need me tonight.'

Lizzie reached forward and grabbed Diana's hand. 'Please take care of yourself, Diana, you're right in the middle of it out there. It feels awfully serious all of sudden, doesn't it?'

'Well, this is what we signed up for, but I know what you mean, there is a big difference between feeling good about doing your patriotic duty, and seeing the sight of those bombers coming here to wreak destruction.'

Lizzie was finished for the day. And, as Diana had a rare night off, they'd planned to go out to the theatre.

'I'm not sure what to do now, I've got those tickets to *Cottage to Let*,' said Lizzie, staring into her teacup, wistfully.

'You have to go, Lizzie, promise me you'll go, don't let the Nazis stop you living your life. You've wanted to go to the theatre for ages.'

'I know,' said Lizzie, 'but it won't be the same without you. I suppose I'll have to go on my own,' she sighed. 'Oh well. At least it's something different to do. I hope it doesn't mean anything, all of this.' She nodded towards the window. 'But I have a feeling that you're right.'

All at once the air-raid sirens went off, and the girls hugged one another tightly before they parted, the kind of hug that said, *This is significant, but we're in this together.*

'Have fun tonight, and I'll see you later at Julia's.'

'And don't be too heroic, Diana,' Lizzie responded. 'Keep your tin hat on and your head down,' she said as they parted company.

As she headed off back to her barracks, Diana felt the tension mounting inside her. This was what she'd been trained for, and though she had a great deal of trepidation, she also felt a little excitement. She'd have a chance to see her work in action fighting the Germans. Her job was to do something for her country, to protect the boys in the air who were fighting the Battle of Britain and that's what she was going to do.

When Diana arrived at her barracks, there was a lot of activity. 'They want us out at the site,' shouted Maisie when she saw Diana approaching. 'As many of us as are here. They're anticipating a large attack on London tonight.'

Diana nodded, put on her uniform and her boots, got her jacket on and, armed with her metal helmet and gas mask, made her way with her unit out to the site to start flying her barrage balloon as the air-raid sirens continued to scream.

Chapter Eighteen

The first wave of the bombing to target civilians after Churchill attacked Berlin hit London at 4.30 that afternoon, and though it had hit some of London hard, Lizzie was unaware of the damage at the docks. It was only as she got on the second bus on her way to Julia's house that she heard stories from the passengers of what had happened. It appeared that just as everyone had feared, the Germans had stopped bombing air bases and prime targets, and now appeared to be aiming at all areas in the city.

When she got back to the house, Julia wasn't yet home from work, and as Diana had gone straight to her barrage balloon site, Lizzie made herself a cup of tea and stared out of the kitchen window. She noticed, along with a lovely sunset, that smoke was still billowing from the direction of the East End. Hopefully, that was the last attack for the night. Her ticket had been expensive, and she'd been looking forward to it all week, even if Diana couldn't come with her as they had planned.

Changing out of her WAAF uniform, she put on a skirt and a blouse that Julia had lent her since she had lost all hers in the August bombing. Julia's style was classier than her own, but she liked how the clothes looked on her. Running a comb through her new haircut, she put on a pair of Julia's high-heeled shoes, some lipstick, and made her way to the bus.

On arriving in the West End, everyone around her was abuzz with the talk of the attacks. But while many bombs had fallen on the East End, the West End seemed virtually untouched.

Making her way inside the foyer of the auditorium, Lizzie's breath caught as she took in the decor. It was the first time she'd ever been inside a real theatre, as where she'd lived in Scotland there hadn't been one for miles, and the Victorian architecture was dramatic. Looped arches in cream masonry formed domes that reached to the ceiling, where a large crystal chandelier was mounted, encircled with decorative olive leaves. Lizzie stared up at the brilliance where tiny glass droppers glistened with sparkling white light. Beneath her feet, a luxurious, plum-coloured carpet was stretched out along the floor of the lavish hallway that continued up an elegant staircase with gold-gilded railings. Illuminated in a recess on the first landing was a portrait of the king. Lizzie looked about her, and quickly realized she was very underdressed and tightened her raincoat with her belt. People obviously got dressed up in London to go to see a show.

As she strolled around the room to enjoy the decor, she caught snippets of lively conversations all around her, many of them about the war and the attack that had just happened and what it could mean for them all.

Once the house doors were open, Lizzie grabbed a programme and made her way up the stairs and into the auditorium. Stepping inside she stopped in awe as she scanned the magnificent sight. If the hallway had impressed her, the actual theatre itself took her breath away – two tiers of balconies stretched below her with velvet seats in the same sumptuous plum colour, gilded with gold trim. Around the walls, highly ornate boxes looking as if they had been sculpted into the sides of the walls themselves. They were starting to fill with men in dinner jackets and women in long evening dresses and fur coats. All around the building the walls echoed with the excitement as a cheerful usher showed her to her seat. Lizzie had got the cheapest ticket she could, so she was at the very top of the building, looking down on it all. Even though the stage looked miles away to her, the experience of being in such an awe-inspiring environment was overwhelming. Once seated, Lizzie flicked through the programme as she waited for the play to start and enjoyed reading about the actors and a notice telling the audience there would be sirens and bangs during the performance and not to think that the Germans had attacked, but that it was all part of the show.

As the lights dimmed, people started to settle around her, a collective hush coming over the whole audience as the thick maroon curtains, decorated with gold trim and fringing, gathered slowly up to reveal the set of *A Cottage to Let*.

They were only about thirty minutes into the performance when she sensed something wasn't right. There were indeed bangs and crashes, but they appeared to be coming from the outside rather than inside the building. All at once, even though she was far inside the theatre, she heard the screech of the air-raid sirens outside. Suddenly, the whole theatre shook, and the stage lights flickered. The actors onstage looked nervously at each other as they continued to perform. A second shudder and bang appeared to cause the glass chandelier to fall from the ceiling in the foyer and shatter into what sounded like a million pieces, which generated gasps from most of the audience. All at once, the curtain came down and an older man with his sleeves rolled up walked out onto the stage. He introduced himself as the stage manager.

'Ladies and gentlemen, I'm sorry to tell you this, but apparently Herr Hitler has decided tonight's the night they're going to attack us. If the reports are correct, there are bombs dropping all over London, and to be safe, we need you all to move downstairs into the basement. It's huge, the whole length of the building, and should accommodate everyone. Please could you leave your seats in an orderly fashion and make your way downstairs until this raid is over.'

Around her, people started murmuring in hushed tones as they made their way out into the aisle. As Lizzie rushed down the stairs into the foyer, she noticed the real damage. The enormous chandelier had shattered all over the carpet, leaving glass everywhere, and pictures had also been knocked from their frames. Programmes lay scattered about, and a plinth with a bust of Shakespeare had toppled over and crashed to the floor. Following the crowd, she hurried down the next flight of stairs into the basement of the theatre. The bangs and crashes, as well as the wail of sirens, continued to filter in from outside. In the basement, though it was enormous, it still was quite a squeeze for them all to get in. She hoped the raid wouldn't last very long. Downstairs there was very dim lighting, illuminating dark brick walls and a threadbare, brown carpet. Very different to the rooms above ground. As her eyes adjusted to the light, she realized the basement was an overflow storage area for the theatre – all around her, large flats from past shows were stacked up against the wall. A Roman scene, Victorian manor houses and pantomime sets all sat haphazardly gathered together along with an augmentation of bigger props, shelves of instruments, and also a practice piano and a row of costumes covered in plastic.

Even with the covering, she could see policemen's uniforms, clown outfits, long frock coats, and crinoline dresses. Above the rail, shelves of top hats, flat caps and wigs of every description. The room smelled of a mixture of scenery and greasepaint mingled in with the dust. After a while, tired of standing, many of the audience sat down on the carpet as the bangs and crashes continued to roll above their heads, shaking the dust from the plaster and making the lights flicker on and off; while the wail of sirens reminded them that there was a war going on outside.

One particularly loud crash caused some brass instruments to fall down from a shelf, and people all around her gasped with shock. Lizzie covered her ears to drown out the sound of the crashes outside. She was amazed at how loud it was, even though they were all the way down in the basement, about ten times the sound of thunder. Her thoughts went to Diana, who was out there, in the midst of it. The sound of the bombing was hard enough, but what was also disconcerting was the cracking and creaking of the building above her head.

Suddenly, she feared a fire. What if some incendiary bomb came down on the theatre and set it alight, and they were all in the basement? She tried to put the thought out of her head and think of better things. She thought of her uncle Hamish and his tweed cap and coat, out on the land with his sheep. He was probably in front of the fire right now reading his paper. She thought of Fiona and Margaret, playing a game of Scrabble, innocent in this world, and her aunt Marion comforting and loving with arms that could hold her and make her feel the world was safe. She concentrated on the last dinner she'd had with her family. That last night when they'd all sat and eaten lamb stew together. She focused on the feelings she had had that night and felt insignificant and foolish that she had been so full of bravado, coming down to London to find her daughter and do war work. And though she hated to admit it, she'd actually been looking for a little excitement as well. She hadn't been in any way prepared for the realities of war, crashes so much louder and tremors so much harsher than she could ever have expected or imagined. This was just the first wave. What was it going to be like if the Germans came back again and again?

All at once, they were plunged into darkness, and Lizzie noticed her heart started to quicken and her mouth was bone dry. What if she died down here, alone? Taking in a deep breath, she counted to ten, as she had as a child whenever she'd been afraid. 'One, two, three, four, five.' Crash, bang, went another explosion above her head. 'Six, seven, eight, nine, ten.' She took another deep breath and tried not to think about what her life would be like if the Germans took over here, and she concentrated on what she had to do. She had to believe they could win; that this land would remain free. That would get her through all this fear. Lizzie continued to breathe as her whole body trembled. It took every inch of her willpower not to scream.

Chapter Nineteen

Diana looked up at the fiery sky and tried to will herself to breathe. London had been under attack for well over an hour now, and she'd never known or felt anything like it in the whole of her life. Why did it feel like her lungs weren't able to expand, weren't able to take in air? It was as though her chest was bound tightly by an invisible chain, and no matter how much she sucked in air, she didn't seem to be able to get a good deep breath. All around her, the sights and feel of war was so much more intense than she could ever have imagined. Every time a bomb dropped, the sound was deafening, and if they dropped close by, she could feel the reverberation below her feet that shook her whole body, jarring every bone and placing her teeth on edge.

It had taken every inch of their strength to focus to get the balloon up in the air. They had almost had an accident on the way up. They had been so distracted by the noise and the threat, when all at once the blast from an explosion close by had veered the climbing balloon sharply to the right. Her three-woman team had quickly pulled it back into position. As they did so, Maisie stepped in front of the wire, and before Diana could stop her, it had wound itself around the girl's waist and lifted her off her feet.

Reaching out, Diana had grabbed hold of her and pulled her down with all her might as she screamed with the pain and the shock. Jean had started tugging at the cables to loosen them, and between the two of them, they'd managed to unhook the girl, who was shaking with fear.

'Thank you,' she'd whispered with a quiver in her voice.

But Diana hadn't even had time to comfort her. She had to go back to her own position. Now it was flying again, Diana was amazed at how much her body was shaking, not just with the fear, but with the heightened emotion that was racing through her body as she heaved on the wires to keep the balloon where it needed to be. Huge searchlights had snapped on all over London, criss-crossing one another as they prowled through the darkened skies looking for enemy aircraft. As they bobbed and rolled, London landmarks flashed into view along with the German warplanes that hummed steadily through the night: the Houses of Parliament, Big Ben, Westminster Abbey. Once a plane was detected, the lights stayed trained upon their enemy. Then the rat-a-tat-tat of the ack-ack guns, as the anti-aircraft guns were known, would release a volley of return fire, their line of bullets leaving a fiery white trail that would light up the sky.

Whenever the ack-ack gun close to Diana's balloon fired, not only was it deafening, its missiles concussed the air around her every time. It took all of her concentration to stay on her feet as the wail of the sirens intermingled with the drone of the planes that hummed overhead. What she hadn't expected was the amount of black smoke and brick dust that grew and rolled all around them from the bombs and fires springing up all over the city. Every time she shook her head, a scatter of rubble and dust would fall from the top of her helmet. To cope with the experience, she focused on the training they'd all been given and was grateful now for those nights she'd been woken at three in the morning and the many scenarios Sergeant Daly had put them through to prepare them. As usual, she was situated on the port side of the balloon, a pale-faced Maisie and Jean gripping the cable behind her. They'd got it up quickly, but keeping it flying took all of their attention. She listened carefully through the dark to the quivering voice of Kathy on the megaphone as she continued to shout out instructions to them all.

Diana kept hoping it would stop, but it seemed to go on forever, rolling through the night, and with every bomb drop, she could see fires breaking out all over London. As the night wore on, a bright glow of light formed a ring around the whole of the city that was punctuated by the sounds of the bells of ambulances and fire engines as they tore through the city, saving people's lives.

Diana was so thirsty, but with all her focus on the balloon, she didn't have a moment to take a drink until Sam Daly came around and hastily gave them all some water.

'Keep it up, girls,' he encouraged. 'I'm proud of you all. You're doing great,' he said in his chirpy way.

Diana hung onto her wire and willed the noise and the onslaught to stop and hoped and prayed they would all live to tell the tale, they would all live through the night.

Chapter Twenty

Lizzie opened her eyes and looked around the basement of the theatre to try to make everything out in the dark. Somebody was handing out candles at the far end, but all around her, it was still pitch-black. As she sat rigid on the floor, a shadow passed in front of her, and someone tripped over her feet before she had time to make them aware that she was there. Grabbing out for whoever it was, she felt the rough fabric of the uniform on the person's arm as they toppled to the floor beside her. 'So sorry,' she whispered in the darkness. 'I keep doing that, tripping up people. Are you okay?'

As her eyes started to adjust, a face swam into view, and she noticed the person was wearing a Royal Air Force uniform.

'Now, that's one way to fall for you,' said a voice, and even though she couldn't see it, she could tell he was smiling. His voice was warm and calm, everything her inner voice wasn't. As she became aware of how close his presence was by her side, she felt a little self-conscious being this near to someone she could hardly see.

Somebody arrived with a candle and lit it for him. He took it from the outstretched hand and as he did she got her first look at the person sat next to her on the floor. He had dark hair and kind eyes, and by his insignia on his uniform, she could tell he was a squadron leader.

'My name's Jack Henson,' he said, reaching out his hand to shake hers.

'Lizzie Mackenzie,' she responded, taking his hand in hers. It was warm and strong and comforting. She automatically felt at ease with him. Usually, when she was around superior officers, she felt tight and uncomfortable. But Jack made her feel relaxed and calmed her with his reassuring smile.

'Do you mind if I sit here for a while? There's not a lot of space in here. I was making room for a lady who was older than I was and I was just trying to find another spot when I ended up here. I'm not too close, am I?' he asked, almost at a whisper in her ear, the hint of his spicy aftershave scenting the air between them.

'It's fine,' responded Lizzie. Their arms grazed and she was extremely aware of the weight and the warmth of his body next to her that caused the hair on the back of her neck to stand up. Politely, she tried to manoeuvre away to give him more room, but there was nowhere to go.

Jack didn't seem too concerned. 'Do I detect a Scottish accent?' he enquired.

'I'm from the Highlands,' she said, 'down here to work for the war effort.'

'I have distant family in Scotland,' he replied as he pulled the candle closer so they could see one another better. 'It's so beautiful up there. One of my most favourite places to visit in the world. I like the open spaces.'

'So do I, especially right now,' said Lizzie with a chuckle as she stared out at the heaving mass of bodies. 'I must admit I'm missing it and the quiet. It's much noisier down here.'

'Only when Jerry comes to the party,' joked Jack.

They both laughed.

'I see you're in the air force. I am too. I'm part of the WAAFs. I work as a filter plotter out of Kenley.'

'Well, now I see why they call it the beauty chorus,' he responded, staring directly into her eyes and using the nickname given for the female plotters. 'I'm based over at Biggin Hill. Squadron 111.'

Blushing slightly at his compliment she nodded. 'I know of it.'

'You must be one of the people tracking my direction in the air.'

'Well, my superior does. I just push you into position on the map.'

'And I never felt a thing,' he joked back.

'It's a minor role really, but I enjoy it. It's like watching the war unfold in front of me.'

'There are no minor roles, Lizzie,' he whispered, meeting her eyes with great sincerity. 'You are doing a critical job. You are our eyes on the ground, and we would be lost up there without that overview. So, don't belittle what you are doing. I, like all the squadrons, am very grateful you are down there watching over us.'

She suddenly felt valuable, seeing her job through his eyes. So much of the time she was so intently focused on making sure all the planes were where they were meant to be on the map, it had slipped her mind that individual pilots were counting on the work to get them into battle.

They talked effortlessly through the night. And it was amazing how easy it was to deal with the ongoing onslaught over her head with someone kind to pass the time with. In a way, he reminded her of her uncle Hamish, the same calm, thoughtfulness and sincerity to everything he talked about, coupled with a great sense of humour. There was an aura about him that everything was going to be okay.

He told her all about his home and family in Essex. She, in turn, about her life in Scotland. The food they liked to eat, films they'd enjoyed, books they'd read. It was anything but a first date, but as the night rolled into the morning, Lizzie felt like she knew Jack better than any man she'd known apart from her family.

There was an ease between them as they conversed. She wasn't nervous around him. It was as if they had known each other forever; and even though the bombs continued to crash overhead, some taking their breath away and making them gasp, simply to have some real human connection, another person there with her, made such a difference. The last thought she'd been thinking before he tripped over her feet was *what if I die here, alone with all these strangers?* Now she felt she'd made a real friend.

At about two o'clock, the stage manager came down to check on them all. 'We've opened up the bar the next floor up, if any of you want to go up for a drink. It has been a while since a bomb dropped close by. The all-clear hasn't sounded yet, but it appears the bombers are making their way to the other side of London. If you feel you need to get a drink, please feel free to do so. It's still underground, so you'll be safe in there.'

Jack looked across at Lizzie. 'Can I buy you a drink?'

She nodded. 'I think we've earned one, don't you?'

They made their way into the bar, and she found a little table where she placed the candle. All around, on surfaces, other candles had been lit, and if it hadn't been for the rolling, crashing, and banging above their heads that still came intermittently, though sounding further off now, this could have been the perfect romantic situation.

She looked around the room. The cast were there, still in their costumes, drinking beer and gin and tonics, as she and Jack continued to sip their drinks. The all-clear didn't come till 4.30 in the morning, at which time people had started to fall asleep and the rolling crashes had ceased.

Making her way upstairs, she found out when she got outside that all London transportation had been suspended for the time being, so she'd have to walk home. The air was filled with dust and smoke, drifting from areas that had taken the hardest hit. And even all the way over in the East End, the fires on what looked like the docks were still raging, illuminating the sky with an eerie orange glow.

Jack turned to her. 'Well, it's nice to be outside,' he said, thrusting his hands in his pockets, 'though the air doesn't seem to be as fresh as when we left it. Can I walk you home?' he enquired.

She shook her head. 'It's about three miles.'

He shrugged the distance off. 'It will be good to walk after being cooped up for so long.'

On the way back to Julia's house, they continued in their comfortable conversation as they crossed the river and walked along the

South Bank to Vauxhall and then down towards Brixton. By the time they reached Julia's street, the glorious pink light of morning was rolling in and the dawn chorus was in full voice. How odd, she thought, to go from a thunderous bombardment to the beauty and the sounds of nature in only a few hours.

On the doorstep, Jack seemed to be looking for the right words. 'Lizzie, thank you for keeping me company this evening.'

'And thank you for walking me home,' responded Lizzie, politely. 'I'm glad you tripped over me.' She laughed.

'I had such a good time.' He paused and became almost coy, something she hadn't seen in him all night. She waited for him to speak again. Finally, he looked up. 'Would you mind if we saw one another again?'

'I think that would be a terrible idea,' she joked, keeping her face straight, then seeing the panic in his eyes shook her head, laughing. 'I'd be delighted, I hardly know anyone in London.'

The relief was evident in his face.

'There's a dance at the RAF station at Biggin Hill next week. I was wondering if you'd want to come with me. I'm not sure what time I will be finished with work but I could meet you there?'

'I would love to go,' said Lizzie.

'Next Friday, then,' he said, offering her his hand again, and as she slipped hers into his, he covered it with his other hand. 'Lovely to meet you, Lizzie from Scotland.'

She nodded. 'You too, Jack from Essex.'

As she stood in the doorway, Lizzie watched him walking up the street. He moved with a comfortable stride, one hand in his pocket, his cap thrust back on his head, and she felt something, something odd, as though she was going to miss him even though she'd only just met him.

Once inside, Julia was relieved to see her. 'Thank goodness. I've been worried about both of you. Diana's still not back, she was going to stay here tonight. How are you, Lizzie?'

'I was trapped in the theatre. They kept us for hours even after the bombing stopped.'

'How awful for you.'

'It wasn't so terrible,' said Lizzie, with a coy smile.

Julia frowned. 'What do you mean?'

'Well, I met somebody. And I'm going to meet him at a dance next week.'

'You're incorrigible,' said Julia, shaking her head.

'Right now, I'm just tired,' she said with a yawn. 'I might try and get a couple of hours before I have to go back to work.' Lizzie made her way upstairs. Her bed felt comfortable, and as she drifted off to sleep, her mind ran over the highlights of her conversation with Jack and she felt a glow. She really liked this new friend. And his warm smile was the last thing she thought about as she drifted off to sleep.

Chapter Twenty-One

At six in the morning, Diana came off a long duty and made her way back to Julia's house. She was exhausted. It took all of her strength to put one foot in front of the other. Nothing could have prepared her for the realities of a bombing. She knew it was going to be loud, but she hadn't expected the physical impact on her body, not just from the concussion from the bombs, and the ack-ack guns, but also the sheer exhaustion of flying the balloon during the attack. At around 5.30 the previous day, an hour into the attack, a German plane had been hit by one of the ack-ack guns right over their heads. All the girls had screamed with the sheer terror of it as their commanding officer had shouted to them to stay on task.

It had been a horrific sight to see the plane burst into flames and plummet down into the city, landing on buildings and exploding. But with true female grit, they had carried on. As the night had gone on, the fires had become worse, and it had become so bright that by the end of the evening, the glow from the London docks alone had lit the whole sky, as if it were a raging orange sunrise, plumes of rolling fire reaching up into the air, filling it with ash and smoke that coated everything and everyone and choked the back of their throats. As she looked down at her hands, she found they were filthy; she was covered in soot and dirt.

Turning into Julia's street, Diana looked up from under the metal rim of her grey helmet. A perfect dawn was stretching up the road to greet her. It brought tears to her eyes. It was so beautiful. And she realized that all night there had been a fear in the back of her mind that she would never see one again, let alone one this lovely. At one point, in the early hours of the morning, as the bombing had started to cease, Diana had looked up at a sky that was awash with a million stars and wondered how the two could survive together. The ravages of war and the beauty of nature. The sky feeling endless and tranquil, like a deep black ocean. How could it stay so calm, watching over the devastation of the world below it?

She couldn't believe she'd been working all night. The second team had come to relieve her at four o'clock, but it appeared that the night's trauma was over, except for the sounds of ambulance bells and firefighters as they continued to respond to a city alight.

How long would it take to put out so many fires? Diana wondered.

Once the all-clear had sounded, Diana had decided to come straight to Julia's, as she had arranged, instead of going to her barracks. She wanted to talk to someone, and the rest of her crew would have just gone straight to sleep. But she needed to reach out and find some comfort, her centre, feel some normality, to draw on the feeling of home in the midst of a world gone mad.

She opened the gate, shuffled down the path, and knocked at the door. As she waited for Julia to answer, she stretched out her neck. The whole of her shoulders was knotted, and her back was aching, her feet sore. When Julia opened the door, she was ecstatic to see Diana, and concerned at her exhausted, traumatized appearance. She helped her into the house, took off her coat and her helmet, and pulled off her boots. Diana was glad to be inside. Bringing her into the kitchen, Julia poured her a brandy as Diana sat down at the table. Even her arms ached as she tried to lift the glass to her mouth.

'Well, that was fun,' she joked as she shook her dark curls and inadvertently scattered brick dust around the kitchen table. 'Is Lizzie all right?' she asked.

'She arrived just before you. She's gone to bed,' said Julia as she fussed around the kitchen, making tea.

'It's pretty bad out there,' Diana told her.

Julia slumped down in a chair at the table next to her. 'Agnes knocked on the door at two o'clock to tell me a friend of hers had told her that the docks took quite a beating.'

'It's been slammed over there,' Diana confirmed. 'We could see it from where we were in Westminster. The fires were that high. Hard to believe this is real, isn't it?'

Julia nodded.

Diana looked down at her hands and couldn't believe the amount of grime and dirt under her fingernails and even plastered up her arms. After her tea, she stood up. 'I'm going to go and have a wash.'

'Why don't you have a proper bath?' said Julia.

Diana nodded. 'That actually sounds really good.'

'I'll run you one,' said Julia as she went upstairs.

Diana was so grateful, and could see Julia liked taking care of her and imagined she must be really missing her family. When Diana went up half an hour later, she couldn't believe that Julia had surpassed the water level past the six inches they had been told they must abide by.

'I think you need a good soak and to relax,' said Julia with a smile.

Diana nodded, making her way into the bathroom, undressing, and sinking into the hot water. She tried to push from her mind all the sights and the sounds, but her ears were still ringing with the impact of the bombs and flashes continued to roll around in her memory. And suddenly, she thought of her dad. No wonder he had not wanted her to join the war effort. He had lived through this too, except he'd been in a trench like a sitting duck. She could only imagine what it would have been like to have bombs dropping literally on your head in a trench. No wonder it had been so hard for him to watch her leave. Tears started to roll down her cheeks as she thought about it. She could never have imagined anything this dramatic. But as she wiped them away, all it did was make her more determined to keep going, to keep fighting for herself and for her family. This was a night she would never forget but she girded herself with steel. Britain was counting on her and so many other women like her and she would have to be ready for the next onslaught because she knew the Germans would be back.

Chapter Twenty-Two

As Julia travelled to work on Monday, the transportation system was still in much disarray from the second night of bombing. A lot of the roads were shut down due to either dangerous buildings that were still unstable from the bomb attack or others that been entirely destroyed. There were remnants of them scattered about on the road, stopping her from getting through. She had to go across town on a different route, having to change two buses to get her to work. It took her a while to get just from Brixton into Whitehall. Still, the bus driver had to put her off early, and she had to walk nearly half a mile to get to the office, but she noticed something very interesting as she went. There was quiet defiance around everywhere. People were not just clearing up the debris; there was a determination in how they spoke to one another and how they were.

She wondered now that there had been two nights of bombing if this was going to be a regular occurrence from now on and was suddenly very glad her children were safe. Her thoughts returned to the day before, and the message that had been on the wireless about Churchill's visits to the East End, to an area that had taken one of the hardest hits. A woman whose house had been destroyed was being interviewed, and the resilience in her tone had impressed Julia. 'They will not tear us down,' she'd said in a firm voice, and it echoed in Julia's mind as she made her way through the city streets. Everywhere there were the WVS and air-raid wardens who were helping wherever they could. Outside one of the stations, she passed a makeshift tea stand that had been erected by one woman, who was handing out cups of tea to weary travellers to bolster them up. 'Keep going,' she was saying. 'We're not going to let him intimidate us.'

On the way to the gate at Whitehall, she noted, security was much more intense today. It took her a while to get through, and once she got down to the war rooms, the energy inside was electric.

Everyone was busy trying to come to terms with the situation. There were more people in the bunker than she'd ever seen before. As she passed the map room, someone opened the door and inside she could see a large group already in, talking, quietly whispering around the map, obviously attempting to get a read of what was going on in the air and in France. Ready to assess the damage and what needed to be done. In her own typing office, there was a hush and a buzz as all the girls quickly moved to type up assessed information being filtered through from the main office.

'We'll have our work cut out for us today,' said Linda as she lit a cigarette. 'I don't suppose we'll be going home tonight,'

Mrs Scriber suddenly appeared.

'Sorry I'm late,' said Julia, pulling off her hat and coat and sitting down at her typewriter.

'No time to spare,' she snapped. 'Mr Churchill wants to see you right away.'

All the girls stopped typing and looked across at Julia.

Mrs Scriber continued. 'He wants you to type up his speech for the broadcast on Wednesday.'

Julia scanned the room at all the other girls' faces as they nodded their encouragement.

Nervously, picking up the typewriter, Julia followed Mrs Scriber at a clip to Churchill's office. Balancing her typewriter on her knee, she perched on the edge of a chair outside the door, to wait for him. All at once, the prime minister himself appeared, chatting in a loud, animated way with a member of his cabinet. 'I hear your point of view, and it's not that I'm against it,' he was booming as he rushed past her, 'but sometimes, you have to fight to create the peace you want.' Pushing open the door, he stomped inside and then, turning to Julia, signalled to her to follow him. Clutching her typewriter to her chest, she hurried into the room, hanging back in the corner, awkwardly, while they finished their conversation.

'I just think that you'll live to regret it,' said Lord Halifax, the foreign secretary, as he left the room and closed the door behind him.

Julia was then left in the room, just her and Churchill. She tried not to think about what an unusual situation this was and tried not to be in awe of her prime minister.

'Sit down, girl, sit down,' he snapped in his abrupt, no-nonsense way.

Julia quickly moved to the desk and placed her typewriter on it as he fished around his office for what he was looking for, which turned out to be a bottle of Scotch. Opening it, he poured himself a generous glass, and Julia fought back the temptation to check her watch. It couldn't be more than half past nine, maybe ten o'clock at the latest. Oblivious to her surprise, he lit one of his usual cigars, sat back in his chair, and sighed deeply. He seemed to be taking time to collect himself in his own world before, all of a sudden, he remembered she was there and came to life.

'I need you to type the speech for a broadcast to the nation,' he stated solemnly.

Then, Julia sensed a difference in him as he contemplated the words for his speech. He seemed more reflective than the times that she'd passed him in the office; he'd always been an eager, forthright kind of a person, a man who she felt was in control. But there was a difference in his countenance now and a deep concern, she could tell. Even though he'd clearly disagreed with Lord Halifax, she could see he was considering many things. He took another a deep long drag of his cigar and stared at a propaganda poster on the wall, reminding them all to be vigilant and not to trust anyone.

Julia held her breath as the blue smoke swirled around her face, blurring her typewriter in front of her.

'Ready?' he muttered in a low tone.

Julia nodded and, with her trembling fingers, removed the cover from her typewriter. Hastily rolling in a sheet of paper, along with the carbon and another page, she prepared to type.

But instead of beginning his speech, he stopped, turned, and looked directly at her. 'What's your name? I don't think I've had you in here before, have I?' he asked, his deep, guttural voice measured and thoughtful.

'Julia Sullivan,' she said in a tight, dry voice, swallowing down the anxiety caught in her throat as she tried not to cough because of the smoke filling the room. She was knocked off-guard with his personable approach. She'd expected him to start speaking for her to transcribe straight away.

'Julia,' he repeated in a low grumble, rolling it around in his mouth as though testing it to see if it was acceptable. 'Are you well?' he asked. 'After the last two nights, I mean. Is your family all right? Everyone is safe?'

'My husband is away serving, and my children are in the Cotswolds.'

He nodded, considering her words. 'Awful sight,' he said as he spun his chair around, almost as if he was talking to himself as he looked up at the wall to a place a window may have been if they hadn't been underground. He took another sip of his Scotch. Then to clarify his train of thought, he muttered, 'The East End yesterday, terrible mess.'

Julia nodded to the back of his head.

He swivelled back around then morphed into the Churchill she knew. 'But we have to keep going, don't we? It's the right thing to do.'

Julia nodded absently, her fingers hovering over the keys. Was she supposed to be typing? She wasn't sure if their conversation had finished or whether he'd started transcribing. She then wondered if he regretted his decision to retaliate for the Croydon raid with the bombing of Berlin. Julia wanted to tell him that she thought he'd done the right thing. The Germans were going to come anyway. But she didn't feel it was her place to be so forthright with him, even though she still felt he needed a little reassurance.

'They won't get to us, sir. They won't destroy us or crush us. We'll all just work harder.'

He turned to meet her defiant gaze, and his forehead relaxed, the look of worry that had been lining it since he had arrived in the room disappearing for a moment as he gave her a watery smile of connection. 'Yes, that's right. That's the attitude we want. Well done. Good girl.'

Julia felt relieved. She'd felt a little bit insubordinate being honest. Still, she could see that she'd seemed to bolster him with her words.

He nodded at her, and then started to dictate: 'When I said in the House of Commons the other day that I thought it was improbable that the enemy's attack could be more than three times greater than it was in August, I was not, of course, referring to barbarous attacks upon the civil population, but to the great air battle which is being fought between our fighters and the German air force.'

He then went on to outline what the British forces were doing to combat the onslaught of Hitler, informing everybody how the Nazi invasion of England was proceeding, with hundreds of self-propelled barges moving down the coast of Europe from German and Dutch harbours towards the ports of northern France and to Dunkirk and Brest and beyond.

Julia felt her chest tighten as she typed the reality of those words.

'Behind these clusters of ships or barges, there stand very large numbers of German troops, awaiting the order to go on board and set out on their very dangerous and uncertain voyage across the sea,' he continued in his rolling, booming tone. 'We cannot tell when they will try to come; we cannot be sure that in fact they will try at all; but no one should blind himself to the fact that a heavy, full-scale invasion of this island is being prepared with all the usual German thoroughness and method, and it may be launched now – upon England, upon Scotland, or upon Ireland, or upon all three.'

Julia swallowed down the fear as she continued to type his message, realizing once again the significance of the time they were living in. It wasn't that she hadn't known beforehand that they'd been at war, even without bombs dropping on bases and watching the Spitfire pilots in the air, but it had felt somehow removed from her, with the constant waiting and preparation during the 'phoney war'. Now, somehow, it felt more real and as if, at any moment, the barges he talked about could be sailing across the sea, from any number of ports, to attack the British people.

He continued and then said in a low whisper, 'Every man,' and then stopping and catching her eye and acknowledging her with a slight smile, 'and woman, will therefore prepare himself to do his duty, whatever that may be, with special pride and care.' He nodded at Julia then, apparently remembering the words she had said to him, he paused again and stared at the floor, collecting his thoughts. 'Little does he know the spirit of the British nation…'

Julia found herself nodding as she typed.

'… or the tough fibre of the Londoners whose forebears played a leading part in the establishment of the parliamentary institutions, and who have been bred to value freedom far above their lives.'

Julia felt proud. She was one of the Londoners he was talking about, and yes, they may have to get to a place where they would value their freedom above their lives. All at once, she knew she was prepared to do that. They all had to be if they were going to get this job done. As she continued to type his words, she was struck by the next line.

'What he has done is kindle a fire in British hearts, here and all over the world, which will glow long after all the traces of the conflagration he has caused in London have been removed. He has lighted a fire which will burn with a steady and consuming flame until the last vestiges of Nazi tyranny have been burned out of Europe, until the Old World – and the New – can join hands to build the temples of man's freedom and man's honour, upon foundations which will not soon or easily be overthrown. This is a time for everyone to stand together, and hold firm, as they are doing.'

He continued offering his admiration and thanks to the fire services and the different work people were doing to maintain order in London before finishing up his speech.

'But that we shall rather draw from the heart of suffering itself the means of inspiration, survival, and of a victory won not only for ourselves, but for all; a victory won, not for our own time, but for the long and better days that are to come.'

Finishing his speech, he sat back in his chair and emptied his glass of whisky. Filling the air with more blue cigar smoke, he seemed pensive, as though he'd once again forgotten that Julia was there.

Then all at once, he came to his senses, barking out instructions on where he needed the speech to go.

She rolled the paper out of the typewriter and separated the carbon and the copy, then placed the original on his desk as he pulled out a pen and started to make the edits he wanted. 'Will that be all, sir?' she asked in a quiet voice.

He grunted, nodded his head, absorbed by the words on the page. As she got to the doorway, his voice reached out to her. 'Thank you, Julia. I'm very grateful for your service.'

She nodded, and as pride sprang up in her heart, she closed the door behind her.

Going back to the typing pool, she felt encouraged, strengthened by the work she was doing and knowing that, in her small way, like so many others, she was encouraging her own prime minister to do the job he needed to do. But deep inside she wondered, was all of this futile? Would England be overrun by Germans one day? Would she see Nazis goose-stepping down the Strand or taking over Buckingham Palace? She couldn't even think about the Houses of Parliament with Nazi flags flying over the top of it. It just couldn't happen. One thing she knew about her nation: the people of Britain would fight to the death to preserve their freedom. They may be just a small island, but they had a mighty history of fighting for what was right. Taking in a deep breath, she strode back to the pool, put the extra copy of the speech on her desk, and started her day of work.

Chapter Twenty-Three

The first time Lizzie heard his voice over the radio, two days after they had met, her heart skipped a beat. She'd always felt the extreme importance of her job, plotting the pilots' movements during their air battles, but now to hear Jack's voice through a headset made her stomach flutter.

'Red Leader moving into position. I can see three enemy planes from here. I'm going in,' came his calm delivery.

Lizzie hadn't seen him since that first night and she suddenly felt close to him, imagining his smile, his eyes on her, that warm kind voice calling her by her name and she wondered if he thought about her down here listening in. However, she didn't have long in her reverie, as she was pulled sharply back into the present and the need to do her job.

'Acknowledged, I see all three,' came back Jack's counterpart.

Praying for his safety and holding her breath, she pushed the three enemy planes into position on the map. It was hard enough when any of the British pilots were in the middle of a dogfight, but now to have the man she couldn't stop thinking about up there put her heart in her throat. His wingman, Alan, answered him, 'Falling in behind Red Leader.'

'I'm going to veer right and come down below them,' Jack stated, and Alan replied in the affirmative. She listened intently as the battle unfolded in the sky above her.

When the rattle of gunfire disrupted the transmission, Lizzie froze as she listened for his voice.

But it wasn't Jack she heard, it was Alan saying in a frantic tone, 'Watch out three o'clock, Red Leader! Three o'clock!'

Lizzie paused. As she waited for the response, there was the sound of another round of bullets.

'Coming around. I'm coming around.' Alan's voice again.

Where was Jack? Another rattle of gunfire. All of a sudden, it was him, he sounded intense, but assured. 'I'm going to climb higher, see if I can shake them off.' The sound of his engine as it climbed steeply whined through her headset.

Then all at once the sound of an explosion. Lizzie couldn't help but suck in air and thrust a hand to her throat. Below it her heart was beating rapidly and she felt light-headed.

'Please, God, let him be all right,' she whispered to herself. The radio crackled in response, and there was no more communication for about thirty seconds, but it could have been two hours as far as Lizzie was concerned. She closed her eyes to listen more intently as machine-gun fire rattled the airwaves, trying to picture what was going on as she kept praying.

All of a sudden, another explosion and the sound of a plane careering to the ground. Then Lizzie felt sheer relief as his voice cut in.

'Okay, that was a close one, Red Two, but we got him,' and all at once she was able to let out the breath she didn't realize she'd been holding. Thank God he was all right. She knew how often they lost pilots, and sometimes only one in five returned, but not today, not Jack.

Later on in the day as she was finishing work she saw him on her own base. He had obviously been sent over and was talking to another pilot. She raced across the square to intercept him. His eyes lit up as he spotted her.

'Lizzie! From the theatre! This is a nice surprise,' he started, greeting her with a kiss on the cheek, so unruffled without a hair out of place. 'I thought I wouldn't see you again till the dance on Saturday.'

She was shocked at how blasé he was being.

'I realized it was you in the sky today. And my God, it was very close, Jack. I was listening in,' she spluttered out, not wasting time on pleasantries.

He turned to face her, a curious expression crossing his face. 'You were worried about me?'

'Of course, it is very dangerous up there.'

'How sweet to know someone is thinking about me in that way.'

'I was praying,' she confessed, not even trying to play it cool.

He studied her face intently as if taking in all of it and then raising his hand, he brushed away a stray curl that danced across her cheek.

'My very own angel on earth keeping me safe in the sky,' he whispered. He looked deep into her eyes and for a minute she thought he might kiss her as he drew his head close to hers and his gaze wandered to her lips. Then apparently realizing that it would have been inappropriate with them both on duty in uniform and in view of everyone else on the airfield, he pulled away reluctantly and drew in a long slow breath. 'It all sounds much more dramatic than it really is,' he stated hoarsely, trying to remain casual.

And Lizzie felt tongue-tied by the intensity of their exchange. It was only their second ever meeting but it felt like his heart was already heading in the same direction as her own, and as concerned as she was about his close call today, her heart soared with that knowledge.

He quickly changed the subject.

'Would you like to go for a drink? Alan and some of the other lads are going to the pub; it may be a little raucous but I would love it if you could join us.'

Lizzie smiled and nodded, noticing how quickly she slipped into feeling comfortable around him and with the prospect of doing things together. It was a strange dance in her heart between the warmth of the friendship that was building between them and the stirring emotion she felt coursing through her body just being close to him. But as they walked to the lift he had arranged, the unease of the earlier event hadn't entirely left her.

'How do you do it, Jack? How do you go into the sky time after time and be okay? Aren't you afraid?'

He seemed thoughtful for a minute, and stopped walking. Looking down at the ground he seemed to concentrate on her words.

'Honestly, Lizzie, I don't think about it. If I did, I probably would be afraid. But fear is a luxury we cannot afford. We are making split-second decisions, any of which could be our last. Shooting from the hip, going on instinct, and if you were to dwell on that fact you would be frozen, unable to do your job. So, I go up, and I do what I need to do to win this war. Every one of us does, and it's really tough when we lose pilots and friends. But that's what sends us into the air again and again. We see the faces of all the men we have lost and want to make their deaths mean something, make sure that their sacrifice was not in vain.'

She nodded, understanding, and purposely she threaded her fingers through his. He gladly accepted her reassurance and acknowledged that by lifting her hand to his lips and brushing her knuckles with a gentle kiss. A thrill ran up her spine and squeezed the back of her neck.

When they arrived at the pub, it had a warm lively ambience. A high wooden bar was mirrored and backlit with shelves of spirits, the grey stone walls decorated with brasses and various hunting pictures. The strong smell of beer and nicotine permeated the atmosphere as jovial servicemen were everywhere, some playing billiards and a lively game of darts in the corner, their raucous interactions competing with a gramophone on the bar playing a cheering big band number.

Pushing their way in through the smoky atmosphere, Alan was already at the bar when Jack introduced her.

'So, this is Lizzie,' Alan said, jabbing his cigarette into the corner of his mouth and stretching out his hand with a knowing glance in Jack's direction. Lizzie got the distinct impression he already knew her name and the bashful way Jack responded only compounded her belief that he had already told Alan about her. As Alan shook her hand with a crooked smile a curl of blue smoke circled its way into the corner of his eye, making him squint and contort his face. He was tall and slender, a wiry figure, with curly, unruly sandy-coloured hair that seemed to have a life of its own. All of them were still in their uniforms, and they were given their first drinks for free by the pub owner.

'Keep shooting them down, lads,' he said, as he slopped the two pints of frothy amber liquid onto the bar in front of the men and a gin and tonic in front of Lizzie.

Jack led them back to a quieter spot in the far corner of the pub and they huddled close together to hear each other.

'Close one today,' stated Alan, taking the first sip of his bitter and pushing his cap back on his head. 'I honestly thought he'd got you for a minute.' Lizzie gave Jack a sideward glance as if to ask him why he'd been so nonchalant about it all. Jack took a sip of his pint, trying to play down the severity of it, apparently for Lizzie's sake.

'All in a day's work, Alan. All in a day's work.' Alan must have caught Lizzie's look. 'Don't worry, Lizzie. No one is going to get Jack. He's got the luck of the Irish,' he said, a smile lighting up his face.

But Lizzie saw something in Jack's eyes, even though he joked along, and she suddenly realized how difficult this was going to be. War was hard enough, but now knowing the man who was making her heart pound would be making life and death decisions was agonizing. Just the knowledge that the slightest wrong move could take him away from her filled her with dread.

After a couple of pints during which Alan regaled Lizzie with some of Jack's most notorious escapades in training, including flying upside down just to see if he could, much to Jack's embarrassment, but at which Lizzie laughed heartily, she started to feel really relaxed in their company. She noticed a freedom in the pilots that she hadn't known before in her male friends in Scotland or other members of the armed services she had met since she had been in London. They seemed to have no problems letting down their guard, having a good time. She wondered if this devil-may-care-spirit came because of the job they were doing. Nothing brought your vison into clearer focus than knowing that out of five of you in the air, only four were coming back. She had seen it in Jack in the intense and completely absorbing way he connected with her and she saw it in Alan in his over-the-top exuberance for life.

At the end of the evening, Alan and Jack drove her home, and Jack jumped out to see her to her door. She would have loved to have kissed him goodnight but with Alan honking his horn and making kissing sounds out of the car window, any chance of an intimate moment was lost as they both laughed with the awkward embarrassment of it. Coyly she kissed him gently on the cheek and squeezed his hand.

'Don't forget the dance on Saturday,' he reminded her. 'I won't be bringing Alan,' he added with a raise of his eyebrows.

Lizzie laughed, then waved from the door as he jumped back in the car and tore off into the night.

Chapter Twenty-Four

A few nights after the first raid on London Diana trudged to the sentry box, and she was miserable. It was pouring with rain, which had been hard enough the last few nights with the balloon, but she had learned to harden herself to the terrifying world around her to do her job and at least the activity had kept her warm. But the thought of having to stand on guard duty at the camp in the cold, damp, gloomy, musty sentry box – where, no doubt, it would be wretched and freezing all night – did not fill her with joy. She was also frustrated because it wasn't even her regular shift. Diana had been woken by Sergeant Daly at two o'clock to inform her that one of the other girls was ill and she would have to step in. Pulling herself up out of her warm bed, she hadn't even bothered with her uniform, reasoning no one was going to see under her coat. So, slipping on her oilskin trousers and long mac over her pyjamas, she'd shoved her feet into her gumboots. Then, tucking up her curlers under her sou'wester, wrapping a scarf around her neck, and armed with a truncheon, Diana had shuffled out into the cold to go on duty.

She stepped inside the sentry box and shook off the rain from her mac, as another girl greeted her as she stepped outside, at the end of her own shift. 'Good luck, duck,' she said. 'I hope you like to swim.' And with a chuckle, she disappeared into the night.

Once alone, Diana yawned and, staring out the rainy window, tried to focus and get her bearings. Then, tucking her curlers further up under her hat, she mused how she'd never have been seen dead dressed like this at home, where how she looked had been very important as a hairdresser.

As the clock in the tiny room ticked away the minutes, it was a reasonably quiet night, and Diana tried to stay out of the rain as much as she could.

A few recruits came through the gates, many coming back off their own shifts, and whenever they sidled up, she would step out of the booth, pull down her scarf that was wrapped around her face, look at their pass, and nod them on, most of them thanking her and being sympathetic to her duty.

At four o'clock, Diana was still stamping from foot to foot, trying to bring life back to her freezing feet, her hands stuffed up her sleeves inside her pockets, and her eyes closed, when someone approached the gate. She didn't hear the person at first, who was on his bicycle, until a jovial voice greeted her, 'Well, hello there, how's it going tonight, aircraftwoman?'

As a superior officer stepped into the sentry box to get out of the rain, Diana's eyes flashed open, and she was surprised to see not her own officer in charge, Sergeant Daly, but a different officer altogether.

The first name to enter Diana's mind was Cary Grant. Soft brown eyes, a similar build, and a warm, kind smile.

Blinking away her dismay, all at once she remembered she was supposed to salute him, as she'd been thinking how self-conscious she felt stood here in her curlers.

Quickly, pulling her hand from her pocket, she saluted him and flicked rainwater straight into his face. Diana was mortified.

'I'm so sorry,' she gushed, forgetting to use her posh voice and letting her strong Birmingham accent slip out.

'A Brummie if I'm not mistaken,' he said with a smile as he pulled out a handkerchief to dry his face. 'I haven't met many people from the Midlands during this.'

Diana could have kicked herself. She'd been working so hard on keeping her accent neutral, as people often ribbed her about it. And now here she was, in front of the best-looking man she'd seen in months, looking like something that had just been dragged through the mud.

'Are you keeping warm, Aircraftwoman...?' he asked.

'Ah, yes, sir,' she said. 'It's Aircraftwoman Downes, sir.'

'Aircraftwoman Downes,' he said, nodding. 'I'm just out checking on all the duty officers tonight. I guess you picked the short straw.'

'One of the girls was sick.'

'Well, at least you're a little drier than me,' he said. 'I didn't think to grab my coat before I went on duty tonight.'

Diana looked down at his sodden uniform and instantly felt sorry for him; he was soaking wet. 'Here,' she said, 'there's a spare mac. Why don't you put that on?' She handed him a mac that was hanging on the door, and he smiled at her.

'That's very kind of you. Thank you, Aircraftwoman Downes.' He slipped on the mac, stepped back outside the booth, and nodded to her before getting onto his bicycle and riding away as Diana watched him.

Before he came back two hours later to return the coat, she tried to make herself look a little more presentable by pulling out her curlers and shoving them in her pockets.

'Thank you, Aircraftwoman Downes,' he said, handing the coat back to her, as it had now stopped raining. 'That helped keep me dry.'

'Anytime,' she said, smiling. 'Corporal...?' And she waited for him to fill in the blanks.

'Shelley,' he said. 'My name's Corporal Shelley. Nice to meet you. I hope to see you again sometime. Maybe at one of the dances.' He looked down at her boots, and she felt very self-conscious. 'Guess you won't be doing much dancing in those,' he joked with her, and Diana knew that she blushed. Why did she have to meet someone this good-looking when she was dressed like someone on a trip to Antarctica?

She shook her head and smiled through her embarrassment. He stepped back out of the sentry box and started to cycle away. As Diana watched him go, she thought how friendly and easy-going he was, and she hoped she might see him again.

When the next girl arrived for the shift, the weather had improved.

'Sorry, Diana. It looked like you got the rough end of the stick last night.'

'Not necessarily,' said Diana. 'I met some fascinating people.' And with that, she sauntered off to her barracks, thinking about that warm smile, hoping to get another couple of hours' sleep before she was out on parade. As she closed her eyes she tested the name for fun: *Diana Shelley*, yes, that could work she joked with herself if she ever met Sergeant *Cary Grant* again; and she dropped back off to sleep thinking of those soft brown eyes.

Chapter Twenty-Five

When Diana arrived on Saturday, Julia and Lizzie didn't hear her come in because they were both in the bedroom. Glenn Miller was playing on the wireless in the front room.

'Are we having a party?' Diana asked finally, finding them.

Julia shook her head with a smile. 'Lizzie is going out for the night with that nice airman she met last week. Do you remember? He's invited her to a dance over at Biggin Hill. So, she started getting into the mood early.'

Lizzie looked at herself again in the mirror. She was trying another one of Julia's outfits on, a green dress that set off the colour of her hair perfectly and cinched her in at the waist with a black belt, a perfect cut for her figure.

Diana whistled. 'You look gorgeous.'

Lizzie threw her arms around her friend's neck, giving her an extra squeeze with all her excitement. 'I'm going to see that pilot again,' she said, her eyes wide with the excitement. 'Keep your fingers crossed that Jerry doesn't screw it up for us. I just want one dance with him before tonight's raid, that's all.'

Julia sat on the bed. 'Well, it's not so terrible if you have to go into an air-raid shelter together. You could sit on a bunk next to each other.'

'We already did that. Don't you remember?' said Lizzie with a wink, brushing off her skirt. 'I want to dance with him now. I'm so nervous,' she admitted, pressing both her hands into the space in the middle of her ribcage and taking a deep breath. 'He's so good-looking and sophisticated. I'm just a country girl from Scotland. I have no idea what he sees in me.'

'He sees what we all see,' assured Diana, looping her arms around her friend's waist and hugging her from behind. 'You're so much fun and loving and caring. Plus, you have the best haircut in the world,' she added, joking with her as they all laughed. 'You must have a fabulous hairdresser.'

Lizzie felt the apprehension tug at her stomach. 'I'm so nervous about going there on my own. Diana, would you come with me?' she implored. 'Or Julia, could you come?'

Julia shook her head, 'I promised Agnes I'd keep her company tonight. I've been so busy, and she's been feeling very neglected, she told me yesterday. I promised John that I would spend time with his mother. So, unfortunately, I can't come.'

'Diana, do you want to come with me?'

Diana looked down at what she was wearing. It was a smart skirt and a blouse, but she hadn't planned to go out for the night. 'I'm not really dressed for it. I've got no stockings on,' she said, looking down at her bare legs.

'I have a jacket,' said Julia, swinging open the door of her wardrobe. 'Here. It'll go lovely with that skirt.'

Diana tried it on, and Julia also handed her a pair of beautiful earrings and a necklace, which really made the outfit look amazing. 'But what about my legs?' she persisted.

'Don't worry,' said Lizzie. 'I've been reading about this in a magazine, what people are doing.' She ran to her make-up bag and pulled out an eyeliner. 'Come on, turn around, Diana, I'm going to draw you a line in, and they'll never know you're not wearing stockings.'

The girls laughed as 'Pennsylvania 6-5000' played on the wireless and Lizzie tried her best to make a straight line down the back of Diana's legs. 'The things we do for beauty,' bemused Diana, shaking her head. An hour later, the two girls set off arm in arm in the dark towards the bus that would take them out to near the Croydon base, where a friend of Lizzie's had promised to pick them up and drop them out at Biggin Hill.

When they eventually found the dance hall at the camp, it was in full swing. A long brown wooden building practically pulsed with the noise that was coming through the doors, even with the blackout curtains they could see all the rows of windows around the outside were already steamed up with the heat in the room.

Inside, the dance hall was packed with service members and their girlfriends and dance partners, not just airmen but from all the fighting forces. Lizzie squeezed Diana's hand for reassurance as she looked around the room to see if she could find Jack, but it was so crowded she could hardly see anybody.

They pushed their way through the packed, sticky room, battling clouds of blue smoke and the smell of beer, then across the heaving dance floor towards a table. It was just as they reached it that somebody tapped Lizzie on the shoulder, and she spun round. It was Jack.

'I've been waiting for you,' he said, his smile lighting up his face. 'I was hoping you would come.'

'Of course,' said Lizzie returning the smile. She had forgotten just how handsome he was. 'This is my friend Diana. She thought she'd like to get away for a few hours and have some fun too.'

Diana nodded at Jack, and he smiled at her too. 'Well, I hope you'll save a dance for me, Diana, if you get a chance.'

'Of course,' she responded cordially.

'Let me get you both a drink,' he shouted as the band in the corner stopped playing and everyone around the room started clapping. They shouted back their orders, and Jack strode off to the bar. Sitting down at the table Diana stared at her friend, her eyes wide and her mouth open in mock exasperation.

'He is so handsome, Lizzie.'

'I know,' she responded with a tiny squeal, 'can you believe it?'

'He seems so charming, like the prince in a fairy tale.' They both roared with laughter.

As the music picked up its pace Lizzie sat tapping her foot to the music, surveying the hall; it was very warm inside but everyone was having such a good time. Dances were the one place they could relax and really enjoy themselves. The room was a long, narrow building similar to a Scout hut, with a brown linoleum floor and trestle tables. At the far end was a five-piece orchestra playing swing and a mixture of all the latest tunes. As people shuffled the best they could around the tightly packed floor, laughter and conversation filled the air with electricity. It felt so wonderful just to get away for a few hours, away from the intensity of war. The music stopped, couples left the floor and as the crowds parted Lizzie noticed her friend went pale.

'What is it Diana?'

'Across the room, I think I saw someone I know.' Lizzie looked across. At the bar was a group of NCOs smoking and joking with one another. One turned around, and next to her Diana drew in a breath.

'Who is it?' Lizzie was intrigued, Diana was blushing.

'Don't look over, it's a corporal I met on duty, Corporal Shelley, I lent him a mackintosh when he was soaking wet,' she hissed, not moving her lips.

Lizzie was amused; it was the first time she had seen Diana so unhinged.

'Well that doesn't sound too scandalous,' she giggled.

Surreptitiously Lizzie stole a glance and as if drawn by her gaze, he suddenly turned and noticed Diana, and his eyes lit up.

'Oh no, please don't come over. I'm so embarrassed,' Diana hissed again.

'What's wrong?' Lizzie was intrigued by her friend's reaction.

'You should have seen the way I looked the other night, I was a mess; surely he wouldn't recognize me.'

But apparently, he did, as, stabbing out his cigarette in an ashtray, he leant across and said something to his friend, which made the man look over at Diana, and smile. Then the corporal made his way across the dance floor towards their table.

Lizzie watched him approach as Diana squirmed by her side. He was about six foot tall, with thick brown wavy hair and brown eyes that looked kind. Arriving at their table, he smiled down at her friend. 'Aircraftwoman Downes, isn't it?'

'I don't have to salute you if I'm not in uniform, do I, Corporal Shelley?' Diana asked nervously.

He shook his head and stretched out his hand. 'No, and you can call me Len off duty.'

'I'm Diana,' she responded, taking it gingerly.

'Diana,' he said, rolling her name across his tongue. 'That's a beautiful name.'

'And this is my friend Lizzy,' she said quickly, apparently desperate to get the attention off herself.

Lizzy shook his hand and was thoroughly enjoying this. 'Would you like to join us?' she enquired, being mischievous.

Diana shot her friend a look.

'Thank you, I would love to,' he said, sitting down next to Diana. 'I was hoping I would see you again, Diana, just to make sure you didn't catch a cold.'

Diana shook her head. 'I'm amazed you even remember me.'

'You're very memorable; it's not often I get to meet a member of the fighting service in a nightie and curlers,' he quipped back with a cheeky grin.

Diana glowed as she attempted to laugh off her embarrassment.

Jack arrived back with the drinks and Lizzie seized her chance; she wanted to get Jack on the dance floor before the sirens sounded. Besides, she wanted to give Diana and Len a chance to get to know each other better.

'Come on, Jack, ask me to dance,' she said, jumping to her feet. Another big band number was in full swing, and he seemed more than happy to oblige. He was a good dancer, and as they circled the dance floor, she liked the feel of being in his arms. They chatted easily about everything, just as they had in the theatre, and whenever Lizzie looked over at Diana, she too seemed to be getting on quite well with her new acquaintance.

After they'd been around the floor a couple of times, and after a particularly fast quickstep, they decided to sit back down with Len and Diana. Len decided to buy them all a round and disappeared off to the bar. When he arrived back, Jack and Len got into a lively debate about the war and Lizzie grabbed Diana by the hand and whispered, 'I think we need to go to the toilet, don't you?'

Both girls got up. 'We're just going to powder our noses,' announced Lizzie with a smile, and they disappeared to the cloakroom.

Once they were inside, she turned to her friend in the mirror. 'Well, Diana, you are a sly fox. Who's that good-looking fellow?'

'Believe it or not, he's one of my superior officers. I can't believe that he even remembers me, let alone wants to sit and talk to me.'

The girls stared in the mirror as they reapplied their lipstick.

'He seems nice, a lot of fun.'

'So does Jack,' said Diana.

'At least this war is giving us the chance to meet people we'd have never met before,' said Lizzie, pressing her lips together.

Diana laughed. 'I'm definitely warming up to that part of it.'

Both the girls made their way back outside to enjoy their evening. They all danced till their feet hurt and were glad that Jerry came late that night. In fact, Lizzie and Jack made it all the way back to Julia's before the bombing started. Jack had borrowed a car from the base to drop Lizzie home.

As they drove through the dark streets together with just the pinhole of light the headlights projected with the blinds on, Lizzie couldn't help but stare at him. He was so good-looking it made her stomach cramp. But it wasn't just his looks that she found attractive, it was the way he treated her, the way he talked to her, as if she was the most important person in his world.

Arriving at Julia's, he escorted her to the doorstep.

'Thank you for coming tonight, I wasn't sure if you would.'

'Of course, I wouldn't let a friend down.'

He looked earnestly at her then. 'Is that how you see us, Lizzie, as friends?'

'Is that how *you* see us?' she responded, throwing the question back at him.

'Yes, but also so much more than that. From the minute I met you in that theatre, I felt a connection I couldn't really explain…' He paused and seemed to be struggling to find the right words. 'But I would love to… explore that.'

She smiled to herself. It was such a formal way to ask her to go out with him. He was always so confident and assured, she was interested to see him so tongue-tied around her in the intimacy of this moment.

'If you are asking me to be your girl, then the answer is yes.' She giggled, nervously.

A look of relief crossed his face and he drew himself closer to her, and even in the pitch black she could see the sincerity in his gaze as he studied her face. The attraction between them charged the air; he appeared to want to kiss her, but was nervous to make the first move. She slipped her arms around his neck to encourage him. That was all he needed; all at once his lips were upon hers. Soft and gentle but also with a depth of intensity. Lizzie had kissed before; she and Fergus had kissed often before they parted. But nothing prepared her for how this felt. It wasn't just the butterflies that were flip-flopping in her belly, or the wonderful scent of his aftershave or the incredible feeling of him so close to her, but there was a rightness between them she couldn't explain, a feeling of coming home. As though in this man's arms she could feel safe for the rest of her life.

Chapter Twenty-Six

Two days later, Lizzy looked at the blackened building and her heart sank. It would be a wild goose chase, trying to locate where the children from the orphanage were now and she had no way of knowing where to start. After she'd found out that St Barnabas had been moved, this had been the latest address she had found in the telephone directory. Though she assumed Annie might have already been adopted by now, she knew they would have records. Records that had probably been destroyed, because the address she was looking at was now a blackened shell, obviously bombed in the recent attack. As if to mock her, the sirens wailed into life. Hurriedly, Lizzie looked around her. She was in a part of town she didn't know and so she followed the running crowds as she rushed down into the bomb shelter that was the closest.

One hour later, Lizzie emerged from the underground and clambered up the steps. Her ears were still ringing, and her bones jarred. No matter how many times she went through this, she would never get used to it, even though now it was becoming a familiar event. It wasn't just the deafening explosions and concussive experience of the bombs dropping above her, but also the re-emerging into a world that was utterly changed. At some point every day she found herself heading for a shelter, then huddling, sometimes for hours, with a group of strangers as they all held their collective breath.

As furrowed brows and concerned eyes studied the ceiling with each new thundering crash above them, their thoughts were not only directed to the destruction being wrought outside but to absent loved ones. If they caught one another's eye in between bombardments as worried faces and nervous smiles swept the shelter, they didn't need words to know they were all wondering the same thing: was this unknown group of people the last they would see in this world?

Once the all-clear sounded, it was as though fresh air swept the room, and everybody could breathe easily again. But once they emerged, another world was waiting for them all above ground.

Now, in the street, Lizzie tried to find her equilibrium again; she was disorientated as she tried to navigate her way with so many buildings and landmarks now in rubble or on fire. More than anything, the heat and the dust and the debris still flying around presented so much continuous danger.

Wiping the back of her hand across her forehead, Lizzie could feel the crust of dirt that had already started to coat her face as she peered out into the smoky grey darkness. Concrete dust was swirling around her, the only illumination provided by the eerie glow of thousands of blazes haloed by the fiery fog. Working her way carefully through the debris, she coughed as the brick dust and smoke combined into a heavy dry powder that caught in the back of her throat. Tentatively moving forward, unable to see more than a few feet in front of her, she continued to peer through the smog as the high-pitched, repetitive, rolling screech of the all-clear competed with the jangling bells of fire engines and ambulances. The whole experience creating a surreal, but now daily occurrence. The constant bombing was now being called the Blitz, after the German word for lightning war, *Blitzkrieg*.

As she staggered forward, many buildings were still on fire, flames leaping into the air, some reaching over one hundred feet, their searing heat heightening an already fractious night. Around her, weary people were trying to make their own way the best they could, no doubt desperate to check on family, friends and property. In front of her, firefighters stumbled across the roads, clambering through the rubble and pulling their heavy hoses, calling urgent instructions to one another as they tried to do their duty. Moving forward, carefully, Lizzie's eyes began to adjust to the eerie atmosphere when something caught her eye.

In the middle of the road, a small figure stood stock-still, not moving or breathing, head tilted up to the sky. Lizzie stopped, drawn to the odd spectacle. Frantic people hurriedly pushed past the figure as they went on their way but no one seemed to see her, it was if she was not there. Lizzie was fascinated at how she could stand so perfectly still in the midst of so much activity, seemingly paralysed, unaware of the danger all around her. Lizzie scrambled towards her to see if she could help her and realized with surprise that it wasn't a short adult, it was a young child, right in the centre of the road, dressed in a blue flannel nightie, her feet bare and dirt-spattered. Her blonde flyaway hair was golden, aglow from the fires that lit her up from behind. Lizzie looked around for her parents, but no one seemed to be searching for her, and she seemed to be entirely, completely alone. Stumbling over the bricks of what used to be an old church building, Lizzie reached her side and noticed that the girl's eyes were firmly closed, her head tilted up, her palms facing upwards. If she'd been in church, you would have thought she was praying.

Lizzie reached out to her tentatively. 'Hello there,' she said in a quiet, calm voice. Hard for her to achieve when all around them, the aftermath of the bomb was creating hysteria.

Slowly, the young girl's eyes opened, her blonde eyelashes blinking away the coat of dust that swirled around the two of them. Seeing Lizzie in front of her, her eyes widened and then she threw her arms around her waist, taking her breath away and almost knocking her down to the ground. She gripped Lizzie so tightly, she was afraid the young girl would lose sensation in her arms. A lump caught in her throat. She must be frightened to death. Taking hold of the tiny fingers and gently peeling them away from her waist, Lizzie bent down to talk to her eye to eye.

'What's your name?' she asked gently, trying to keep her tone light and sound as English as she possibly could.

But the girl seemed to like the way Lizzie spoke and cocked her head to the side like a dog listening to the way she was speaking.

'Is your mummy or your daddy about?' continued Lizzie, asking quietly. Still, the girl didn't answer. 'My name's Lizzie,' she continued, and with that, the tiny child threw her arms around Lizzie's neck and wrapped her feet around Lizzie's waist, burying her head firmly into her shoulder.

Lizzie could hardly leave her now, she thought, as she heaved herself to her feet and, hugging her close, she started walking. With the little girl wrapped around her body, she scanned the street again, to see if anybody was looking for her or a house that she may have come from. Lizzie was in a part of town she didn't know, quite a way from Julia's house. Holding the little one in her arms she stumbled up and down the street, trying to figure out what to do.

As she did so, she felt fear tug at her heart. Virtually nothing was left standing in the road she was walking up and down. Wherever the child had come from obviously didn't exist any more. She must be terrified.

An air-raid warden rushed across the road in front of them. 'Excuse me,' Lizzie shouted. 'I found this little girl. What should I do?'

Barely acknowledging her, he shook his head. 'Oh, love, I can't stop and chat. There's too much work to do tonight. For all we know, Jerry'll be back later. It would be best if you took her to the Red Cross. They'll take her off your hands.'

Lizzie felt the small person grip her even tighter, and from a head buried into her shoulder, she heard a gasped sob.

Lizzie slowly rubbed the tiny back, cooing to her. 'It's going to be all right. Don't worry. You're safe with me.'

As she held her close, Lizzie's thoughts returned to the daughter she'd given up all those years before.

She'd have been about this age, she thought. This was what it would have felt like if she'd stayed with her. She'd have hugged Lizzie like this, her tiny little body wrapped around her with her heart fluttering ten to the dozen against Lizzie's breast. This was what it would have been like to hold her child, to be a mum.

All at once, she fought back her own emotion. She was being sentimental. More than likely, Lizzie's child had her own adopted mother now. Annie was living somewhere lovely, having an incredible life, she hoped. As she looked all around her at the devastation, that dream started to waver. The hope that her daughter was happy was what had kept her sane all of these years. Helped assuage her guilt. But how could Annie be safe in all of this? What if her own daughter was wandering the streets somewhere in a nightie looking for someone to take care of her? The thought was too difficult to even contemplate and Lizzie swallowed down the acidic pain that rose from her stomach and stung the back of her throat. She had never felt more determined to find Annie at all costs.

As Lizzie continued to stumble through the streets, every police officer or warden she met was busy. They didn't have time for her, so without any other option, Lizzie decided to take the child home. At least in the warm there she could give her something to eat and drink, and she could get some sleep while Lizzie worked out what to do with her.

Walking the two miles back to Julia's, even though she was tiny, waif-like, she grew heavier as Lizzie carried her. As she finally stumbled down Julia's path, Lizzie hoped that Agnes wasn't watching her through the window. She had already had one or two interactions with the older woman and could tell by the way Agnes looked down her nose at her that she didn't approve of Julia's friends, and Lizzie didn't need any kind of confrontation tonight. But next door was quiet, with no twitch of the curtains as she opened Julia's gate and it creaked on its hinges.

Inside the house, it was empty and dark; Julia must be working late. Lizzie took the little girl into the front room and, laying her down on the sofa, noticed that she had dropped off to sleep. She turned on a table lamp: in the light, Lizzie could get a really good look at the child's face. She was cherub-like, with a small, round face, red heart-shaped lips, and strawberry blonde hair that curtained her dirt-spattered features.

All at once, the door jangled with the sound of keys, and Diana walked in behind her. Julia had given her an extra key in case she wanted to stay the night in her own room. Lizzie heard her kicking off her shoes, hanging her tin helmet up on the hook, and shaking out her dust-filled headscarf wrapped around her hair underneath.

'Anybody in?' she called out.

Lizzie met her in the hallway and explained the situation in hushed tones as Diana pulled off her heavy air-force coat.

Following Lizzie into the front room, Diana stared at the new arrival. 'Look at her,' she exclaimed in a whisper. 'Poor thing. Someone must be looking for her. There was no one around who knew her parents?'

Lizzie shook her head. 'It was as if she just appeared there out of thin air.'

The two of them tiptoed into the kitchen to make a drink.

'What are you going to do?'

'I'm going to go to the authorities tomorrow,' Lizzie responded. 'They were too busy this evening.'

Lizzie felt a drop in her heart as she outlined her plans to Diana. For just a minute, just a tiny sliver of a second before Diana had arrived, she'd pondered that maybe it would be possible for the child to stay with her, but of course, that was ridiculous. She had a family somewhere, no doubt desperate to get her back.

As the tea brewed, Lizzie covered the tiny feather-like body with a blanket and contemplated the world they now lived in, where along with bombs, little girls dropped out of the sky.

*

The next morning when Lizzie woke up, she could feel the tiny body curled in front of her. She had tried to settle the young girl in Tom's bed, and Julia had even given her some of his toys for comfort, but in the middle of the night, Lizzie had felt the girl crawling into the bed beside her, and she hadn't had the heart to take her back. Now she looked down at her, breath rising and falling in an easy rhythm, wisps of fair hair grazing her scarlet cheeks. Lizzie was in awe of the innocence of her, the pure perfection of her tiny features. It would be hard to take her to the Red Cross today, but Lizzie had to do what was right. A parent could be heart-sick and looking for her, and Lizzie knew how it felt to live with that kind of anguish.

Once she'd got her up and dressed, Julia gave her some of Maggie's old clothes, and they had walked to the local Red Cross building. All the way there the wide-eyed child had clung to her, a tiny hand tight and clammy in Lizzie's own. As she waited her turn, Lizzie looked around at all the people in line with her. Many looked bereft or heartbroken; she knew a lot of them were there looking for news of a loved one that was missing.

When she finally got to the front of the queue, the Red Cross volunteer had informed her that this wasn't the right building, that she needed to be taken to another place across town where they were taking in the orphans. Just hearing the word 'orphan' made something in Lizzie's stomach tighten. Maybe it was because of her own experience with her daughter, or perhaps it was just the thought of placing this precious little child into a system she wasn't even sure could really support all she needed right now.

'It's the best we can do until her parents are found,' the Red Cross worker informed her, looking down at her charge. 'What's your name, dear?' asked the woman in a chirpy, friendly manner.

The girl's eyes just widened with fear and she buried her head into Lizzie's skirt.

'She hasn't spoken since I found her,' explained Lizzie in a whisper, smoothing down the mane of blonde flyaway hair.

'Poor little thing,' responded the woman, shaking her head and pursing her ruby red lips. 'We have two or three of them a day, you know, children, waifs and strays turning up lost. But most find their parents.' She tried to reassure Lizzie. 'She seems to be attached to you though,'

Lizzie didn't like the sound of the word 'most', and suddenly she felt even more connection and obligation to this little lost soul. She thought of her own daughter out there somewhere amongst all this terror and hoped that she wasn't wandering about looking for a place to belong, being labelled a waif and stray.

After they left the building, she had walked them to the park, and Lizzie realized she needed to find out the child's name. She hadn't managed to get any words out of her, even though both she and Julia had tried to coax her over breakfast, asking her what she wanted to eat. The child had just shaken her head, and eventually, Julia had managed to get her to eat some toast and jam.

After she had played on the slide and Lizzie had pushed her on the swings for a while, Lizzie went to sit on a park bench, and the child followed her, sitting close by her side. Lizzie smiled down and stroked the tiny cheek.

'You know, I'm going to need to know your name if I am to help you.'

The tiny face tipped up to her own, eyes wide.

'Do you think you could tell me what you are called?'

The little girl continued to stare up at Lizzie as tears formed in the corners of her eyes, and Lizzie didn't want to push her to speak.

'How about if we play a game? You can trace the first letter of your name in my hand – do you know your letters?' Her eyes widened which gave Lizzie hope.

She looked down at Lizzie's open palm, watching with interest as Lizzie started to trace letters with her finger.

'You see? My name is Lizzie, and it begins with an "L".' Lizzie traced the letter L. The young girl was fascinated. 'The second letter is "I", and then I have a "Z", and another "Z", and an "I", and an "E". Do you think you could write your name in my hand?'

The little girl looked hopeful. She slowly took Lizzie's hand, and with feather-like fingers she started to trace the first letter, A. 'A?' said Lizzie as she began to try out different names. She caught her breath. Could it be Annie? Her own daughter?

'Is your name Annie?' she asked breathlessly. The little girl shook her head, and Lizzie felt an overwhelming disappointment. There had been a tiny part of her that had hoped this had been some sort of miracle. The sort you saw in movies and read about in magazines, that brought about happy endings.

'Why don't you start with the next letter?' Slowly her tiny finger traced the letter, B.

'A, B. Abbie? Abigail? Is your name Abigail?' The girl slowly started to nod her head. 'Your name's Abigail? How about your last name?' Abigail just shook her head and looked confused as she stared out across the park; maybe it was a hard name to spell, Lizzie reflected. Whatever it was, it appeared that her first name was all she was willing to share, and Lizzie wanted to give her some time. 'Well, Abigail, I'm glad that you told me your name. Now we don't need to be strangers any more.' She stared down at her tiny charge, who looked up and, for the first time since she'd found her, smiled.

Chapter Twenty-Seven

Lizzie woke up early the next day and looked across again at the tiny person in her bed. The sun was just starting to creep its way through a gap in the blackout curtains, and it had formed a triangle of light across Abigail's face. The night before, Lizzie had tried again to put her in Tom's bed and had even read her a story, but at two o'clock in the morning, she'd heard the patter of tiny feet and once again felt the bed dip as the waif-like child crawled in beside her, her little arm hooking itself around Lizzie's waist, her blonde head burying into her chest. Lizzie's heart melted. She'd been through so much trauma. And Abigail so obviously needed the comfort. She would never get tired of watching her sleep, the wisps of blonde hair pressed onto her hot red cheeks, her chest rising and falling with a little whiffly snore. It was going to be hard to take her again today and give her up to the Red Cross orphanage, but she kept reminding herself that Abigail must have a family and people that loved her and somewhere out there somebody was looking for her and was heartbroken. And more than anything, Lizzie knew what it felt like to have your child torn from your life. It left an empty space in your arms that could never be filled.

The night before, they'd bathed her and put her to bed in one of Maggie's old nightdresses. She seemed well-cared for and fed, just totally alone, but no matter how much they tried to coax her, Abigail didn't seem to want to speak.

After she'd fallen asleep in Tom's bed that night, she and Julia had stood at the bedroom door, whispering from one to the other as they watched her slumber. 'So sad that she is so traumatized that she can't even tell us anything about herself,' sighed Julia.

'At least we know her name is Abigail,' whispered back Lizzie, trying to hold back the emotion in her voice. 'I had a friend with that name. It means "source of joy".'

'Source of joy, it suits her,' Julia mused quietly, closing the bedroom door.

As they crept carefully down the stairs, the house was pitch dark with its blackout curtains in place but so far there hadn't been a raid that evening. In the front room Julia had the wireless turned down low and Vera Lynn was crooning out 'Yours' and filling the darkness. In the kitchen she turned on the low light that was permitted and Julia made them both a cup of cocoa. A rare treat, and a gift from her supervisor, as they huddled around the table to continue their conversation.

'I know I have to take her to the authorities tomorrow and hopefully, they'll find her parents,' Lizzie surmised reluctantly.

'Such a strange time we're living in,' reflected Julia, shaking her head, as she took a sip of her drink. 'Everybody I know has sent away their children and so many have even had their animals put down. And now children are turning up alone. With this relentless bombing, night after night... so many beautiful buildings destroyed, so many people lost.'

Lizzie sighed. 'I have this terrible feeling that her parents may have been killed that night in the bombing. All the buildings on the street where I found her were flattened, Julia; there wasn't a house standing. I don't even know how she made it out unscathed. She barely had a mark on her, and she couldn't have walked that far in her bare feet. I just keep thinking how hard all this must be for her and I don't want her to go through any more heartache.'

Deep in thought, Julia drew in a long slow breath.

'I had a letter from Tom this morning,' she shared in a halting voice. Going into her kitchen drawer, she pulled it out and placed it on the table for Lizzie to read. Lizzie unfolded the wrinkled blue paper.

Written in big looped writing with the 'Y' back to front were the words 'Dear Mummy.'

It continued, 'We are all right, and Auntie Rosalyn is very good to us, but, Mummy, I miss you very very much.' And then he'd drawn a sad face with a tear on it.

Lizzie put a hand to her chest. 'Oh, Julia.'

Her friend shook her head despondently. 'He feels everything. Tom worries about everybody. And I hoped he'd settled by now, but I can tell he's really pining for home. But I can't bring them back to this, can I, Lizzie? I hope I did the right thing, sending them away. Every single night when the bombs drop, I thank God they're somewhere where they're safe. But it is so hard. I miss them so much, I just didn't think it would be like this.' Julia welled up with the brimming emotion inside her.

Lizzie reached out and took her friend's hand. 'Of course you did the right thing, and none of us could have prepared for what this was going to feel like. How could we know what it was going to be like to have bombs drop out of the sky every day? When I left Scotland, I was naive. I wanted to do something for our country, for the soldiers away fighting. I knew there was a chance Hitler might invade here but up till then the danger all sounded so remote and far-off across the sea in Europe. Never in a million years did I expect to have bombs dropping on London night after night like this. Only being able to sleep for a few hours at a time in our beds or cramped in a shelter. Watching a city turn into rubble and hearing the roll call every day of all the people who have died. But what it has shown me is that strength is built by doing; it's not something you're born with, strong is what you become by getting up after being knocked down day after day. Even for your children; they are becoming strong in their own way, too.'

Julia nodded, wiping a tear from her cheek. 'I hope you're correct, because there don't seem to be any right choices. Everything has its costs. If I brought Tom back here, I would worry about him every single day. But if I leave him there, I'm worried he'll continue to pine for home. I have to do what feels right to me, and what feels right to me is him being safe in the country. And I just hope this war doesn't take too long and break his heart.

'I keep hoping that in a year or so, we could be in a whole new situation. We'll have defeated this awful enemy, and they can start their lives again, and this will just be a tiny moment in time for them. I think you should do what feels right with Abigail. Do what feels right to you. Lizzie, she's really fond of you. And if she has lost her parents, it might make sense for her to stay with you for a little while until she feels better. I can't imagine if the authorities do take her that it's going to be any better than being here with us. We can all take care of her between us when I'm back from work, and there's always Agnes to help out. As much as she's a worrier, she adores children, and then you can see her every night when you get back. You could even enrol her in the small school down the road for a few months until the Christmas holidays. It might do her good to make some friends, and maybe she'll start to talk.'

'Well, let's see what tomorrow brings,' said Lizzie, shaking her head. 'I'll take her to the Red Cross orphanage because maybe her family is waiting for her and all of this will be sorted out. But thank you, Julia. Thank you for offering her a home here.'

'Of course,' said Julia. 'You and Diana are like family to me now. I miss John and my children with all my heart, and my goodness, I was lonely before I met you. You have been both such a rock through all this madness.'

As if on cue the air-raid siren screeched into life and they both sighed deeply. Julia put the cups in the sink and prepared the bags they kept packed by the back door while Lizzie went upstairs to get Abigail to take her to the shelter.

Lizzie thought about all this as she lay there in bed the next morning, and as she looked over at this little cherub, she knew with a sinking heart she'd have to be prepared to give her away today.

As she dressed, Lizzie tried once more to coax her to speak, asking her what she would like for breakfast or whether she'd like a toy or something to drink. Abigail just stared up at her mutely, blinking wide blue eyes through her blonde hair.

After they finished breakfast, Julia offered to come with Lizzie to the Red Cross station, as she wasn't working that day. Getting their coats on and picking up their gas masks, they made their way down to the address that she'd been given by the Red Cross office the day before.

Nothing could have prepared them for what would greet them: lines and lines of people all looking for loved ones or dropping off children. It was so busy. They had to stay standing in line for two hours before they finally got to the front of the queue, where a rather tired-looking woman with a curt attitude looked at the three of them. Lizzie explained the situation, and peering down at Abigail, the woman sucked in a breath and blew out her cheeks.

'We have so many of them,' she sniffed. 'God, I don't know how we're going to feed half of them. Fill out this form, and if you want to leave her here, you can sit her on that bench over there.'

Lizzie looked across the room where a whole line of labelled children were sitting on a bench. She couldn't imagine leaving Abigail over there and just walking away.

Sensing her horror, the woman spoke again. 'It's the best we can do,' she retorted defensively. 'I know it's not ideal. On the other hand, if you fill in this form, tell us about the little girl, where you found her, et cetera, you could take her home, temporarily. Then if somebody's looking for her, they can contact you as long as we have a record of her and you don't mind keeping her for a couple of days while they're digging people out or identifying people in hospital. And we'll keep looking for her parents.

'Honestly love,' she said, leaning forward and lowering her voice to a whisper, 'it's a much better idea than putting her in the home here. The people are kind, but we're really overcrowded. It's an unfortunate time for everyone at the moment, and the children are crying all the time.'

Lizzie looked in shock across at Julia, who seemed to make the decision for them.

'Thank you very much. We'll be taking Abigail back with us. We'll fill in the form.'

'Best option,' agreed the woman. 'Here's your form. Fill it in and leave it over there in the basket.'

Julia and Lizzie moved aside, Abigail gripping Lizzie's hand so tightly as she glared at the line of children sat on the bench; she had obviously been wondering if that was to be her fate. Lifting her into her arms, Lizzie kissed her on the cheek.

'Don't worry, Abigail, you're going to stay with me for a while. At Auntie Julia's. We're not going to leave you here.'

Abigail buried her head into Lizzie's shoulder, and it was as if her whole body relaxed; she must have been so tense and worried. Filling in the form, they got out of there as fast as they could and made their way back to Julia's.

On the way home, Lizzie used some of her rations to get Abigail some sweets, and she started to cheer up as she skipped along, sucking a lemon sherbet hand in hand with Lizzie all the way back to the house.

'Are you sure about this, Julia? It is a big commitment.'

'There's no choice,' she responded, decisively. 'You couldn't have left her there. That was awful. I'm sure they're doing their best, but that would be so heartbreaking for her, particularly if you know they can't find anybody,' Julia whispered to Lizzie.

They settled Abigail back at home, and Agnes came round with a jigsaw puzzle. It was the only time that Julia ever saw her smile, when children were about. And she and Abigail started to work on it as Julia shepherded Lizzie to the door and off to work that afternoon.

'She'll be fine; we will keep her busy.'

All the way to work on the bus, Lizzie thought about Abigail and the fact that she'd lost her own little girl and that now she'd found this one. It seemed like a strange twist of fate in her life. However, the thing she was struggling with the most was that she knew she was getting really attached to Abigail. Lizzie knew on some level her maternal instinct was kicking in, but she couldn't seem to help it. She reminded herself they'd probably find her parents and that she should just enjoy her for as long as she could; and at least until then, Abigail would have a safe place to live, a warm bed, food, and the little family of women to take care of her.

Chapter Twenty-Eight

After the dance Jack saw Lizzie briefly at Kenley one afternoon and he invited her to the cinema. A Charlie Chaplin film was playing, and they both needed to laugh. The relentless bombing campaign from the Nazis was not stopping, and it had now been weeks of being attacked every single night. Nearly two months, in fact, of bombs dropping on London, sometimes more than two or three times a day. And almost every day, Lizzie had been in the operations room and Jack had been in the sky, fighting for Britain. So they were both glad of the distraction.

As they sat down to watch the film, Jack reached across and took Lizzie's hand and gently kissed it. She loved being with him, and she knew he felt the same way because whenever he looked at her, the depth of feeling in his eyes was so evident.

They were about halfway through the film when Lizzie, skimming the room and enjoying the communal laughter, caught sight of someone across the aisle, someone familiar to her. Lizzie turned back to focus on the film again, trying to recall who it might be. She looked across again. The memory of her face was strong but entirely out of place to her here, as if it didn't fit in this part of her life. She was from somewhere else, but she also knew it was somebody important to her.

Lizzie tried to comb through her memory of all the people she'd met since she'd arrived in London – people at camp, different service members, or people she had met with Julia or with Diana – but no one was coming to mind. All of a sudden it hit her, and it was like running into a wall of pain as her past emotions slammed into her, and she had to hold her breath to stop herself from crying out with the realization.

She looked across the aisle again to confirm her suspicions. As the flickering of the black and white pictures blazed across the woman's face, she laughed again and glanced randomly in her direction, and Lizzie knew. All the blood felt as if it was draining from her body, and what replaced it was a cascade of ice-cold water. She was sure. That woman was one of the nurses who had been there when they had taken her daughter from her, her baby, so long ago. This young nurse had been training at the time and Lizzie had seen compassion in her eyes.

All at once, with a shudder, her thoughts returned to that night. The oppressive darkness in the room that hung with the sweet and sticky heat from a night of summer labour, and the eerie quietness following hours of prolonged pain and screaming agony. Her head on the pillow as she attempted to catch her breath, her hair matted to the sides of her face, sweat dripping between her breasts, her emotions a mixture of relief and deep, deep sorrow. Lizzie remembered her whole body shaking and her throat red raw. The exhaustion and the tearing pain still ripping through her body had been nothing compared to the wrenching she'd felt as they'd taken that baby away from her.

But this was the kind nurse, the one who had allowed Lizzie to hold her daughter briefly, even though it was against the rules. When the senior nurse had stepped out for a minute to talk to a doctor, Lizzie had pleaded with this young woman. She'd just wanted to hold her daughter for a second. Eventually, the young nurse had relented, and when Lizzie had looked into that little face, felt the warmth of the tiny bundle in her arms, something had happened in her heart, something that she didn't have words for. Something that had left a longing inside her ever since. In that moment, when she'd held her daughter, there had been a rightness, a completeness, a connection that was stronger than she had ever felt in any form before. And even though Lizzie knew everything they had told her about being young and how she had her whole life ahead of her, it was as though she could have thrown all of that out of the window at that moment.

If she hadn't been so physically broken, and in so much pain, she would have jumped out of bed and run away with her baby, run until she'd found a safe place to hide. But she was in agony, her limbs still shaking violently, and she'd needed stitches. On returning, the older nurse had snatched the baby from Lizzie's arms and, with a look of disgust at her young protégée, had marched out of the door, taking the biggest part of Lizzie's heart with her. This young woman had lingered at the door saying in a whisper, 'I promise you we will take really good care of her.' But when Lizzie had howled in response, the woman had bowed her head with sadness and disappeared from the room.

Back in the cinema, Lizzie shivered again with the memory and noticed her hand was shaking slightly. Jack noticed too. ·

'Are you cold?' he whispered into her ear.

She nodded, not wanting to let him into her private thoughts right at that moment. And he slipped his arm around her shoulder and gathered her in close to warm her.

Lizzie tried to concentrate on the screen in front of her, but knew she had to talk to this woman. It was agony as she waited, biting her lip, until the end of the film, lost in distant thoughts and pain. As soon as the lights came up and people started to filter out, she jumped to her feet. Jack glanced up at her in surprise.

'There is someone I need to speak to over there,' she mumbled to him, as he looked at her, puzzled.

And not waiting for a response, Lizzie stumbled out of the row and tried to find the woman, but she'd slipped out quickly and was already further up the stairs and Lizzie couldn't get through. She took a mental picture of everything the woman was wearing so she could find her in the crowd again. In the foyer, she was hurrying to the door when Lizzie called out to her, 'Excuse me, miss!'

Many people in the foyer turned around, including the woman she was following, and in seeing Lizzie, she didn't stop but hastily left the building. Lizzie fought her way through the heaving crowd, wondering, had she known who she was? Was that why she'd left so quickly?

When Lizzie finally got out onto the street and looked around, the woman had vanished. She ran up the road to see if she could see her anywhere and raced back down the other way, but she had disappeared. As she made her way back into the foyer, Jack came over to her.

'Is everything all right, Lizzie?'

'I just thought I saw someone I knew. I really need to find her.'

Jack furrowed his brow with concern. 'Are you sure you're all right? You look so pale.'

She nodded. 'This person's just very important to me.'

He smiled and put his arm around her shoulder. 'Then let's look again together. We'll find her.'

She looked in tea shops and up and down the streets for a while but it was evident that the woman had gone. As she strode briskly alongside Jack, hot tears stung Lizzie's cheeks and she felt the wretchedness of her loss all over again.

Jack noticed and took hold of her shoulders and turned her to face him. 'Lizzie, what is it?'

She shook her head and buried it into his shoulder and started to sob.

He enveloped her in a hug and held her tightly, gently rocking her and whispering words of assurance into her ear. But she just knew she couldn't risk telling him. He was starting to mean so much to her and she didn't want to risk losing him. When she finally managed to pull herself together, he gently wiped the tears from her cheeks with his thumb, the concern obvious in his eyes.

'Do you want to talk about this, Lizzie?'

She shook her head. 'Maybe one day, but not now.'

Chapter Twenty-Nine

Len and Diana started seeing one another regularly. As they were living on the same base it was easy to arrange. He would drop by for a walk with her if they were both off duty or she would invite him to eat with her and the other girls in the canteen. He was very popular as he would chat easily with them and make them all laugh. But then the other WAAFs would politely excuse themselves after a while with a knowing nod and smile in Diana's direction.

He was sat finishing a plate of scrambled egg one afternoon as she was on washing up duty when he mentioned casually he would love to take Diana home to meet his mother who lived in Bow.

'She's quite a character, my mum,' he added with a smile. 'I think the two of you would get on great.'

Diana stopped drying the cup she had in her hand as a thousand thoughts flew through her mind. Did this mean something? Was this Len's way of saying he wanted to take this relationship further? She thought about Lizzie and Jack and how fast that relationship seemed to be moving. And she and Len hadn't even kissed yet. But Diana wasn't like Lizzie, she didn't let her heart rule her head and she just wasn't sure that she wanted to get too serious too quickly. She adored Len, he was funny and friendly and great company. But he didn't wear his heart on his sleeve as Jack so obviously did with his love for Lizzie; Len was quieter, more controlled emotionally, hard to read sometimes. All at once, the picture of her father sat in his chair the day she left swam into her mind, so sad, so lost that his daughter was leaving, imploring her to settle down with someone close by, someone from Birmingham. What if this was no more than a fling for Len? Something to pass the time during the dark days of war. And if this was more than that, how could she bridge her two worlds: this new world she was living in, and the world she had left behind? Len must have taken her contemplative pause as reluctance.

'We don't have to go this evening if you would rather stay here. We could go another time.'

Diana turned and smiled; maybe she was just thinking too much about it all. 'No, tonight is perfect, give me a chance to powder my nose and I'll meet you outside in a little while.'

When they arrived at the tiny, tidy house an hour later, the front door was already open and, in the kitchen, a petite, buoyant woman with a mass of dark brown curls and lively hazel eyes greeted her, telling Diana not to stand on ceremony and to call her Amy. She didn't seem a bit put out with Len turning up with his new friend unannounced. In fact, within minutes she had handed a tea towel to Diana and guided her to a pile of washing up that needed drying. Diana felt very comfortable in this warm bright room with Len's energetic mother, who started recalling for her son all the activities of her neighbours.

Within ten minutes of arriving at her house, a face appeared around the kitchen door.

'A treat for you, Amy,' said a perky cockney voice. A man with twinkling eyes and a flat cap came into the kitchen, placing two pears into the older woman's outstretched hand.

'Where did you get those from, Ron?' Amy asked, one hand on her hip as she eyed him suspiciously.

'If you don't ask, I won't tell,' he joked with her. 'See you later.' He nodded and then he was gone.

Five minutes later, somebody else appeared with a joke and a story and then another person to update her on a child in the neighbourhood who had been ill. Then one returning a borrowed plate, another with some seeds. Diana watched in bewilderment as one person after another funnelled in and out of the house, which was a constant hive of activity.

Len's mother seemed to know the whole neighbourhood, and they all seemed to come via her house on the way to wherever they were going.

As the kitchen filled and emptied, Len introduced Diana to numerous people, uncle this and auntie that. Many, she suspected, weren't even really related. Len seemed to know all of them by name, and they all chatted in a happy, carefree way. Diana watched him: Len was so comfortable with people. He was kind and funny as he joked with them all and was so thoughtful with his mother, helping her whenever he could. However, Amy was fiercely independent, with tireless energy as she moved around the kitchen with such speed it made Diana dizzy. When Diana had a chance to chat to Len alone, she asked who everybody was.

'It's my mum,' he said with a smile. 'She just draws people. She knows everybody, and they all know her.'

Diana thought about her own family. Because of her dad's illness after the Great War, there was an unwritten rule about people coming over. Her mother didn't want too many people in the house in case somebody popped a cork or cracked a loud joke and set her dad's nerves on edge. Also, he wasn't always good at talking to people any more with the weakness in his chest. He couldn't speak comfortably for very long, and it created a void in any conversation he was having.

Her home life was the direct opposite of the way Len had grown up. They'd both grown up as only children, but Len had lived in this revolving front door of a life with numerous friends and family sharing the same space, and she'd been brought up in a loving, but much more solitary environment. Amy seemed to know everyone by name and was continually feeding people. Where she was getting the food from, Diana wasn't sure, but people seemed more than happy to repay her kindness if the pears were anything to go by.

After a while, Amy pulled on her coat and said, 'Come on, let's go and get a drink.' Off they streamed to the local pub where the same thing happened all over again, as Amy made her rounds in the room, Len behind her, and Diana tottering along behind them both, meeting what felt like hundreds of new people. Everybody eyed Diana with interest and smiled knowingly at Len, who seemed more than proud to show her off to his friends.

'This is my... friend, Diana,' he would announce.

Not 'girlfriend' Diana noted with a little disappointment, feeling the wariness of earlier return.

'She's down from Birmingham, working on the barrage balloons.'

People would nod their heads with admiration and appreciation as they shook her hand warmly.

Finally, Amy settled down at what was obviously her usual table, and it wasn't long before one of her many friends was on the piano, and the whole table joined in singing old-time music-hall songs. Others started to get up and dance around the room, hitching skirts onto their hips, some even shuffling around in carpet slippers as they crooned and circled to tunes about coppers and chorus girls.

Diana just watched in amazement. She loved the camaraderie they all seemed to have with one another. The love they had for each other; it was contagious. But did Len just see her as someone to add to their tribe? Another friendly face in their crowd?

Len whispered in her ear, 'Not too much for you, is it, Diana? They can be a bit much when you first meet them all.'

Diana shook her head. 'No, I think it's wonderful. I'm so glad that your mother has so many people that care about her, particularly as she lost your dad in the last war.'

Diana thought about Agnes and how angry and upset she'd been about her own husband's death, how it created so much bitterness in her, and Amy was the opposite. She hadn't let it keep her down, and now she was the life and soul of her own party.

On the way home, Len told her hysterical stories about many of the people they had met, but she noticed he didn't take her hand, and when she got back that evening, he didn't offer to kiss her goodnight, just gave her a friendly hug.

All these things reinforced her concerns. Was he just shy? Or was it nothing more for him than friendship? As she bumped along on the truck later that evening to set up the balloon for the night, she listened to the other girls around her talking of their own romantic endeavours. The war seemed to have a way of making so many relationships more intense; as they faced life and death every day, people moved more quickly, like Lizzie and Jack.

Also, some of them talked about the heartache from meeting soldiers who viewed the war as a good opportunity to meet women. Diana kept quiet as she listened to both sides, not sure about where her friendship with Len fitted in. Was she simply someone he saw to spend time with on lonely nights or did this mean more to him? She needed to know soon, because the longer this continued the more that was at stake for her. Even in holding back her feelings, she was starting to care deeply for him and she did not want to get her heart broken.

Chapter Thirty

When Julia arrived at the War Office on 9 November, the mood at Whitehall was sombre. She'd picked up a newspaper on the way in to work, and walking into the bunker, the air was thick with grief. Stephanie was already in and at her desk.

'Did you hear about Mr Chamberlain?'

Julia nodded, showing her the headline on the paper under her arm.

Carol slid in behind her, glancing at Julia's paper. 'Awful, isn't it?' she said, pushing a platinum curl out of her eyes. 'Didn't think he would go so quickly.'

Sally arrived in the bunker, her face red from rushing and out of breath.

'Did you hear about the former prime minister?'

All the girls acknowledged they had.

'It's a sad day,' Sally sighed as she uncovered her typewriter.

'Anyone know when the funeral will take place?' asked Carol.

'They'll probably keep it a secret,' responded Stephanie, practically, and Julia sat down at her desk.

They'd all known that Neville Chamberlain had cancer, but it still came as such a shock that he was dead. It wasn't long before Julia's boss found her.

'Julia, the prime minister wants to see you in his office.'

Julia nodded and picked up her typewriter; she had been expecting it. Churchill would probably want her to type the eulogy. Following Mrs Scriber to the office, she knocked on Churchill's door and his gruff voice called out to her to enter. Inside, he wasn't seated at his desk as she had expected, but she saw through ribbons of wafting blue smoke that he was sitting up in bed, still in his pyjamas, breakfast tray in front of him. His glasses were perched on the end of his nose as he perused his vast collection of newspapers and finished up what was not his first glass of Scotch, by the looks of the bottle.

'Come in, girl, come in,' his gravelly voice called out to her as she made her way into her position at a table near his bed. This arrangement wasn't unusual. She'd heard from the other girls that they'd all had to do this once or twice, type for him while he was still in bed, but it still felt awkward to her. The two of them squeezed into this intimate space, that still had the odour of stale air from being slept in swirling around it.

He lay back on his pillow and stared at the ceiling, inhaling a deep draw from his cigar then slowly blowing out more blue smoke around the small room, which made Julia's eyes water as she set up her typewriter. She was getting less nervous around him after doing this numerous times. However, the smoke still made her nauseous.

'Very sad business, Julia. Very sad.'

'It is, sir. Mr Chamberlain was a good man.'

'Didn't deserve it. Served his country well,' added Churchill, wistfully.

'Yes, sir, he did.' She rolled in her papers and carbon and sat with her fingers poised above the typewriter keys.

'Got to think of a lot of nice things to say about him now for the funeral. We didn't always get on, but I had a great deal of respect for the former prime minster.'

'Yes, sir. Of course.'

Churchill shook his head. As she waited for him to start, Julia thought about what she knew about Neville Chamberlain. She knew that he'd been opposed to the war, had wanted appeasement, pursuing talks with Mussolini, the Italian dictator, to try and bring about a peaceful solution. He had presented some of the same arguments when she had taken notes in the war room before they had bombed Berlin. She also knew that the king had offered him the Order of the Garter, the highest British honour that could be bestowed. But Chamberlain had refused, saying he'd prefer to die plain Mr Chamberlain, like his father before him, rather than being adorned with a title.

But everyone knew he'd been ill. The last time she'd seen him had been on 19 September when he was leaving London. He had come down to the bunker to speak to Churchill, and she'd passed him in the hallway. He hadn't looked well then, pale and thin with hollowed-out cheeks. He'd looked like he'd been in pain, half the man he used to be. He had given his resignation on 22 September, and she knew that Churchill had wanted him to stay on after being prime minister to supervise the work on the home front. But he'd just not been well enough, and now he was gone. Another significant loss for their country.

Churchill's voice brought Julia back into the present moment. As she began to type, she was struck by one particular passage:

'Whatever else history may or may not say about these terrible, tremendous years, we can be sure that Neville Chamberlain acted with perfect sincerity according to his lights and strove to the utmost of his capacity and authority, which were powerful, to save the world from the awful, devastating struggle in which we are now engaged. This alone will stand him in good stead as far as what is called the verdict of history is concerned.'

She wished with a saddened heart the former prime minister had been successful with his pursuance of peace.

She carried on typing as Churchill talked eloquently of his relationship and admiration for the man who'd often been very opposed to him, particularly at the beginning of the war.

After he was finished, she made her way out of the room and back to the typing pool. Carol looked up from her typewriter. 'You heard anything from John?'

She and Julia spoke every day, as both of their husbands were in North Africa together.

Julia smiled. 'I got a letter this morning. He sent some funny jokes for Tom and a drawing for Maggie. I'll be sure to post it all on to them. What about you?'

'Nothing for a week now.'

Julia felt the sting again of missing her family. Her children's faces swam into her thoughts and it hurt so much to think none of her family were around her for comfort when news like this hit. No special cuddles with Tom or thoughtful acts from her daughter, who would do things to cheer her mother, like picking flowers when she was sad. Worst of all no husband's arms to hold her in the middle of the night when she felt so desperate.

Sally sat back in her seat. 'I'm glad I haven't anyone in the war. It'd be horrible waiting around to see what happened to them. Mind you, there may not be much left for me to pick over if this war keeps on. I might die an old maid at this rate,' she chuckled, rolling in a sheet of paper, and her infectious laugh made the whole typing pool smile.

Julia finished the address and read it over, and three days later read it again in the newspaper. Chamberlain's funeral had been kept secret for safety's sake. But he'd been buried at Westminster with all the pomp and ceremony of a state funeral, and the nation had grieved once again for another good man who had been taken before his time.

Chapter Thirty-One

A few days before Christmas, Lizzie was just leaving the operations room when she noticed someone waiting. She knew who it was, even with his back to her. As he turned, a smile lit up Jack's face. Even though they had been going out now for three months her stomach still flip-flopped when she saw him.

'There's my girl,' he said, stamping out his cigarette and walking towards her. Even with other air-force personnel around, he didn't hesitate. He put his arms around her and gathered her in for a gentle kiss.

A couple of the operators whistled and hooted their encouragement as they passed by, and they parted, laughed, then walked together, hand in hand.

'This is a nice surprise,' said Lizzie. 'I thought we weren't seeing each other until next week.'

'I managed to get a couple of days off. That's why I wanted to see you,' he said with a smile, stopping and turning her around to face him. 'Could you get the night off tomorrow? Is Abigail still with you?'

'She is. We've been in touch with the Red Cross again, but there's still no news on her family.'

'Could you get someone to take care of her tomorrow night and on Saturday? I have somewhere special I want to take you, but it's a surprise.'

Lizzie raised her eyebrows with delight. 'I'm sure Julia can help out. I love surprises. Is it a surprise I will like?'

'I think so,' he said. 'And pack an overnight bag.'

Something inside Lizzie's stomach tightened. As much as she trusted Jack, there was a side of her that was fearful of ever getting into a situation as she had with Fergus. Quickly, she dismissed the thought. This was Jack. She loved Jack. He was one of the most honourable people she'd ever known, and she knew he would never hurt her or put her in a position where she would feel any kind of pressure.

'All right,' she agreed. 'I'll meet you here after work.'

'See you then; I have to go and arrange something.' He kissed her gently on the lips, and she could tell he was excited as he moved away.

Even with the apprehension, she was thrilled to spend the evening with Jack and maybe the next day. Where could he be thinking of taking her? Lizzie didn't sleep well that night, and visions of Fergus came back to haunt her. She couldn't believe after all of this time that she could still be so affected by the experience. The pressure, the feeling of guilt, then her daughter being torn from her arms, all returned to torture her as she tossed and turned through the night. She was almost glad when the raid started, and the three of them made their way down to the shelter. In the garden, Abigail curled up in Lizzie's lap, cat-like, and fell straight back to sleep, and as the bombs rattled the walls of the little metal Anderson shelter, Lizzie shared with Julia what Jack had said. Julia was excited.

'He must have something special for you for Christmas,' she said. 'What a lovely thought. Abigail will be fine with me. Besides, I'm really missing my children; I can't believe it's been six months,' she sighed. 'I have so wanted to go down and see them again before Christmas, but we have been so busy at work. Also, the last time I saw Tom he was so upset when I left, I wonder if it is harder on him when I visit. I'm looking forward to hanging a stocking with Abigail and have her help me decorate the tree. It's a bit of a pathetic one this year, but at least we'll be celebrating Christmas all together.'

The next afternoon Jack was waiting for Lizzie again when she came off duty. As she came out of the operations room, he was standing there, hands tucked in his pockets, a broad smile on his face. Slipping his arm around her shoulders, he walked with her to a car he must have borrowed. But he didn't drive to the main gate; instead he turned and drove to the aerodrome. She curiously raised an eyebrow. 'Are you going to tell me where you're taking me?'

'Not yet,' he said, smiling. When he pulled the car to a stop beside one of the hangars, she became even more curious. He came round and opened the car door for her, and she took his hand as he helped her out. In her months with the WAAF, Lizzie had never been this close to the aeroplanes themselves; even the compact fighters seemed huge compared to how they looked in the air.

As she stood admiring the display, a Spitfire turned away from her down the runway, and she held on to her hat as it moved past her with the swift blast of air from the propeller. Walking her out onto the airfield, he headed towards a row of other aeroplanes that were parked. They arrived at one that was nondescript, without the usual camouflage colours of war.

'I thought you might like a little joy ride,' he announced. Lizzie looked up at him with surprise. And then back at the trainer aircraft. There were two seats in it for training, unlike his Hurricane, which only had one seat.

'We're going up in this plane?' she said, with shock.

'We are,' he said with a smile. 'We borrowed this from 12 Group, and it needs to be returned. Wing Commander asked me if I'd be willing to fly it up to Coltishall over the weekend, and as I was due time off, I requested to take a guest, and by a miracle, he agreed. Come on, let me help you in.'

Lizzie's stomach clenched with anticipation. Never in her wildest dreams had she ever imagined flying in an aeroplane, even though she spent most of her days talking about them or guiding them. The actual thought of flying above the clouds was unbelievable.

Jack helped her into the seat and buckled her in. He gave her a headset to wear so he could speak to her. Securing himself in, he pulled down the canopy and giving a thumbs up to the ground crew that appeared to remove the chocks they began to taxi down the runway. Lizzie couldn't control her enthusiasm.

'Jack, this is unbelievable!' she squealed as she looked around her.

'Well, you're easily pleased,' came back the voice in her headset. 'We haven't even left the ground yet,' he added with a laugh.

'I never thought I'd ever do anything like this. Wait till I write to my cousins. They won't believe it.'

The plane started to gain speed, and Lizzie gripped her seat straps as it sped towards the end of the runway. She'd never moved so fast in her life and feared that it wouldn't get off the ground in time, and she held her breath. Just when she thought they were going to crash into the hedges at the end of the runway, she felt the plane lift beneath her, taking her stomach with it, and an enormous pressure bore down on her chest as it climbed into the air. Lizzie couldn't quite believe it. It was exhilarating and frightening, all in the same moment. The noise of the plane's engine roared in her ears, causing the inside of the plane to vibrate with the pressure. Lizzie was pinned back in her seat as the plane headed through the clouds, bumping its way through the heavy air. It continued its ascent as swirls of white surrounded the plane, making it impossible for her to see anything around her, and it reminded her of the thick fog that sometimes descended on the loch at home in the evenings. It gave her that same sense of isolation as it did in Scotland, as if she and Jack were utterly alone, the only two people cocooned in a magical world.

All at once, they broke free of the cloud, and she sucked in a breath with surprise as above, the sky was blue. She instantly relaxed, unable to believe the feeling of calm, of beauty, of total serenity. No wonder Jack loved this so much. Down below, it had been grey, and the clouds had been dark and heavy, but up here there was nothing but a china blue sky, illuminated by the fiery globe of the sun, whose rays glinted across the wings and warmed her face.

'Jack, this is amazing,' she gushed into her headset.

'It's nicer when the enemy is not chasing you,' he responded, laughing. 'I feel very fortunate to be a pilot. We get to see the world from a very different perspective.'

As they made their way north of London, Lizzie settled, lulled by the roar of the engine and the beauty of the sky. Below her, fluffy white pillows of clouds rolled out ahead of her as far as she could see. Occasionally they cleared so she could peer down at the ground. She was spellbound by how different the world seemed from above. For months she had been living in the turmoil, the dirt, and the smog of war. But so far from the ground, it all looked so perfectly still – a quilt of calm and beauty.

As they left London behind and made their way north-east towards the airfield in Norfolk, Jack pointed out landmarks to her. Beautiful estate houses, crumbling castles, and vast silent lakes. As they drew closer to the east coast the clouds began to thin beneath them, and she noticed that there was a light dusting of snow on the ground as they headed down into East Anglia. The land below was so beautiful as the sun glinted off it, highlighting a herd of glossy black horses galloping on frozen fields, and a miniature train that was winding its slow way through the crystallized landscape. She'd never imagined in the whole of her life that she'd ever see anything like this.

It took about two hours before he finally started to head down towards the airfield, not far from the Norfolk coast. Jack called ahead to alert the tower he'd be landing there. As they began to descend, Lizzie's ears began to pop and crackle with the changing pressure, and her stomach tightened again with each new step down.

Although she had watched the planes landing at her airfield, she hadn't realized how precarious it felt heading towards the ground at such a rate, having to get the airspeed just right so that the plane would land the right way. As the ground rose to greet her, she clung to her harness one more time and prayed it would be a smooth landing. Jack touched down so gently that Lizzie didn't even realize they were down until she saw the ground beneath the wheels, and she breathed a sigh of relief. Slowing the plane, Jack taxied the aircraft to a hangar.

Helping her out, she noticed her whole body was trembling with fear and exhilaration. He held her close, then lifted her chin to meet his gaze. He looked concerned.

'You're shivering, was it that awful?'

Lizzie shook her head, tears brimming in the corners of her eyes. 'No, Jack, it was magnificent! What a wonderful gift you gave me today. Something I will never forget. No one in my family has ever been in an aeroplane before. Up there in the sky, it is as if the world is at peace, and I haven't felt that feeling of calm for a very long time. It was as if time stopped, and all I had to do was enjoy all the beauty of this world.'

He nodded, understanding her experience. 'I sometimes forget how awe-inspiring it can be, so much of my time above the clouds is spent just trying to stay alive.'

Once he'd signed the plane over to the commander in charge, Jack commandeered a car, and they drove east to the coast.

'I used to come to a beach here as a child,' he said, smiling over at her as he drove. 'We have relatives here, and there's nothing quite as beautiful and breathtaking as the stretches of the Norfolk coastline. There's a guesthouse in a little tiny place outside a village called Sea Palling, and I took the liberty of booking two rooms for us tonight. I thought you'd like it. We could have dinner and walk to the beach. The parts that aren't mined, of course,' he added with a smirk.

She nodded her head, felt a sense of relief when he talked about two rooms; of course, he was the perfect gentleman, she had never known him to be anything else. As they drove alongside the Norfolk Broads, a vast network of ancient waterways, Lizzie stared mesmerized out of the window, marvelling at the unfamiliar landscape, so very different from Scotland but so beautiful in its own way. A vast expanse of clear, still water and along its banks proud stone windmills and waving sheaves of high winter grasses. As far as her eye could see were flat straight fields that disappeared into the expansive horizon that seemed to stretch to the very ends of the earth. She hadn't realized till right now how much she had needed this. Just a respite, a window of time away from a constant fear of bombs dropping on her head, and as she looked over at Jack, his eyes steady on the road, she felt beyond happy.

When they arrived at the guesthouse, Jack pulled the car to a grinding halt on the grey gravelly driveway as Lizzie looked out of the window, admiring the beautiful stonework of the building which was perched on the edge of some rising ground. It was solid yet welcoming with a peek-a-boo view of the sea through sand dunes and spirals of seagrass that cavorted in a brisk sea breeze.

As he helped her out of the car, the fresh, salty smell of sea air filled her lungs and the sound of gulls reached her on the edge of the sharp northern wind that whipped her curly cropped hair across her cheeks.

Jack gathered up their luggage, and slipping his arm around Lizzie, pulled her close to keep her warm as he escorted her to the door.

Inside the guesthouse, a pleasant mahogany-panelled hallway greeted them along with the smell of beeswax. Beyond the hall, a door opened onto a lounge room with large picture windows that also overlooked the sea.

An older woman, neat and well put together in a sensible tweed skirt and a cream blouse, introduced herself as Mrs Barton as she greeted them in the foyer.

'Jack Henson,' he said with a smile, 'I booked two rooms.'

The landlady chuckled as she pulled out a pen for him to sign the guest book. 'I know who you are. You're the only people staying this time of the year. So, you're fortunate you get the best rooms in the house.'

Lizzie mused that Mrs Barton was unexpectedly modern. About the same age but so different from her own parents, who would certainly have frowned on the two of them staying together unmarried, even in separate rooms.

'Wonderful,' responded Jack as Lizzie stroked a friendly tabby cat that had leaped up onto the welcome desk to meet them. After Jack signed the guest book, he paused to consult their host. 'Is there anywhere nice nearby we can go for dinner?' he enquired.

Mrs Barton shook her head. 'Unfortunately, we're very cut off here on this part of the coast, but if you like home-cooked food, I'd be more than happy to make you something warm and filling for dinner. A local farm has been keeping us well-stocked, and we have a dining room with a lovely view of the sea.' Jack looked at Lizzie as she enthusiastically nodded her head.

'That sounds lovely.' She smiled.

They settled into their rooms, and Lizzie had to pinch herself that there was even a war going on. She would've thought she was on holiday if it weren't for the spare gas masks in the room and procedures for what to do in a bombing raid. Meeting Jack downstairs, they decided to go for a walk to enjoy the last rays of sun that was starting to set in a tangerine glow. The wind was bracing, so she dressed up warm and was happy to cuddle next to Jack, who had changed out of his uniform and was now looking very handsome in a cap and scarf and a dark blue knitted sweater. Exiting the guesthouse, they walked along the low hillside and down onto the beach.

They avoided walking too close to the water because of the mines, and warning signs were everywhere, so they sauntered along the top of the sand dunes instead.

As they wound their way around the coastline, they talked about everything, their families, their friends, their hopes for a world in peacetime.

'I love it here,' mused Lizzie as she stared out to the sea. 'I've missed the quiet since I left Scotland.'

'I bet it is beautiful up there,' added Jack.

'I would love to take you. You would love my uncle, the two of you would get on so well. Maybe if we get extended leave someday, you could come with me?'

Jack pulled her close, and she could smell the fresh spicy scent of his aftershave and feel his warm breath on her cheek. He turned her to face him and kissed her on the lips with such tenderness it made her heart pound. Sliding her arms around his waist and up under his sweater, she nuzzled her head into his warm shoulder as they watched the final rays of the day disappear.

'I love you, Lizzie,' he whispered into her ear to be heard above the wind, 'and I can't wait till this is over so we can start our life together.'

Lizzie felt a tingle of exhilaration. He hadn't talked about plans for a life together after the war in such intimate terms before. But she really hoped to have the chance of a life with Jack.

When they arrived back at the guesthouse, Lizzie went up to change when Mrs Barton informed her on the way up the stairs that dinner would be served in the tiny library at seven o'clock. 'It's warmer in there,' she insisted. 'The dining room can get a little chilly. We're going to set up a nice table in front of the fire for you both.'

Lizzy nodded and made her way upstairs to get changed.

An hour later, after taking a bath and changing her clothes, she made her way downstairs. The smell of leather, polish, and the warmth of an open fire greeted her as she opened the panelled wood door. It was a grand space with dark polished mahogany shelves stacked from floor to ceiling with leather-bound volumes of books. An elegant, highly glossed writing desk with a crystal inkwell and a cream-coloured blotter was positioned in front of the picture window fitted with its blackout curtains. And next to a roaring, crackling fire, a table was adorned with a cream damask tablecloth. In the centre, a spray of winter foliage of scarlet berries and evergreen leaves was gathered in a vase alongside an elegant red tapered candle.

Jack was already there waiting for Lizzie and pacing the room, and she noticed he looked preoccupied, but broke into a smile when she arrived. They soon settled down to eat, and the intimacy and smell of the books all around them, the warmth of the fire, the delectable home-cooked food that Mrs Barton served them, lulled them into a happy stupor of peace and contentment. It was as they were finishing their dinner that Jack leant forward and took her hand.

Lizzie looked up at him, trying to read his expression.

Finally, he spoke. 'Lizzie, I have something I want to give you.'

She smiled and thought about what Julia had said about him wanting to give her a Christmas present while they were gone.

'Wonderful,' she responded, reaching both hands out to accept her gift. She hadn't seen any parcels on the way into the room. Maybe he had smuggled it in under the table. 'I must admit,' she said regretfully, 'I've been knitting you something for Christmas, but I haven't quite finished it yet and didn't want to bring it with me half done.'

Jack smiled and took her outstretched hands, he kissed her palms. 'You're the most beautiful woman I've ever known, not just physically, but with the kindest heart and the most beautiful spirit.'

Lizzie started to blush with his compliments and was just about to pull away when she sensed something more serious was happening. Jack reached into his pocket and pulled out a small velvet box and placed it on the table in front of her.

Suddenly she realized what this was, and though she had dreamt many times that they would get married, she hadn't even thought about them getting engaged until after the war was over.

'Lizzie, I want you to be my wife. One thing about being in battle every day is that if you know something for sure, you don't want to wait. And I am sure of something: you're the only woman in the world I ever want to spend the rest of my life with.'

He opened up the box and took out a ring.

'This was my grandmother's. I would have asked you before, but I've been waiting for it to arrive, and it did a few days ago, and when this came up this weekend, I thought it would be the perfect opportunity to get you alone and ask you.' He took a breath. 'Lizzie Mackenzie, you would make me the happiest man in the world if you would agree to be my wife. Over the last few months, I have faced some of the darkest days of my life, but through it, you have given me a reason to hope and a reason to want to live. Meeting you and sharing this incredible connection is something I never thought would be possible. I am actually grateful to this war that brought you down to England, so I could meet you, and if you say yes, I will be the luckiest man alive, and I will try to make you happy every single day of our lives together. So please say yes.'

He held out the ring towards her, and the sapphire and diamond setting glistened in the firelight. Lizzie stared at it, trying to take it all in as she listened to the crackle of the fire and the thud of her heart that seemed to want to beat its way out of her chest.

She started to shake, crying with the sheer joy. Finally, she spoke, and she had to force the words out; his proposal had taken her voice and breath away. 'Oh, Jack, of course I'll marry you.'

He came around to her side of the table, swept her up in his arms and kissed her passionately, and pulled her so close to him he lifted her off her feet. She laughed breathlessly as she finally pulled away from him. He gently took her hand and slipped the delicate white gold ring onto her finger.

They were in the middle of another embrace when Mrs Barton came in with the pudding and didn't seem to be too taken aback to see the two of them in each other's arms.

'Now that's nice to see,' she said, stopping in the doorway to admire the picture of them together as Lizzie wiped tears of happiness from her eyes and held out her hand towards the older woman as an explanation.

'Oh, bless my soul,' the older woman retorted. 'Has he just proposed to you?'

Lizzie nodded, trying to believe it herself as she locked eyes with Jack's own, so full of love.

'Well, we have to celebrate!' said the landlady dropping the dessert unceremoniously down on the table and bustling out of the room, remarking over her shoulder, 'Mr Barton has some home-made brandy put aside for an occasion like this.'

As Lizzie held Jack close again, Mr Barton, a short, balding man, arrived, clearly having rushed from his own dinner table, as he still had his shirtsleeves rolled up to the elbow and a cloth napkin tucked in the top of his shirt. In his hand was a bottle of red, syrupy liquor.

'I was keeping this for when the Germans surrendered,' he informed them as Mrs Barton handed out crystal brandy glasses. 'But this seems a much better use for it; I can always make another batch for when we see off the Hun.'

He poured generous glasses all round and lifting his own, toasted them.

'To your excellent health, and I wish you as many years of happiness together as Mrs Barton and I have enjoyed.'

Lizzie smiled. *Years*, no one talked about years any more, when you weren't sure what would happen from moment to moment. But she would take any happiness she could. After the brandies were downed, the Bartons tactfully excused themselves, and Jack walked over to a record player in the corner and slipping an Al Bowlly record out of a paper sleeve, placed it on the turntable. Holding each other close, they turned slowly together in front of the fire. Lizzie closed her eyes and listened to Al Bowlly crooning on about forgetting everyday things because of the strength of his love, trying to absorb the whole experience. And something struck her, it was as if nothing else mattered in the world, not the war, not Scotland nor the air force, nor even her family. All that mattered was this incredible love she had with Jack and this stolen moment of bliss together.

Chapter Thirty-Two

The next morning, Lizzie woke to the sound of the gulls and rays of weak morning sunlight shining through chinks in the blackout curtains. And for one minute she thought she was back in Scotland because it was so quiet and such an airy room. Then the memory of the night before came rushing back, and her stomach tightened with the excitement of what had happened. She was going to marry Jack.

To prove that it hadn't been a dream, she quickly pulled her hand out from beneath the covers to make sure she was still wearing the engagement ring he had placed there the night before. And there it was, an exquisite sapphire surrounded by an oval of diamonds in an elegant white gold setting. She rolled it around on her finger with her thumb, trying to get used to it. It was the first piece of real jewellery she had ever owned, and amazingly it was a perfect fit. She thought about Jack's grandmother who'd worn this ring. Who would have guessed that, years later, her grandson would be giving the same ring to the woman he loved, and that woman would be Lizzie?

There was only one thing that threatened to rob her of her happiness. The truth about Annie. She felt awful not telling him about her daughter, but what if he couldn't accept her past? 'Sinful and used goods,' that's what her father had called her in the front parlour where the main decor consisted of the large leather Bible on the plinth in front of the cross-stitched picture of the Ten Commandments. As he'd paced in front of the fire berating her and making sure she knew how thoroughly disappointed they were, her mother had sat in the high-backed chair next to him sobbing into her handkerchief. What if Jack was more conservative about those kinds of things? Men wanted to marry pure women, that's what her father had made clear to her in no uncertain terms. What if that was what Jack wanted? Was she being fair to him not to tell him? She pushed the thoughts from her mind; she wasn't going to let her past rob her of the joy of this moment. Lizzie would worry about that another day.

Slipping out of bed, she made her way to the bathroom and after getting ready, went downstairs. It was quite early, but Mrs Barton was already up, and the dining room had a little table already laid with home-made jam and butter on a white lace tablecloth.

'Good morning, my dear,' sang out her host, as she bustled into the dining room and set down a tiny jug of milk on the table. 'I hope you've got a good appetite. We managed to get some bacon today,' she exclaimed with such vigour it was as if she'd just struck gold, which in some ways it was. Lizzie hadn't had bacon since she'd left Scotland, and she settled herself down happily to look out through the window and wait for Jack. The water was choppier today. It was rolling onto the shore in powerful grey waves that crashed down onto the creamy white sand. Hovering above, gulls danced in the wind before diving to fetch an early morning catch.

All at once, someone was behind her, a hand slid across her shoulder, and warm, soft lips brushed her neck.

'Well, if it isn't Mrs Henson-to-be,' Jack whispered into her ear, and a shiver ran down her spine. Lizzie turned and stood up to hug him, and as she ran her hands down his neck, he noticed his hair was damp and his face was pressed against her cheek, smooth and soft from a close shave. Pulling back, he cupped her chin and tipped her face up to meet his lips. Then he kissed her deeply. Finally pulling away, he broke into a smile. 'I hope you haven't changed your mind,' he toyed with her.

Lizzie laughed and shook her head. 'Never,' she responded as she locked her hands around his neck and pulled him in again for another quick kiss. 'I know when I'm on to a good thing.'

Slipping out of her arms Jack made his way around to the other side of the breakfast table, but didn't let go of her hand as he sat down.

He admired the ring on her finger then finally looked up. 'It suits you, Miss Mackenzie.'

'It will look even better when it has a gold band to keep it company,' she responded with a quirk of her eyebrows.

Mrs Barton entered the room with the full breakfast for them both, and they settled down to enjoy it. After they'd eaten a very hearty meal, they decided to go for one last walk along the coast, before they made their way home. Jack would drive the car back to the aerodrome, where one of the other commanders would hopefully give them a lift to the railway station.

They walked the beach again, which with the blustery weather, was dramatic and awe-inspiring. And standing on the top of a dune, Lizzie closed her eyes and drew in a breath, drinking in all the beauty around her as she realized how much she loved being on the coast. The lochs were beautiful in Scotland, and they did have their own small tide, but nothing as dramatic and as breathtaking as the movement of the sea.

All the way home on the train, they talked about their plans, where they would live, how they would tell their families.

'I want you to come to Scotland with me as soon as we have leave,' said Lizzie as she stared out of the window watching the icy fields rush by.

'And you must come and meet my parents and my brother too,' responded Jack. 'They're going to love you.'

Lizzie curled up on the seat next to him and put her head on his shoulder. And as they made their plans, it was as though there was no war on at all. She tried not to think about what it would be like to be back in London, with him in the clouds, fighting the enemy.

*

Lizzie couldn't wait to get home and show the girls her ring, and when she walked in the kitchen and thrust her hand out to show them without saying anything, they both squealed with delight.

'This is so wonderful,' exclaimed Julia, 'I'm so happy for you.'

'Jack is such a lovely man,' Diana added, 'and what a beautiful ring.'

'It was his grandmother's,' Lizzie stated proudly as she stretched out her arm and spread her fingers in front of her to admire it herself.

Julia made a cup of tea as they sat around the table, and Lizzie filled them in on how he had proposed to her and the incredible adventure she'd been on.

'He is such a romantic,' gushed Julia, and Lizzie caught a shadow pass across Diana's face.

'Don't worry, Diana, you'll be next. I'm sure Len's thinking along the same lines.'

Diana shook her head. 'It's not that,' she responded thoughtfully, 'I was just thinking what I would say if Len did propose.'

Julia, who was placing water in the kettle on the stove, turned to look at her with surprise. 'I thought you really liked him.'

'Oh, I do,' affirmed Diana, 'I really do like him. In fact, I think I'm in love with him. It's just that he's so different from us, from my family, and I just wondered how my parents would feel if I were to marry him. He comes from a really gregarious family, and we're so quiet. Also, my dad has always wanted me to marry someone close to home in Birmingham, and he'd always had his eye on some chap down the road who was as dull as dirt.

'But I'd always thought that was how my life would end up too. Me marrying someone down the street at home and seeing my mum and dad every day. But Len loves living here in London, and he has so many friends, and he's very close to his mother, I'm sure he would want to settle here. I'd just never really given it much thought before, but now, being here and being with him, it's like a new world has opened up to me about family. I've realized how amazing having lots of them can be. But I love my dad, and in some ways I feel if I was to walk away and marry Len, I'd be leaving him behind, and I feel so guilty about that.'

Julia sat down at the table and took her hand. 'You have to do what's right for you, Diana, not what's right for everyone else. Your dad would come round.'

'I know you're right,' said Diana, shaking it off. 'And, of course, he hasn't even asked me yet, but it's just when I think about it, I feel a bit unsure.'

'I would do anything to have John back right now and wouldn't let anything or anyone stand in our way,' sighed Julia wistfully.

'I'm sorry, Julia,' said Lizzie. 'We shouldn't be talking like this with your husband away. You must be feeling rotten.'

'Not at all,' responded Julia. 'I miss him, of course. But I love the fact that you two are finding love in such a dark time. John has been with me my whole life. I can't even imagine what it would be like to meet someone at my age. John is all I've ever known, and since he went away, it's been so strange. It's like half of me is missing, a huge part. We grew up together. As long as I can remember, he's been there, and it's like something isn't right without him by my side. Something is missing. Not just because he's the love of my life, but because he is part of my history, part of my growing-up years, part of every thought or experience I've had, and I can't imagine my life without him.'

As they sat at the table, Lizzie grabbed both of her friends' hands and squeezed them, feeling so grateful once again for how close they had become and how much she truly loved them both.

'John will come home, I will marry Jack and Diana – you will find a way to marry that wonderful kind man. And once this is all over, we will all find a way to be together with the people we love, forever.'

Chapter Thirty-Three

Because all three of them were working on Christmas Day, they decided to go out to celebrate Christmas Eve together and splurged on an expensive meal in town, complete with turkey and Christmas pudding. It was nice that some of the restaurants didn't have as much restriction on food as people did individually.

'I'm stuffed,' said Lizzie, sitting back from her plate, wearing the party hat she'd pulled out of her cracker. 'I won't need to eat for a week.'

Paying the bill, they looped arms and made their way home. They'd only got halfway when the sirens wailed, and they quickly looked around for the closest shelter, which was an underground station close by. Racing towards it, they clattered down the stairs with hundreds of others. Even though they were under attack, everybody was in a jovial mood because of Christmas.

'Is it Father Christmas?' said an older cockney as they arrived on the platform, and people around him laughed.

'If it is,' responded another, 'I don't think much of his presents.'

Moving down the platform, the girls took off their coats and laid them on the cold, hard concrete, and sat together, their backs against the wall, staring at the brick arches that formed the station.

'You'd think Jerry would give us a night off,' shouted somebody else. 'Isn't it Christmas in Germany?'

As the underground platform filled up, it was an interesting sight. People caught in the midst of celebrating the holiday. Children dressed in angel costumes, obviously coming from a nativity play, a group of carol singers standing with their candles, a group of musicians, and plenty of mothers with children dressed in their Sunday best, probably on their way back from visiting Father Christmas.

Abigail was spending the night with Agnes, who had assured Julia that she would go into the Anderson shelter if the sirens went off, even though she was vocal in her dislike of it.

Somebody stepped in front of the girls with a box of chocolates. 'Ee' ar' from my family in America,' said a woman with a round face and a cheeky grin as she offered the girls the box. They thanked her, and all took one.

Lizzie couldn't remember the last time she had eaten chocolate, and it tasted so good.

Suddenly, a girl rushed down the stairs in a wedding dress, her veil tucked under her arm.

'God, you'd think the enemy would give us the night off so I could get bloody married,' she said. 'I'm only half-dressed.' Lizzie stood up and helped the woman by zipping up the back of her dress. 'I didn't even have a chance to do my hair,' sighed the bride-to-be as she pulled out the curlers, still arranged in a neat row on her head.

'Well, fortunately, my friend is a hairdresser,' shared Lizzie with a smile.

'I'm getting used to working on the go,' added Diana, sorting through her bag for a comb. 'Come on, let's see what we can do.'

Somebody produced a chair, as some people carried them down to the underground, and the young woman sat down as Diana started to comb through the bride's hair as best she could, styling it in a way she thought would be attractive. Then, lifting her veil onto her head, she started to pin it into place for her. Young women and young girls gathered around to watch Diana work as the bride-to-be continued.

'We thought it'd be romantic getting married on Christmas Eve. I thought the Nazis would give us a night off. My fiancé's probably still all the way across town. I hope he's all right, and let's hope the church is still there when I get above the ground.'

As Diana adjusted the bride's veil, Lizzie thought about her own wedding and when it would happen. She hoped soon. They hadn't got around to talking about a date yet. She wanted to tell her family first. But something about living in a time where the veil of life and death was so thin made everything polarized. She could see so clearly through the superfluous to what really mattered. And if she only had months, weeks, or even days with Jack, she hoped to spend them as his wife.

'There you go,' said Diana, finishing off the bride's hair, and someone produced a compact mirror from their bag so she could admire Diana's handiwork. Lizzie thought the young woman looked beautiful.

'God, I look gorgeous, thank you. Let's hope we get a lull so I can go and say my vows.'

All at once, the violinist from the orchestra started playing a heartfelt version of 'Love is the Sweetest Thing', another popular song by Al Bowlly, and all around her, people started to sing, and to wish the bride good luck. It made Lizzie miss Jack more than ever, as she remembered dancing with him and she couldn't wait to see him again. A couple of people even came over and pressed money into the bride's hands or little gifts they had been given already for Christmas. Somebody even gave her an orange. 'Not much of a wedding breakfast,' said the well-wisher, 'but at least it'll be something.'

Diana turned to her friends. 'I've been thinking since you got engaged, Lizzie, and I can't see it ever being possible for me to marry at the moment. Dad would be heartbroken if I got married down here in a register office without a church or all the family around, not that I have the opportunity. Dad would want me to get married in Birmingham, but how would that be possible when we are in the midst of all this? The war has changed me,' she said wistfully. 'It makes me think differently about life and just how fragile it is.'

Both the other girls nodded their agreement and sat back down, huddled together with the usual hum of bombs banging and crashing above their heads. The violinist started to play a lovely rendition of 'Silent Night', and Lizzie smiled at the irony. But it wasn't long before they all began to join in and sing, and the echo of hundreds of voices up and down the platform while the whole of the world was being destroyed above their heads felt spiritual, somehow, like all being together in a cathedral. There was a connection with one another, a real sense of camaraderie. Lizzie noted Julia crying; she'd been putting on a brave face while she was busy, but now her guard seemed to be down and Lizzie knew she was really missing her husband and children. She slipped her arm around her friend's shoulders and pulling her close, offered her a handkerchief as they sat huddled together. She was sad as well, picturing her uncle and aunt and cousins gathering to exchange presents without her, but she was also heartened. They were a city that was battle-worn, but not divided. They were exhausted from night after night of disturbed sleep, but awake and invigorated by a sense of resilience and sheer determination, a determination that would keep them going for as long as it took. They were continually fighting to keep their spirits up, even as a cruel enemy attempted to chip away at that day after day. A whole country was fighting to preserve the very elements that made them British. And even though so many of the buildings in the city had been destroyed, they all carried a vision of its former glory in their hearts, and would do so until they could rebuild again. In the meantime, they never ever forgot who they were.

They sat there till two in the morning, and though it was a strange way to spend Christmas, there was also a sense of community.

'If I were at home,' said Lizzie, 'my aunt would have made a big feast of food. I'd have been doing the plum pudding tonight and hiding coins, wrapping gifts for the girls. Of course, Hogmanay is much more celebrated in Scotland than down here, but Christmas is a special time. I miss them.'

Julia held her hand. 'I was thinking about Tom and Maggie as well, spending Christmas in a strange place. As soon as I get some time off, I think I'm going to go to the Cotswolds and see them just for a few days. I can't imagine not being with them tomorrow for Christmas morning. I thought about bringing them back for a couple of days, but it looked like it would prove impossible with work, and I didn't want to make them a promise only to have to break it.'

Diana nodded. 'I hope my mum and dad are doing okay on their own, I do miss my family as well.'

'We're family for each other now,' said Julia, taking hold of her friends' hands and squeezing them. 'And I, for one, am grateful for both of you.'

They put their arms around each other as the carollers started to sing 'O Come, All Ye Faithful', and the girls joined in until the all-clear sounded. They made their way back up to see what was waiting for them above ground.

It was as they were leaving the underground station that Lizzie saw her again. The woman must have been a long way further down the platform, so she hadn't seen her until now, but it was undoubtedly the same woman she'd seen at the cinema. Hurrying away from the girls, she grabbed hold of the woman, who swung round, startled, and then with recognition dawning in her eyes looked sheepishly into Lizzie's own.

'I know who you are,' Lizzie said. 'I know exactly who you are, and by the looks of it, you know who I am too.'

The woman nodded.

'Look, I'm not angry or anything. I just want to know. I just want to know she's safe. I just want to see her. This war has made everything crystal clear to me, and all I have in my life is her. I'm not going to try and cause any trouble. I'm not going to upset her. I'm not even going to tell her who I am, but I'm begging you, please let me see my daughter. Let me see Annie. At least tell me, is she here in London?'

The woman seemed to deflate, and then she nodded. 'Such a beautiful little baby. I'll never forget her or your face when I left you. But you need to know she was homed with a lovely family. She has two brothers, and I'm sure she's happy.'

'You've got to tell me where she is.'

'I'm not supposed to.'

'Look, she may not even be here. She may have been sent out of the city. At least let me try and see her. There has to be a reason that I've seen you again. Please. I'm begging you.'

The woman seemed to relent; she sucked in air. 'I can't remember the address. I have to go to work and find it for you. It's closed over Christmas, so you can give me your address but I can't promise you anything. I'm no longer a nurse. I left the job that organized the adoptions because I thought it was very wrong taking babies from young girls and I now work in a different office and I reunite families instead. Occasionally I have to go to my old office and if I'm left alone I could possibly have access to the older files, but you can't tell anybody. I'm not supposed to do this, but I will try my best. Like I said, I can't promise anything. Your daughter may not even be in London any more.'

Lizzie couldn't stop herself. She hugged the young woman as tears streamed down her face and hurriedly gave her Julia's address.

'Thank you so much.' And Lizzie felt a sense of relief. She might finally get to meet her daughter again.

Chapter Thirty-Four

The truck rattled along the road on the evening of 29 December, and as its wheels jarred into potholes and crunched through rubble from the raid the night before, Diana prepared herself for the night ahead. It took them longer to get there now, because they had been moved from the playing fields to one of the many bomb sites, and she was closer to the Square Mile, the financial district of the city. As she listened to the girls laughing and joking with one another, Kathy recalling a particularly disastrous date she'd just had, Diana bounced with the rhythm of the truck and was thoughtful. Even though it was impossible for her to describe the sounds and the intensity of war to anybody who had never been through it, she herself had got used to it now. Though the anticipation of what would happen that night, what they would have to deal with, always sat like a stone in the pit of her stomach. The evening was bitterly cold and as an icy blast whistled through the gaps and flaps of the truck, she tucked her hands into her coat pockets, closed her eyes and dwelt on happier things: her plans for New Year's Eve.

She and Len both had the night off, and he'd talked about taking her to the cinema, then out for something to eat. Maybe even some dancing as well, if they had the energy for it. And her mind was filled with warm thoughts about him so she didn't feel the truck rattle to a stop.

'Come on, Diana,' encouraged Mavis, the girl who drove them and managed the winch. Diana blinked her eyes open away from her daydream. 'Are you coming or not?'

Diana suddenly realized that everybody was off the truck but her.

'She's miles away,' Kathy retorted, 'no doubt dreaming about that young corporal, aren't you?'

'Wouldn't you like to know?' Diana quipped, leaping down from the back.

As she joined Maisie and Jean at the staging area they all moved into their comfortable rhythm, Kathy on the megaphone, Mavis on the winch, the rest of the girls on their cables. It was a clear night and Diana shivered as clouds of her white breath rolled into the air. The team guided their silver bullet into the sky and as there was no serious wind tonight, they all fell swiftly into a swaying rhythm together with Bertha, who danced like a kite on the undercurrents.

As the first siren sounded far off and the searchlights all over the city flicked on, one of the girls started humming a new song by the Andrews Sisters, called 'Boogie Woogie Bugle Boy' and they all joined in, tapping from foot to foot to keep warm. Then the sound came towards them, as it always did, like a thousand bees buzzing through the night. Diana swallowed down dry, stiff air and got ready. She could hear that they were close, obviously planning on hitting central London again.

All at once, the sky was filled with ugly bombs, their black casings clear to see silhouetted against the night's full moon. These were the type, she knew from experience, that split open and dropped thousands of other tiny bombs called incendiaries. They were often sent ahead of the high-explosive bombers because on impact, they would explode and would start fires all around the city that could blaze a trail for the bombers coming in so they would know where to hit.

The bombs started to fall en masse and Diana wondered if it was her imagination, but there seemed to be a lot more of them than usual. All around her, they rained down, hitting the ground with a crack and bursting into life with their eerie green light, like fizzing fireworks. Fire marshals raced about them, stamping them out as fast as they could. But no matter how quickly they worked, more fell from the sky.

'God, they're lively tonight,' shouted Jean.

'Hopping,' responded Maisie. One arrived right beside the girl next to Diana, and she screamed as it fizzed around her feet. Diana stamped it out the best she could before another followed it. She looked up in exasperation, trying to make sense of it all. Why so many? Surely not just to light the route; there must be an alternative reason, as there were literally thousands upon thousands of them. They all seemed to be centred on the area they were in. Lots of fires were already taking hold and erupting into life all around the local streets.

'What have they got against us tonight?' shouted Kathy, as the girls stamped violently, gasped and swore all around her. No one could snuff them out quickly enough. All at once, the balloon yanked to the right and twisted in the air, and some of the wires severed on Diana's cable.

'Someone's got to splice it,' shouted Jean.

'Great,' responded Maisie sarcastically.

This was always really painful for the girls to do, especially when their hands were cold.

'I'll do it,' Diana volunteered. But as she reached up to gather the cables, above them, a flood of incendiaries landed on the top of the balloon, spitting and sizzling with their fiery green anger.

'That's not good,' whispered Maisie, echoing what Diana was thinking as they watched in horror and shock.

'Should we bring it back down?' suggested Mavis in panic to the group.

'I don't think there is anything we can do,' responded Kathy.

Sergeant Daly called to them, 'Stand your ground, girls. Stand your ground.'

Then, in horror, they watched as all of a sudden, three of the incendiaries penetrated the balloon. Instinctively, they all dropped to a squat and wrapped their hands over their helmets, knowing what was coming next. The effect was incredible; the balloon burst into flames, becoming an enormous fireball in the sky, illuminating the night before rolling and dancing its way to the earth. As they huddled together, long fiery silver ribbons of balloon rained down on their heads, followed by unfettered cables that fell haphazardly about, barely missing them all as they clattered to the ground.

Fire marshals were upon the bombs quickly, stamping out any fires that ignited.

Slowly they all rose, and instinctively their collective gaze was drawn skyward to stare in astonishment at the large black void where the balloon had been.

'Rest in peace, Bertha,' whispered Kathy into the icy night air.

'At least it saved my hands from splicing that wire,' added Diana.

They didn't have long to muse about their new situation because all at once their collective reverence was cut short by another barrage of the tiny, fizzing green bombs, reminding them that though their balloon was gone, the German onslaught was still continuing viciously all around them.

'Get yourself back to the barracks,' ordered Sergeant Daly.

Hurriedly, they all started to file onto the truck. Diana turned to her sergeant. 'Permission to check on a friend who may be caught in this bombing sir, if you won't be needing me for the rest of the evening?'

Daly shook his head. 'Granted. Just make sure you're back on duty first thing tomorrow, Downes.'

She agreed. Because it was such a wild night she wanted to check on her friends; Julia worked not too far away from here and Diana wanted to make sure she had made it home safe. Bombs were raining down everywhere tonight.

She started to race across town. All the buses were stopped, and what greeted her was devastating. The whole of the City's Square Mile was an inferno, a ring of fire around St Paul's Cathedral.

Holding a handkerchief to her mouth and nose to stop herself from coughing and protect her from the caustic, dense, black smoke that billowed around her, she kept moving forward. One building was roaring, and she enquired of one of the firefighters what it was. He shook his head with distress. 'A Victorian book depository. What a sad, sad thing.'

No wonder the fire was taking hold so strongly, thought Diana as she watched pages and pages of different books burning up in the intense heat then floating down to the ground like little black feather bats that disintegrated into a thousand pieces above her head. Picking her way through the rubble and avoiding the numerous fires was slow going, but when she got to St Paul's, there was a great deal of commotion.

As she passed one of the firefighters, she overheard him talking to what appeared to be a group of volunteers.

'We've had a direct command from Churchill himself. He believes that the Nazis are targeting St Paul's tonight. The formation the planes are coming in and the way the incendiaries are landing, we think they're going to try and burn the cathedral to the ground. Mr Churchill has sent us a message, "Save St Paul's at all costs." We need all the help we can get. All hands to the pump. The prime minister is counting on us.'

Diana stopped and approached one of the men that rushed in front of her with a hose. 'Can I help at all?'

'Yes, love. You can. Get inside, up onto the roof and put out any fires that you can see up there.'

Diana raced inside the building; the walls and banners were charred and thick, black smoke was everywhere. In the crypt, the dean's wife had set up a first-aid camp, that was already overflowing with people being treated for burns and injuries. All around the church building, a small group of church volunteer firefighters, including the dean himself, his face, hands and dog collar blackened with the soot, were manically trying to put out the fires. They all looked exhausted. She raced up the stairs and joined a line with a group of people as they chained water to wherever it was needed. On the roof the smoke and heat were intense and the sight was unbelievable. St Paul's was completely surrounded by burning buildings with flames leaping high into the air all around them.

The man next to her informed her in breathy rasps as he sloshed full buckets to her that, though the dome was made of lead, inside it was a wooden structure, and if that caught alight, the whole roof could be lost.

Diana continued to work shoulder to shoulder with the other volunteers, fighting the choking, acrid smoke as the incendiaries continued to land all around them.

At one point, the dean came rushing up to them and informed them they had just had a call from Cannon Street station. The dome appeared to be on fire. Diana raced up more stairs with a group of volunteers into the dome. There she could clearly see the green glow of a burning incendiary from the rafters: the bomb had lodged in the outer lead casing and was burning towards the wooden rafters.

'Bloody hell,' exclaimed one of the volunteers. 'If that hits the wood, the whole thing will go up.'

They all watched with bated breath as one of the other ministers, dressed in his tin hat, shimmied across one of the support beams trying to reach the fizzy green flare that was causing the wood to smoke and blacken around it. Diana prayed he would be safe and reach it in time, it was such a plucky and precarious thing to do as she watched him hang from the beam, creeping towards it. All at once, like a miracle, it moved, rolled down the side of the building, and was able to be put out on one of the roofs.

They continued all night, as the Germans were relentless. It was apparent they wanted to tear down the morale of the British people by destroying one of London's most famous landmarks. But no one in her line was going to let that happen. They worked through the night until the bombing stopped, and then even afterwards. Diana didn't make it to Julia's; instead she went back to her barracks, not reaching her bed until four in the morning. She was exhausted and blackened with the soot and the dirt, but was jubilant. They'd saved St Paul's, but the whole area had been absolutely razed to the ground.

After first washing off the grime, she got into bed for a few hours' sleep, knowing that she'd done the best that she could and grateful for the many firefighters and the brave people at St Paul's Cathedral, many of whom were simply clergy, all of them working to save one of the most famous cathedrals in London. Hitler was trying to wear them down, destroy their resolve, but as she went to sleep that night Diana felt the opposite. Now she was even more determined to defeat this horrific enemy.

Chapter Thirty-Five

One frosty morning in February, Julia dropped down into the chair in the kitchen and reread the words over and over again. Surely it wasn't true. She'd just been on the way out to work when she heard the letter box rattle and the post fall onto the mat. Picking it up, she was excited to see there was a letter from John and also one from her aunt Rosalyn in the Cotswolds. She'd been writing to Julia a couple of times a week to inform her how the children were doing. Apart from Tom feeling a little bit sad, all the reports were that they were growing and were healthy and well during their time in the countryside. She opened that letter first, to read about this week's adventures, and instead, there were just a few lines scribbled onto the paper. Abigail sat quietly, eating her breakfast at the table, watching Julia as she read and reread the lines.

Dear Julia,

I have sent a telegram but just in case it hasn't reached you I thought I would also write a quick letter. I'll come straight to the point. I'm sorry to tell you that last night Tom disappeared. We think he's run away, as he's taken a bag, his teddy bear and the postal bonds you'd sent to him. Unfortunately, we didn't find out until this morning. He must've crept out of one of the bedroom windows overnight. We got the local constabulary out straight away. Julia, I don't want you to worry. Maggie is safe and we are doing everything to try and

*find him. Please call me as soon as you get this note though.
Hopefully, by then, we might have already found him. But
I wanted you to know, not least in case he is trying to make
his way back to London. I didn't want you to be shocked if
he suddenly turned up on your doorstep.*

Lots of love, darling. Call soonest.

Aunt Rosalyn

Julia scanned for the date on the letter: two days before. She looked at Abigail's little face. It reflected the worry that was obviously in Julia's own. She touched her tiny hand. 'Everything's all right, Abigail. Finish your breakfast. Lizzie will be down in a minute, and Agnes will be around to take you to school.'

Julia had managed to enrol Abigail in the local school. Though there were very few children left in London, the authorities had informed her that it was best to keep her in the immediate area until her relatives were located, and they were doing everything they could to find them. Julia quickly put on her coat and her shoes and slipped out the door. Racing to the phone box, she swung open the door and quickly dialled the number.

It was picked up on the third ring, and she heard Maggie on the other end.

'Hello,' said the tiny, faraway voice, then she recited her aunt's phone number as she'd obviously been taught.

'Maggie, it's Mummy.'

'Oh, Mummy,' spluttered Maggie, and then she dissolved into tears. Oh, God. It was something bad. Something had happened to Tom. Julia waited what felt like an eternity for Maggie to stop sobbing so she could get more information out of her. 'I miss you, Mummy,' she muttered through her sobs. It tugged at Julia's heart and once again came the guilt. What had she done to her children? She reined in her emotion to calm her daughter.

'I miss you too, darling. Is there any news?'

'Tom's run away.'

'Yes, darling, I know. Have they found him yet?'

'They're looking everywhere. The policemen have even been here, Mummy. They asked me all sorts of questions. He was very sad and missed you.'

'Is Auntie Ros there?'

'Just a minute,' Maggie said, and Julia heard the phone go down on the table and in the background, she could hear a lot of people in mumbled conversation. Coming to the phone, her auntie picked it up. 'Oh, Julia, I'm so sorry.'

'Have you found him?'

'Not yet, but we're doing everything we can. The police are here right now, just updating me with all that they're doing. A little boy fitting Tom's description was seen at one of the local stations yesterday, but no one reported seeing him on the train. So we're searching the area right now, but there is a chance that he did try to make it back to London.'

'I want to come and help with the search.'

'We're doing everything we can, Julia, and the fact of the matter is he may be on his way back to you. It might be better for you to stay there, at least for another day. It could have taken him a while to find the right train and get to the right place.'

Julia's heart sank. She should never have sent her children away. This was all her fault. Abigail was doing fine here; they just took her to the shelter during a raid. Why had she thought her children would be safer in the country? Tom was so close to her and so clingy. Of course he'd want to get back here.

'Julia? Are you still there?'

She realized her auntie was still speaking.

'Yes. Yes, I'm here.'

'They're searching the countryside now, and they're talking to a lot of people in the area who may have seen Tom. Even with all the evacuees, it's not easy for a little boy just to walk into town and not be spotted. Call me again in a few hours, and I'll give you an update.'

Julia nodded blankly at the phone. 'I'm so sorry.'

'It's not your fault, dear girl. I'm the one that should be sorry. I thought all the windows and doors were locked, and I knew he was sad. We talked about going on a walk today, and he seemed excited about that so I thought it was just a mood. But I think he'd been planning this for a while. Maggie said she'd seen him slipping food from the kitchen, and she thought he was just having midnight snacks, but now we wonder if he was actually packing food for his journey. Julia, I don't want you to worry. People are lovely here. Someone will find him if he's not on the train, and maybe you could go along to the train station there and let them know to look out for him.'

Julia nodded to the receiver; this was a good idea. She could do that. 'I'll call again in a few hours,' she said and hung up the phone. Once again, she felt the weight of this war. As if it wasn't hard enough fighting for your life during every bombing campaign, she had to try and figure out how to keep her family together as well.

She rushed home, and when she got inside, Lizzie had arrived downstairs after having a late night out with Jack, and was sitting at the table talking to Abigail as they waited for Agnes to take her to school.

As soon as Julia walked in, Lizzie knew something was wrong. 'What is it?' she asked as she stood up to greet her friend and instinctively put her arms around her.

'It's Tom. He's gone missing. He's been gone for two whole days. My aunt thinks he might be on his way back here.'

'Oh, Julia, I'm so sorry,' said Lizzie.

All at once, Abigail, sensing the desperate atmosphere in the room, came up and put her arms around Lizzie's waist and held her tightly, and the three of them stood there in silent communion.

There was a knock at the door, and Julia wiped her face. 'We can't tell Agnes anything. She worries enough as it is. I don't need her going on about this for two days.'

Lizzie nodded and started to put on Abigail's coat, ready for Agnes. They had only been gone for about fifteen minutes when the door knocker sounded again. Julia walked out into the hallway, opened the door, and stood in surprise as an older, official-looking man on the doorstep asked her in a sombre tone, 'Mrs Julia Sullivan?'

She was taken aback. Oh God, what was this? She was so scared. She nodded her head, 'That's me.'

'I'm so sorry to tell you. I have a telegram for you.' He handed the small brown envelope to Julia, and she looked down. It could be the one that went astray from her auntie. But it looked more official than usual and then it hit her. Was it possible that when she was already feeling so wretched that this was about John?

The person on the doorstep looked at her sympathetically.

'Sorry, love,' he murmured as he walked away.

Lizzie joined her in the doorway. 'What is it?'

Julia looked down. Her hand was trembling, her own name blurring in and out as she stared at it on the outside of the official-looking envelope. 'I can't open it, Lizzie. I can't take any more bad news today.'

Lizzie led her friend back into the kitchen and sat her down. 'Take a deep breath, Julia. Do you want me to open it for you?'

Julia nodded and then stopped her halfway through. 'I'm not ready yet. I'm not ready to know that he's dead.'

Lizzie's eyes flicked up to hers as she started to sob. Lizzie waited patiently as she squeezed Julia's hand.

Finally, Julia nodded. 'All right, I'm ready now. You can open it.'

Lizzie slowly sliced the envelope open and pulled out the sheet of paper that was inside, unfolding it. It felt as though it took her forever to read it, but when she did, Julia saw that her shoulders didn't sink. The look on her face wasn't anguish. 'It's not bad, Julia. He's not dead.'

Julia collapsed then onto her forearms, sobbing on the table. She didn't care what the rest of the letter said; she just hadn't wanted to hear the words that he was dead. After a good cry she blew her nose in a handkerchief that Lizzie fetched for her, and took the telegram from Lizzie.

'Dear Mrs Sullivan, we are sorry to inform you that John Sullivan is missing in action...' and then she felt the cruel twist of fate, like a knife carving out her insides. So, this was just a precursor letter to the one that would tell her he was dead?

Lizzie must have sensed her fear. 'You've got to have hope, Julia. Lots of people are missing in action and come home, are wounded or captured. Don't automatically think the worst.'

Julia nodded her head, knowing that what Lizzie was saying was sensible, but the cascade of emotions that were going through her body right now made her feel like her whole family was being torn apart. Tom was missing, dear sweet little Tom, and somewhere out there in some godforsaken foreign land her husband, the only man who could make her smile, the only man who could make her laugh until she cried, the only man who could love her in a way that made her weak at the knees, was who knows where, alone and lost.

'How can they lose people? That sounds ridiculous,' she sobbed as she blew her nose again.

'Oh God, Julia, what a horrible day. Look, if you want to go down to the Cotswolds, I could stay here today.'

Julia shook her head. 'I'm going to go to Marylebone station though. Maybe they've heard something or they know something, I can at least tell them about him. I'm going to wait a little while. I know he may be back already but I need to let the police know here to look out for him, just in case.'

Lizzie nodded. 'I'm not on duty until later. You go ahead and do that. And, Julia, we're going to be okay. I promise you, we're all going to be all right. You know why? Because we're women, that's why. And even though some men will never take us seriously in this war, we have a secret weapon. The one thing that those men have little appreciation for because it's a bit unglamorous, and that's our spirit of endurance. Women are experts at holding on. It's woven into the very fabric of our being through centuries of just… holding on. It might not sound as impressive as valour, but it is that grit and determination that will keep this nation together.'

Her friend's words stirred Julia. It was so true. In a time where men were sent to war to fight, it was women who had to stand in the gap emotionally for their families, in the storms of war, holding all the threads of their lives together. No man went to the front with his children, home and family, but women here on British soil were expected to fight while considering all of that every day. Julia wasn't going to give up now, she told herself sternly. Putting on her coat and her shoes, she hurried out of the door and headed into the city, towards the train station.

Chapter Thirty-Six

Across town, Diana was receiving bad news of her own. She'd been in the little kitchenette at the barracks, as they all took it in turns to cook when they didn't feel like going to the canteen and this was her week, when one of the girls came in with the mail.

'You got a letter, Diana, from your mum,' she called out, waving it in the air.

They had all got used to each other's family letters, and Diana got a letter every few days from her mother. But she'd heard nothing from her father, which had made her sad. But Jessie kept her updated on all the things that were happening at home. Drying off her hands, which were soaking as she'd been peeling potatoes, Diana took the letter from her friend and slipped it open. Reading the words, she sat down hard at the kitchen table. All the girls gathered around her.

'Are you all right, Diana?' asked Kathy. 'You look pale.'

'It's my dad. He got injured in the last bombing campaign in Birmingham.' She turned over the sheet of paper to reread it. 'Apparently, he broke his leg falling down the stairs in the blackout.'

'Is he all right?' asked one of the other girls.

'He'll be being a nightmare for my mother. He hates being idle. I wish I could go and see them. He wasn't pleased about me joining up and he hasn't written to me since I got here.'

'It's hard for a lot of them,' put in Mavis, wistfully, 'older people, particularly those who went through the Great War. My dad's the same, so angry about me leaving to come and join up. I think he just wanted to keep me safe.'

'Why don't you go and talk to Sergeant Daly and see if you can get some compassionate leave? We'll be all right without you,' said another member of the team. 'Besides, last night, Jerry gave us a night off. First time in forever. Maybe he's finally giving up.'

Diana nodded and, putting the letter back in the envelope, hurried out to find her commanding officer. Knocking on his door, she went inside and told him about her situation.

'Could I get some leave just to go and see him? My mother says his spirits are very low.'

Sergeant Daly nodded and stamped her pass. 'I'm giving you twenty-four hours. Be back as soon as you can, though, Downes. We need you here.'

She nodded and, quickly gathering her things together, set off to catch a train.

It was as she was walking inside Marylebone Station that she saw Julia, whom she knew should have been at work. But when Julia told her what had happened with Tom, she was heartbroken for her friend and put her arms around her.

'I will look out for him. Maybe I'll see him on a platform. Julia, I'm so sorry. There's a lot of kindness out there at the moment. People are taking care of each other. They will do the same for Tom.'

Julia nodded. 'I hope if somebody sees him, they'll take him to a bobby. I spoke to the authorities here. I've given a description, and they said they would watch out for him and they promised me if they see him here, they'll bring him straight home.'

Diana smiled. 'Sometimes it feels like our world is being torn apart, doesn't it, the longer this goes on? It's not just buildings being destroyed by bombs and all the fires. It's as though Hitler is trying to destroy our families too by putting us all under so much stress, but he won't get us. We're stronger than that. He doesn't know how bloody-minded the British can be.'

The girls hugged, and Diana made her way quickly to the train. When she got into Birmingham, she was shocked at the devastation. She had left before the Birmingham Blitz, and everything had been intact then. Now, the bomb damage to the city centre itself was horrendous.

Strolling across town to get her bus, she felt so much sadness. So many memories she had: the times she'd been up here with her mother shopping for clothes, birthday parties, walks in the park. Many famous landmarks in the city had been damaged. On the bus home, she gazed out of the window, seeing the familiar and unfamiliar; houses she knew along the way, and substantial bomb craters where other homes no longer stood. Diana considered how different she felt. She couldn't believe it had only been a few months since she'd gone away. She'd changed so much in that time and viewed her world so differently now. It wasn't that she didn't see the value in hairdressing any more, but living, breathing and working with people who put their lives on the line every single day for her – as she put hers on the line for them – had changed the way she thought about her world and service in general.

She wasn't sure she could go back to being a hairdresser when the war was over. She thought about Len and the relationship that was just beginning with him. She was saddened by the knowledge that she couldn't tell her parents about him. She just knew they would be disappointed. He was from London and they would want her to marry someone from Birmingham.

When the bus came to a stop, she got off, and as she walked down the street, she spotted one of her friends she'd grown up with, pushing a baby in a pram.

'Hello, Diana. How are you?' Her friend hugged her, and then launched into a long account of her life as Diana tried to mediate her two worlds. As the woman droned on about nappies, teething and local gossip, Diana tried to reorientate herself to this world when she had been living with such a different intensity and speed. It was as if her own world was bigger now, and trying to squeeze it into the world she had come from felt unfamiliar and uncomfortable. It wasn't that Diana saw this world as lesser. In fact, she envied her friend's more traditional life. But Diana had seen so much and been through so much that she knew her own life would never be the same, and in that way, she couldn't relate to what her friend was telling her. It was a new, unexpected feeling for her and she didn't know what to make of it.

Leaving her friend, she was thoughtful, thrown off-kilter by the experience.

Then she saw her home, thankfully still intact. As she opened up the green wooden gate that led up the path to her house, it creaked on its hinges with its familiar squeal, welcoming her back, and she suddenly felt excited. Her heart skipped with the joy of being home. Putting the key in the lock, she opened the door to a familiar world. The same smell of lingering pipe tobacco and lemony waxed flooring that her mother liked to buff to a shine.

'Anybody in?' she called down the hall.

As always, Jessie was in the kitchen. 'Diana,' she said, the joy unmistakable in her tone as she bustled down the hallway to greet her daughter. 'We weren't expecting you home.'

'When you told me Dad was laid up in bed, I wanted to come and surprise you both. It's been a while. They gave me twenty-four hours' leave.' Diana found herself enfolded by the soft, flowery embrace of her mother, the scent of lavender as always on her mother's hair. She followed her into the kitchen, which was where Jessie spent most of her time. Horace tended to dominate the front room, and the other sitting room was kept pristine and untouched, especially for guests.

'I'll put the kettle on. And you can tell me all about your time in London,' said Jessie.

'First, I want to pop up and see Dad,' said Diana. 'How's he doing?'

Jessie's smile wavered a little. She tried to cover it up, but Diana caught it.

'He's not doing very well, is he, Mum?'

'He's struggling, love. This war is bringing back a lot of memories for him. Those bombs are not helping at all, and since they started bombing Birmingham, he's been in a terrible state.'

Diana nodded. 'I understand so much more about his experience now. There were times when I was growing up when I wondered what kind of a thing could have made him so ill, but after living through it myself, I can't even imagine what it must've been like for him, with the gas attacks as well.'

Jessie nodded. 'War is a terrible thing,' she said, drying her hands on a tea towel. 'Maybe one day women will rule the world,' she added, looking out the window wistfully, 'and then war will never be declared again. Because there's no woman who has ever seen a son or a daughter, husband, or a brother suffer or die because of war who could ever put another mother, even of an enemy, through the same pain.'

Diana nodded at her mother's wisdom; a woman who had seen her husband go away to war but come back broken, and then sent her only daughter off to war too. She certainly felt Jessie's strength. She'd always admired her mother, getting up and taking care of the family when her dad couldn't. Still, she'd never really thought about how valuable her stamina was, and how she knew she'd found that same strength in herself. She looked out of the kitchen window to the victory garden. It was now February and her dad had been covering plants with sacking to preserve them from the frost over the wintertime, and she thought how quickly the time had gone. When she'd left, it was just starting to hit full season, and now he was right. She had missed the cabbages.

The kettle boiled, and Jessie made tea for Diana and Horace.

'Why don't you take that up to your dad? He'll be so glad to see you.'

Balancing the two cups on saucers, they rattled against the tea-spoons as she crept up the stairs. Diana stood outside his bedroom door, and drew in a deep breath. Putting a teacup down on the landing table, she knocked, the voice from inside sounded frail as it beckoned her inside. In the darkened room, the sadness clung to the air, and the curtains were closed. In his bed, her dad looked so tiny and fragile and half the man he had been when she'd left.

He didn't see it was her, as he was lying with his eyes closed. She walked over to the bed and sat on the end, putting both teacups on the side table next to him. When she didn't speak, his eyes flicked open and grew wide when he saw who it was.

'Diana?' he enquired incredulously, almost as though he thought he'd seen a ghost. 'What are you doing here?'

'Oh, I knew you'd do anything to get me home, even break your leg,' she joked. 'I've come to see you, Dad.' She tapped his hand. 'Make sure you're all right.'

Tears filled his eyes. 'My girl's home,' he whispered to himself. She moved forward and folded his frail body into her arms and gave him a huge hug. 'I've missed you, Diana. How are you keeping?'

'I'm doing all right, Dad,' she said. 'Never mind about me. I've come to see you. Tell me everything that's happened since I left.'

He shook his head and gave her one of his favourite comebacks. 'Have you got a postage stamp? I'll write it down for you.'

She smiled with the familiarity as she plumped his pillows and helped him into a sitting position to drink his tea.

'Stupid,' he said, 'falling down the stairs like that. There's all the world out there fighting, and your old dad managed to fall down the stairs, wasting the doctor's time. They've got so many more people to take care of. Diana, love, why don't you pull the curtains open so I can see you properly?'

Diana drew the curtains and came back to sit next to him as he smiled broadly, and asked for his pipe. Lovingly, she packed it with tobacco and handed it to him and then struck a match.

Blue, earthy smoke surrounded the pair of them. It was a scent so familiar to her and made her know she was home.

'How are you doing in London, Diana?' he asked.

'Oh, you know.' She didn't want to tell him the truth: that she loved it there and that she'd met a man that meant a lot to her. 'I work on the barrage balloons, Dad.'

'Your mother told me.' He lowered his voice, suddenly full of remorse. 'I'm sorry I haven't written. I've tried many times, but every time I start to write, I just feel all the sadness and loss. And the last thing I wanted to do was discourage you. I'm so proud of you, Diana, so proud of what you're doing for the country. I know it was hard for me to come to terms with it. It is for any parent. After what I went through, I never wanted my own child to go through anything like that.'

Diana took his hand, understanding. She wouldn't want her children to go through it either.

'This will be the last one, Dad. There'll be no more wars after this one. No one would be that foolish after this loss of life.'

He nodded. 'Let's hope so. I have something I want to give you,' he said as he rested his pipe and sipped his tea. 'I meant to give it to you before you left, but I didn't have the courage. I kept hoping you wouldn't go.'

Diana looked at him quizzically.

'Over there in my chest of drawers, second drawer down, there's a little box inside. Bring it over to me.'

Diana walked over to the chest of drawers that was so familiar to her. It had been in the room for the whole of her childhood. Opening up a drawer, she took out the box he had asked for and brought it over to her dad. He opened it and sorted through it until he found what he was looking for. Taking her hand, he placed something in her palm.

'This is my lucky sovereign. This is what got me through my war. I know it sounds ridiculous, but there are times when life feels like it's hanging on by a tiny thread. And it was during that time I needed something to hold on to, to anchor me because everything around me was disappearing. Like a little good luck charm, I would hold on to this and hope for a better day, for a better tomorrow. I want you to have it, Diana. I want you to hold it if you need it.'

Tears started to brim in her eyes. She felt the cold coin in the palm of her hand and thought about the nights he would have spent in the trenches holding on to this charm as though somehow this tiny bit of metal was going to make the difference between life and death. Still, she realized maybe that it was a symbol and it had helped give him courage, the courage that he needed to go on, to believe there would come a day the war was over.

'Thank you, Dad,' she said, fighting her tears. 'I'll keep it with me all the time.'

He closed her hand around it. 'Diana, I owe you an apology. I realized something really important since they started bombing Birmingham, which is that all I had wanted was to keep you safe. I wish you were still little enough to fit under my arm inside my overcoat. But you aren't, and there's nowhere safe at the moment. And the only thing you can really do is fight back, and that's what you are doing, and I'm really proud of you for doing that.'

She hugged him then and kissed him on his smooth, red cheek, feeling, at last, they were getting back the relationship they used to have, and that she had missed so much.

Chapter Thirty-Seven

After their engagement, Lizzie felt as if her relationship with Jack had changed; it became something so much deeper. There was only one thing that haunted her, that woke her in the middle of the night and cramped her stomach: Annie, her dark secret. The dark secret that she hadn't even shared with her friends yet. Every time she considered telling anyone here in her new life she felt overwhelmed with the guilt and shame. She would see the picture of her father so disgusted with her and hear the sound of her mother crying herself to sleep and she couldn't bear to go through anything like that again. What if they all rejected her? What if Jack walked away and her friends disowned her? These relationships had been the most important of her life. She didn't want to jeopardize anything. But as this war was building strength within her, her secret was starting to hollow her out from the inside.

On 14 February there was a knock on the door, and when she opened it, Jack was standing on the doorstep, smiling. She shrieked with surprise; she had her head wrapped in a towel, having just finished washing her hair, and she wasn't wearing any make-up. She was on duty in the afternoon and she'd thought that he'd been called in that morning.

'What are you doing here? I thought you were flying.'

'Happy Valentine's Day! I've got three hours off,' he said with a smile, 'so I stole my friend's car. I thought I would take my fiancée out for a picnic.'

She grimaced. 'Where are we going to go? It's freezing.'

'Where's your sense of adventure? Put on something warm. I'm sick of being inside. I want to get out, and I've got a surprise for you.'

'What about my hair?'

'It will dry on the way.'

She shook her head with dismay. Pulling on a sweater and her coat, she followed him out to the car.

'Where did you get this?' she asked.

'I'm helping out. Someone was needed to run a couple of errands in town, and I offered my services as long as I could get a couple of hours off afterwards.'

Opening the door for her, he helped her in and got into the car and turned the key.

Lizzie looked round – behind her was a picnic basket and a large wrapped box. 'What's that?' she asked.

'It's your surprise.'

'Is it a surprise I'll like?' she enquired.

'I think you'll like it,' he said, laughing as they drove off.

Arriving at Brockwell Park he parked the car, and rubbing a circle to look through the icy window, Lizzie noted how strange it looked. The vast metal gates and all of the railings that had marked its boundaries had been pulled up and were being melted down for the war effort. The park felt exposed, open, but crisp and beautiful in the winter morning's light.

Stepping out of the car she shivered not just with the cold from her damp hair but also the exhilaration of this stolen moment with Jack. Making their way along the path – where many of the flowerbeds were now filled with vegetables, becoming victory gardens – they headed for one of the ponds at the far end of the park. Even from a distance she could see that gliding silently on the water, undeterred by the cold, was a flock of swans. They moved with such peace and grace, only occasionally disturbing the icy stillness and sending gentle ripples across the surface as they plunged their heads into the water to search for their food.

Entwining her frozen fingers into his own, she stole sideways glances at him as he carried the box under one arm and she brought the picnic basket. He was so handsome in his blue air-force uniform, his dark hair cut short under his cap, his strong chin and kind blue eyes always so attentive whenever they met hers.

Arriving at the pond, he pulled her towards him and slipped his arms around her waist.

Brushing her cheek with a kiss he whispered into her hair, 'I don't know how I got to be so lucky, Lizzie Mackenzie. And the only thing I can thank Hitler for is that he brought you all the way from Scotland so we could meet. I'm never going to stop counting my blessings whenever I look at you. I can't believe you're going to be my wife.'

He drew her in for a gentle kiss on the lips, and she felt a shiver down her spine. Every time he kissed her now, she was starting to feel rippling emotions surging through her body that wanted more than was possible at this time. She guessed he felt the same way because quickly, before the electricity between them became too hard to bear, he pulled away from her and held her hands.

She shivered again.

'I hope that wasn't you grimacing because I kissed you,' he joked with her.

She shook her head numbly. 'That was me freezing!' she informed him, her teeth chattering.

He drew her in close again, and she slid her arms under his jacket and around his waist.

'All part of my evil plan to make sure I get to be closer to you,' he whispered into her ear.

Lizzie laughed and placed her head on his chest, lulled by the rhythmical beat of his heart and the clean, spicy scent of his after-shave, her breath slowed to mark time with his own. She delighted in how she felt so safe in his arms, so complete, as if she had waited her whole life to feel this way. This overwhelming feeling of being so comfortable this close to him, along with the thrill that raced through her body, was a sensation she never wanted to get over.

Turning her head, she gazed out at the expanse of beauty all around her and noted that, bar the two of them, the park was completely empty. In the distance, a low-lying morning mist was still swirling along the ground, masking trees and low-lying shrubs. Above, a weak winter sun, a perfect circle of white framed by heavy clouds, attempted to warm up the February chill.

Lizzie had forgotten how much she'd missed being outside like this. Whenever she was in nature, it took her straight back to Scotland. Every tree, every bird, every blade of grass was where her heart felt most at home.

Finally slipping out of her arms he produced a blanket from the basket and flung it out onto the ice-cold ground.

'You can't be serious,' Lizzie said, shivering again.

'Come on, shouldn't be hard for a tough Scottish lass like you. Besides, I can keep you warm.'

She shook her head as they snuggled up on the blanket together, spirals of icy breath circling between them.

Opening the picnic basket, he handed her a sandwich.

'I managed to sneak this from the canteen,' he said. 'Cheese and tomato.'

Her eyes widened. 'How did you manage that?'

'Someone owed me a favour,' he said, passing her an apple.

As they ate their lunch, watching the swans circle the pond, Lizzie sat forward and wrapped her arms around her knees. 'Amazing, isn't it?' she said. 'Nature just goes on as though nothing's happening. They're not worried about the next bomb attack, where they're going to get food from, whether they will live or die. They just keep building their nests and raising their families as though nothing is going on. It gives me hope when I look at them. It reminds me of what peacetime looks like, what peace used to be like.'

Jack nodded. 'It will be again soon. I think we're winning, no matter what the fearmongers are saying. I don't think this war will last forever. And then you and I can live like these swans because they mate for life, you know, we will be together always, like them.'

Lizzie stomach tightened, and all at once she couldn't stand it any longer.

She sucked in a huge icy breath, then blurted out, 'There is something I need to tell you about me. Something you may not like. And you may not want to marry me after I tell you. But it's only fair that I'm honest.'

His brows furrowed with concern, instantly realizing that this was something serious, and he looked fearful of what that could mean.

Lizzie tried to calm the quiver in her voice. 'You need to know that there was someone in my life before you.' She paused to gauge his reaction.

He reached forward and took her hand in his, worry in his face moving to compassion and relief. 'We all have a past, Lizzie. You shouldn't worry about that.'

'This is slightly different.' She swallowed, pulling her hand from his, not wanting to meet his gaze. Gulping back air, she decided to just say it quickly. 'I was walking out with a boy at home where I live, and one night... something happened, and I became pregnant with his child.'

Jack sat back from her on the blanket, the weight of what she was saying seeming to press him down and take the air from his lungs.

Lizzie flicked her eyes up to meet his to try and get a sense of how her confession had been received but saw nothing in his own, only the fact he appeared to be considering her words carefully. Was he angry? Was he judging her? She couldn't be sure; Jack was just so silent.

Lizzie continued the story; she may as well get it all out now. 'That was when I moved in with my aunt and uncle. But I had to give up my daughter for adoption. They took the baby off me, and it was the hardest thing I have ever done. Even thinking about it is still incredibly painful for me.' Lizzie's voice petered out to a tiny whisper as fresh tears streamed down her face and pooled on her chin.

Jack stood up, and for a second she thought he was going to walk away from her, just leave her sitting there in all her exposed pain, and instantly she regretted telling him. But instead of heading for the car, he bent down and pulled her gently to her feet, and enfolded her in his arms, holding Lizzie so tightly she could barely breathe.

'Oh, my love. I'm so sorry you had to go through something so hard. I wish I could take all this pain from you,' he whispered into her hair.

Lizzie couldn't believe what she was hearing. Was he loving her even though she had not only had a baby out of wedlock but had also kept this secret from him even after they were engaged? It appeared he was. Letting it all go, she collapsed into his arms and allowed the grief to flow. This was all she had ever wanted; to be accepted and loved. Acceptance from her parents, from a world where she was seen as sinful and used goods, but mostly from this man she loved.

Now, with the truth out and his acceptance of it, Lizzie allowed herself to sob, long and hard, as he gently rocked her in his arms and stroked her back.

He kissed her damp cheek softly, and whispered tenderly into her ear. 'I never, ever, want you to worry again about anything that has gone on before, anything you did or were before; our love is stronger than anything in your past or mine. It is all about now, Lizzie – war has taught me that. It's all about living and loving in this very moment. Because that's all we truly have.'

Lizzie felt her heart leap with the realization of what his words meant. The chains of fear and loathing that had kept her heart captive with the belief she was unworthy of this kind of love melted away. There was now nothing standing in the way of her happiness; she would have someone of her very own to love her forever. She drew even closer and buried her head in the chest of the man she was going to marry and couldn't imagine him not being in her life. How had she managed to live this long without knowing him? Knowing the complete and utter fulfilment of having a person that she loved and who loved her back and who accepted her exactly as she was.

They stayed there in each other's arms for a long time, as long as she needed, Lizzie feeling all his acceptance in his embrace. Eventually, reluctantly, she pulled away and blew her nose, and as she did so she noticed something over his shoulder.

'Are you going to tell me what the box is for?' she asked, her voice still hoarse from crying.

'Why don't you go ahead and open it?' He grinned, pulling her back down to the blanket and handing it to her.

She placed the box in front of her and undid the packaging.

'It's a gift for you,' he added as she released the red satin ribbon that was keeping the brown paper in place.

'For me?' she whispered, gratefully.

Under the paper was a square mahogany box with a highly polished veneer. She looked over at him curiously, and undoing the silver clasp, pushed up the stiff heavy lid. Lizzie was thrilled and totally taken back to see it was a gramophone.

'You bought this for me?' she asked, her eyes widening with shock.

'I did. Somehow music makes me always think of you, your laughter, the joy you always have. It felt right that you should have music to enjoy.'

Lizzie stroked the smooth, dark-grained wood, admiring the silver-engraved arm. There was a record already on its turntable. Al Bowlly, 'The Very Thought of You'. The one that he had found at the guesthouse and played the night he had proposed.

'Whenever I hear that song, it will always make me think of you, Lizzie. The words express exactly how I feel about you. I thought that because we didn't get to go dancing lately, we could maybe dance here.'

'In the park?' she responded, frowning, looking around her with embarrassment, but there was no one to be seen.

'I don't think the swans will mind,' he stated confidently, standing up and offering his hand to her. She wound up the gramophone and carefully placed the needle on the glossy shellac disc. And as the orchestra started up, she got to her feet, and slipped into his arms. Al Bowlly's melodic tones crooned out into the damp, crisp morning, singing about how he was living in a daydream and that the love of his life made him forget all about the ordinary, everyday things.

Lizzie circled Jack's waist with her arms, placed her head on his shoulder and they swayed gently as she absorbed all the words.

As they moved rhythmically together, the song summed up so much of how she was feeling, how her love for Jack made her forget everything else in her life, especially the sadness she had known because of his tenderness and now his complete acceptance of her. She wasn't sure if the intensity and finality of war contributed to the immense gratitude she was feeling, but as they circled the blanket in the middle of the park in the middle of winter, with swans as their audience, she felt nothing could rob her of her happiness.

As she closed her eyes to enjoy it, it was as if they became one. Lizzie wasn't sure where he ended and she began, and it was as though she could sense exactly what he was feeling and thinking. Nothing about this felt like it had with Fergus; that had felt so immature compared to this. This was so much deeper. And as her cheeks reddened, her mind drifted to what it would be like once they were married and they could be closer than they were now. She imagined him slowly undressing her in the moonlight and she unbuttoning and pulling off his clothes. Then she would draw him closer, feeling his smooth warm skin next to hers as they indulged in long lingering kisses until they were both breathless. She would run her hands through his thick dark hair and make him shiver as she danced her fingertips up and down his back. They would take their time to find what gave each other the most pleasure. Until, unable to bear their desire any longer, they would finally become one in body as well as spirit. Lizzie just knew without being told that nothing about what she had experienced in the past with Fergus would compare to what it would be like with Jack. This was already so different. The feeling she had for him so much stronger, the desire to be closer unbearable and she couldn't wait until they could take that desire further.

He must have sensed something because he looked at her. 'You look flushed. Are you getting warm now?'

She nodded, not wanting to let him into her intimate thoughts.

'I was just wondering about us actually, and wondering if you loved me as much as I love you.'

He stopped dancing and stared at her and for once, gone was the playful expression in his eyes. It was replaced by an intense gaze fixed upon her as he searched her face.

He ran a finger down the side of her cheek, his eyes following its journey. 'I love you, Lizzie, more than I will ever be able to show you,' he whispered, his emotion visible. 'I've been in love with you since the very first night when we sat huddled together in the basement of a theatre. There was something so right about us, something that just fitted, that was easy, that was destined to be. I couldn't explain it then and I can't explain it now. I could have proposed to you that very first night but I didn't want to frighten you off. Scotland's an awfully big place to try and find you if you ran away, and I sensed there was some reason you were holding back and now I know what it was. Your daughter. As you told me about her I felt the shift. Just now, I've felt that last bit of distance between us fall away. As if you finally feel safe enough to get close to me.

'Sometimes I wake in the middle of the night with the realization I may never see you again, because of the danger, and I feel this panic come over me. I want us to be married so the next time I wake like that I will be able to reach out and feel you next to me. Once I am in the plane I have to push these kind of thoughts away, because if I thought of the loss I wouldn't be worth much up there. But before I met you, dying in battle didn't really mean anything. There was no real cost. Now, it is so different. I know it has been fast and it's hard to believe we have only been together a few months, but that doesn't affect the intensity of what I feel.'

Lizzie felt tongue-tied, her heart beating wildly as she listened to his confession.

Finally, she spoke. 'I feel the same way,' she whispered back, 'and you're right, I was holding back because of my daughter. I knew if you couldn't accept my past that we could never have a future.'

Pulling her into his arms he kissed her with great depth of feeling.

All at once there was a quack from a wayward duck behind them, and Lizzie laughed, remembering they were in a park. She had been lost in the world they were creating around them. A world without war. As they stepped back, both of them were breathless.

'I should get back,' he whispered, hoarsely.

'Me too.'

'But, it's not going to be easy concentrating on flying this afternoon,' he laughed. 'I'm counting on you, Lizzie. Don't let us down now.'

She smiled.

They packed up the basket, and she carried her gift under her arm as they walked back through the park hand in hand. 'This was lovely, Jack. Thank you.'

On the way home, she told him about the woman in the cinema and how she'd met her again in the underground; how she'd been the first clue to her daughter's whereabouts.

'I was fourteen then, just a child myself. And back then I felt I didn't have the choice, that I had to give her up. But now I want to see her, just to know she is happy and loved and cared for, and that woman is the key to me finding her. My daughter might even be here in London.'

Jack nodded his understanding. 'And I am going to help you in any way I can.'

On Julia's doorstep, she looked up into his eyes. Something had changed between them since she had shared this part of her life.

Lizzie slipped her arms around his neck and pulled him in close, feeling his body relax into hers with the new intimacy between them. Slowly his lips moved towards hers, his eyes not leaving her face, and as Lizzie closed her eyes, she felt the warmth of his mouth upon her own. It wasn't the first time he had kissed her, but somehow it felt like a beginning. It completed the deep and strong bond between them that had been cemented in the park. As she eventually pulled away and they parted, the warmth and glow of their connection made her heady with the love that was growing so strongly inside her for this man she never wanted to be apart from.

Chapter Thirty-Eight

Julia had been working in the bunker, trying not to think about Tom. She had already called her aunt that morning and been by the station before she went in to work. It had been four days since he had gone missing and still there was no word; work was a good distraction. She had decided that if there was no word today, she was going to the Cotswolds to search for him herself. All at once Carol had arrived at her desk, her face pale. She had shown Julia what she had been working on and it had been in black and white. John's battalion had taken heavy losses and many had been killed and were still not identified. Seeing it written down had been jarring and she hadn't even felt Carol put her arm around her as she had started to sob. Both their husbands were missing in the same area. Hearing the news, Mrs Scriber had given Julia and Carol the afternoon off to deal with this terrible shock, and Julia headed home early for once.

Halfway home the air-raid sirens sounded and she took cover in an underground shelter. Her thoughts were many thousands of miles away with the man she loved, who might be alive or dead, and closer with the pain of her missing son; she felt in a daze. But as she turned the corner of her street she couldn't believe what she was seeing. She'd lived for twenty years on this road with enchanting little terraced houses that sloped away down a hill, tiny front gardens, and a tree-lined path. Now, as Julia stood on the brow of the hill, she didn't recognize what she was looking at. It took her a minute to even understand where she was standing in relation to her home because in front of her were just piles upon piles of bricks and rubble.

Moving tentatively down the street, Julia stumbled over vast chunks of stone, tripping on her neighbour's belongings. As the wind picked up, the remnants of a singed, flowery apron blew towards her and wrapped itself around her ankle, and what looked as if it had been a glossy film magazine with charcoaled pages fluttered in the wind. She continued to stride through the bomb wreckage, feeling sick as she noticed all people's beloved belongings: a chair, a candlestick, a birdcage, a smashed vase.

Julia tried to hurry to get closer to her home, which was much further down the street, her heart in her throat. But as it came into view, she could see her house was still standing, and she breathed a sigh of relief.

However, sadly, she could see across the street that the home of the couple who had moved in not long ago was a hollowed-out wreck. Not only destroyed by the direct hit of a bomb, but it was also in the final stages of burning to the ground. Firefighters had already arrived and stood stolidly getting it under control. The air was filled with the smell of burning, smouldering wood.

As she continued to wade through the debris that was now her road, Julia noticed that all the windows in the phone box on the corner were smashed, and with a sinking heart, she saw as she approached her own home that her windows too were all gone. Blowing about in the street were many of her belongings, along with everyone else's. As she got to what would have been her gate, there was now a pile of rubble from the house across the street. One of Maggie's blouses had wrapped itself around the gatepost and was rippling in the wind like a flag. She spotted her own kitchen equipment, books, her mother's tablecloth, her whole life seemed to be out here in the street. For some odd reason, maybe the shock, Julia unhooked Maggie's blouse, even though Maggie hardly wore it any more, and held it to her chest as she tried to suppress the sob that was just hovering in her throat.

Suddenly, an awful thought struck her.

Agnes, John's mother. She glanced at the house next door. Its windows, too, were blown out. Agnes had a real fear of the shelters and so hardly went anywhere. Surely, she would still be in there.

'Agnes!' Julia shouted out. 'Agnes!' She stepped over another remnant of what looked as if it had once been one of her neighbours' dining tables and made her way round to Agnes's front door. The door had been blown open with the blast, and she could get in there easily. The hallway was strewn with dust, clutter and bricks, but she was relieved to see, as she went from room to room, that Agnes wasn't there.

Climbing over the mountain of rubble as she made her way carefully back to her own house, Julia coughed, choking on the clouds of brick dust being swirled about by the wind, the smell of the smoke in the air clinging to her hair and her clothes. Pushing open her front door, it was as though it had been ransacked. Lots of her furniture was gathered towards the back of her house, obviously with the force of the blast. Carefully, she started to pick her way in; glass was everywhere. As the wind ripped through the broken panes, it continued to whip letters, documents, and newspapers into a spiral that cavorted around the room – book pages whipping and snapping their disgruntled displeasure on the floor where they had fallen from the bookcase. She didn't even know where to start.

All at once she heard a noise coming from inside the kitchen. It was tiny but unmistakable. Her heart started to thump. Abigail? Could Abigail be here? Surely she'd still be at school. Julia waded down the hallway, noticing broken pictures, the photograph of her and John, and the one with the children smashed on the living-room floor.

When she got into the kitchen, the table was turned on its side. The noise was coming from behind it. 'Abigail,' she called out. She could see someone stirring with dust-filled hair, a tiny person. *Oh God, don't let Abigail be hurt.*

She reached the table, and the person moved, their eyes blinking away the dust. Suddenly she realized with a shock who it was. 'Tom? Tom, is that you?'

His little green eyes flicked open as he heard the voice of his mother, and automatically he burst into tears. She kicked the debris out of the way, the fierce mother's instinct in her finding all the strength she needed to get through everything that was now lying in her way in the kitchen. Quickly she leaned down and picked her son up into her arms and held him, feeling as if she were snatching him from the jaws of death. He started to sob into her shoulder.

As she held him tightly and felt his tiny heart beating against her chest, she suddenly felt all of the tension, all of the fear and the breath she'd been holding that had clenched her stomach since the news of his disappearance starting to release. 'Oh my God, Tom, we've been looking everywhere for you.'

'I missed you, Mummy,' said the little voice that was buried in her blouse. 'I'm sorry that I left Aunt Rosalyn's. I know now I shouldn't have. I should have stayed there. I was so scared without you and so scared without Maggie, but I just wanted to come home. I got on the wrong train and went the wrong way, and couldn't find the right one. I didn't want to tell a policeman as I knew they would have been angry.'

Quickly she pulled her son down on her lap so she could look at him as she squatted to the floor. He had a nasty cut over the top of his eye. There were scratches and bruises on his knees. His jacket was ripped, but apart from that, he seemed in one piece. It was only then that she could allow the tears to fall. 'Thank God,' she said. 'Thank God, Tom.'

Tom looked up at his mother's face in surprise. 'Don't cry, Mummy. I promise I won't do it again. I promise I'll stay where I'm told to stay.'

'I'm not crying because I'm sad, Tom,' she said. 'I'm crying because I'm happy.' He looked at her quizzically. 'I'm just so happy to see you.'

He threw his little chubby arms around her neck and held her tightly then. Julia picked him up, pulled out a chair that she managed to un-mangle from things on the kitchen floor, sat him down, and went to find her first-aid kit. She cleaned up the cut on his head. Once she had removed the blood, it wasn't too bad after all. She put a plaster on it and also some cream on his knees.

She carried him up to his bedroom then. Miraculously the windows hadn't smashed in there at the back of the house, so she sat him on his little bed. 'Tom, I need to grab things that have gone out of the windows before they disappear. It's windy, and there might be important papers and things. Can you stay here while I do that?'

He nodded his head, pulling his knees up to his chest and looking so tiny in the corner of his bed.

She went to his wardrobe and pulled out two of his comics. 'Why don't you read those till I get back?' she said, pulling down a blanket from which she shook off the dust and covering him. 'I'll be back in a little while. Do you need anything to drink?'

He shook his head. 'I'll be all right, Mummy. I'll just wait for you here.'

Julia went out into the street then and started to gather anything that was theirs. More of Lizzie's things. Poor Lizzie had already lost so much; she couldn't bear for her to lose even more. Also, Julia noticed a lot of things that didn't belong to her. She wondered if they had come from the people across the street, as their house had been bombed. She wondered, numbly, if they had survived.

As she continued to gather personal belongings, she went across to see if she could see anybody there, but the street seemed to be desolate apart from her, so she went on clearing up as best she could. It was as she was lifting up a pile that something fell out, some correspondence. A type written note that was blackened. She tried to read it to see if she could figure out who in the street it was addressed to.

But as she read through it, Julia started to feel a chill. This wasn't a regular letter. This was a letter or a document that described important things about England. Locations of military bases, famous landmarks, and some sort of a diary of things that were happening daily. She realized as she read it that this was something that would be very important to the enemy. She went cold.

Shaken, she looked around the street, as if the very person who owned it might have been there in front of her, but once again, she was alone. Somebody on her street, or maybe even living in her home, was a traitor. The word sat heavy with her. She thought about Lizzie, with her outgoing and warm personality, and Diana, who was so kind-hearted and loving. Surely neither of them would be working undercover for the Nazis? What about the couple across the street though? They had been new to the neighbourhood. Could they have been working for the enemy? The older man next door? All these people she knew, or she thought she knew. She shuddered.

She was still contemplating all of this when she heard somebody call out to her. Quickly she shoved the letter into her pocket and turned around.

'Oh, Julia,' said Lizzie's distraught voice as she looked at the mess that had been their home. 'What happened?'

'The house across the street,' said Julia, trying to get her mind back from what she'd just read. 'It took a direct hit, by the looks of it. I've been trying to retrieve things out here in the street. Also, Tom's here.'

'Oh, thank God,' said Lizzie.

'The little blighter made it all the way back from the Cotswolds. He's upstairs on his bed. He's pretty shaken up. He looks exhausted, and I hope he'll curl up and go to sleep.'

'Let me help you. Did you find much?'

All at once, Julia was hesitant. She suddenly felt different about the people around her. She would have to report this. What if it was Lizzie or Diana? Surely it couldn't be. But wasn't that how they were trained? To blend in? It could be anybody.

'Not much,' she said absently.

Lizzie nodded and waded her way into the house, treading her way carefully to the kitchen.

'Good news,' she shouted as Julia stood in the front room, looking around, trying to decide where to start with her thoughts so far away.

'What?'

'The stove is still working. I'm making us a cup of tea.'

Julia smiled. It couldn't possibly be Lizzie, and it definitely wasn't Diana. It had to be somebody else. She would need to report this at work, but she'd like to know who it was first. Julia needed to sit with this information for a short time to figure out what she was going to do.

Chapter Thirty-Nine

It was a beautiful day on the last day of February 1941. Lizzie travelled to Kenley for her next shift on duty, enjoying the warmth of the sun that was shining as if it was spring. Even though the bombing of London continued, the intense daily bombing they had experienced the year before had ceased, which meant they occasionally got a whole night's sleep. Hopping off the bus, Lizzie was in a buoyant mood because she'd been out dancing with Jack the night before. And she remembered with great fondness the conversation they'd had on Julia's doorstep. For the first time, they'd talked about children and about where they would live after the war was over. Just before he kissed her goodbye, they'd decided the next time they had leave together, in a week, they would go to visit his family in Essex. He wanted his mother and father to meet Lizzie and get to know her.

Then he had slipped his arms around her waist, pulled her in close, and left her breathless with a long lingering kiss. 'I love you, Lizzie, and I can't wait for my family to meet you. I know they will fall in love with you as much as I have,' he'd said before he left her. She had watched him walk away all the way up the street, until the echo of his footsteps had faded away and his shadow, cast by a bright clear moon, had disappeared completely from her view.

So, as she travelled to work that day, her spirit was alive as she thought about Jack and marvelled at the beauty of the season all around her. Tulips and daffodils were defying the war and pushing up through the cold, dark earth, and the sun was attempting to warm the day. Arriving at the operations room, she resumed her usual position. Her job had become second nature to her now, and she enjoyed what she did. Putting on her headset, she plugged herself in.

'Morning, Stan,' she said, greeting her counterpart on the other end.

'Morning, Lizzie,' came his chirpy response.

'Jerry's been keeping you busy?'

'Not yet. Looks like they're all waiting for you,' came back Stan's comic reply.

Retrieving her plotter, Lizzie started work. The day started slowly, with only a few German planes being spotted, but then around midday, they got their first real action. Three bomber formations had been spotted over the Channel on their way in, en route to London. Lizzie listened in on the action as she pushed the hostiles into position on the map.

Hurricanes had been scrambled from Biggin Hill, and as she tuned in, her heart skipped a beat when she realized it was Jack's squadron that was in the air. She recognized his voice straight away.

'Red Leader here, bombers down at nine o'clock. Okay, gentlemen, let's see them off.'

She watched the WAAF next to her push Jack's squadron into position as Lizzie inched the bombers forward.

As Stan gave her new instructions, Jack's wingman, Alan, whom Lizzie had met, answered Jack with a crackle on the radio. 'See you down there, Red Leader.' Then Lizzie heard their engines roar.

She pictured Jack in the sky with the other eleven planes making their way down to try and take out the bombers before they reached London. German fighter planes always accompanied their bombers, but the hope was that the British Spitfire squadrons, who were also out there, would deal with them in the air.

All at once, the sound of a stream of bullets peppered the airwaves. Lizzie hoped the sound was of Jack's squadron attacking the bombers themselves. Her breath hitched as she listened. Even though he did this every day it was never easy when it was her call.

The battle continued in the air. From what she could tell by the conversation, some of the German fighters had broken free of the Spitfires' engagement and had headed down to intercept Jack's squadron.

Suddenly, a concerned transmission from Alan. 'One on my tail! Red Leader! There's one on my tail!' This was followed by the sound of another rattle of bullets on metal, like hail on a tin roof.

Jack's calm voice came back. 'Coming down, Alan, I'm coming down.'

Alan sounded frantic. 'I can't shake them, Red Leader! They're all over me! My wing's been hit! My wing's been hit!'

'Nearly there, Red Two, hold on, I'm nearly there.'

Lizzie held her breath as there was the sound of another round of fire. There was no way to tell who it was coming from: the enemy, or the friendlies.

Everyone around her was listening intently as Stan cut in carefully to add a new vector for her to move the bombers ahead. Numbly, Lizzie moved the hostiles along the map.

Jack's calm and controlled voice was on the airwaves. 'Sharp right, Alan, turn right. I've got them. I've got them in my sights.'

'They're everywhere, Jack!'

'I'm not leaving you, Alan. I've got him. Veer right and I'll finish him off.'

There was another long transmission of gunfire that seemed to last an eternity. Lizzie listened, the fear swelling in her throat. She attempted to unclench her jaw and under her breath she whispered, 'Come on Jack, see them off.'

Just then, her intense concentration was interrupted. 'Lizzie, are you hearing me okay? Bombers have moved position.'

Stan was talking to her, and she hadn't heard him. She looked at the girl next to her and realized that she hadn't listened to the last two instructions. Lizzie pushed the bombers along on the map into position as she continued to listen to the fierce battle being waged in the sky.

Suddenly she realized she must have been holding her breath because she became light-headed. She quickly sucked in air.

There was an explosion and then she heard, 'You got him, Jack, I'm free. Thank you, Red Leader.'

Lizzie breathed a sigh of relief. He did have the luck of the Irish, as he always said. She heard Jack's breathless tone come back with deep sincerity, 'I'm always here for you, Red Two, you can count on me, Alan. Let's go back in again and—'

All at once, there was an intense crackle and another spray of bullets, and another explosion and Jack's transmission cut out halfway through what he was saying.

'Pulling up, Jack, I'm pulling up. Jack? Jack? Red Leader?'

Everybody waited. The girl next to Lizzie was listening to the same conversation, giving her sympathetic glances, knowing that Jack was her boyfriend.

All at once Alan's frantic voice. 'He's been hit! He's been hit! He's on fire. Bail out, Jack! Bail out! Red Leader, can you hear me? You have to bail out!'

The transmission crackled and cut off. Lizzie was going to faint. She reached out to the girl next to her and grabbed her arm as Alan's sombre voice came back. 'I've lost sight of Red Leader in the cloud cover… Anyone see him bail out?'

The transmission was silent, the long ominous crackle confirming everyone's worst fears. Lizzie didn't hear any more; nothing was registering; it was if her mind had just shut down. Looking around her for reassurance, she shouted to the whole room, 'Did anyone hear if he got out? Please, someone, did you hear! Did you hear!'

Lizzie searched frantically from face to face, looking for someone to reassure her. To tell her that they had heard something else, something about him being safe. But the whole room of women were frozen, as if turned to stone, the horror on all of their faces. Many of them knew she was engaged to Jack Henson.

Then a calm voice came over her headset. It was Stan. 'He may well have bailed out, Lizzie. Just because they didn't see him doesn't mean that he's not okay.'

Lizzie yanked off her headset and threw it down on the table. Why was it so hot, and why was the room spinning? She thought she was going to pass out.

All at once, one of the other girls was beside her with a chair, helping her down onto it. And somebody else arrived with a glass of water.

She held it, her hand shaking uncontrollably, staring at the glass, not knowing what to do with it, waiting for somebody to tell her what to do. Her mind was reeling with a thousand thoughts. This was not supposed to happen. They were going to be together forever, he had promised her. He was lucky, Alan had told her. This was just some cruel joke, maybe just a nightmare, she would wake up in a minute. There had to be a mistake. He must have got out. The weight of the alternative was too monstrous for her mind to grapple with.

Someone must have called her superior because Sergeant Wheaton's face suddenly swam into her view.

'Come on, Lizzie. Let's go to my office. I'll make you a cup of tea.'

Lizzie didn't remember the walk back up out of the operations room through the long dark tunnel. She didn't remember going into the office. The next thing she remembered was the heat of the cup in her hand. All around her, everything was dark and moving slowly, as if she were deep underwater. When people spoke to her, the words didn't make any sense. Nothing seemed to register. Sergeant Wheaton was telling her things, but they just washed over her. Then, there was a knock on the door.

Her superior must have called Diana, who was listed as a contact in Lizzie's files because all of a sudden, she was there with

Lizzie, lifting her from the chair, walking her outside, placing her in a vehicle, and putting her arm around her as they were driven back home.

She didn't say much. Just held Lizzie as they went. Words just weren't possible. What could either of them say? Diana was helping her into the house. They were still clearing up from the recent raid but the kitchen was now in decent enough shape for Diana to sit Lizzie down and make her a strong cup of tea with lots of sugar, as she quietly sobbed into a handkerchief.

'He's all right, isn't he, Diana? Tell me you think he's all right.'

Diana looked out of the cracked kitchen window, resolutely, appearing not to be able to quell Lizzie's worst fears.

'We'll know soon enough,' she said quietly. 'Sergeant Wheaton told me as we headed out of the door that as soon as they had any news, she would let us know.'

Lizzie burst into tears and howled. She collapsed forward onto her arms and sobbed, her shoulders heaving with the pain that came from the pit of her stomach. Diana was beside her again, saying reassuring things, but Lizzie was crying so hard she couldn't hear any of it.

Once she had cried herself dry she lifted her head. This was all wrong, there had to be a mistake, he had to have bailed out and no one had found him yet. In her mind's eyes she saw him strolling through a field, his parachute tucked under his arm, thinking about regaling them all with his story over a pint.

She looked into Diana's concerned eyes. 'I know he's fine,' said Lizzie, blowing her nose. 'This is all going to be a great joke that we talk about in the pub later. He and Alan will be reliving it, just like we did before. He has to be okay. There's nothing wrong.'

When Julia arrived home hours later, there was still no news. As Diana and Julia spoke in hushed voices in the kitchen, Lizzie wandered aimlessly around the house, her arms folded across her chest, tears periodically gliding down her cheeks. Whenever Lizzie would tire of pacing, Abigail, now home from school, would find her and curl up next to her or put her arms around her waist and bury her head into Lizzie's neck. It was as though she sensed the sadness that Lizzie was feeling. Lizzie sat slumped in the front room, watching the hands on the clock move. Sometimes the minutes took an eternity to tick away, sometimes it felt like a whole hour passed in a minute. Nothing felt real, her whole world was just somehow out of sync. Every time there was a noise, Lizzie would think it was a knock at the door, and would jump to her feet to check out of the window. But nobody was ever there. As she watched the day move into the evening she became more and more angry. Where was Jack? Why hadn't he come to tell her he was all right yet? Had he forgotten she would be waiting to hear? How cruel. They would be having their first argument when he finally made it over to her.

Trying to fill the void in the house, Abigail walked over to the radio and turned it on. It was the Home Service, giving a cold roll call of the dead from the day before. Just vast numbers that they had all become numb to. Lizzie suddenly felt a shiver run down her spine. Tomorrow, would Jack be one of those? No, she wouldn't let it happen to them, they were Lizzie and Jack, they were perfect for each other, surely fate could not be that cruel. She started practising in her mind what she would say to him when he did turn up. About how glad she was he was alive and how scared she'd been. Then she would thump him on the arm for not coming sooner and leaving her so long without word. All at once, the crystal voice of Vera Lynn drifted across the airwaves, singing 'We'll Meet Again'.

Julia rushed in to turn it off, but it was too late; already the words had hit home. Lizzie collapsed into a chair, her head in her hands as she sobbed.

It wasn't until very late into the evening that they finally got word. The whole night the three of them had hardly spoken. They'd just sat, waiting, knowing that the news was coming. As soon as she heard the knock on the door, Lizzie rushed to it. But when she looked into Alan's face, she knew it was the worst. Lizzie crumpled onto the floor in the hallway before he could even get the words out, and the two girls rushed to support her.

'I'm so sorry, Lizzie. Really. I'm so sorry.'

Someone screamed the word 'No!' Was it her?

He carried on speaking, even though it wasn't making any sense to her.

'His plane came down, and for reasons we'll never know, he didn't bail out. We don't know why he couldn't. But I'm afraid he's gone, Lizzie. We have retrieved the plane.'

She could no longer see Alan. Tears filled her vision, streaming down her face, and a darkness was growing in her eyes. Her pain inside was suffocating her, strangling her, a huge weight pressed on her chest and she gulped for breath; something was growing around her, threatening to engulf her behind a dense black cloud. But there was also part of her that couldn't believe it. Alan's words just wouldn't sink in. Jack couldn't be dead. There was a mistake. They were getting married. No one had seen him bail out. He could still be alive, she started to bargain with herself.

Alan knelt down in front of her. 'I want you to know something, Lizzie. He talked about you all the time. He spoke about you this morning as we were leaving and how he felt he was the luckiest man alive.'

The world 'alive' hung in the air like a stone.

Alan's voice started to crack. 'I'm so, so sorry, but I wanted you to know how much he loved you. He was the bravest and kindest man I've ever served with, and I'll miss him too.'

Alan, evidently not wanting to be emotional in front of her, squeezed her hand, got up quickly, replaced his cap, and left the house.

Lizzie started to become light-headed as her friends helped her upstairs, as she sobbed into Diana's arms. Julia closed the curtains, and helped her undress and get into bed. Lizzie didn't sleep. She just lay there, numbly looking at the ceiling, trying to let it sink in. Pain and grief washed over her, and she felt irreversibly broken, as if there was nothing that could fix this; only the arms of the man she loved that would never hold her again, and the pain of that realization was just too much for her to bear.

Chapter Forty

Diana had returned to base that night and after hardly any sleep and not wanting to go to the canteen she had been trying to prepare breakfast the next morning in the little kitchenette, when the door had opened. Thinking it was just one of the girls she didn't look up when all at once arms were around her waist. She started with the shock but when she turned Len was in front of her.

'Diana, I just heard. I'm so sorry about Jack. Lizzie must be beside herself.'

Diana burst into tears. She had been holding back her feelings to be strong for Lizzie but now as Len folded her into his arms she allowed the emotion just under the surface to pour forth like a flood.

As she sobbed on his shoulder, he rocked her gently and stroked her hair, and it felt so good to be close to him. This was the first time he had been really demonstrative with her and once again she wondered if he was just being kind in that moment or if this was something more for him.

Once she'd had a good cry, she sat blowing her nose at the table as he made her a cup of tea. As he placed a mug in front of her the whole story of what had happened and the agony of the wait they'd had the night before poured out of her and she noticed how he listened so attentively, saying just the right thing to make her feel better. This was the first time she had been with him when he hadn't been joking or being light and she saw something in his eyes – a real concern and care for her. And she started to believe that maybe he did consider her more than just as a friend.

He had sat with her until she needed to be on duty and then kissing her on the cheek had squeezed her hand before he went off to his own side of the base. It had been a nice moment and she had been grateful for his friendship.

After he left, Diana had slowly prepared to go on duty with the balloon, when the sirens went off. She was making her way to the truck with her team when suddenly the whistle of the bombs overhead seemed really close. Before they could even get into a shelter, the attack was upon them, a bomb dropping really close by. Throwing herself to the ground and crawling towards a wall, she pressed herself against it and covered her head with her hands while she scrabbled for her tin helmet and thrust it on her head. Though the bomb had dropped nearby, it had missed the building they were in.

'That was bloody close,' said Kathy as they all sat slammed against the wall, breathing a sigh of relief, and then suddenly Diana looked up, and her blood ran cold.

The bomb had hit one of the other barracks, and with a sinking heart, she knew which one. Len's barracks had taken a direct hit; she could see it on fire from here. He had not long gone back. Could he still be over there?

'Len!' she screamed out and jumped to her feet, then she started to run towards where the fire was leaping into the air. *Please don't let him be in there, God.* Not after Jack. Could fate be that cruel to both of them? She thought about Lizzie's pain, and she realized all at once she really loved Len. It hadn't been like Lizzie for her. She hadn't fallen madly in love; it had crept up on her. Diana thought of Len's warm, kind personality, always having a joke and being there for her, and now the last thing in the world she wanted to do was attend his funeral.

She pulled her dad's coin from her pocket and clutched it in her hand, squeezing as hard as she could. Maybe it could work for her in the same way. As she ran as fast as she could, the hot, sticky, smoky air racing in and out of her lungs, tears sprang to her eyes again as her heart tried to thump itself out of her chest. Were the Nazis going to take everyone? All of their men? She raced across the grounds. Then she saw a figure running down towards her.

And she knew who it was. The relief she felt almost took her legs from under her as she started to shake with the adrenalin coursing through her body. They both slowed to a walk, coughing with the smoke, out of breath. They met halfway across the parade ground. She threw her arms around his neck and held him so tightly he started to laugh.

'I thought I had lost you like Lizzie lost Jack, and I couldn't bear it. I couldn't have taken it. I couldn't have taken that news.'

He pulled her into his arms. 'We can't do this, Diana,' he said, haltingly, trying to catch his breath. 'It's too hard.'

She pulled back. What did he mean? Was he saying he couldn't bear the strain of them being together and that they needed to part? Just when she felt they were really starting to connect?

He repeated his words. 'We can't do this. You racing up to check on me, me racing down to check on you. After I left you I got thinking about what I would do if I lost you, and I realized I would regret many things but mostly about not telling you how I feel. I love you, Diana, and I think we need to get married.'

She drew in a breath. Had she misheard?

'Sorry?'

'We have to get married. Diana, I love you. I've been trying to tell you that for weeks but I was so afraid you would reject me and that you saw this as just a friendship.'

'I thought the same,' she said, laughing, the relief obvious in her tone.

She threw her arms around his neck again and burst into tears with relief. 'Of course I will marry you! I love you too.'

He swung her around in the air and pulled her into his arms for a crushing hug.

'After what happened to Jack, and to so many of my mates, I realized that we really don't have time to spare. Look at my barracks.

I'm hoping that everyone got out, but the only thing I could think about was you. As I was racing over here, all I was thinking of was, "This is ridiculous. We've got to stop doing this. We need to be together so we can really take care of each other." Because I really love you, Diana.'

He kissed her passionately then, right there in the middle of the parade ground. The first time he had really kissed her. Once they pulled away, they both started to laugh.

'I've been wanting to do that for weeks,' he rasped. 'I just wasn't sure how you felt. I don't want to wait long now though. Let's get married right away – as soon as we can get banns read! We can get married in the register office. I don't want us to go any longer without being together.'

Diana's thoughts went straight to her parents. What would her dad say if she suddenly got married quickly? How would her mum feel if she wasn't at her own daughter's wedding? They would be heartbroken, and getting them down to London seemed impossible with her dad's leg and his nerves.

'I don't know if I can do that. What about my family?'

'I don't want us to wait, Diana. I can't go through this again. I want to be together if the worst happened, not living separately. When we are off duty I want to be close to you. Wake up with you. By the time we organize getting leave together and then get up to the Midlands to arrange the wedding, it could take months. I just want to get married as soon as we can.'

Diana caught her breath. 'But I need a little bit of time, all right? It's not a decision I want to make quickly. This has all happened so fast, and there's a lot to consider. I do love you, but this is just so sudden. I can't think about anything like that right now, especially my own happiness.'

She saw the rejection on his face, but how could she run away to get married when her best friend was in so much pain and her parents were so far away?

He nodded, but there was sadness in his tone as he said, 'I guess I did take you by surprise. I've felt like this for a long time, just wanted to make sure you felt the same way. But I do understand.'

Diana felt conflicted as she looked into his disappointed eyes. But he knew how she felt –that even though this felt right for them, everything else was wrong right now.

Chapter Forty-One

Lizzie stood staring blankly down the aisle of the church, and even though it was positively balmy outside for a spring day, the whole of her body was chilled. She could barely feel her feet, and her hands, even though they were thrust into gloves in her pockets, were two blocks of ice.

She tried to focus. She knew the minister at the front of the church was speaking because she could hear his voice from the pulpit bouncing and echoing off the stone walls. And though the sounds he was making were reassuring to her, almost like waves rolling over a sea wall, for some odd reason his words drifted in and then out of her consciousness without anchoring themselves to any meaning.

The only thing she could be sure of in the fog of emotion that saturated her was that Julia and Diana stood on either side of her, supporting her, because she could feel their arms linking hers. But even so, she was still unable to stop feeling jittery, and she had felt sick all morning. Her knees seemed to have a life of their own as they trembled, and her chin quivered like there was a fluttering bird trapped in her throat as she fought back the waves of grief. But for once in the last few days, Lizzie wasn't crying. She seemed to have cried herself completely dry.

As the vicar continued talking in his rolling, melodic tones, Diana started to rub Lizzie's back in long slow circles, and it instantly comforted her. It also made her so homesick for her aunt Marion that it hurt. It was something she would always do whenever Lizzie was in pain.

Unable to concentrate on the service, Lizzie's attention strayed aimlessly around the church. It was a beautiful building of smooth grey stone with a high vaulted ceiling and a classical Norman tower. Running in neat rows along both walls were large arched, leaded windows that had not been exempt from bomb damage. Their cracked, broken panes were illuminated by the midday sun that streamed through the remaining stained glass, creating jagged patterns on the floor in a kaleidoscope of colours.

Each window depicted a Bible story, or she supposed they had once. Only one remained intact so she could understand it.

The story of when Jesus walked on water, telling the fisherman not to be afraid of the storm and to have faith. Even that one was riddled with blast holes, and strips of tape were holding the window in place. It seemed ironic that this one representation had been spared. The Bible story in which Jesus asked his followers to stretch their faith beyond what seemed possible was the only window that was still relatively undamaged.

Lizzie stared at the picture of Jesus wading on the top of the water, his hand stretched out towards his followers in the boat. She needed that kind of extraordinary faith right now. Her hope was at an all-time low, and all she could think of was what was the point any more? The point of holding on, the point of fighting? All that they were doing seemed so futile. The German bombs and bullets were going to have their way, no matter what the British did. They would take and destroy whoever or whatever they wanted, so why bother? Why not lie down and wait for the bomb with your number on it?

Lizzie's attention was drawn forward down the aisle to the people gathered in the front pew. People she imagined were Jack's mother and father were huddled close to the coffin. His father with the same angular build and the hint of dark hair that was peppered with grey. His brother shorter and squarer than Jack but when he turned his head Lizzie caught her breath to see him hold his head at the same angle as Jack. Lizzie felt the loss. She also felt sad that she didn't know them. Her relationship with Jack had been so quick and so intense. Lizzie hadn't even had the opportunity to meet his family and right now she couldn't bring herself to say anything to them.

Behind his grieving parents, pews were filled with more family and friends. Behind them, row upon row of smart-looking pilots, including Alan, hair cut to regulation length, shoes shining, all standing solemnly together, a wash of air-force blue, the same air-force blue that Jack used to wear.

All at once, Lizzie realized people were singing around her, a song that was familiar to her; she fought the fog in her brain to remember the title. Then it came to her through the murky depths of her mind: 'I Vow to Thee My Country'. It was a song she'd heard at school, but now the words seemed to evade her, and no matter how she tried, Lizzie couldn't seem to be able to focus on the hymn sheet in front of her that Diana held between the three of them.

So, she just listened to the words as people sang quietly around her – and they struck her in a whole new way. The words were talking about Jack: 'The love that asks no questions, the love that stands the test, that lays upon the altar the dearest and the best.'

Lizzie's eyes were drawn to Jack's coffin. That's where her dearest lay, not on an altar but in a wooden box. And though the words of the hymn sounded noble, she didn't feel the same devotion to her country right now. It was one thing to sing about it, to talk about it, be inspired by it; it was truly another to be a victim of it.

The congregation continued to sing around her, and the pointed words stabbed at her as they continued to roll around in her thoughts. 'A love that asks no questions, a love that asks no questions...' What exactly did that mean? The one thing more than anything Lizzie wanted to do right now was to ask questions, questions such as, *Why?*

Her beloved Jack was lying in his coffin, which was draped with a British flag, like a badge of honour. Right in front of her was a man who had paid that price. And she wasn't allowed to shout out to the world: 'Why?' Because it suddenly became really crystal clear to her that there were no winners in this charade of valour they called war. She just knew that on the other side of the water a German girl was standing in front of a swastika-draped coffin asking exactly the same question she was.

Lizzie closed her eyes as her thoughts drifted back to the day she'd flown with Jack. That crisp perfect day, the sun resting above the grey clouds in a china blue sky. Then his words of love when they'd been dancing in the park and the feeling of holding him in her arms when he'd told her he'd loved her and accepted her, and how the experience of all that still felt so tangible, so real to her. If she closed her eyes, she could conjure up the feeling of him close to her, the weight of his hand on her waist, the smell of his skin, the feeling of his breath grazing her cheek, his words of love in her ear. How could all that feel so real, but this funeral didn't? Lizzie swallowed down the tears that rattled inside her chest, swallowed down the pain past the dryness in her throat and her aching stomach. Her cheekbones hurt from crying, and all the time now she felt as if she had grit in her eyes.

Julia touched her arm, and Lizzie was grateful for her friends. Strangers to her mere months ago, they were now the rock she relied on. With great sensitivity, neither one of her friends spoke to her; it was as if they knew she wasn't in any fit state to actually hear or process what they were saying. But just them being there and holding her up was all she needed, and it was amazing how their touch reassured her.

As the hymn ended, Jack's wing commander walked to the front of the church, his shiny black shoes echoing on the black and white tiled floor as he stood up behind the high stone pulpit with the purple banners of Lent draped from it. Staring down at the floor,

Lizzie fixed her eyes on one spot to try and concentrate on what he was saying. The words rang out to the congregation in a booming resonance as he told stories about Jack, stories that his parents and friends had shared with the commander to prepare for the service. Stories from his childhood that described his adventurousness and his devil-may-care spirit.

And Lizzie acknowledged the many smiles and nods from around the building from people who had known him longer. She recognized there was so much they hadn't talked about. So much that had been left unsaid. But as his commander brought up stories of Jack's young life, Lizzie could see elements of the man she'd loved in all of them. See him doing the very things they were talking about.

A tear slid down her cheek, and even though she didn't notice it, Diana did and handed her a hanky. Lizzie blew her nose as the commander went on to talk about Jack's bravery as a pilot. He spoke of the kind of leader he was. He spoke about how in his last moments, he'd laid his life down for one of his fellow pilots. She watched Alan look down at his shoes and could tell by the way his shoulders were lifting and falling that he was having trouble containing his emotion as well. The wing commander finished the eulogy by reminding everyone how Jack had a tremendous sense of humour. 'I almost expect him to jump out of the coffin and say, "See, wasn't that a great ruse?" The man bowed his head then, adding almost in a whisper to himself the words, 'If only.'

As he stepped down, the minister finished the sermon by quoting Churchill's speech about the airmen: 'Never was so much owed by so many to so few.' Lizzie thought about those words; they took on a whole new meaning for her now.

The congregation started to sing, 'The Lord Is My Shepherd'. All at once, the sirens wailed out into the air, a cruel reminder that the war didn't stop, even if life did.

Automatically, there was activity in the church. The vicar, with what was obviously a well-rehearsed performance, commanded them all to the front and down into the crypt under the church, which would be a safe place for them to be during the raid.

Slowly, people started to file forward out of the door at the far end of the church behind the altar as the sirens continued to ring out.

Diana and Julia escorted Lizzie down the aisle. But when she got to Jack's coffin, she found her legs wouldn't move. She couldn't leave him here. Not during a raid. It just didn't seem right, somehow.

'I just need a minute,' she told her friends. 'Go ahead. I'll follow.'

With a look between them, Julia and Diana stayed where they were.

As bombs started to drop all around them, the coffin began to rock on uneven ground, and Lizzie placed her hand on it to steady it, feeling the smooth fabric of the British flag beneath it.

Julia touched her hand.

'We should go down, Lizzie,' she whispered into her friend's ear.

Lizzie shook her head. 'I'm not going anywhere,' she said. 'I'm going to stay here with Jack.'

She was surprised at how calm her voice was.

'You won't be safe up here,' implored Diana. 'Jack would want you to go below ground.'

'I don't care what you say. I'm not going to change my mind. If you want to go, then go. One thing this awful war has taught me is that you have no choice of when you die. You can think you're safe in a shelter and die or you can fight the enemy head-on and be taken fighting in the sky. You can't hide from it. Shelters are just things that we put in place to make us feel better; nothing can hide me from the hand of God if He wants to take me. If it's your time to go, it's your time to go. And if God wants to take me, He can take me right here next to Jack.'

She laid her hands on the coffin and felt the vibrations under her feet and through her arms as the bombs dropped and rattled the very fibre of her being.

As Lizzie listened once again to the whole of London splintering and shattering above her head, she'd never felt quite so safe as she did there with Jack at that moment. *Is that what the window meant?* she wondered, as she looked up at it again. *Trusting even when there was nothing physically in this world you could count on?*

'Oh, Jack,' she said as the flood of tears that had stayed away started to find their way down her cheeks again, dripping onto the new, stiff flag.

Diana placed one arm around Lizzie's waist, the other on the coffin to steady it, and Julia did the same on the other side. The three of them stood in their mutual solidarity as the sound that echoed around the church was deafening; they had proved they were strong, they had all been through the worst of what life could offer, and it was as if Lizzie knew all of their thoughts. One was thinking about the man who had just miraculously been spared, one about the husband who was still missing, and Lizzie about the man she would never see again.

Chapter Forty-Two

It was as they arrived back from Jack's funeral that Julia saw it, and she froze, her keys still in the lock, the door half-open. The telegram, screaming at her from the mat inside the hallway. Surely, after they'd just been through so much sadness, surely bad news wasn't waiting for her here at her home.

Diana followed her gaze and, knowing automatically what it was, looked to Julia. 'Would you like me to pick it up?'

Julia shook her head. She'd been dreading this telegram. Telling her that John was dead. She could do this. This was just something they had to do now. Deal with the death of their loved ones.

Her thoughts went straight to her children. Maggie's tiny tear-filled face and Tom's trembling lip, both of them on the doorstep saying goodbye to their father. That would be the last time they would ever have seen him. This suddenly felt so final. Scooping it off the mat, she walked into the kitchen and placed it on the table.

Diana helped Lizzie into the house, saying, 'I'm going to put her in bed.' Lizzie nodded, apparently oblivious to what Julia might be facing, or maybe she just couldn't take any more sadness. No more pain this day.

As Diana and Lizzie went upstairs, Julia went into the kitchen and stared out of the window. She fixed her gaze on the corrugated Anderson shelter, the same bullet-grey as the sky today. Everything in her world was constantly there to remind her that there was no escaping this war; it surrounded her, trying to suffocate her at every turn. The cracked window pane she stared out of, the shelter in front of her and the telegram behind her on the table. Numbly, she started to fill the kettle with water as she stared at the shelter. Julia remembered that day in the spring when John and one of his mates had built it. His shirtsleeves rolled up, he'd been wearing his thick brown gardening trousers and his heavy work boots. They had both been being playful with one another as she had stood at the open window resting on her elbows, shouting out her instructions to her husband.

'How about putting some pink frilly curtains on that escape hatch for me,' she had joked.

He had given her one of his wry smiles, his thick hair matted with sweat as he drove a shovel into the ground.

'How about you stop giving me so much lip and instead come and dig this hole for me,' he had joked back as he flicked soil up the side of the building.

It had been such a lark then, this phoney war, before bombs dropped, before the call-up papers and telegrams arrived.

'I just wouldn't want to show you up,' she had cracked back. 'I would do it in half the time. Wouldn't want to show you up in front of your friend.'

He had rushed into the house then as she squealed with the anticipation of their confrontation and tried to escape him. He'd chased her down and before long she had been swept into his strong arms; as he carried her out to the garden she had protested, kicking and screaming in mock horror. He had taken her right into the shelter, past his mate who rested on his own spade to watch the performance.

'Welcome home, Mrs Sullivan,' he'd joked, as he had kissed her on her neck playfully and she had attempted to squirm away from his sweaty face. He had laid her on the little bunk bed then and moved close to his wife, a playful gleam in his eye.

'Cosy, isn't it? Might be quite intimate on those nights when you're frightened and need to get close to your big brave husband to protect you from those scary Germans.' He raised his eyebrows. 'Who knows what could happen, maybe if we had another baby we could call it Anderson?'

'Oh yes, very romantic,' she had barked back, in a sarcastic tone. 'With all five of us in this bed, two children and your mother if we ever managed to convince her to get into the shelter.'

'Where there's a will there's a way.' He had smiled and kissed her again.

She had heaved him off her and raced from his grip. And into the house where she had locked the back door, laughing, and then had flicked water out of the window to cool him off.

All at once she could feel the water. Coming back into the present and looking down Julia saw that the kettle was overflowing and running down the back of her hand and she hadn't even noticed.

Diana was suddenly there, taking the kettle from Julia and placing it on the stove.

'Come on, Julia. We can do this,' she said softly.

Julia nodded blankly and then walked to the table, sat down and picked up the envelope. She turned it over in her hand. For some strange moment, she thought about the people who had to write these. How hard would it be to do this day in, day out? There were thousands upon thousands of these arriving every day, all over the country. Such a difficult job.

Julia slipped a finger under the flap of the envelope and tore it open. Taking a deep breath, she unfolded the piece of paper. She read it, and then again to make sure she hadn't just imagined it. Then she jumped to her feet, her hand to her mouth.

Diana jumped up beside her. 'Julia, what is it?'

Julia couldn't speak. She just shook her head as tears rolled down her cheeks.

Diana grabbed the telegram from her quickly and read it, then she threw her arms around her friend.

'Thank God. Thank God.'

Julia nodded. 'I was so sure that it was bad news. I was so sure I was going to be planning his funeral too. They say he's wounded,' she said, repeating the words again so that they would sink in. 'What does that mean, Diana?'

'It means he's coming home, Julia. It means he's coming home to you.'

She nodded her head, and couldn't believe it. John wasn't dead, and he wasn't missing. It didn't say the extent of his injuries, but she imagined if they talked about him coming back, then hopefully it wasn't too bad. But whatever it was, she didn't care. She would nurse him and take care of him herself.

'I must tell Agnes. And Tom!'

'I'll make the tea,' responded Diana. 'You go and tell them. She'll be overjoyed.'

Julia raced next door, noticing once again the taped windows after the blast. When nobody answered her knock, she pulled out the key that Agnes always kept under a flower pot in the garden, and putting it into the lock, she stepped inside. She realized with a sense of guilt that she hadn't been over to Agnes's house in a long time, as Agnes was so often in her own house. So she never really bothered to pop over. It was such a gloomy place, always dark, and Agnes hardly ever heated it. It was as if the inside of the house reflected the inside of Agnes.

She raced down the hallway, calling her mother-in-law's name. Then up the stairs. Maybe she was resting. But the rooms were dark, and she suddenly remembered that Agnes – who'd been babysitting – had talked about taking Tom and Abigail to the park while they were at the funeral, as it was Saturday.

She was on her way back to the stairs when something caught her eye. The spare bedroom door was open, and on the wall was something red and black. It seemed familiar to her. She knew she probably shouldn't pry with Agnes not being there, but she suddenly had a chilling thought that she had to prove wasn't right.

Pushing the door open, it creaked on its hinges. She looked inside the darkened room and then gasped. On the table were leaflets, booklets, all about the fifth column: the group of people that were anti-war, anti-British, and supported Hitler. Meetings, places they were getting together, and she realized with a shiver that the letter she had found in the rubble had been Agnes's.

Was Agnes working with the enemy? That was impossible. She was an old lady. Her son was fighting in this war. There had to be some mistake. Julia continued to flick through the leaflets. 'Why would Agnes do this?' And then something chilling hit her. She would have to report Agnes to the authorities here. They'd probably arrest her, probably put her in prison, and suddenly her thoughts went to John. John coming home injured. John asking her to take care of his mother. How could Agnes do such a thing?

She turned to leave, and suddenly she heard a rattling at the front door. But before she could move downstairs and out the back, Agnes was on the doorstep. She seemed shocked to see Julia up there.

'I just dropped the children off at your house. I thought you'd be there,' she said in an accusatory tone as she climbed up the stairs to meet her halfway to where Julia had been.

'I wanted to tell you I have some news,' said Julia, trying to drag her thoughts back from the spare room.

'Diana said you had something to tell me, but she thought it better that you tell me yourself. What is it? Is it John? Have they taken him as well? Is he dead like everybody else is in my life? Just like my husband? Is that it? Is that what you want to tell me?'

Julia shook her head and just held up the telegram to Agnes. Agnes scanned it, and then looked up with her piercing glare.

Could she not even be happy to know her son was alive? Julia thought to herself.

'He's probably wounded beyond recognition. This could mean anything. He could be broken in so many ways. His mind could've gone. Could be missing parts of his body. How is this good news?'

For once, she wanted to shake the woman. Shake her until she rattled. 'Because, Agnes, it means he's alive, and that's all that matters.'

Agnes glanced past her up the stairs and appeared to notice that her spare bedroom door was pushed wide open. Realization crept through her, and she narrowed her eyes as if she was trying to read what Julia knew. Julia swallowed. She had to confront her. She had to. She worked at the War Office. How would this look? Besides, it couldn't possibly be real, could it?

Agnes pushed past her on the stairs.

'What were you doing up here in my private things?' she snapped in a quiet, calculating tone.

'I was looking for you. I wanted to share the good news. Agnes, what are all those leaflets in there?'

Agnes's eyes widened, and it was as if she was now proud. She'd been found out. Instead of being upset or trying to hide it, she just walked in and turned the light on. 'This is the only way we will stop this madness. Sending young men off to their death.'

'Agnes, you're helping the enemy!'

'I don't see it that way,' she snapped. 'There are people here in England doing everything they can to stop this war, and if Hitler wants this island, then let him have it. Then at least people can come home. Wives can have their husbands, children can have their fathers, and then...' she added in barely a whisper, 'mothers can have their sons. It is easy for you. You have never sent a son to war. My heart was ripped out when I lost my husband and he wasn't even a very kindly man. But my son is everything to me. He has taken care of me for years, making this house a home, and together we became a family. I will do anything to save him, to bring him back, to end this war. Even if it means doing things that in other people's eyes don't appear right. I love him. Do you understand?'

Agnes started to cry. Julia really didn't know what to say or what to do. She saw the fear and terror in the woman's eyes and knew that it was that that had pushed her to do what she'd done, but how could she sit on information like this? She worked for the government. Suddenly she felt totally conflicted. What was the right thing to do?'

Julia knew this was the bitterness affecting Agnes. The bitterness of losing her husband in the Great War. She'd never ever been able to get over it. It must've poisoned her. Made her this way. She wanted to reach forward and grab the scrawny little woman. Hug her or something. But Agnes would have never allowed it; everything about her was prickly. Apart from the children who seemed to win her heart; the adult world to her was the enemy.

'Agnes, you've put me in an impossible position. I'll need to report this.'

Agnes's eyes widened. 'You would do that? You would report your own mother-in-law?'

'It's my duty, Agnes. I work for Mr Churchill, and you are working against us.'

Agnes became angry. 'He should never have married you. I told him not to marry you,' she spat. 'You with your high and mighty ways, even though you grew up right here you always thought yourself a cut above the rest of us. *Get yourself a nice girl*, I said, *who will cook your dinner and take care of your children*. But no, you had to go and work for Churchill. Work at the War Office. Work above your station.'

Julia was shocked. She'd never heard Agnes talk like this, and though she'd always sensed that things weren't right between them, she'd had no idea she felt this way. 'I can't stay, Agnes. I have to go. And you know I can't sit on this information.'

As she reached the door, Agnes sent her last crushing blow towards her. 'If you do that, if you tell anybody about this, John will never forgive you. I'm his mother, and he might love you and your children, but he'll never forgive you for putting his mother in prison.'

The words made Julia freeze because there was a side of her that knew Agnes was right. The guilt that John felt for his mother, the need to protect her and coddle her because she'd lost her husband, was so intense in him that he was blinded to who she was.

He would excuse her behaviour, saying she was probably scared or fearful or trying her best. What frightened Julia, though she didn't believe John would leave her, was that it might drive an impossible wedge between them. Would he ever be able to truly forgive her? As she walked out of Agnes's house, Julia knew there was no one she could trust with this secret, but she couldn't see how she could not report it. It was her duty, wasn't it?

Chapter Forty-Three

Lizzie awoke with a start. She hadn't slept for more than a couple of hours at a time since Jack's death and had finally dropped into a deep sleep, but someone was pulling on her arm. She dragged herself back from the thick fog of exhaustion and forced her eyes open; it was Abigail. As she focused on the concerned look on her tiny face, Lizzie became aware of a noise. Was it coming from the hallway? Trying to orient herself, she pushed up into a sitting position and realized someone was knocking on the front door.

Stumbling out of bed, she made her way out of the bedroom and down the stairs. Pulling open the door, it took her a moment to remember who the woman was who was staring at her, and then the realization came back in a rush. The nurse! The nurse from the night she'd given up her baby. She felt the sting, again. Lizzie hoped this was good news. She didn't feel strong enough to take any more bad news right now.

'I found her,' the woman assured her. 'They'd moved out of their last house. But I tracked her down. Their last name is Henshore.'

Fresh tears clouded Lizzie's vision. She had lost one love and found another.

'I have her address,' the woman continued and handed her a piece of paper.

Lizzie stared at the address in her hand. 'Thank you so much,' she said, noticing her voice was still croaky, her throat still sore from the crying, mind still blurry from the lack of sleep, but she felt a surge of momentary joy. The woman nodded and scuttled away.

Lizzie looked down at the address in front of her with renewed hope.

She dressed and, as she went to put her shoes on, Lizzie noticed Abigail standing in the hallway staring at her. They were on their own together. Julia had gone to do some shopping and Agnes had disappeared earlier. Lizzie didn't want to waste a minute, so she would have to take her.

'We have to go out, darling,' she said hastily to Abigail, fetching their coats. As she did Lizzie allowed the realization to wash over her: she had found Annie. She was going to see her daughter again. It was hard to believe because this was something she had wanted for so long, an impossible dream. She hoped more than anything to be able to gather that little girl into her arms, to draw her into the space that had been left forever empty by the tiny baby she'd held so long ago.

Looking down at Abigail now, she thought how strange the world was. In front of her was a child who didn't belong to her but was with her; out there was her own daughter who couldn't be with her. Both of them holding a piece of Lizzie's heart.

She quickly put on Abigail's coat. They grabbed their gas masks, and off they went.

It wasn't too far away to the address she had been given, and as they got off the bus, Lizzie's heart was in her throat. This would have been hard enough as it was, but now that Jack was dead, it felt like she had no skin, no barrier, no fortitude to hold off any emotions she might be overwhelmed by. She held Abigail's hand tightly, grateful for even that small feeling of reassurance.

Walking down the street, something about it felt familiar to her. She looked at the number on the piece of paper. Some of the houses in the road looked as if they had been bombed not long before, and though a lot of rubble was now cleared away, the homes were marked with the usual bomb damage.

Lizzie turned a corner in the street and started to speed up, count-ing the houses as she went. The house number she'd been given on the piece of paper was 78. But as she approached that number, a fearful realization started to twist in the pit of her stomach. She glanced down at the address and then double-checked the houses around it. But here it was in front of her – number 78, between 76 and 80. But instead of a neat terraced house like the ones either side, there was a gaping black hole, a pile of rubble where a home used to be, and behind it, the Anderson shelter was flattened. She put her hand to her mouth and gasped. She was too late; her daughter was gone.

Tears started to stream down her face, her heart felt as if it was being squeezed in a vice; Lizzie had missed her chance. She stood there, looking at the devastation, as though maybe her child was going to materialize from under a pile of bricks. Turned on its side was a little pram smashed almost flat and missing a wheel, and she wondered if it had been her daughter's. This wasn't how her journey was supposed to end. Lizzie had given her up for a better life, not to die in such a horrible way.

By her side Abigail seemed agitated, alert somehow, looking around her. Did she sense Lizzie's pain? Did she sense how important this place was to her?

All at once, a voice broke into her thoughts.

'Hello, there.'

Lizzie turned, wondering who it was.

'How are you?' continued the friendly voice.

Then she caught sight of someone. Lizzie realized an older woman was walking towards her and calling to her, but then she noticed she wasn't looking at Lizzie, she was looking at Abigail.

'Do you know her?' asked Lizzie, following the woman's gaze.

'Of course I know her. That's Abigail, my little granddaughter's friend. How are you?'

Abigail's eyes widened. She looked at Lizzie and then back at the older woman, as though trying to reconcile her two worlds.

'I'm so glad to see she is okay. We'd thought the worst when her house was bombed. I'm so happy I was wrong,' the woman continued, as if she believed Lizzie understood what she was talking about, whispering to Lizzie over Abigail's head: 'Sad about her grandma, wasn't it? Are you a friend or part of Abigail's family? I always thought she only had her gran.'

Lizzie's brain was moving slowly, still deep in the grief of all of her loss, but she suddenly started to put the pieces together. That was why this place was familiar, it was just down the street from where she'd found Abigail. She suddenly remembered the day she'd come to look for the orphanage. That same day she'd met her.

And somebody here knew her. 'I'm sorry,' said Lizzie. 'You're sure you know her?'

'Like I said, she's my granddaughter's friend. They used to play together all the time. Would you like to see her? She's down at my house today.'

Abigail's face lit up.

'Yes. We would love to see her,' said Lizzie, a little bewildered. 'Do you live close by?'

'Just down the street, love.'

The two women started to walk side by side as Abigail skipped ahead of them.

'Do you know what happened to the family that lived in that house?' Lizzie enquired, pointing towards the bomb site.

'Of course, that was my daughter's house. Living with me now, they are, all of them, just down the street.'

Lizzie froze with the understanding of what she was saying. There was a chance that her own daughter wasn't dead.

Her voice became hoarse with emotion as she asked her next question. 'What's your granddaughter's name?'

'Annie, Annie is Abigail's friend,' she answered, oblivious to the impact her words were having on Lizzie. 'Didn't she tell you about her?'

Lizzie shook her head. 'Abigail hasn't spoken since the night her home was destroyed. We didn't know who she was or where she was from.'

'Oh, the poor little mite. How awful for her, and she has already been through so much. She lost both her parents in an accident, you know, when she was tiny, and she has been living with her grandmother. When I heard Maureen was dead, I just assumed the worst for Abigail. It will be good for her to come down to my house. I'll put the kettle on. She can play with Annie for a while. My husband Fred is home at the moment and I've got all the kids over there. Annie and the two boys, her two brothers. Their mum is working in the aircraft factory and their dad's away fighting.'

Lizzie followed the woman blindly down the road, trying to comprehend all of this. Abigail had no family left. But she and this woman's granddaughter were friends? And the granddaughter might be her own Annie. If she hadn't had Abigail with her, this woman might have never even stopped to talk.

The little house at the end of the road was teeming with life. As they went inside, two boys rushed past them running out into the garden, playing a game of war, shooting at one another as they went, and Abigail rushed ahead and ran into the front room.

She'd obviously been here before. Lizzie's heart stopped in her throat; she was going to meet her daughter for the first time. How would it feel? Her hands started to tremble as she turned the corner of the hallway and caught her breath. Sitting on the floor colouring was a little girl with wild red hair like her birth mother's, and when she looked up, she was the spitting image of Fiona. Tears brimmed in Lizzie's eyes and her heart was wrenched in two as she looked at her daughter for the first time.

'Hello,' whispered Lizzie, her voice cracking with the emotion.

'Hello,' the young girl responded then beamed. She was missing a front tooth. 'Thank you for bringing Abigail over! I haven't seen her since my birthday, that was ages ago.'

Six months, three weeks and four days ago to be exact, thought Lizzie to herself. There wasn't a day she hadn't counted, though she didn't say it. She just nodded, unable to say anything.

Annie jumped to her feet. 'Come on, Abigail, let's go and play.' She sounded like a Londoner. That had momentarily surprised Lizzie. She'd looked so much like Fiona, she'd expected her to sound Scottish, but of course, she wouldn't. Taking Abigail's hand, Annie pulled her outside to play in the garden. Lizzie watched the gleeful pair disappear as she joined Annie's grandmother in the kitchen.

'She seems like a happy little girl, your granddaughter.'

'Our Annie, oh, she is. She's an absolute joy. Her father dotes on her, he does. She can wrap him right around her little finger, and don't you be fooled about her being the smallest. She keeps her brothers in order as well. They couldn't have children of their own, you see, they are all adopted, but you'd never know it, they are such a happy family.'

Lizzie watched through the window, fighting back the tears, recognizing that Mackenzie spirit. Annie pulled out two skipping ropes and handed one to Abigail so they could play. All at once, the sun broke through the clouds, and Annie's hair became a flaming halo around her head. She was telling Abigail a very animated story, and they both giggled as they skipped. This was all that Lizzie needed. She wasn't sure why it was so vital for her to know Annie was okay, maybe because she herself had never felt okay. There'd been so much pain and sadness the last time she'd seen her. Annie had been frozen in Lizzie's mind at that age, and she'd had this terrible fear that Lizzie had broken her irrevocably and the loss and sadness that Lizzie had always felt had somehow stained her daughter.

But Lizzie knew now, she knew she could move on, knew she could close the door on this part of her life and not worry about it. This little girl, her daughter, was happy.

As they were going, Lizzie promised to bring Abigail again to play with Annie another day, and the little red-haired girl ran up to her and threw her arms around her and hugged her. As Lizzie's arms were filled with the young person who had left them so deprived, it took all of her control not to burst into tears and never let her go. She closed her eyes to enjoy the feeling of completeness, the tiny feather-like heart beating against her chest, the candy floss of hair so similar to her own brushing her cheek. She must have squeezed her a little too long, as her daughter wriggled out from beneath her grip, and ran to say goodbye to Abigail. As Lizzie said goodbye, she felt at peace. A huge part of her heart was reconciled and something stirred deep within it, something she hadn't felt in a while: a glimmer of hope.

Chapter Forty-Four

It was two weeks later, and as soon as Lizzie opened her eyes that morning, she felt the sinking feeling she'd been dreading. Slipping out of bed so as not to disturb Abigail, she went to the window and peeled back a corner of the blackout curtains. Lizzie took a deep breath to prepare herself. Since losing Jack, which was still so painful, she could barely breathe when she thought of it. Having the love of Abigail had been her only solace.

Looking down Julia's garden past the Anderson shelter towards the centre of London, Lizzie noted the city was still smoking from the night before. A rather brutal attack in the Mansion House area had come as a shock after a few days without being bombed. They had all hoped that maybe the constant onslaught was over, but that was not to be.

Lizzie thought back; it had been the week before when a somewhat official-looking lady from the WVS had stood on her doorstep to inform her that Abigail was being sent away. As soon as Lizzie had established Abigail's true identity, she had told the authorities in case she still had family somewhere. But no one had come forward. Abigail appeared to be alone in the world.

'All our children are being sent to the country now,' the stern woman had told her the week before, 'and because your charge is an orphan, as we have been unable to find any living relatives, we have an orphanage in Wales that will be taking our children from the city. So we need you to take Abigail to Paddington Station next week at this time.'

The woman handed Lizzie a piece of paper as Lizzie tried to protest. 'Surely Abigail is safe here with me?'

'I think Abigail,' retorted the woman, 'is better served in the place where she can be rehomed with a family, with a mother *and* a father.'

Lizzie felt the snub. The abrupt way the woman phrased it made it pretty obvious that she didn't think that Lizzie was a proper guardian for her young charge.

'But she's happy. She's settled here,' Lizzie pleaded with her.

'Nevertheless, this is the law,' said the woman as she puckered her lips and rolled back her shoulders. 'So, we will expect to see you and Abigail at the station next week, and I'll bid you a good day.' And she was gone.

Lizzie had sat looking at that piece of paper and felt the terrible loss. Abigail had become so much a part of their family now. The littlest member of a group of four women, all surviving together.

Julia was already in the kitchen when Lizzie came downstairs.

'Like a cup of tea?'

Lizzie nodded. The sadness and loss was palpable between the two of them.

Julia voiced her own thoughts. 'We've all grown accustomed to having her in the house. Having her around helps me stop missing Maggie, who is getting quite settled in the country, though I think Tom misses her, but Maggie seems to like having all the attention to herself. I'm not sure it's for the best, sending Abigail away,' she said, putting the kettle on. 'But unfortunately, we can't argue with bureaucracy.'

All at once, there was a scampering on the stairs, and a tiny waif-like creature raced into the kitchen. Abigail's hair was a mess, and she was yawning and wiping sleep from her eyes. She automatically climbed onto Lizzie's lap. Lizzie had told her she was leaving the night before, and though Abigail, as usual, hadn't said anything, she had clung to Lizzie's neck, shaking her head defiantly. Lizzy knew it was going to be a battle today.

'Did you sleep all right, darling, when we got back from the shelter?' she asked, smoothing down the little girl's hair.

Abigail nodded.

Julia prepared her some breakfast and Abigail sat on Lizzie's lap, eating it. Lizzie enjoyed the feel of having her there and being able to wrap her arms around her tiny body and wondered how she'd feel tomorrow when she was no longer with her.

Julia had to go to the War Office, and she gave Abigail a big hug goodbye. Lizzie could tell by her expression she was fighting her own emotions and that Julia didn't envy her task that day.

Lizzie got her dressed and prepared to leave, hooking Abigail's gas mask on her arm and placing over her head the address that she'd been told to add. She tried to avoid the girl's sorrowful face as she buttoned her coat and left the house.

As Lizzie walked, she thought about packing the tiny suitcase the night before and laying out Abigail's clothes to pack – a new red pinafore and new black shoes she'd bought for her to wear on her journey. She plaited Abigail's hair into two braids and used the shiny red ribbon that Julia had found.

Now, she looked adorable as they walked up the street, but her eyes didn't leave the ground. And even though she still didn't speak, Lizzie knew how she was feeling.

On the way, Lizzie tried to make cheerful conversation, telling Abigail all about her own childhood and how she'd loved being in the country. How she'd had a dog and what it was like to have sheep. When they arrived at the train station, there were children everywhere, many of them from the orphanage, a couple of whom she'd seen the day that she'd been there enquiring about Abigail. Her heart sank. Abigail was to become one of these, a mass herd of children, who could be moved like cattle from one place to another.

While she waited her turn to go through the gate, Lizzie straightened Abigail's ribbons smoothed down her coat with the shiny black buttons and pulled down the woollen hat Lizzie had knitted for her. Reaching in her bag, she pulled out the letter she'd written and put it in Abigail's pocket.

'I have a photograph in there of me, so you won't forget me. And I will write, Abigail. And try and draw me a picture of where you are.'

Abigail just looked up, a deep sadness like a dark well of sorrow in her eyes.

The same starchy-looking woman greeted her with a clipboard. 'Ah, yes, Abigail, come along.' The woman automatically started to shepherd Abigail away from her, and Lizzie felt a huge sense of loss.

'Can I just say goodbye?' she asked.

'Well, hurry up, please. We've got a lot of children to organize today.'

Lizzie grabbed hold of Abigail and hugged her tightly. 'I love you, darling, and anything you need, anything, you can let me know. Julia's address is in the envelope. I'll make sure I follow up on you and send you lots of wonderful letters.'

Abigail just looked at her sadly.

'Bring the orphan this way,' the woman instructed.

That stung Lizzie. 'Do you have to be so harsh?'

Abigail looked at Lizzie's face for understanding, as if she was trying to get her mind around this new word she was being called.

'There's no point beating around the bush, is there?' said the woman emphasizing her point, seeming to have no tolerance or tact for the job she was doing. She quickly pulled Abigail from Lizzie's arms. 'Come along now, dear. You're going to be a good girl, aren't you? I'm not going to have any trouble with you, am I?'

Abigail looked grief-stricken. Panicking, she pulled her hand straight out of the woman's and ran back towards Lizzie.

'Now that's not being a good girl, is it? Come along,' the woman barked, gruffly.

Lizzie didn't know what to do. But she had no choice.

Before she could do anything, the woman had already grabbed Abigail and pulled her towards the group on the platform, Abigail let out a howl, and the woman shouted, 'We'll have none of that, young lady. Now you get yourself into line.'

Lizzie raced to rescue her, and the woman pushed her back. She was a large woman and held Lizzy by the shoulders. 'She is not your concern. She is a ward of the government. You, my dear, need to control your emotions.'

Lizzie suddenly realized she could tackle this woman and grab Abigail, but what would that serve? Abigail was already so upset, and the woman was right, so she spared her energy and instead shouted over to her, 'Abigail, it's going to be fine, I promise you. I'm going to come and see you really soon.' Even though she couldn't be sure that was the case.

Lizzie continued to shout encouraging things to her. 'Don't forget the letter and don't forget to write to me. There'll be lots of lovely children who you're going to meet. You're going to have so many adventures.'

A kinder young woman came up to work out what the fuss was. She looked at Lizzie and assessed the situation straight away. Coming to Abigail's side, she put her arm around her and spoke gently to her, and Lizzie was so grateful. 'She'll be all right with me,' said the woman as she gave the other woman a stern look. 'I'll take good care of her.'

She took Abigail's hand and led her to the group of children. If only Lizzie was married, if only Jack wasn't dead, If only... Before she knew it, Abigail was herded onto the train, and Lizzie searched frantically through the train teeming with children, but couldn't locate her anywhere. When she realized she wasn't doing any good to Abigail or herself crying her eyes out, she moved quickly through the station, tears now streaming down her face.

It was as Lizzie was halfway down the road that the siren sounded, and she started to look frantically for shelter. Had Abigail's train left? She didn't know whether to run back. Would the children be taken to a shelter there? She felt the acute loss, and she almost went back, but it was too far. Hopefully, Abigail's train had already left. She ran into an underground shelter as the first bomb hit, very close to where she was, and as she raced down the stairs they were all thrust forward with the impact of the blast.

The group, in a panic, moved as fast as they could. An elderly lady had fallen. Lizzie helped her to her feet. Another bomb sounded close by. The impact sent them wheeling onto the platform. It was a hard, swift bombing campaign, but after thirty minutes, the all-clear was sounded.

Quickly, she hurried up the stairs out of the underground station and looked towards the train station. Her heart leapt to her throat. It had taken a direct hit. Firefighters were already there on the scene, their hoses spraying long streams of freezing water from every direction.

As she got to the entrance, injured people were being helped out of the building. An older man who was holding people back from going inside spotted her.

'Can't go in there, young lady, it's dangerous.'

'My daughter's in there,' she pleaded with him, and the warden, seeing the absolute panic on her face, nodded and directed her to a side entrance.

'Don't tell anybody I let you in.'

She shook her head and raced inside. But nothing could prepare her for what she saw. She had just been here, and now it was like a building site: rubble, smoke, fire, heat from the flames streaming up from the very place she'd been with Abigail. She raced down the stairs to the platform.

People were shocked and dazed and making their way out, being helped by the services. When Lizzie got down there, her worst fear was realized. Abigail's train was still there, and scattered about the platform were piles of tiny belongings: teddy bears, scarves, caps, small suitcases. Lizzie stumbled through the rubble. She looked around and then she saw a red ribbon caught in the stones. Was that the ribbon she'd put in Abigail's hair just that morning? Please, God, don't let it be.

Finally, she found an air-raid warden who was on duty. 'The children, where are the children that were being evacuated? Do you know where they went?' He pointed to a shelter further down. Inside was a whole group of children and the woman who had been so rude to her before. 'Abigail, Abigail,' Lizzie shouted into the shelter.

All that echoed back to her were children's sobs and the women in there trying to comfort them in cooing and reassuring terms. She looked through the whole shelter, all the children, one bleak little face after another, but Abigail was nowhere to be seen. All of the grief slammed into Lizzie. The loss of her baby, the loss of Jack, and now the loss of Abigail. How could this happen to her again? She recognized the same sense of panic that she'd felt when they'd taken her baby from her. The fear of never seeing her again and a deep maternal instinct to protect her.

Lizzie tore out of the shelter and started searching again. And all at once she saw Abigail, just as she had that first day, standing right at the end of the platform. Her eyes closed, her hands out, as though she was praying. Lizzie raced to her and picked her up in her arms.

As Abigail grabbed her neck and held on tightly, Lizzie didn't wait. She moved through that station as fast as she could. She didn't care what they said. They were never taking Abigail away from her again. Even if she had to hide her in the house, even if she had to fight, be arrested, or battle for her through the courts, Abigail was going to stay with her no matter what.

'It's all right, darling,' she repeated to her over and over. 'It's all right, you're coming home with me. They'll never take you away again.' Her little body relaxed in Lizzie's arms as she had on the first night she'd found her. And Lizzie knew it would be true. She would find a way; and Abigail would be hers.

Chapter Forty-Five

On 10 April – Julia's birthday – the girls were celebrating when the wail of the sirens blasted out into the air just as they brought out the cake they had pooled their rations to make. Julia quickly raced into the hall. 'Abigail, Tom, put on your shoes and coats, we have to go.' All three women jumped into action, a well-prepared team grabbing hats, coats and supplies for the shelter, and with the children headed off down the garden. Julia didn't even bother to call out to Agnes, who never came to the shelter.

Diana carefully carried the cake.

'We will not leave this behind for the Nazis to blow to smithereens,' she joked as they closed the door on the little corrugated iron Anderson shelter.

Julia quickly found the lamp and lit it, and Diana organized the children into the beds, while Lizzie prepared something for them all to drink. The children settled down to play a game of Snakes and Ladders as the women huddled together on the other bed to celebrate.

Lizzie lit the candles on the top of the cake. The gentleness of the candlelight was quite beautiful in the tiny room.

'You need to make a wish, Julia.'

Julia held the hands of her friends. 'There is only one wish for me this year, that we will all stay safe and that John and Maggie will be home soon.' She blew out the candles and Diana cut slices for them all to enjoy.

But the celebrations were short-lived because it wasn't long before their world started to rock, bombs showering down all around them. The sound was tremendous. The girls could tell this attack was very close, and every time there was an explosion, it rocked the ground below them, rattling everything inside the shelter.

About thirty minutes in, one came down with such force it knocked them all to the ground. The explosion above their heads was deafening, followed by a shower of debris raining down on them, crashing down on the tin roof. The impact snuffed out the light and Abigail started to scream. Lizzie reached for her in the dark, trying to feel for her small body. Finding a shoe and a sock, she tugged the little girl's leg towards her and pulled her into her arms.

'It's all right, darling, it's all right. I'm here.'

Abigail sobbed.

Lizzie could hear Julia scrambling around on the floor, trying to find the light, and Diana felt around in the dark looking for Tom, who was also calling out.

Suddenly, they all heard a tiny voice, a tiny voice they'd never heard before. Lizzie looked down, wondering if she'd imagined it. Abigail spoke again, her little bird-like voice creeping through the layers of Lizzie's coat.

'I'm scared of the dark.'

All three women heard it and froze. This was the first time Abigail had ever spoken, and Lizzie could hear the tremble in her voice.

She cupped Abigail's tiny tear-stained face and pulled it close to her so she could see the whites of the child's frightened eyes. 'You don't need to be afraid of the darkness, darling, because you know why? Because I have learned something in this war, and that is inside of us, we all have our own very bright light. Close your eyes and look for it. It's there.'

Abigail's eyes closed. Instantly, with her eyes closed, she seemed to calm. She stopped screaming.

Lizzie continued to whisper. 'You can make that light as bright as you want because I want you to know a secret. The darker the night, the brighter we shine. Keep your eyes closed and make that light as bright as you need to.'

Abigail nodded her head. 'I can see it. I can see it, Mummy.'

Lizzie gasped. She just called her *mummy*. Next to her, Diana grabbed her arm. Right in the middle of this tremendous disaster, this was a precious moment between the two of them. She wasn't sure whether to weep with happiness or feel the fear. She did not want to let this little girl down. Right now, Lizzie wasn't her mother and she didn't know how to deal with that; but instead she chose to pull her close and hold her tightly and rock her in her arms.

All at once, Julia found the lamp, and behind her, Lizzie heard a match strike, and suddenly, the shelter was illuminated again.

As Julia held the light up, everything was a mess; supplies, food and clothes knocked from the shelves. Bedding had been thrown down from the beds. Diana automatically started to tidy up as the bombs continued to roll.

'That bomb was so close,' said Julia. 'I just want to check if I can see anything.' She went to the shelter door and tried to open it, but after pushing a couple of times, she turned around to her friends and looked afraid. Obviously not wanting to say anything in front of the children, she said, 'I'll check it later.' Then she went to the side door and tried to check the escape hatch on the side of the building. But nothing seemed to shift as she pushed on it.

There was undeniably a problem. Fortunately, the children didn't see, as Abigail was still in Lizzie's arms and Tom was preoccupied with picking up the pieces and trying to find the dice from his Snakes and Ladders game.

Julia shook her head at the girls, and then mouthed to them over Tom's head, 'We're locked in.'

Fear registered on both the other women's faces. Lizzie suspected the bomb must have hit the house and some of the walls had come down right on top of them. She looked up at the roof. She saw it then, huge dents all the way over it. There was no doubt. It had been loud, but it wasn't until it was illuminated they could see the damage to the top of the shelter. Lizzie sat down on the bed and waited. As the sky above them quietened, both Tom and Abigail became sleepy. They snuggled the children down in bed, and soon they were asleep. As they waited for the all-clear to sound, they all knew of stories of people who had been trapped in Anderson shelters. It was a dangerous situation.

To calm herself, Diana made them all tea. They sat there drinking it, the all-clear sounding, and they were still locked inside.

'Do you think there's enough air in here?' whispered Diana.

'Of course there is,' said Julia, but Lizzie could tell by her tone that she wasn't sure. Would they suffocate inside if the debris above them shifted? If another raid happened and brought more bricks down upon them, would they all be crushed? She suddenly felt terrified.

After some time had passed Julia seemed to get agitated and started to pace the tiny space.

'What is it?' asked Diana.

'I've done everything wrong,' hissed Julia, wringing her hands. 'Everything, and now my family's falling apart. Maggie and John are gone, and Tom could die in here with me. I should have sent him back to the country, what was I thinking? I should have gone myself. If anything happens to me, Maggie will be alone. When John comes back, he won't even have his mother.'

'What do you mean?' whispered Lizzie.

Julia looked at the girls and sat down. They could tell something lay heavily upon her.

'I found out that Agnes has been collecting information for the fifth column.'

Both the girls gasped. 'Agnes?' said Diana. 'I would never have thought she had it in her.'

'All those nights she was going to bingo. Didn't you notice she was gone more evenings? Well, I think she's been going to meetings and handling information for them.'

'I can't believe it,' said Lizzie.

'What's John going to do when he finds out that his mother has been arrested for working for the enemy?'

'Arrested?'

'I have to go to the authorities, don't I? I mean, it's the right thing to do, isn't it? It'll pull my family apart even further. Maggie won't remember me. Tom will probably be killed in here, and if not, John will never forgive me. I'm going to be alone for the rest of my life.'

Lizzie had never seen Julia so unhinged. She got up and stopped her friend, taking hold of her by the shoulders.

'Julia, stop. Just stop. You are always trying to hold everything together. It's all right to let go sometimes. You don't always have to have all the answers, and you are not responsible for every single thing that has happened to you. Agnes is old enough to make her own decisions. And if John loves you, he won't care about what his mother's done. You didn't make Tom get on the train and come home. You're not responsible for all of this. You didn't start this war, Julia. Stop trying to hold all the pieces of your world together.'

Julia's bottom lip started to tremble, and she burst into tears. 'I envy you, Lizzie. You wear your heart on your sleeve. I wish I could be more like you. I wish everybody knew how I felt. I just don't know any other way to be. What will happen when Agnes goes to prison? I feel rotten about that.'

'Do you *have* to tell anybody?' questioned Diana.

'What do you mean?' asked Julia.

'Well, John's coming home soon. Why don't you just tell him and then the two of you can make the decision together?'

'It would break his heart. Besides, I have to do the right thing. The right thing to do would be to tell the authorities.'

'But if it destroys your family,' said Lizzie, 'there must be another way. Because you know what, Julia? Sometimes doing the right thing isn't the right thing to do. And I'm not saying you don't report this. I just think you need to take a step back, just see what happens. And trust. You don't always have to be the one putting the whole world right.'

Julia collapsed into Lizzie's arms and started to sob. She sat her down on the bed.

Once she'd had a good cry, they sat in the quiet.

All at once, Diana spoke. 'Len proposed, you know.'

They both turned to look at her.

'What?'

'Len proposed, asked me to marry him over a month ago.'

'Oh, Diana, that's wonderful. You did say yes?' enquired Lizzie.

'Kind of, it all happened so quickly and I wouldn't set a date, I have been putting it off. I didn't think it was fair on you, Lizzie, with all you're going through, and I'm worried about my mum and dad. Len wanted to get married right away in a register office and it would destroy my dad. He always wanted to walk me down the aisle in a church. And the ones that aren't damaged have a long waiting list. I was so conflicted, and if I die in here, Len will never know how much I love him.'

Diana started to cry.

Lizzie turned her friend to face her and took her by the shoulders.

'Listen to me, Diana. I don't know about your family but I don't ever want you to hold back embracing your happiness for one single day because of me. I want you to go and grab it with both hands and hold on to it. Because I never got to spend even one night in the arms of the man I love as his wife. And you have no idea how much that grieves me, not to have loved him in all the ways I wanted to. I will never get him back and you have an opportunity for love and to be with someone who loves you. So please marry him! Tomorrow, if possible!'

Lizzie then took both her friends' hands and squeezed them. 'We're not going to die in here. Because I'm not going to let us. We'll figure out what to do about Agnes, and you're going to marry Len. You're not going to put it off, Diana. You're not going to give this a second thought.'

Diana nodded. 'I've just been so uncertain, with my family. You are lucky, Lizzie, to have such a simple life back home.'

Lizzie felt her stomach tighten; she still hadn't told them about Annie. She knew they cared for her, but having a child out of wedlock was seen as something very taboo. She remembered her friends back in Scotland when the rumours of what she'd done had filtered through to them, how they had reacted. And when she had confessed her secret to her very best friend, the friend she had known all her life, she'd turned her back on Lizzie. There had been a distancing, a need to hold her at arm's length as if getting pregnant was something she could catch from her. She found that women in her village had been the cruellest with her and it had broken her heart. She had been shocked when Jack had been so accepting, but would that kind of acceptance have stretched to these new friendships?

She made a decision that she didn't want to go forward with anyone in her life who didn't accept her for exactly who she was. She couldn't do that, so she drew in a deep breath.

'I have something to tell you both.' Her two friends looked across at her, as the words tumbled out. 'It was more than just the war that made me leave Scotland and come to London. When I was fourteen I got pregnant and had a baby. That baby was sent here to London and… a few weeks ago I met her for the first time.'

The shock on her friends' faces was palpable, but she couldn't look at them. So, she carried on. 'I've wanted to tell you before, but I have lost friends because of this and I didn't want to lose you both. I told Jack and he was accepting of it, but I just wasn't sure how you would both react—'

'Stop,' stated Julia sternly, lifting a hand. 'Stop right there.' Lizzie was shocked to suddenly see her friend looking angry. Julia continued. 'Lizzie, I can't believe you don't know how much we care about you, and something like this would *never* change that. We are a family: you, me and Diana. This is a friendship forged in the fire and those friendships, I have found, are the strongest.'

Diana nodded her agreement. 'We love you, Lizzie. Please tell us all about your daughter.'

So, with grateful tears in her eyes, Lizzie did so, and as they waited out the hours she told them everything she knew about Annie, and her journey to find her. And the friendship between them all grew, became something even stronger, because of the acceptance they all felt that night.

Lizzie finished her story saying, 'One thing I've realized through being here, and being independent and alone, is that I see I have more strength than I ever thought was possible. Going through this Blitz day after day. Getting up and carrying on after what happened to Jack. I've realized that I have a lot more courage and strength than I knew. I have that partly because of what I have seen in you two. Every day I see you, Julia, juggling all of this and keeping us all together as a family, and Diana, when we're all running to the shelters, you're running out into the bombs to fly the balloon. You have both inspired me; I'm very different to the girl that left Scotland. When we get out of this, I'm going to apply for adoption, and I'm going to take Abigail home with me. I don't care what people think of me.'

The three of them wrapped their arms around each other and held each other tightly.

'A three-stranded cord is not easily broken,' Diana whispered into the huddle, quoting a well-known proverb.

*

Lizzie was just dozing off when she heard someone on the roof of the shelter. Both Diana and Julia were asleep at her side. She woke them quickly. 'Someone's here.'

Lizzie banged on the roof above her, and someone banged back.

'Oh, thank goodness.'

It took about another hour, but eventually their rescuer managed to pull away enough debris from the escape hatch, and a face leaned down inside. The sun shone through the gap, blinding them all. It was already late morning. 'So that's where you're all hiding,' said Len's cheerful voice. 'I've come to reprimand Diana because she didn't turn up for duty this morning. She'll be peeling potatoes for the rest of the war.'

'Oh, Len!' screamed Diana, reaching up to kiss him. 'Yes, I will marry you. As soon as you want me to.'

He looked stunned, shaking his head. 'Well, you should get trapped in an Anderson shelter more often! It seems to be good for you, and definitely good for me.'

They all laughed.

He leaned down, and the women first lifted up the children, who were just starting to wake up with all the commotion. And once they were all out, they saw the extent of the damage, and they were shocked.

It wasn't Julia's house that had been hit though. It was Agnes's. And it was completely gone. They rushed around to the front, where a solemn warden informed them of her death.

'Oh, Agnes,' Julia said shaking her head with regret. 'She would not get in the Anderson shelter.'

As the ambulance men and women brought out the stretcher, Agnes's body covered with a white sheet, the girls put their arms around Julia. Julia felt heartsick, for though she and Agnes had never been close, Agnes had loved her son dearly and been a wonderful grandmother to their children.

'Poor Agnes, it'll be so hard on the children and break John's heart.'

'He'll be all right. He'll have you and the kids,' soothed Diana.

As the ambulance left, the three of them stood there and looked up and down the street at the devastation. They would never, ever get used to what the bombs could do. It was a terrible sight.

Chapter Forty-Six

Three weeks later, Julia woke up and couldn't believe the day was finally here. She opened her eyes and just stopped herself from squealing with joy.

How she wished Maggie was with them, but she was so settled at Aunt Rosalyn's and was helping out at a fete in the village this weekend. Pulling the curtains and looking out on the day, she was happy the sun was shining, matching her mood. Today she would see her husband. She hadn't seen him for ten months. And though they hadn't told her the extent of his injuries, he was obviously not sick enough to be taken straight to the hospital and would be arriving by train that morning.

Though she couldn't wait to be with him, she also felt the weight of the terrible news she would have to share with him about Agnes's death. Julia felt a stab of guilt again about how their relationship had ended and also what Agnes had done. But John would never know that his mother had been a traitor.

The girls had been right to talk her out of it. After the bomb that had levelled Agnes's house, she'd sorted through the wreckage of the bomb blast, pulling out everything that connected Agnes to the fifth column that she could find.

She didn't want John walking in there, stumbling upon documents that showed support for Hitler, and discovering what his mother had been. Even though Julia understood in some ways what had driven Agnes to do it, it would be such an awful shock to John, and with Agnes dead, hopefully the secret could die with her.

She moved downstairs, Tom not far behind her, rubbing his little eyes, his hair ruffled, flattened on one side, sticking up on the other, showing that he too had had a restless night.

'Is it now, Mummy? Is it today?'

'Yes, Tom, it's today, come on. Sit down at the table. You need to have some breakfast.'

'I can't wait to see Daddy,' he said. 'I wish Maggie was here.'

'I do too, Tom. And she will be soon. I spoke to Aunt Rosalyn. Now the bombing has lessened she's travelling to London with Maggie herself and will be here in the next few days.'

'I've missed Maggie, Mummy.'

'I know, Tom, I have too,' she said, kissing her son's head. The boy so loved his family to be together. And finally, they could bring back the last missing member. John was so good at making them all feel like a unit, as though they all belonged together, the way he jollied them along, told jokes to the children and played with them.

She had missed that. She had missed John, who did that for them all. She prepared some breakfast for Tom, and he sat, scooping it into his mouth.

'I'm going to talk to him about all my adventures, Mummy. About coming on the train and finding my way across London. I know that I shouldn't have done it, and you were very angry with me, but I think he'll find it interesting, don't you? And I think I've grown,' he continued, jumping up and standing up next to the table, stretching up his neck. 'Don't you think, Mummy?'

She nodded.

'I'll also tell him that I've taken care of you. That I've managed to be the man of the house while he was gone,' reaffirmed his small voice, the last sentence making Julia smile. Tom had her heart, all right. The boy who loved everybody, whose family was the most important thing to him.

Once Abigail was up as well and dressed, Diana joined them. She had the morning off, and had offered to come with them. She came down with little Union Jack flags for the children.

'Look what I found,' she said, handing one each to Tom and Abigail. 'You can wave them when the train arrives.' As the children practised waving their flags, Diana came over to talk to Julia. 'How's Lizzie today?' she asked in a quiet tone.

Julia nodded. 'She's all right. She wants to go back to Kenley tomorrow. She feels she needs to get back on the horse. And between you and me, I think it's a good idea. Her commanding officer, Sergeant Wheaton, came by to check on her yesterday. As she told us stories of what was going on, Lizzie felt as if she was missing out a little bit. I think getting back will help keep her mind off Jack.'

Diana nodded. 'It will be good for her.'

Once they had finished breakfast, they all started to get ready, and Julia counted with relief. It had been three days since the last bombing campaign over London. They hadn't stopped, but they seemed to come more periodically now. Not every day, as they had during 1940. Still she couldn't believe they'd been bombed for fifty-six days out of fifty-seven when it had been at its height. And there was still so much to clear up in the city, but at least now they could get a full night's sleep occasionally. And her husband was coming home. God, she hoped this war was turning.

There was talk at work of Hitler withdrawing his armies from France. She hoped it was true. Maybe he'd given up on his hopes of invading their island.

Once they were all ready, they made their way up the street. And they were a happy band, the children waving their flags, Lizzie with Abigail, and Diana and Julia arm in arm.

'How are you feeling?' asked Diana.

'I am so excited, I am beside myself. I've had butterflies in my stomach all morning. You know how it is when you first fall in love?'

Diana nodded. 'I'm the one that's getting married.' She smiled.

'I know,' said Julia, 'but I've missed him so much. There was so much I took for granted when he was here all the time. Little things I didn't even think about. And my family doesn't work right when he's not here. It doesn't feel right. It feels out of step somehow.'

Diana nodded, understanding.

Julia had called Maggie as soon as she'd heard and told Rosalyn what was happening and when John would be arriving. But when they got to the station, she hadn't expected to see Maggie and Rosalyn waiting for her on the platform. They must have left the Cotswolds at the crack of dawn to make it in time for John's train.

'Surprise!' said Rosalyn as she came up and hugged Julia. And Maggie threw her arms around her mother's waist, squeezing her so tightly, Julia had to release her grip so she could breathe.

She pulled her daughter into her arms and hugged her so deeply. 'Maggie, I've missed you so much.'

'I have so much to tell you,' responded Maggie. Instantly, Julia sensed Maggie had grown up. This wasn't the little girl she had put on the train ten months before. There was an independent streak about her as she started to tell her of all the things that she'd been doing in the country. And even though this made Julia a little sad, she pushed it from her mind, now there would be their whole family to greet her husband.

As they waited for the troop train to pull in, Maggie, with great excitement, caught Tom up with all the things in the country that he'd missed out on while he'd been in London. She also chatted away to Abigail and didn't seem to be bothered that Abigail didn't speak much back. She was still finding her feet in that regard and just nodded as she listened to Maggie telling her stories.

Many families were waiting up and down the platform, and there was a great excitement as the train arrived. Julia gripped

Diana's arm so tightly she was worried she would hurt her. As the train pulled to a stop with its hiss of steam, a great cheer went up at the station. Further down the platform, a group of relatives was singing a lively version of 'We'll Meet Again', made famous by Vera Lynn as, slowly, men started to step off the train.

Julia sucked in her breath as she saw on their faces what the ravages of war had done to so many men. They looked battered, exhausted, wounded, all trying their best to smile, to put on a happy face for the homecoming.

Instantly she wondered if it had been the right thing to bring the children. What if John was not himself? Would it be too frightening for them, if he wasn't the dad they remembered? Diana seemed to sense her fear.

'He's going to be okay, Julia. If he's walking, he's going to be fine. And they said he didn't need to go to the hospital.'

The train completely emptied of men into the arms of mothers and wives. And all at once Julia thought maybe there'd been a mistake because John wasn't getting off. She looked frantically up and down the platform that was now full of reunions but she couldn't see the man with a shock of black hair anywhere.

Then all at once she saw him. His smile, that twinkle in his eyes. His arm was in a sling, and he hobbled off the train.

But it was her husband, her John.

The children automatically ran to greet him, and Abigail, not really understanding, followed them and threw her arms around him as well. As he did his best to stoop down and hug them all, he looked quizzically at Abigail.

'We have a new one? Is there something you want to tell me?' he joked with his wife. Then he shuffled to Julia and threw his arm around her. And there was that smell. The smell that was so familiar to her.

'It's a long story. And it's been a long few months. I'll have plenty of time to tell you all about Abigail, and my new friends

Diana – who's there, and Lizzie who I wrote to you about.' said Julia, stroking the little girl's hair.

He pulled back and looked at her then. And it was as if the others around them didn't exist.

'God, Julia, you can't believe how much I've missed you. And your cooking,' he joked.

Julia cried with relief, tears of happiness streaming down her face. And she held him so tightly she did not want to let him go. In fact, she probably would have stood there for an hour if the children hadn't tugged on her skirt and his trousers.

The whole group of them walked along the platform with the kids running out in front, dancing around them as they made the way home.

It was on the way back that she told him the news about Agnes. She didn't want him to see his childhood home and not know.

'I'm afraid your mother…'

He stopped and looked at her.

'A bomb.' She added in the details. She hated to tell him.

The joy in his face crumpled into sorrow.

'They say it was quick. She wouldn't have felt anything. Unfortunately, we didn't know when you'd be home, so we've already had the funeral.'

John nodded. 'I'll take some flowers to her grave. But I will miss her. My dear old mum.'

Julia swallowed down her guilt. That's how she wanted him to remember Agnes. The truth: well, there was no need to burden him with that.

Chapter Forty-Seven

John had been home for nearly two weeks when Diana and Len got married. With no time to really look for a wedding dress and with very few to be found in London, they had opted to get married in their uniforms. Her parents had been disappointed and also concerned by the speed, but they had come round to it, and sent a telegram saying they looked forward to meeting their new son-in-law. The war had changed people. Len's stream of family and friends made up for the absence on Diana's side and her two best friends and her fellow WAAFs were all there to support her.

And when the day arrived, the sun had shone on London and they'd all counted their blessings, with what appeared to be a halt in Hitler's constant bombing campaign on London. Lizzie even seemed to rally and genuinely felt happy for her friend, though it was bittersweet when she thought about the fact this could have been her own wedding. But slowly, gently, painfully she was making her way back, back into the world again. Abigail was a huge part of her healing. When she wasn't on duty, she was at Julia's house, with the little girl curled in her lap, sitting by her side or holding her hand. It was as if Abigail understood that she had a special place in mending Lizzie.

That afternoon they had all stood at the register office, Diana and Len opting for an easy wedding. That morning, Julia and Lizzie had fussed with her hair, then Diana just took the comb off them and eventually did it herself.

'I'm so glad you're going to be happy,' said Lizzie. 'We deserve happiness. All of us, and though I know that I don't feel that yet, I know that one day, hopefully, I'll make my way out of this tunnel. I've started the process to adopt Abigail now. I have to try.'

The women hugged. 'I'm so glad. I can't imagine her not being in your life.'

Lizzie nodded. 'She is my one joy in all of this. I'm so grateful for her every day. At first, I was worried that I was using her to replace the emptiness I felt from losing my own daughter, but now I think differently. Yes, I feel maternal instinct towards her. But now I've seen my real daughter again, things have changed. Seeing how well she's doing. As soon as I looked at her, I knew she didn't belong to me. Her journey only started with me; her path has never been with me. Abigail is different. She needs me, and I don't care what they think of that, here or in Scotland.'

All the girls nodded. After the ceremony itself was over, they had a little get-together and something to eat and, as Diana and Len left, they all threw confetti.

John had gained weight and was on the mend, and the women watched him play with the children as Julia looped Lizzie's arm with hers. 'I know this war will probably be the worst thing we will go through in our lives. There's also something it's given me, a true sense of what matters. I don't think that will ever leave me for the rest of my days. I will just be content to be healthy, to be alive, and to have the people around me that I care about. It's not that I didn't feel that before. I did love my family and my friends, but now it really means something, and I know I will never take it for granted even once this war is won, which I hope it will be, the way it's going. I fear we have a long way to go still, but I can only be optimistic. Promise me we'll always be friends.'

Lizzie hugged her. 'Always.' And the two of them watched Diana wave from the car as Len whisked her away.

Chapter Forty-Eight

7 May 1945

The day the end of the war in Europe was announced, Lizzie, Julia and Diana had been standing in the kitchen, washing dishes, listening to the wireless that John had turned up in the front room. With Churchill's announcement, tears streamed down all their faces.

'We did it!' yelled John, hobbling into the kitchen with the limp he had been left with and grabbing Abigail, now ten, and Maggie, fourteen, by their hands. He twirled them in circles under his arm as they giggled. Tom, now a willowy twelve years old, left the book he was reading and came downstairs to find out what all the commotion was about.

Diana, who was very pregnant with her second child, was so glad she had been at Julia's for the announcement. She had left the air force three years before and now lived up the road, but visited Julia's often, as Len was still stationed in London.

'We did it, girls!' screamed Julia, hugging both her friends tightly. 'We made it through.'

They all whooped with joy.

'I couldn't have done it without you two,' said Julia, her voice quivering.

'Women of endurance,' stated Lizzie.

'A three-strand cord,' added Diana. 'We all held each other together.'

'Yes, we did,' whispered Lizzie thoughtfully. 'Yes, we did.'

Epilogue

Once she was demobbed, Lizzie returned to Scotland with her daughter, whom she had now officially adopted. After the bomb at the train station, the authorities had allowed Abigail to stay on with Lizzie for a while, and it wasn't long after that, with so many orphans, that the government had relaxed their rules about who could adopt. So, she had finally become Abigail Mackenzie in the summer of 1944. Not long after Lizzie left for Scotland, Diana had moved back to Birmingham to be close to her family, with her first child, Carolyn, and her new son, whom she'd named Jack in memory of their friend. Which left only Julia in London. Reunited with her family, she continued to make a home for them all, while still having a successful career in the civil service after her time in the war rooms.

Over the years, the girls stayed the best of friends. Lizzie had never gone back to Barra but had returned to her uncle and aunt's farm to work. She had married a salesman who came to the farm to sell animal feed, and who was devoted to both her and Abigail. Dick was so much fun and accompanied Lizzie often when she came down to London to visit. He had brought joy back into Lizzie's world, though she confessed to her friends she always kept a tiny part of her heart just for Jack.

'Whenever I hear Al Bowlly, I think of him,' she confessed to them. 'He was the best of men.'

They all agreed.

John had pulled up the Anderson shelter after the war, and in its place, he and Julia had planted a beautiful garden with hollyhocks and delphiniums, old roses and poppies. And every year on Julia's birthday, all the girls would meet up again in London to celebrate not only Julia turning a year older, but that birthday of hers at the end of the Blitz when their relationship had been truly cemented.

And on those days after they'd had cake and talked and caught up with each of their lives, the three women would walk outside where John would put out three chairs for them in the garden. And they would sit in the place where the bomb shelter had been that was now a place of peace and beauty. They would sit there with their glasses of wine and talk about their time during the war. Talk about their bond of friendship, the people they'd lost, the people they'd loved, and the people they'd become.

Then they would look up at the sky above them, peaceful and endless, sometimes with a full moon. And they would remember the nine months of the London Blitz, especially those first fifty-six out of fifty-seven days, from 7 September until 3 November 1940, when they were under attack every single night, and tens of thousands of bombs were dropped out of the same sky. They had lived every night in fear, the fear of death, the fear of losing loved ones and the fear of emerging into a world of unknowns. Then when the stories were told and the healing continued they would make a toast, to the British spirit, their own bond of friendship and the hope of a peaceful tomorrow which had been forged in that fire. Then they would thank God for the beauty and the quiet that now surrounded them, vowing never to take it for granted, and then they would pray that what they had lived through would never happen again.

'We have to keep these stories alive,' vowed Lizzie as they held up their glasses in a toast one year. 'The world must never forget, otherwise the same mistakes will happen all over again.' The girls nodded their agreement.

They carried on this tradition until they died, Lizzie being the last one to go. She came down to visit John and his growing family of grandchildren one last time on Julia's birthday when Julia would have turned ninety. Lizzie sat in her friend's garden, herself an old lady now too, looking up to the darkening sky and remembering with fondness everything she had been through. Lizzie remembered the fear of that first night she was bombed and Jack's steadying hand that had reached out to her in the darkness. She remembered the thunder of the bombs and the peace of the singing on Christmas Eve, she remembered flying above the clouds in a plane, and dancing in a frozen park with the man she had loved. Al Bowlly's voice drifted into her memory, the words she still remembered by heart, about deep longing and moments that moved too slowly until they could be together again.

She hummed them to herself as she thought of him. Lizzie had only love left for Jack now, no more pain. Even though the moments had moved a lot more slowly than she could have ever imagined, she would see him soon, she mused; she didn't have that many birthdays left herself. Lizzie thought about the people she had shared that time with, the daughter she had lost and the daughter she had found. But mostly she thought about her dearest friends Julia and Diana and how they had all found their own strength, forged in that furnace, become women of endurance in the most trying of times. She stared into that same dark endless sky and marvelled at the stars and the moon; as she remembered just what it had been like to fight for their freedom, night after night, under a sky on fire.

A Letter from Suzanne

I want to say a huge thank you for choosing to read *Under a Sky on Fire*. If you did enjoy it, and want to keep up to date with all my latest releases, just sign up at the following link. Your email address will never be shared and you can unsubscribe at any time.

www.bookouture.com/suzanne-kelman

As I reflect on the three historical fiction novels that I feel privileged to have written about World War Two, I'm forever humbled by the incredible bravery of the men and women of this era. This book, though, more than any other, touched me on a profound level. Not only because it turned a spotlight on the work of women at war in Britain, but also because my own grandmother's experience during the war inspired Diana's story. Like Diana, she was working at night, flying the barrage balloons during the bombings. My nan very rarely talked about the horrors of war. She only really ever talked about her love for my grandfather, whom she met just as Diana did on sentry duty, and the much-loved story of how he proposed to her right in the middle of a raid. Though, as I started doing the research, I was shocked to read about what she endured through the intense training, the dangers of the equipment, and the sheer physical exhaustion of flying the balloons.

What I wasn't surprised to read was that she was one of the people keeping the world safe while everybody else was running for safety. It was so like her to be so selfless and gave me even more love and gratitude for my amazing grandmother and also my grandfather, who both humbly gave during that time and to their families for the rest of their lives.

So, it was with great excitement I prepared to write this book without any idea of what was waiting around the corner. I started the first draft on 14 January, 2020, and less than a week later, on 20 January, the first COVID-19 case was diagnosed in Washington state where I live. Over the months that followed, I tried to capture the feelings of being in the midst of the uncertainties of war. As I did so, I found I was waging a mini-war of uncertainties of my own, but instead of what I wanted to do, which was go to bed till it was over, I threw myself into my characters' experiences. It was cathartic to live through these women's lives and be inspired by their bravery during this pandemic. Grief in the real world was around every corner. As we all dealt with the collective losses, I processed my own sadness through the writing, with my courageous grandmother holding my hand the whole way. I've never been so emotional writing a book and I felt all of their feelings of loss, even though my own were minuscule in comparison. When Julia said goodbye to her husband and her children, I cried. When Diana dealt with the aftermath of wounds left from a past war, as my own family did, I cried. When Lizzie grieved Jack, making the ultimate sacrifice for his country, I cried.

Though I would never dare to compare having to stay in lockdown in my home in peacetime to living through the Blitz, in a small way, I got the chance to experience the feeling daily of what it was like to live with the fear of the constant unknown of what tomorrow will bring. I hope that as you are reading this, we are at the end of this strange time. If not, and we're still amid this pandemic, I hope this book will give you courage. The courage to know that we have faced far worse as a world and still managed to make it through. And remind you that often the strength comes through the journey. I also hope my characters will inspire you to make the greatest generation proud, just as they made us proud, serving their country so their children and grandchildren could have the hope of a better world.

I hope you loved *Under a Sky on Fire* and if you did I would be very grateful if you could write a review. I'd love to hear what you think, and it makes such a difference helping new readers to discover one of my books for the first time.

I love hearing from my readers – you can get in touch on my Facebook page, through Twitter, Goodreads or my website.

Thanks,
Suzanne

 suzkelman

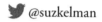 @suzkelman

 www.suzannekelmanauthor.com

Acknowledgements

To my wonderful husband, Matthew Wilson, the love of my life, and my favourite historian. Thank you for coming along on this journey again from the meticulously constructed timeline that we followed to guiding me back into reality when my fictional mind wanted to create a world that lived outside the boundaries of real history. I so appreciate everything that you do, and I'm grateful to walk the path of life with you.

To my son, Christopher, my other lockdown buddy. Thank you for your great sense of humour. For graciously dealing with what was possible for a twenty-first birthday party while I was on an editorial deadline, and also while we were under a pandemic. You give me so much joy every day, and I'm grateful and proud to call you my son.

To my amazing friends whose friendships have meant more to me during this pandemic than anything. All those who have been there for me in the hard times and the good. To Melinda Mack, Kim Weatherall, Shauna Buchet, and K.J. Waters, you are all so special to me, and I'm forever grateful for my little family of cosies.

To my editor, Audrey Mackaman. Thank you, Audrey, for all your fantastic work.

Also, I want to acknowledge the music of Al Bowlly, who sadly died during the London Blitz, and to Vera Lynn, who passed away while I was writing this book. Both of their music was an inspiration and a comfort as I attempted to immerse myself in this time.

I also want to thank my amazing Bookouture team. What a privilege it is for me to work with you all every day. I have to pinch myself that I got to be so lucky – it is pure joy to work on an ongoing basis with the very gifted Isobel Akenhead and all the rest of our incredible team. They include Jenny Geras, Peta Nightingale, Alexandra Holmes, Kim Nash, Noelle Holten, Sally Partington, Alex Crow, and the amazing Oliver Rhodes. Thank you all for your support and ongoing faith in me.

And lastly, thank you to you, my reader. Thank you for once again coming on this journey with me and for sharing in the emotional highs and lows of a journey back through World War II. I'm grateful for every one of you. Thank you so much for continuing to read my work, and for all the amazing emails and messages you send me, I so appreciate your thoughtfulness.

Made in the USA
Middletown, DE
10 October 2020

21557913R00186